CW01429868

CONVICTED FOR COURAGE

BY

KEVAN POOLER

First published in Great Britain in 2018
by
The Lime Press

Copyright © Kevan Pooler

All rights reserved. No part of this publication may be reproduced,
stored in a retrieval system or transmitted, in any form or by any means,
electronic, mechanical, photocopying, recording or otherwise,
without the prior permission of both the copyright owner
and the above publisher.

The right of Kevan Pooler to be identified
as the author of this work
has been asserted in accordance
with the Copyright, Designs and Patents Act 1988.

A CIP catalogue record for this book
is available from the British Library.

10 9 8 7 6 5 4 3 2

ISBN 978-1-9993664-3-8
Amazon Print ASIN: 1999366433
Kindle eBook ASIN: B07MZ779L5

Lime Press edition printed in England by
CLOC Bookprint Ltd, London N17 9QU

Published by

The Lime Press
1 Lime Grove
Retford
DN22 7YH

This is a true story.

The stories of every named character are true,
from original testimony to me, Kevan Pooler.

I have re-created the situations and way they were told as if told
contemporaneously to Eric Chapman. Eric was a Conscientious
Objector from Sheffield whose sentence was to be billeted away
from home on a farm.
Italian Prisoners of War were billeted with him. He took a keen
interest in them.

I know very little about him, so I have created his back-story and his
family. To keep to the historical truth, they are not named.

The full story of World War Two Conscientious Objectors remains
untold. This book is an attempt to correct this, so Eric's experiences,
though they did not necessarily happen to him, are all true and
authentic, taken from research.
The story of the Prisoner of War Camp situation during World War
Two in Britain has also not been fully told outside of academic
journals. This book tells the story of the complete system, based on
the original testimony to me, of those who were POWs, their families
and friends, and camp guards and officers.
Though set mainly across Eastern England, the same
system prevailed across the whole country.

The stories of all named characters are true.

For
Josie/Pina

Josie Sanderson née Giuseppina Gallucci

Contents

Part One - June 1943   Awakening to Reality   3
Part Two - Summer 1943   The Italians   9
                              A Prisoner of War Camp System
Part Three - Autumn 1944   The Germans arrive   108
Part Four - May 1945   The War is Over   163
Part Five - Spring 1946   The Italians go home   207
Part Six - June 1946   My Sentence ends   219
Part Seven - Christmas 1946   Enemies become Friends   233
Part Eight - Summer 1947   Ukrainian POWs Arrive   255
                              Displaced Persons fill the camps
Part Nine - Autumn 1948   Prisoner of War status ends   283
                              Thousands remain and some return

Background to writing the book   311
Main Characters
       Family   313
       Featured Camp witnesses:
       Italian, German, Ukrainian, Polish Free Forces   313
       Camp and military personnel, Farmers and civilians   314
Main appearances by witnesses in the text   315

Prisoner of War Camps featured   319

References   321

Sources of background material   325

Reader suggestions   329

Kevan Pooler biography   337

CONVICTED
FOR
COURAGE

What I, and many others, really did in the war is not being spoken about. I started my story well into the war when I realised that there were lots of Italian Prisoners of War here, and they were almost invisible to the people.

When I was sent to prison, my wife gave up on me. After my release, I was told she was pregnant and I thought I should write up what I experienced and how I felt about it, from my own perspective, at least for our children, the future generation of war or peace.

Alone, I decided our child would listen to me. It would be a girl and I would call her Giuseppina, 'Pina'.

As the Prisoner of War situation inside the British Isles developed at an astonishing rate, so has my record.

Since completing it I have been able to discover that what I have discerned from my immediate locality can be applied to the whole country. Everyone lives not too far from: at least one huge, 5000 capacity Prisoner of War camp, mainly for sorting, transit and greater security; at least one standard camp of 36 huts with a total capacity of 1500; and around a dozen satellite camps, hostels and billets, many hutted, some in old factories and warehouses, and most in disused and fading country houses and estates.

I now know that there were 168,000 Italians, 402,000 Germans, around 200,000 East Europeans, conscripted from territories Germany successfully invaded, and 8,000 Ukrainian POWs. Finally, as most of these were being repatriated, many of the camps were given over to house around 200,000 Polish free fighters who could not go home to their devastated home country, now controlled by the hated Russians.

As to my own situation, as one who still thinks that mechanised war is inhuman, inhumane, and such a waste, I hope you will identify in some way with me. Looking around you wherever you are in the British Isles, and even across the whole Empire and America, you will recognise alternative future possibilities which must give hope for peace for our loved ones.

I offer this story as a contribution to the discussions on disarmament, democracy and the Unity of Nations. We can all look around us and see that enemies are friends, and we each need others, including those from foreign lands.

Eric Chapman, Christmas 1952

Part One - June 1943

Awakening to Reality

1μ
Summer 1943

He cycled towards Retford. He felt freedom. He felt peace. He felt the wind in his hair. As the lane from Rampton weaved down the steep Idle Valley side, with no need to pedal, did he fly? Did he spread his wings and fly?

He flew headlong into an oncoming bus ... and died.

His death will go unreported, but it changed my life.

In the middle of England, in the middle of summer, in the middle of the war, what could the British public be expected to feel about the loss of one enemy, when his countrymen are still mowing down 'our boys' in their hundreds?

Back at Camp 52 Nether Headon Prisoner of War Camp, Palmiro La Banca felt the loss as sadly ironic. Many of his thousand or so fellow Italian prisoners at Nether Headon had been reluctant combatants in the folly of Mussolini's empire building adventure in North Africa. Indeed, many had been captured without firing a shot – there had been no shells to shoot. A hundred and thirty thousand of them had been captured by the British, who had no need to even disarm them.

Capture took them out of the war and mostly out of harm's way.

No, it won't go unreported. I will write it down. I don't know who will read it. They've shut me up good and proper. Sent me out here to this godforsaken place. Actually he forsook the world long ago. Eden was it?

No one will read it, but I'll have to *tell* it to you one day. Even you will want some explanation of what the hell I did in this ... hell of war. Your Mummy won't read it either. But she will certainly listen to a bit ... one bit at a time, before storming off in a fizz. Again.

I do hope I will get to tell you and see a light in your eyes. A light your mother will have passed on to you. It has passed out of her eyes ... to you, Pina.

She will never call you that, either.

So this is between you and me, and after a while, after time has passed, the time that heals all wounds... All? We can hope. We will hope. These boys are showing me. They have hope. It maybe all they have. No - they have a childlike joy, these Italian Prisoners of War. They sing all the time. They sing of home. They sing of love. 'Bella, Bella, Bella!'

What am I doing this for if it gives me no joy?

That's a fair question, and I will be called on to answer it - not least by your Mummy. Actually I think she may have asked it already. 'But why Eric?'

Hope. You are my hope and I do hope for better for you.

Doesn't look like it at the moment. 'What *are* you doing? Just what the hell do you think you are doing, Eric?'

Hoping. All these sad and broken men ... they are men, not boys, though they remain children. They look into my eyes ... yes Pina, tell your Mummy, somebody looks me in the eye. They look into my eyes and they must see hope.

I don't want to talk of it, but they have seen some horrors. Just like my Daddy, all over again. Why all over again? It's money. Not ours of course, but theirs. It's not our coffers they drain, but our blood. We carry back riches from their empires. Those of us with any blood left, they chain us back up to our mills and lathes and make better weapons for them to keep hold of what they have stolen - for us.

Piss in our time, Mr Chamberlain.

I had hoped that my Tribunal would have been a victory. (Oh dear, even I can't avoid slips like that can I?) Yes I definitely gave some hope to fellow prisoners. I did. I did. I'll tell you about that later.

These boys, boys again now, they are frightened, sad and broken men. They cheer me up every day.

I go back to tell you about the boy on the bike. I don't know his name. Palmiro didn't know him. But Palmiro in his broken English said he flew.

Did he fly? Of course he did - for a few seconds. Was it worth it? Were those few seconds worth it? In the midst of this shambles, we have to say yes. Look at his mates, thousands of them beside him, so scared that the teeth rattling in their heads drown out the sound of the machine guns. Drown out the machine.

They are still out there in the desert, their last thought was sheer unthinking terror. His last thought was freedom, the freedom of flight, light flight, he simply flew away.

Sadly ironic, I said Palmiro said. He didn't actually. He is a man of few words. But I knew what he meant. I didn't want to know, but he had to tell me. What am I doing this for if all I hear is about war ... killing ... death ... maiming ... of body *and* mind? Poor Dad, they can't see his wounds.

I know what my Dad did, so one day you might ask me 'what did you do in the war, Daddy?'

2μ

'Don't tell me!' I said to Palmiro, 'I don't want to know.'

This POW's name is Palmiro La Banca.

Another day has passed and I can see the poor lad looking at me. It's bursting out of him.

You should see him, you would like him. The image of soldiers is short back and sides - and the POWs just the same, but not him. He's more like a clown with his shock of curls sticking out from under his cap. He's not the clown with the smiling mask, but the tragic one, the one who gets the bucket of water thrown over his head, gets clonked by the ladder. Yet his eyes have the twinkle ... though today even that has gone.

They may say I don't want to know because I am a coward, nay they do say it. I say I've seen enough, and I know enough. I know it in my heart, and that throbs between my ears sometimes. Dad crawling under the table when I dropped a book...

By way of side-tracking Palmiro, I asked about the hair. Were all his locks cut off? (It was fun explaining that: he thought that I thought they had been in chains like a slave and with locks, see? We were at cross purposes for a few minutes before we both realised and ... well I got him smiling again.) So - had his head been shaved? Several told me that on capture from trenches, tanks, etc, months on the march, that the first thing we ... not we, not me anyway ... that what the army did to them, was de-louse them, and lice hide in hair.

Yes he had all that. His group have been kept in South Africa - tents, no beds, poor food, nothing to do. I do believe the British - again not me, but your Grandpapa and his ilk - invented this way of corralling humans in what they called Concentration Camps in the Boer War. Palmiro hated it.

He claims they were brought over here on the Queen Mary. Can you believe it? Mummy won't want to believe it, will she? Want that record for herself? I don't think he had her luxury, though. Triple bunking, they crammed so many lads on it that they had to take shifts in the bunks - hot-bedding I think we might call it. Not enough grub to go round, either.

Apparently the Eengleesh, had them shaven and shorn and all new uniforms - dark brown, they are. Orange patches. Quite the clown, I assure you!

He brushed some muck off his leg patch, looked straight at me and burst out, 'Boy kill-ed in camp...'

'Don't tell me!' I shouted with my hands over my ears. 'You boys always telling me about mates blown to bits. I know. I know!' I was pleading with him and we both had tears in our eyes.

I know.

Part Two- Summer 1943

The Italians

A Prisoner of War Camp System

3μ

If I am going to report it, I will need to go back to the beginning. Not the actual beginning, but the beginning of the bit that won't be reported. I bet they don't tell you about us Conscientious Objectors, either.

I've started with Palmiro and boys, but he wasn't at the beginning.

We have had Prisoners of War held on our islands for years actually - yes I know we always have. Your Grandpapa even had a good word for the Napoleonic POWs who built the highest wall in England - on top of Mount Snowdon apparently, but that's another story. (Actually I didn't tell him Snowdon is not in England - I have given up telling him anything.)

The first POWs in this war were caught by the King's cousin, Louis Mountbatten (that's the German Prince Battenberg to me and mine) in December '39. They were U-Boat crew - German Submariners whose boats were sunk. Mountbatten's captives were like trophies and were sent to the Tower of London first.

There were also some Luftwaffe pilots shot down in the Battle of Britain. These were held out in the wilds, furthest away from finding their way to transport and a route home, in places like Grisedale Forest. (Mummy and I went there when we were courting. We visited the Lake District in Cumberland for a trip. We got wet, but our ardour was not dampened.)

When they caught Palmiro and his friends, they had a hundred and thirty thousand at once. That was in December 1940. So what to do with them? There was some panic among Palmiro's friends because they had heard about some being brought to England, but then being sent on to Canada in ships ... which were being torpedoed and sunk by German U-Boats.

At this early point I have to say that the *very first* prisoners of this war were in fact Germans living here in Britain. I remember excitement in the works about some trouble in town and Hermann's butchers getting their windows smashed. The Germans - I think anyone with a foreign sounding name - were rounded up and interned. I recall that many were actually Jews fleeing Nazi persecution, and these were soon released. I don't know where the others were held - perhaps Lodge Moor, in Sheffield.

Then when Italy declared war in 1940, the same happened to them, even more indiscriminately. Apparently Churchill said simply 'collar the lot'. One of the girls was upset that her ice-cream man was among them.

What is certainly true is that thousands were held in prisons, before being deported across the empire and to 'Internment Camps' on the Isle of Man.

The biggest tragedy of this situation was that hundreds ironically died when being transported to Canada. It was reported in all the papers. Their ship, the Arandora Star, carrying around 800 Italians and 400 Germans to Canada, was torpedoed by a U-Boat. Almost 500 Italians and over 200 Germans died along with around 100 crew.

All of the 700 'aliens' who died were actually simply living and working in Britain.

For the purposes of this story, these people were undoubtedly Prisoners of War, as was I. I don't suppose anyone will refer to either those Internees or us Conscientious Objectors as POWs.

It was later in the war when Pam and his friends, first captured in North Africa, were held over there before being brought to England. It was they who had to build standard camps. That was their first job - to house themselves. The Geneva Convention, on the correct way to run a war, says look after your prisoners. It says that. Don't keep them in tents over winter. But they did do - because there were so many, they had no choice.

At least for Palmiro it was warm in South Africa. Warm? It was roasting. They also had nothing to do and hated it.

'We slept on the floor, in the sand,' he told me. 'We had just two blankets each.' He looked confused. 'No, one each,' he said, 'but we shared it so that we had one to sleep on and the other to cover us.'

4μ

Palmiro's compatriots were over here and I had found out where some of them were around Sheffield. I had a shufty round on my way to work to see if I could see any of them. Women at work - yes they were mostly women doing the men's work - very soon into the war when the men joined up ... well some of them. The women at work were chatting about seeing them in their funny uniforms. I knew that Dad's old training camp at Redmires was being used again, and suspected that it was being readied for a possible POW camp.

I was right. I took a ride up that way to work - more than once actually. It meant a nice ride: instead of going from Dore down Ecclesall Road to Don Valley, it's no further and a deal more pleasant right along the edge of the moors. After the Christmas 1940 Blitz, I had to weave through rubble on the old Francis Barnett - buckled tramlines pushed me off the motorbike more than once.

In the end buckled its thin wheels too. Maisie the Matchless with her great suspension to the rescue.

So I'd ride up towards Fulwood and reccie the Redmires Lane area. There's a big POW camp there. A stone wall runs along Redmires Lane - at least a quarter of a mile long and you can see where it has been raised from original six feet to about twelve. Though it'll be fairly easy to climb a stone wall, it is completely straight and they will have guards constantly monitoring it. It's called Lodge Moor Camp.

I couldn't really get any idea of the camp itself - hardly at all - from the road, but from either side it is wire fences. Serious. Barbed wire, guard posts, round huts, square huts, brick, concrete and corrugated iron huts - water tower and a few chimneys.

I saw only guards there myself. They gave me a very stern look when I slowed right down by their gate - a couple of brick walls with sturdy posts, let into the old stone wall. One of them slapped his hand on his rifle as if he was going to line it up on me if I moved in. There's a pub across the road. I might make some time and stop off. Perhaps take a walk round the outside, see what I can see through the wire. Huts and men I expect.

The women at work were saying they had seen Italians round Chapeltown. Another said she had seen them round Norton and Greenhill marching to a quarry on Twentywells Lane. Lovely name isn't it? I hadn't been across the other side of the city, so I didn't put in my two pen'orth.

An argument broke out because one of them knew a family who had been put up in a camp on Barnes Hall site at High Green, and another said they weren't if they 'wunt Eye-ties caught up in North Africa' and stormed off. One of the others cleared it up, and I've sorted it for myself: apparently one camp was built on Barnes Hall estate for around fifteen hundred people bombed out in the blitz. Of course they wanted their own places as soon as they could, and moved in with friends, family and things, *then* the Italians were brought in there.

They have been building some concrete roads up there, Parsons Cross, and maybe even helping put up more pre-fabs - mostly concrete huts pre-fabricated at factories. If the POWs concrete a rectangle floor, the huts can follow on easily with just a little bit of supervision by British builders.

I suppose they will also be putting up huts for themselves. They can't be expected to be in real camps of tents for winter.

Can they?

Here's a little map I traced for you:

A. Grandpapa' s Dore.   B. Mam's.   C. Works, Don Valley.
Camps: 1. Lodge Moor.   2. Parsons Cross.   3. High Green.   4 Chapeltown.
5. Norton.   6. Ravensfield

5µ

I just want everything to stop.

I don't really. It's just one of those things I have heard so often. From a mother at her ruins in the blitz. Her son away at war and her younger children buried in the rubble, holding what was left of her singed hair and crying, 'I wish it would all just stop!'; to the Italians who said that they just wanted all the marching - walk, walk, walking in the desert sand - to stop; and their friends who wanted the shells raining down onto Tobruk, from ships so far out to sea you could only hear them whistle in.

To stop.

And to me...

I do not want you my loved ones to stop. So I do not want the chance to love you to stop.

That's cleared that up a bit. I think as ever, as we all do, I just want this awful war to stop.

Wait a minute! As we all do? Where are all the British men who should be ploughing and reaping with me here? Should have been firing the furnaces and rolling out the steel to make smart new cars and bikes and not left it to the women to make tanks and guns. Lovely women with leather hands.

My fellow workers are all Italian. They transport me back to the fields of our honeymoon. They do when it's a nice hot Summer's day - we have had a few. The POWs are all very sunny, too.

They are now. The hopes they had when Italy first capitulated on 8th September 1943, that they would be repatriated, were dashed when Old Duce decided to carry on his fascist state in the North with the Nazis who had rescued him. The ones I've met after that time are all resigned to waiting now for the whole shebang to finish. And they have stopped the arguing. Or someone has stopped them.

Palmiro said the difference he experienced at Headon, having first been held in Cambridgeshire, was the 'two lots of Italians ... we were all King's soldiers, but there was also the sort on Mussolini's side and in this camp there is a lot of angri*ness* between us.'

His language is not brilliant, so I am translating for you. I am amazed how much I picked up from Mummy - she did all the talking out there on our honeymoon. I did a lot of gesticulating - and listening - and now I hear what Palmiro says. He does say 'angri*ness'*.

He went on, 'The day Italy finished, the commandant got us all out on the square and asked us who would be co-operative, with the British, and who would not be. Them as want to stop on British side go on one side, those who want to stop on Mussolini's side go to the other.'

He drew his hand over his chin. I think he was maybe waiting for me to ask which side he was going to be on. I didn't.

'That's when the angri*ness* really started.'

The Commandant's plan backfired then.

'So I didn't like that, because your friend,' he put the back of his hand to his forehead, 'your friend looking at you with bad eyes - "he's changed flag from one side to the other."'

He still didn't tell me which side he had chosen, though I could easily guess. He really does not understand why he should be fighting. He didn't know any mafia, and his village in the Italian hillsides certainly had gained nothing from North Africa. He simply wanted it all to stop.

'And that's when I asked the Commandant for to go out of the camp. I went out on a farm in Tuxford,' he said.

There were lots. Maybe a hundred or so had been bunked up in an old factory on Eldon Street and some in huts on Lincoln Road. Nice lads.

He then beamed at me and nodding said, 'and from Tuxford to Egmanton, to Alec Fox.'

'And to me!' I patted him on his hand. I'm not sure he's used to anybody touching him, not someone British anyway. The Italians are very physical in their expression to each other ... come to think of it, I'm thinking of over there, aren't I? They are cheery ... and singy, and dancey yes, but actually they don't hug and kiss like men did in Italy. Yes. It's this damn war. For them ... splitting families, brother-on-brother, royalists and fascists. For us too, my darlings?

I just wish it would stop.

'And here we will stop together, eh Palmiro?' I said.

6μ

I have been living here for a while now. Egmanton is a bit south of Tuxford in central Nottinghamshire - that's pretty much the centre of England too.

I've been sent forty miles from home to live in exile. I think you will rightly have to say that it's my own fault. Mummy says, and it is of course my own choice, even if it is a punishment. You must not be upset if other children tell you that your Daddy is a prisoner or a convict. Convict is a word I am very happy with. I'm stealing it back off the people who want to use it as a *totally* bad word. I am here because of my convictions, and not convictions for crimes. What is my conviction?

Oh dear, yes I am, but that's not what I mean even if it's what they mean. It is my *conviction* that people should not kill each other. I have been *convicted* of trying not to kill anybody. You might have to be a bit older before you can work that one out, but I will try.

We live in a country. All people live in a country. Countries mostly have rulers. The rulers use power to get their people to do things, especially to help them rule. Some rulers want the power to get more and better things, riches especially, for themselves. Some do it for their people. They say they know what their people want, then persuade them that to get it, they have to fight off other people who want to take from them.

Lord Acton said, 'Power tends to corrupt, and absolute power corrupts absolutely.' I think he was right. All these Earls and Dukes didn't get what they have from saving a fair day's pay. I think most of them got it by rounding up their peasants to fight, usually for the king. I wonder if Acton was an exception? Maybe he was dismayed with his ancestors, what with him being the umteenth Earl of Somewhere - Acton perhaps. Not a very posh place. But I suppose his father's money allowed him to travel and study, through which he realised that 'Great men are almost always bad men.' Your poor Grandad and the Sheffield Pals. They were certainly the lions led by donkeys.

We would all like to stop people from stealing from us wouldn't we?

I want to stop those people by talking to them and being nice to them. At the moment lots of British people think I mean we should give the Nazis our things and they will be nice and not kill us. They think that our ruler Mr Chamberlain, thought like me and that got us into this war. They call it appeasement. Even though he maybe was a bit silly, I prefer his effort to Mr Churchill's. Sadly he just wasn't quite clever enough and the German ruler, Mr Hitler, cheated him. He lied.

You will know that the Nazis are the rulers of Germany. I hope that when you read this they won't be any more. If they are, you probably won't ever see this, because I will have to hide it from them, maybe even burn it or something.

Sadly, our rulers say all of us healthy men must fight, unless we can show that our convictions are real and that we feel justified in not fighting. All of our convictions come from our conscience. That's a bit of us that thinks about good and bad and makes decisions about them. It may not actually be in our brain, but in a spirit. If you say that at your Tribunal, they let you off. But I'm a scientist, and I'm not sure that my spirit is not part of me. I'm sure if old Fritz shoots me, my spirit will be pretty well dampened, don't you?

Who's Fritz, you might ask; and my Tribunal for that matter?

But I'm jumping ahead. I'll tell you about that when I come to it. My candle's about puckering out.

7μ

Sally has brought me fresh washing, sheets and a supply of candles. My country Mum. She's Mrs Fox to you, Alec's wife and Barbara's mother. Barbara is just finishing up school. I hope the war finishes before she gets caught up in it like my cousin Queenie.

Poor Queenie, she did an apprenticeship in hairdressing. Cost her parents a load of money, but they wanted the best for their girls and worked really hard to get it for them. As well as her dad working down the pit, they set up shop in their front room and every penny they made went on the girls' education.

So what's her job? She's making bombs. In exile as well. Bit hair raising. She's turned yellow too. She has to pack cordite, the explosive bit, into shells. Its dust is all in the air, yes and gets in their hair and right inside them as they breathe. Makes them yellow, so people call them Canary Girls.

Queenie can sing too!

My exile is out here in the fresh air, working with men who sing all the time, whistle too - at all the girls, cute or not. Queenie is working underground. Yes like her daddy I expect. He's a Bevan's boy. I suppose I could be. I was, sort of. The country needs coal to melt iron to make steel and drive it all over the country in trains to make tanks, guns and shells. So Queenie's dad's job is protected by the Industry Minister Mr Bevan.

My job was protected too.

Queenie has had to go from Thorne, her small village near Doncaster, and live with a family in Leeds, a big city. But the Germans don't like us making bombs to fight back, so they want to bomb bomb factories. The Government have come up with a great wheeze and built the munitions factory in a warren, like a rabbit's nest, just under the ground. The roof is covered in grass. The bomber planes can't see it.

I work *on* the grass so can't complain then. I am not even trying to.

Mr and Mrs Fox understand me, though they are not sure they agree with me. Like me, they wonder if shooting each other until the last man standing decides that he has won, might not be so good for all the people who had to fall. We have some lively discussions ... not like the ones I had at work - or with Mummy and Grandpapa for that matter. These are cheerful sharing discussions, where we each get to say our piece and we each listen. We are not telling anyone to shoot or bomb people, so what we decide doesn't actually hurt.

Sally is trying to make my bed for me, but I am sitting on it and not shifting. The family does too much for me already.

Putting up quite a fight there, Eric.

8μ

Palmiro told me a funny story - he's told me a few sad ones, about his other prison camp experiences - but you'll like this. When you are older. Mummy will *not* laugh.

'While we was in Ely camp, we was really restricted,' he said, 'not allowed contact with any civilians, especially women.'

He nodded at me and I smiled.

'Well you know why.'

We both chuckled.

'To show the British what we could do, we got a woman in a big sack, pack it wi' straw, 'cos at the time we didn't have proper beds, they were straw mattresses full of straw.'

'We call that a palliasse, Palmiro,' I said.

'Palliasse, yeah, I heard that. We had to go out of camp to get new straw for the palliasses, like...' He was holding his nose to try to stop laughing. He may also have been wondering if he should tell me, what with 'showing the British what we could do'.

'...and we brought this woman into the camp.'

He really laughed. I didn't ask him what for, and nor should you. Maybe to help clean it, eh, Mummy?

'Next day,' he went on, 'we want to take her out. We couldn't take her in the straw.'

'What about the old straw?' I asked, rather stupidly. They will just burn that, and anyway it wouldn't be very hygienic for the poor woman would it?

'We brought in the straw, but we weren't going to take it out again ... so she had to come with us.'

'The dispatcher,' I think he called him, 'says, "how's this woman come into the camp?" So we had to show him what we did.'

He laughed and squashed his curls up.

I hope you have curls as springy as Palmiro's.

20

9μ

I have been thinking about Palmiro's hesitancy over 'showing the British what we could do'. These boys are mostly still part of an army that's fighting us. I say mostly because I have decided that the majority of these Italians know they are safely out of the war, but they are the ones who have been captured - some of their units are still fighting ... our lads - Queenie's boyfriend Jack, for instance.

Jack Saunders joined up before the war - in '36 I think - and he's in the Royal Tank Regiment. Of course she doesn't know where he is, as he's not allowed to write into his letters, but we can all make a pretty good guess - and worry. We know he is in the 8th Army, and in the Tank Regiment. They both get reported in the press.

Palmiro was rounded-up - it's not quite true to say he was captured because that indicates some sort of fight - in North Africa. According to him, they never fired a shot. I think he means, as he explained, that *in the end* he didn't fire a shot because he didn't have any shots left to fire ... so he must have fired them off at some earlier point?

They do not talk about any shooting and killing - that's understandable - except of their own friends of course. Some of them have visible wounds and others show them occasionally, like if they have gasped when pulling on them - loading sacks of spuds or swinging a pitchfork for instance.

We can respect the men who do not give up on their ideals. Convictions? Among these Italians are the Fascists of course and I hope I will get to meet some Nazis, if only Jack and his comrades in arms can turn this war around. A few of my CO friends - Conscientious Objectors - have turned around, given up on their ideals under pressure. I've had more than one white feather myself.

You might think that is pretty, and indeed it is - on a swan. In an envelope with my name on it, or left on a bar next to me the one time, it was scary.

So am I a coward to be scared? I hope not.

Who wants a good kicking? I didn't and I'm sorry to say I did get one.

Don't worry, I'm OK and much better than someone who has been caught by a bullet, bomb, or in my Daddy's case, poison gas.

But I am constantly frightened. I am mostly frightened for you and for Mummy. I do not want you to have to grow and find your Daddy a wreck like I did mine. I do not want you to have friends at school whose fathers simply disappeared out there in the desert, or on the beach at Dunkirk - but you will.

So what can I do?

I hope I can show that fighting is not the solution.

People ask what if the Nazis come and get you, yes you, my child. That is the hardest question to answer. The religious people have a world that is better than this one to look forward to. I just don't really know, but as yet, I certainly do not believe that I should join what is essentially a killing machine. These generals do not think of the cogs in their machine, they just pull a switch and start grinding.

Nazism is a great monster tramping across Europe and hoping to take over the world, too. Fascists also started in North Africa, trying to take Egypt off us ... but how did we get Egypt - or any of the countries in the pink of the British Empire?

Do you know Palmiro may have been in the very same camp that Winston Churchill was in South Africa?

Good old Winnie Churchill started his fighting in the Boer War and he ended up getting caught fighting the Dutch Boers, the enemy of the old British Empire. He was a POW there.

Palmiro was not very happy with his conditions out there. I'll have to find out quite why when I get to know him better.

10μ

I hope I am not getting obsessed by this Prisoner of War system. I have got time for a hobby down here in Nottinghamshire - and this *is* about the war, which I can't get away from, but it's not about fighting. Fighters, maybe ... but not any more. I have a standard working week of fifty two hours - evenings and weekends to myself, though not entirely free. The War Office doesn't want me to feel I am any better off than men away fighting. I am and I am not. I envy the esprit de corps - the sense of belonging to a group with a very focussed single aim.

I do have some sense of this of course, but my group isn't here with me. I can't talk to them, to anybody actually, about how I really feel.

That having been said, there is even disparity between us COs. The religious ones have their churches, and members of their congregations visit and support them wherever they end up being sent. Mummy will say it is totally my own choice. But I didn't give up on her. I am doing this for her and for you, Pina.

She will ask if I would fight off Fritz if he were to actually attack her. My thinking is that I would stand in his way, but if I fight, one of us would lose and ... it's not me that's a trained fighter, or holding a gun.

11μ

Farmer Alec's friends in the Farmers' Union are well networked and the issue of pay for labourers is really high on their agenda. Apparently they meet every year to agree on what they can afford to pay. It's been a bit tricky with them getting told by War Ag - the War Agricultural Executive - what they do and don't have to farm. There's not much 'don't' - if it's soil, plant some food in it.

Alec was really wound up about having to plough up some bramble patches and swamp, down towards the Trent, to sew wheat, but after he heard that a farmer down south had actually had his farm confiscated because he refused, Alec backed down. I reckon the offer of a free tractor may have helped!

I did ask if the land was not simply requisitioned 'for the duration', but Alec just twisted his mouth and shook his head at that.

He laughed when he told me that the War Ag had replied to his request for help by sending me. Shaking his head and scratching it.

So with a free tractor and the Italians, not such a shortage of labourers, either.

The gleaming new Fordson tractor arrived. To be truthful, it didn't - it was driven in by a totally clarted-up driver - 'Muck up t'eyebrows'. There was a lovely lad under that mud, another Eric - Ducksbury - so I'll call him Duckie to you. Alec and his family know him as he comes from just up the road at Tuxford. He was desperate to join up and fight, but his eyesight let him down. He was really pleased to discover he could do his bit and get a uniform too - in the Auxiliary Army. He told them he wanted to drive a tractor. They obliged, but sent him to Rotherham. We know about our little sister don't we? It's a steel town, too.

Ah well, we all need feeding. He reckons he's feeding the POWs. He has been sent all over our area - he is a sixteen hour a day plough - yes, *he* is. He just cannot be separated from his vehicle - or ours. Actually he did in the end have to accept that it was ours, but not before he had ploughed a whole (small) field to show me how it works, without once letting me get hold of the wheel.

They won't let the POWs on the vehicles. Malicious ones could do a lot of damage ... and injury, with such a big and lethal weapon in their hands.

After Duckie had cleaned it down completely - like it had yet to turn a spit - and checked all the levels of oil, water and fuel, it was dark when Alec drove him home. He actually gave it a pat on the big wheel before he left. (I couldn't see if he left a muddy handprint. He did not gleam!)

So I am no longer Alec's donkey.

Still an ass?

I don't know if it's because he has only the two women to chat to - lovely as they are - but Alec chooses to muse over the heavy issues like union and labour, and of course the war, with me. Maybe he is saving them from the negativity. I know I am. Yes I am. I know you haven't got me, but like Mummy kept telling me, most of her friends' men are away fighting. I am away helping to feed us all - and I could come home to see you all if...

Anyway Alec lets me in on his 'inside knowledge'. These camps, and the fact that POWs are all over the area is the worst kept secret of the war. The locals are not supposed to tell, and 'Keep Mum' ... ahem ... does seem to work the closer they are to, say, a camp or munitions store. It's the people who are further away who are inquisitive, like the women at the works who were rowing about it. They really hate not being the one 'in the know'.

The farmers share tips on useful and handy opportunities which, sad to say, the war has thrown up for them. Rationing has of course meant they do not have to haggle to get the best price, and they do not have any waste. Is it a boom time?

(Oh dear, that was not meant to be a sick joke.)

The boss having me here shows that Alec Fox is a forward thinking man - and a caring one I believe. Okay, he took me on when he needed men, but there are plenty who would not have, and others who would have liked to take me and flog me to death, working all hours.

He was one of the first to take on a few POWs too. They're just boys - and men - like us, is how he sees it. I'm not sure he did at the beginning, but he has been won over. He didn't billet one straight away, because he thought he had his share with me. When he found out some of his fellow farmers had whole gangs, like the chap in Tuxford who had twenty like Palmiro in a barn...

The bush telegraph to let each other know what is going on and it is amazing how news gets across the country. Alec tells me that the POWs from Headon are being sent all over north Notts. I was stupidly excited to hear that they are being brought into our region through Dad's old camp on Redmires Lane, in Fulwood. They call it Lodge Moor. The POWs know what it's called and that it's in Sheffield. What more would a spy need to know to tell Lord Haw Haw, hey?

There are lots of Munitions Factories - where they make bullets, bombs and shells, as well as the machines that fire and drop them. Their exact locality has to be very secret, so I'm not going to reveal where the one round here is. However, someone told me (that means it may not actually be true), that thousands were bussed in from certain nearby towns and the bus from one had emblazoned on the destination sign '********* Munitions factory'. No, even I daren't put in the name!

The villagers of Headon are probably the only ones in their locality who feel duty bound to not let it out that there is a camp full of Italians in their village - well at the nether edge of it - it's officially Nether Headon Camp. It is also officially - a secret... so if you couldn't read that bit above, then a censor has got hold of my memories.

A bit further afield people get wind of exactly where the Italians are being held. Some because they don't want them over their back fence (that certainly happened in Ecclesfield), while others are on the lookout for any handsome young men.

Alec told me that 'ours' don't go quite over the border to Derbyshire as there's a camp at Langwith. That's halfway between Worksop and Mansfield so I thought it must be in Notts - but though in Derbyshire, they do some work in Notts.

I've brought Maisie the Matchless motorbike down here now. Mam had topped her up with petrol for me with small amounts collected from friends, here and there. Hard to get round the rations - I hope she wasn't siphoning it out of the WVS van for me. Keep Mum - I won't ask. I still brought her from Sheffield to Tuxford on the train.

So over to recce the supposed camp in Edwinstowe - just down a steep hill from Alec's Farm, past Boughton, (increased traffic with American's now - what's brewing there?) through Ollerton and past a pit called Thoresby (on another Duke's estate apparently).

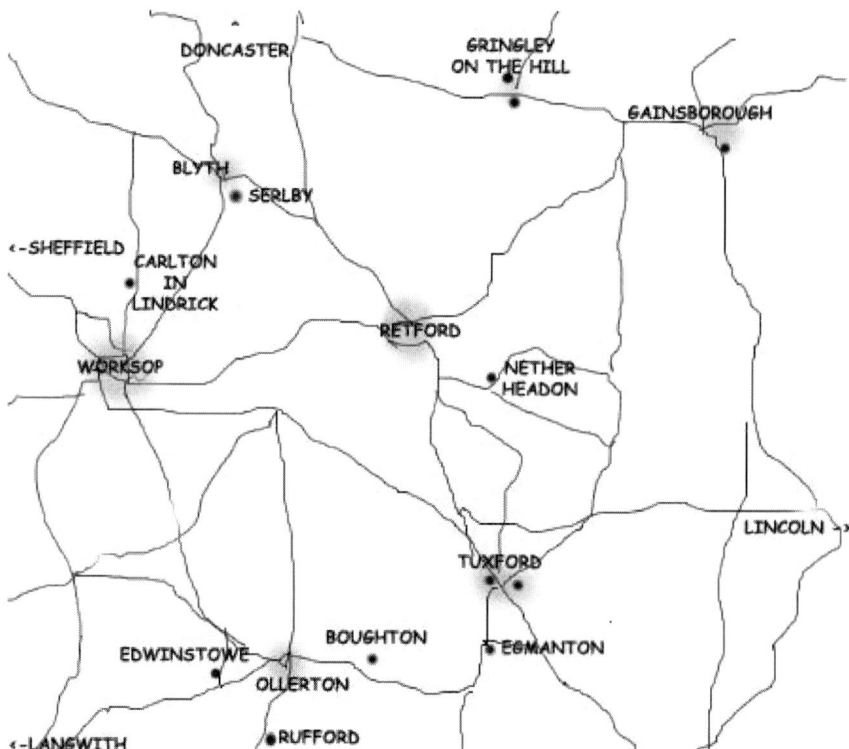

There is a crossroads in the middle of Edwinstowe, and a pub on almost every corner. I parked up and nosied about. Easy - like following an ant trail in the woods. The chocolate uniforms with patches stretched along a road towards Sherwood Forest and Robin Hood's hiding place in the Oak. Only a hundred yards so right next to the village and the school - ooh! About a dozen mixed buildings - wooden huts on brick, concrete ones, one all brick one, and some Nissens. Smiley Ities milling about.

Across to the other side of the pitch adjacent to the school there are two older very big buildings. Cavalry HQ.

I met a Joe Bennett on shore-leave from the Navy. He told me the Cavalry were based there at the start of the war - great place to exercise the horses in the famous forest.

'Posh lot - no wooden 'uts for them.' He thinks they may have moved to iron horses PDQ. (Pretty Dam Quick, Pina.)

Me too.

I steered away from my occupation towards my hobby and told him I was interested in the POWs. He assumed I knew about Edwinstowe's, so asked if I knew about the camp at Langwith and he was gone.

I looked on a map and I thought Langwith would come under Worksop's influence, but when I trundled over there I found it's nearer to Mansfield, which for a very big town, doesn't seem to have any POW camps, though I hear they are building an army camp at Clipstone - maybe even rebuilding a Great War camp.

Adopting my usual pose for drawing a bit of attention, I was lounging on the Matchless outside a pub near a tunnel in what I discovered is one of three Langwiths, not really the same place: Upper, Nether and Junction.

Just what I needed - the Home Guard troop burst on the scene after their Sunday morning practice and they all immediately disappeared into the pub - except their sergeant and a pimply faced young one. He of course drooled over the bike. 'Two bikes', I teased him - back of one and front of the other. He marvelled at the 'Teledraulic' suspension on the front forks springing it up and down to the chagrin of his Sarge.

Sergeant Tom Collis was a bit tight lipped about the whereabouts of the camp in the area, but after some banter he asked me if I hadn't been through the bridge behind us, nodding and winking, then asking what I wanted to know for.

I told him how Palmiro was helping out and even billeted on 'our' farm now, and how that drew my interest on the numbers in particular.

Too many, he grumbled. Said they weren't so well liked in Langwith, quite a few local lads fighting against them in the desert ... and 'our June's not impressed with their...' he looked at the lad, 'well their lewdness and cat-calling.'

He chuckled balefully and added, 'well a chap doesn't much like his teenage daughter being ogled and jeered at on her way to school. Our June says she pedals like mad to get past on her bike.'

I wondered how they could get so close.

'That's cause you haven't had your eyes open, flying about on that machine. Goggles got too many dead flies on them. Suspension's too comfy I shouldn't wonder.' He was nodding over my shoulder again. 'The camps right up to the fence. Didn't you see the Nissen huts?'

Looking towards a bridge I said, 'I thought I'd missed it when I was in open country.

'Wrong bridge, son,' he said. 'There's another over there.'

So there is. Bit like a tunnel, but single carriageway - these great big army lorries must breathe in to get through it, and there it is. He was right. Simple compound of huts among some bushes. Looks a bit like an old factory site.

Thought I'd call straight back at the pub before closing time. Couldn't get much out of the Home Guard even though their sergeant wasn't there.

An old chap smiled at me so I joined him with my pint. He told me there had been a huge chemical (wink) factory in the village for the last war, over a thousand, mostly lasses, working there, so they had a barracks built for them and that became an army camp. 'Camp. Geddit?' he nudged.

I asked him which Langwith and giggled. I thought I was being the clever one.

He laughed at me, then doubled me. Apparently Langwith consists of six villages, not three: Langwith, Langwith Maltings, Nether Langwith, Upper Langwith, Langwith Bassett and Langwith Junction. If they join that lot up it'll be a city as big as Sheffield by the time you've grown up.

I took a ride past - only the huts to see - at Langwith *Maltings* it must be. Sunday afternoon, are POWs allowed an afternoon nap on a Sunday? They'll be used to their riposo.

Nice ride back through a couple of Dukes' estates. Some posh folk live in castles round here. Can't see them from the road either.

What happened to Sheffield's?

Oh, Dore! I forgot.

12μ

Though Alec insists on keeping me updated on the progress of the war, I do not take a newspaper myself. Perhaps that is why he tells me - doesn't want me burying my head in the sand. I would actually like to do that ... but Fritz might sneak in and kick me up the bum. (Fritz is my cheeky name for a German soldier).

In all seriousness of course - Hitler might win. And Alec may be wondering if that is what I want. I am used to being misunderstood.

The POWs don't entirely trust their weekly POW paper Il Corriere del Sabato (Saturday Courier) as many think it is British propaganda, but with constant meeting up with friendly farmers - and some very friendly farmers' daughters - there is no way of stopping the Italian boys getting a clear picture of everything - except what they really want to know - when they are going home.

Palmiro hasn't mentioned it yet, but the war will really hit home - literally - any moment now.

Where is home for Palmiro? I wonder if it is anywhere near where we honeymooned - Sorrento and its hinterland - and that is most decidedly in Salerno's hinterland.

'I come from Potenza,'

Never heard of that.

'Village called Latronico.'

Village - that's better.

'Near Salerno.'

Oh dear. I need a map. I must get onto Barbara - she'll have a school atlas, surely.

'I come from big family,' he's carrying on talking, laughs, 'family of ten.' He hasn't heard yet.

I'll have to look it up, but Salerno was the landing site for the invasion of Italy across from Sicily. I do hope Latronico is not *really* near Salerno, because I think with the Americans and all the other allies, it will almost be trampled flat.

13μ
Late September 1943

It's worse - they haven't only landed in Salerno, but also at Calabria, just down the coast - i.e. south of Potenza, and also on the other side of Italy at Taranto. I've found all three and it looks to me as if the three lots of allies meet up and sweep north, they maybe swept Potenza off the map.

He said he is one of ten children in the family - are there any other soldiers? Have the girls anything to fear from our men? I can't find Latronico on the map.

I asked him if I had the correct spelling. I'm not sure he knows that so well either - our way of saying the alphabet is different. I do think I have it correct. There really is no point in me upsetting him with the news - he can do nothing about it except worry about family at home ... and he will find out soon enough.

'Family of ten?' I said.

'Two girl, only.'

I asked if there were any more at war.

'I were called in the army and sent to Libya. Terrible...' cough '...from both sides.'

He was moved, and had moved from answering my question. On purpose?

'I was in in*fan*try, you had to walk everywhere you went in the war. From Benghazi, we went to Barce.' He choked up again. 'Bardia ... that's where the war really start.'

I didn't interrupt. I didn't want to know this. But like before, I think he will determine to tell me.

'Then we made our first push,' he gesticulated, 'make advance ... in Egypt.'

I know what he means.

'Capuzzi on border of Libya and Egypt, with that near Alessandro. There we stopped for about four month. Four month, never moved...'

I wondered if they didn't do any fighting. They never talk about fighting. I don't want them to be fighting, but I'm not very easy believing these ... well hundreds of them are round here ... were soldiers captured without fighting.

He tendered an explanation: '... for the reason was the Italian army was to have more equipment, more lorry, more tank, more this, more that...' He was rattling.

I could feel his frustration.

'For another push. By that time the British were cleverer than us. They pushed us back as far as Bardia and from there we were all captured prisoner.'

There was a clap of thunder. We both jumped, but Palmiro shook and carried on shaking for a moment, before pulling himself together, grinning sheepishly and swinging his pitchfork. The heavens opened. We had just a few more stooks of corn to get up and let rain run off. Great harvest. Don't let it spoil.

Sally had a brew for us at the back door when we sloshed through the crew yard.

I noticed she didn't look at me at all.

She was measuring Palmiro.

Good lass.

14μ

Family of ten, eh, Pina? And you the eldest? How does that work for Mummy ... or for Palmiro La Banca's mother? At least she knows this boy is alive and well, here in England. What about all her other boys, the ones Palmiro doesn't seem to want to tell me about.

Grandma would have loved some more. I would have liked a brother or a sister ... a brother and a sister. But Grandad is too much of a handful for her - worse than a brood of kids. There's at least some cheer in a child, we hope. Hope is a bit missing for Mam. I am her lost hope. Her last hope I hope. I will show her my worth. I don't think she would have liked me to have gone off ... Dad hasn't got any Pals.

I shouldn't say that, should I, what with Uncle Frank and all, but you'll find out what I mean.

15μ

That has not been a very comfortable two weeks. Palmiro sent me to Coventry. We might have a laugh about that saying one day, but I suppose nobody who knows about Coventry, or anybody who has been in a blitz, who's been bombed, will probably baulk at saying that. Coventry had the very worst single night of all in the blitz. Flattened the Franny B motorbike factory to. Mine just about lasted until I had sorted the Matchlesses which I rescued from our Blitz.

So what I mean is, he hasn't spoken; he has elected mute. He has looked me in the eye, and I have seen his watery eyes - on the verge of tears. Choked. Of course he doesn't know the worst - none of us do - but he can't help suspecting that his family have been trampled in the rush of the Allies up Italy from their three landing points.

He gets mail of course. It comes to the camp and he gets his whenever a gang comes to work here, or maybe if it passes. We have had regular teams to help for this great harvest. Plus women and even children - not toddlers, but some very lithe and hard working young men, volunteering from the village and even from Retford and Newark too. That's been a bit tricky - they can't mix, so Alec has me divvying up teams to different fields. The POWs tend to get less romantic jobs, like hedging, ditching and mucking out the animals and I feel it incumbent on me to work with them to avoid demoralisation and backlash.

They are our regulars after all. And the British forces are not exactly rushing to make sure their prisoners get their post - especially from the lands they are still literally fighting over.

Palmiro has an older brother, but he doesn't know anything about his whereabouts - even if he's in the forces. He thinks they all might be saved through the intercession of a younger brother who is a Friar, I think. Frate - Brother and not a priest.

There is even a joke in there, but he told me about it before. No joking now.

I'll tell you though, Pina, things are a bit serious for my little one. Maybe Mummy will leave out some of the serious stuff, but I hope she tells you what Mr Churchill said. He is a warrior, but I credit him with a very quick wit.

They don't exactly have a wardrobe of clothes to change into, back at camp, and here Palmiro does get to wear a few of Alec's clothes he's 'grown out of' (according to Sally), but he is *expected* to wear his official uniform. You remember it's ordinary army uniform, but dyed dark brown.

Palmiro was cleaning it up as best he could after a bit of muddy work, catches me looking as he kind of steps back to admire himself.

He laughs: 'Mussolini said "I'm going to dress my Prisoners in black as good fascists," and Mr Churchill said "I'm going to dress mine like monks" and that's why...' and he gave me a twirl like Mummy would when she got a new frock to show me.

I was thinking back to around the time he was captured. I remembered that I was in prison and a Christian CO reminded me, (well told me, because I didn't

33

know what the Italians were doing owning Libya) that they had snatched it off Turkey.

Yes it is complicated, that's another reason why I'm not siding with any empire-building nations - not even my own.

Apparently the old Ottoman Empire, based in Turkey, had collapsed by the time of the Great War, so Italy decided to take advantage of its weakness during its final gasp and jump across the Med onto Libya. This CO said an American anti- Imperialist bishop had asked what for - 'To bring to Mohammedan Turkey the blessings of Christianity? Not at all; purely to control the trade of Tripoli?' My sentiments entirely!

16μ
Autumn 1943

Sorry that was a week ago - busy with grain harvest and immediate re-sowing.

Things are looking a little better. Palmiro has heard from home and though there are soldiers from every country on earth seemingly, in the area, his family feels fairly safe as theirs is a hilltop village and not at all strategic - it is no use to the army to guard a pass or a road.

He is not at all comfortable or relaxed; he is rather a shy man. He has to wear his uniform, as we have to remember that he is a prisoner.

Am I? I don't get a free uniform - or wellies for that matter. There has been an issue rankling with the local farm lads about Wellington boots - the POWs are provided with them. Where else are they likely to get footwear from - or any sort of wear, for that matter. Palmiro came here from sleeping in the sand in the desert.

These long days we are actually working all hours, but the POWs aren't - the ones from the camp are picked up when their 48 hour week is up - can be tea time if they were on an early drop off - but Palmiro is 'one of us' so does what Mr Fox needs. It is not unpleasant. Lightened considerably by Land Army girls - for the POWs I mean - not me of course, Mummy.

We even have school-kids who are specially released... I can't be doing with it. Child labour is supposed to have stopped last century in factories and mills, but it still goes on in farming. Yes, yes, you could say they are only playing at it, that they are even in holiday camps (camps!) but in actual fact, my dear, children are working a forty hour week, even on top of schooling sometimes. Realistically it is not a dark satanic mill situation, and for some kids, just to get away from blitz threatened cities cannot be a bad thing.

What did Palmiro do when he was a kid?

He left home at twelve to work in the salt 'mines' in Sardinia. With Granny, twelve of them at home. Sent money to help out.

Now that is *worse* than dark satanic mills - in my opinion. I think of cousin Queenie's ancestors - all miners going right back to lead mining in Wales by the sound of it. Kids pulling carts through tunnels too low for ponies in that black underground.

Palmiro was overground, of course. Not dark, but blinding grilling sun. Wading in lagoons, raking, piling, barrowing; breeze whipping up salt into the tiniest wounds; eyes.

Coal versus salt. No I can't think which is worst.

They would have wanted me to work in the mines - quite a lot of COs do. They may have regarded me as a bit too weedy for mining. But Mummy doesn't go for the Johnny Weissmuller look and that's what counts for me. I've put on some brawn out here on the land, dawn 'til dusk.

Sardinia. I had to look that up on Barbara's atlas again. It's an island! So little Palmiro, at only twelve years old, has left his hilltop village in the centre of Italy, to go to a coast for the very first time, and then get a boat to a large island where there was what seems like a goldrush. Mussolini made new towns in the 1930s and we all know there was a terrible slump for large areas of the world. Whole families went across to Sardinia and settled. Not Palmiro's though - they had some land, a farm. But many boys went with each other's families.

Shaking his head, 'Mussolini,' was all that Palmiro could say.

He moved rapidly on to tell me about being called up - that was better.

It was - before the war.

'I were called in the Army and sent to Libya.' He is a man of few words.

I asked when that was.

'Before the war - 1940.'

'But the war started in 1939.'

He was looking at the floor. He twisted his toe into the ground. He looked up at me and opened his hands. 'But we Italy - not Germany.'

I didn't know about this. I thought Italy and Germany were in this war together.

'In Libya - Italian country - for a few month. Then war really started.'

'When was that exactly Palmiro?'

'Unior ... June decimo...' he coughed.

June tenth 1940 I reckon that is. Nine months after the Germans.

'...terrible. From both sides.'

He *was* involved in fighting then.

'I was in in*fan*try, you had to walk everywhere you went in the war.'

Then he told me, in almost exactly the same words, about the Bardia push to Alessandro, being pushed back, and then captured. I expect he will get to repeat it many times over what I hope will be a long and much happier life.

Or will he want to forget it and tell no one else?

17μ

'What did you do in the war, Daddy?' you may ask - one of my children might, anyway. War might be a bit boring for girls.

If I were as to-the-point as Palmiro is, I might say 'I were called in the army and I were sent here.' The end.

That is true, but there is a longer story, too.

Mummy and I honeymooned in Italy and there was a lot of talk of war. We were in love, not war, so we hardly noticed. The Italians were lovely to us. I even named you after a sweet little girl we met.

When we settled at our new home - at Grandmama and Grandpapa's place in Dore - a war started. The war started.

What was I doing?

Minding my own business - and Mummy of course - working in our research laboratory making metal. We were making all sorts of metal; some new ones, mostly improving steel, brass and some aluminium - that's a very light metal, great for vehicles, especially their bodies - aeroplanes, yes - but not very strong for engines.

You can be very proud that your Daddy, and his Daddy, and even his Daddy before him, made steel and that made Sheffield great. I was lucky that I didn't have to work at the dangerous end - handling molten metal and bashing it into shapes with red hot pieces flying at me.

I was using small amounts to work out which mixture was best for which use. Mixed metals are called alloys. Steel is an alloy: it's mostly just iron with some carbon mixed in. Iron breaks easily, but with the carbon - that's actually what the lead is in your pencil - no it's not lead, because when you chew your pencil real lead would poison you.

Lots of toys are made of tin plate - that's steel mixed with some tin to help stop it rusting.

Lots of POW's huts are Nissen huts made of Galvanised steel - that's steel with a coat of zinc - again to stop it rusting.

I know it's boring boys' stuff again, but really it's very exciting and I hope you will maybe want to be a woman scientist when you grow up.

Our little firm was making a great variety of alloys to try to help big factories make better products. Even my motorbike: it's two motorbikes as you have already heard - the back of one and the front of another. The back bit is from a bike that did not have a springy front, so your arms shook about and it was hard to steer. But because of better metal, Matchless (the makers) were able to make a special spring for the front of new ones. Your clever daddy got two smashed up bikes - both crushed in the blitz - and stuck the best bits together, with very hot metal glue called weld, to make a new bike. I painted it myself - like the new ones - and it gets lots of admiring looks, especially from boys. I call her Maisie Matchless. You'll like her.

But back to the war.

Your Grandad - that's my Daddy - was in a very terrible war and people tell us we won that war. Whatever they say, Grandad did not win anything and he lost lots - thousands - of Pals. When he came back, whoever won did not help him feed Grandma and me. Nor my friends at school in Sheffield. We made lots of the guns for that war, without which they couldn't have won it, but when they didn't need the guns any more, they didn't pay Grandad much to make other stuff.

Even Palmiro knows about that stuff - he was so excited when he realised that I came from the place that made his mother's knives and forks. Sheffield cutlery is the best in the world and that's because of little workshops like mine which made steel that wouldn't go rusty. Also a lot of cutlery that Grandma's mummy had, needed to be polished every week because it was made of silver. That was a chore.

I was making tougher and stronger steel - I was very proud of it and that it was helping make protection for our soldiers.

Then our factories - and most of our houses and even schools - got broken up by bombs in the Sheffield Blitz. Fritz's Christmas present 1940. It might seem silly at first, when I say unfortunately that less factories and more houses were bombed. The German bomber planes came to stop our factories from making guns and shells that shoot them. When they got here the Don Valley, where most of the factories are, was covered in fog so they bombed what they could see - and that was...

Enough of that bit. My factory was untouched and luckily so was our house out at the edge of town in Dore, but my parents' house lost most of its windows and loads of people's houses round about could not be lived in - some were repaired, some not at all, they were too unsafe to mend. If you were old enough, you may have been glad that the majority of the schools in the city were so damaged they had to close.

That made me think about what I was doing to people all over the world. Things I made and helped make were killing people in North Africa - people like Palmiro's friends - and people all over Europe - almost every single country in Europe where Germans are, all except Spain, Switzerland and Eire.

The government wanted me to do that work, so I didn't have to go in the forces to fight.

In the end I refused to do that work ... so they called me up to fight.

And I wouldn't go.

18μ

Palmiro is twenty four years old now - not such a kid - but some of them are just kids.

Probably because there was a very fresh faced lad in the gang who came over today, I had a sudden flashback. It's strange that I hadn't thought of it sooner, but I maybe saw Palmiro on the silver screen earlier in the war.

At the flicks people mostly talk over the short films and some of the propaganda films - 'Be like Dad, Keep Mum!' (Mummy might remember if we weren't still lovebirds kissing during the shorts. Is she blushing Pina?). You don't get many laughs from the serious talk-over man on Pathe news. When someone mentioned seeing Italian POWs walking in Graves Park, a chap retold the news I had also seen. The news hadn't stuck, but I did remember the punch line.

Today I remembered the story: it showed POWs captured in North Africa coming off a ship in South Africa. I remember the commentator saying that 'it's a crime that kids like these should have to face the horrors of war'. I think he said they were starved and emaciated. I took it then that he probably meant that that was how they were found and captured, but Palmiro says he was held in Alessandro (Alexandria) and 'Swiss' (Suez) area for some months, before being transported away from possible release by other Italians in the Panzergroup or Rommel's men. Are you with me? If they were looking so bad, had the Brits been treating them badly? They were Scot's Guards, though because the punch line was: 'Leave it to the Jocks to bring home the garlic'.

19µ

They are well fed over here. They have better rations than you and Mummy you know - POWs get the same as the soldiers and me. Don't begrudge us, though, will you? The soldiers get more to keep them sharp and on their guard, and we need the energy to keep on digging for Britain.

There isn't much garlic. Garlic! We British hate garlic. Not me or Mummy. We found out how to love it, as we found out how to really love each other, on honeymoon. Amalfi coast?

The Scots Guards don't seem to have gone to great lengths to source any for the lads in South Africa.

'They used to feed us on maize,' Palmiro said, 'very little rice, very little bread. There was no work in South Africa. The life it was really misery ... terrible.'

I couldn't say much about that. I should have bowed my head in shame, but I sucked my teeth.

'That was twenty eight months of agony' (There he goes again - that must be from capture to coming over here or else we'd be up to 1946 by now, not forty three as I calculated.) 'You had shower, you had facility to keep clean, but you slept like animal.'

'But then you had a lucky break?' I said, giving him a big smile and pouring him a bit more from the bottle of warm light ale we were sharing (in jam jars).

'That's right. Then we were selected to come here to work and travelled from Durban to Cape Town and then to England on Queen Mary.

'Selected?' I said.

'We were selected by alphabet, mine's L - some men from one camp, some from another ... to come to England.'

'There was more than one camp then?'

He nodded vigorously.

'Came over t'England', he said stopping and scratching his handsome wig, 'Forty two ... *forty three,* ' he stressed.

That's better. He's getting his dates right if not his months and weeks.

'Brought us as *workers.* Came into Scotland.'

'Scotland?' I was a bit surprised. Why travel right up there?

'Glasgow.'

Ah - deep water perhaps, for the Queen Mary and all?

'Then work on land to camp called Ely.'

Ely - I've heard of that - got a big cathedral I think.

'From there moved again on farm, stayed on farm in bungalow.'

'In your own clothes?' I said. They surely couldn't fit them all up, just like that?

'Before this camp, uniform very dark dye, with patch on knee (front of thigh) and on back. But when we went out of camp, when we were asked what side we wanted to be, uniform was changed - was still uniform, but not patch, meant you wasn't on Mussolini's side, was free to do whatever you want.'

'You mean really free,' I said, thinking that the Cambridgeshire experience was in an actual *prison* camp, 'and whatever you want?'

'After you done your work, free to go out,' he said, 'to pubs, to anywhere you wanted as long as you didn't create any trouble.'

That was all a bit strange, because he already told me that he asked to come out of camp to *here*. That being *after* Italy 'came over' to our side - and the Nether Headon Camp commandant separated them out.

'You lived on the farm - back then, Palmiro?' I said.

He gave me a look, one of surprise that I could be so stupid.

'How was that, Palmiro ... for you?' I said.

'Well, you were well treated by the people you worked for because we all used to get a shilling a day and the work what we did were good for them, so they treated us pretty well. Eat with them at same table. They did washing for us, did everything for us. It was alright.'

'Like here,' I said.

'Si.'

Just like here. I had to shake my head. I don't really get it. I had assumed (it seems wrongly) that they were proper prisoners until the capitulation. I thought of Sally doing the washing and that it was special. It is special.

'Thee-ir another couple o'year or so.' (Months!) 'Went back to camp, camp called Friday Bridge which is near Wisbech, isn't it?' He coughed.

Wisbech, in Cambridgeshire. So is Ely. I nodded but said I'd not heard of Friday Bridge.

'And from there I was punished.' He took on his sheepish look, 'because we were working on the river just outside Wisbech ... chucked sludge back in the river as we didn't like it; not treated properly.'

I raised an eyebrow. He didn't smile. This was serious stuff. Proper prison.

'So we refused to work ... that's when I got moved from Fribridge to this camp.'

'How did you feel?' I said.

'Well more or less as punishment, not as really got punished, just got moved from one camp to another.' He took a sup. 'No, I didn't *feel* any different.'

I think the POWs must have been in the right. We Brits like to think that we enjoy fair play and that we treat our POWs right. We are also wary of word getting back to the Axis that we are not treating our POWs well. We do not want to give them any excuse to do worse with all of the lads they have got 'Stalagged' up.

It is my impression that we are treating them pretty damn well, all things considered ... all the invasions, attacks and blitzes.

Oh dear, I am trying very hard to not think like that.

So ... thinking about being moved from friends etc, I am reckoning that out there - on the battlefield - they learn to not get so attached to each other. Maybe it's all very well getting moved away from each other, but not so good to have the man next to you shot, gassed, blown away, like Dad's Pals. Soldiers hopefully learnt to not get too pally. I know the war office decided to abandon the 'nice idea' of recruiting groups of pals together into brigades

I hope you are snuggled up safe and sound in your Mummy's tummy.

20μ

'More or less as punishment,' Palmiro said.

Funny thought about prison, is what I think. Mummy said going to prison was my choice. She is of course right. So it was only 'more or less' a punishment.

Less punishment because I had chosen that rather then simply having a medical. 'That wouldn't hurt Eric,' she said, hand on my shoulder, peering into my eyes. I could look back into hers. But I couldn't say anything because of course it would not hurt - so why was I refusing to go?

More punishment perhaps, because I was being culpably stupid, at fault, wrong, committing an offence and therefore needing to be punished. I was convicted. I became a convict.

Was Palmiro punished? He sees it that he was already a prisoner and he was simply transferred to another prison. He thought they were being mistreated 'not treated properly.' Sorry but I find the thought of him throwing their muddy dredgings back into the river funny. He is so mild mannered. I therefore think that he regarded himself as in the right. In addition, what he ended up with was an improvement in his conditions. Is that a punishment?

The thought of my Dad digging trenches - flinging mud about - makes me tremble. I wasn't even there, but having been there makes my Dad tremble still, over twenty five years later.

Was that 'more or less punishment'? He's still alive. Millions are not. On that one day in 1916 on the Somme, the best of Sheffield's youth was cut to shreds by metal - lead fired from steel.

That was what finally did it for me. I was quite content in our lab and works improving metal for every sort of use, and I couldn't miss that the city was a major manufacturer of weapons ... but I was not.

I was ... naive.

What with Dad going down, along with the Steel City's productivity during the early thirties, Mam needed me to get work if I could. She held on to let me Matriculate, but at eighteen she really could not afford for me to join my classmates in the first real batch of Steelers to get to University. She knew many of Dad's colleagues regarded me as 'the bright lad', and they found numerous opportunities for me to join in the research to find better and more ways to increase production. I loved it. I learnt the theory slower than the practical, but when I *discovered* the theory it was a late dawning. I had to work for Uni chaps and along the way they taught me some theory.

An early seed sewn was that the awful machines gunning down a million men on the Somme were based on a Maxim gun from the last century, improved by our Vickers, and how: by making it both lighter and stronger with improved alloys.

That's me now, I thought. We also invented and improved armour, so our tanks and ships were tougher. Unsinkable. Titanic even? Seriously, it seemed good to provide better protection. Of course.

43

A second seed planted in my brain was that we didn't *win* the last war, the Germans *lost* it. You don't hear that much.

You don't hear that many of Germany's biggest companies developed out of British complacency. A bloke discovered you could get a great dye - a bright purple one - from coal. Yes, black coal, Pina. His assistant was excited and wanted them to see if they could find any more, but the boss was complacent, satisfied enough to make money from his Purple.

One of the 'Profs' (university educated know-it-alls) in the lab, told me all about it. The assistant went back to Germany and tried it for himself - and succeeded. In short, that led to a blossoming of many industries making colours - *farben* in German - from coal, called aniline dyes. With these sorts of discoveries and previously unseen possibilities, the companies researched what other chemicals could be found and what uses. Some great uses - medicines in particular.

That's me again. Am I that assistant?

What was Palmiro doing when he was twelve? 'Mining' a simple chemical - salt.

What a clever chap put to me was that during 1914-18 Herr Hitler realised that he and his pals, and dad and his Pals too of course, were wasting their blood on the battlefield. It was the British Blockade of sea ports that proved the decisive weapon: Germany ran out of oil to run their machines, rubber for them to roll on, and nitrates to make explosives. They had to import all these by sea. The industrialist realised too. They set about ensuring it didn't happen again. They needed to make the chemicals from material they did have. They got together into a partnership - an I.G. - based around their peaceful interests - calling themselves I.G. Farben - Colour Partnership.

Hitler hated them being managed by lots of Jews, but overlooked that because he needed them to make his new German Empire, his Third Reich. He became a partner. What a partnership.

Mummy had high hopes for me; I had high hopes for our love blossoming; I have high hopes for you Pina. I got on with the job and enjoyed all the amazing things that could be made, simply by adding very small amounts of chemical to vast amount of another - carbon to iron makes steel; chrome to steel makes it stay bright and stainless; stainless steel makes lovely cutlery.

It's not just cooking and eating utensils though. If you could see cousin Queenie - the yellow canary girl. She had to pack a yellow chemical - TNT - into alloy metal cases to make shells. She couldn't do that for long as she was too sensitive for it, so she moved to another section of the weapon factory packing the less colourful cordite. She's making shells for her Jack to fire at the Ities and Gerries. Fair play to her, she has the courage of her own convictions.

They are different from mine.

She doesn't agree with me, but seems to respect ... that I did put up with my convictions, without much complaint. (Not to her anyway. Stiff upper lip Chapman?)

21μ

Palmiro has got wind of a couple of other camps where Italians are being billeted - stately homes! I told you about all these dukes round here. These two camps are well the other side of Retford - nearer Doncaster I see on my local map: one at Carlton-in-Lindrick, near Worksop, the other does belong to a Duke - of Galway?

How did he get it? Irish invaders - here? He doesn't need it because he's got half a dozen other castles he prefers apparently, but someone else said it's because he's dead, and anyway it was a hospital in the Great War. Bit of a wreck, then.

The money these blokes must have - at Worksop is another Manor that has been owned by Dukes of Shrewsbury, Norfolk and Newcastle. Then a few miles in the other direction, a Marquis or something of Scarborough has got a place. There's no seaside round here.

I think they are given these manors as prizes for mustering a brigade of serfs to fight - and die mostly - for the king. The Lord of the manor gives his recruiting sergeant a public house - hence all the 'Arms' of a local duke. There's a Galway and Newcastle Arms in Retford - on opposite sides of a road.

I have heard that the most commonly named pub like this is the Granby. They are all over the place. He must surely have built a mountain of cannon-fodder. Pyre? Fodder is feed, Pina. Cannons eat people. Oh, and cannons are big guns, not priests.

Galway's place is called Serlby Hall. It's actually at a funnily named place called Scrooby on the Old Great North Road - at risk from Dick Turpin and other highwaymen.

Scrooby is more famous to the American's because the Pilgrim Fathers set out from there and ended up founding America. Can you believe it? They used to preach in churches round here, but the bishops didn't like their popularity - and their distinct lack of willingness to pay him tithes - and chased them out. The local people are still proud of them though.

Proud to show it off to the GIs who are coming over here now. Bit silly when you think about - their ancestors were actually chased away from here. Not sure where these soldiers are based, but there does seem to be a lot of them. Making a bit of a ruckus in the pubs and towns sometimes.

There's a big old coach stop cafe at Scrooby Top, so I called in to get the local intelligence. Yes Mummy there is a lot of intelligence among your local yokels. *And I'm one now.*

Not much to tell: Italians, whistle at the girls, work on Farms; some of them work hard, some mess about. Just like English lads, eh?

Apparently the old Hall is a farm and has plenty of buildings, but there are tents on a 'parade ground'?

I don't know if it was a Duke who lived at Carlton-in-Lindrick, but he let the Tank regiment use 'The Hall' until very recently, before moving up north somewhere. They left a load of broken down (and maybe shot up) vehicles all over the place. Yet more Italians were brought over as these have been willing and reliable, if not exactly industrious, workers. The lads like Palmiro, from strong peasant stock, have been particularly welcomed by the farmers.

First job - clear the place up, then make yourselves at home. It's a big old farm with lots of buildings that they can bunk up in, and plenty of parkland to put up the usual bell tents.

That's just what they told me at Scrooby. I haven't actually been to Carlton yet.

That jaunt and bit of spying will save for later.

22μ

You'd have liked my Dad, your Grandad. He'd have really liked you. Gentle souls the pair of you. Supported the Blades - that's Sheffield United to you. But Uncle Frank was the one who took me to the matches. I knew why like, my Mam told me it was the noise, from the war and that. I knew all about the noise ... and how I couldn't make it.

1919 was the last league derby there had been. I suppose it was because they were in different leagues or something. But when I could stand on my own two feet and see between a few people who were taller, me and Frank would catch a game somewhere most weeks.

I didn't find out he wasn't my real Uncle until the great 26/27 season. I'd turned eleven that June and Uncle Frank gave me the Steel City derby for my birthday. Course it wasn't *on* my birthday - it's two games - they play at each other's grounds. That's not at Derby of course - I don't know why they call it that. It's where the two local teams play each other. For us that means when we play Wednesday - the Owls. But that year, Mam said it was the right sort of fever that gripped the city, not like in 1919.

After the games, Uncle Frank would take me into the house and bring my dad a bottle of brown - just the one that they would have to share. The twenties did not roar for us - times were always hard after the war.

We'd all sit down and Mam would corral me - almost put reins on me to keep control. She'd sit there while I rattled off who scored this, who fouled who and 'bloody ref', when Mam would clip Uncle Frank round the ear.

'Don't be teaching t'lad your ways, Frank,' she'd tell him. But she'd smile.

Her hands would go back over her mouth as I prattled on, her eyes intent on Dad, sometimes bringing me up short. I would be beginning to notice the shakes for myself by then. Well I weren't a kid n'more, our Pina, were I?

'26 had the General Strike in May, and there wasn't such a thing as strike pay, so for my birthday in June, Uncle Frank was giving a present he didn't have to pay for, yet!

The season opened and it was our long school holidays. Us lads would be out on the street being moved on by one set of neighbours after another: 'Stop banging your ball on our wall,' 'watch out for t'winders, lads, get down t'Rec.' The first derby match was one of the first matches of the season - end of August. We had a bit of a trip out and up to Hillsborough on the tram to play Wednesday away. And we won! We beat them 3 - 2.

My, did us lads have something to talk about when we got back to school. And not a few scraps either. It was big school now - lots of extra lads we didn't know and just as many supporting Owls as Blades.

I got a cut lip I was proud of, but you girls don't understand that sort of thing do you? Mam didn't.

Christmas wasn't so bad for us that year. Mam and I had a heart to heart just before New Year. She was pleased with how I'd settled into the Grammar School, and I think she felt she was at last getting someone in the home she could talk to. I see it as my coming of age, even if most people think eleven is a bit early for that.

She was happy how Dad had held down his work this year 'for the first time since the war, really...' She looked into my eyes and took my hands. 'It weren't good for your Dad, the war, you know.' She paused and looked into my soul. 'Uncle Frank is looking after you, i'n't he? Out there?'

I wanted to tell her how many lads and lasses in my class had dads that had simply disappeared in the war, gone to bits, blasted to pieces, ground into the mud, rotted with rats.... But I think she knew I knew all that. She wanted to tell me something else. Something about Uncle Frank maybe.

'Frank isn't your real Uncle, our Eric.'

Was he my real dad?

She coughed and carried on, 'This footie ... Blades, Eric.'

That's why it's him that takes me to the match. That's what Dads do.

Frank had gone and left Dad a cheery chappy, snoozing off a couple of lunchtime pints by the fire.

Mam was happy. Hands holding mine were soft and dry - not gripping and dripping.

'Do you remember your Daddy taking you when you were about five?'

I didn't. 'Really Mam?'

'Yes love, it was the last time they had a proper Derby match.'

I didn't know that Mam understood football. She was a woman after all.

'It was a stinking, rotten, horrible year. You won't remember that either, will you?'

I thought she was going to let me down gently about the Blades in 1919.

'You know about all the men killed in the Great War and your dad ... you know. Well there was this...' Her voice cracked, but she carried on. 'This great plague they called the...'

'Spanish Flu,' I said. 'We did it at school. Killed more people than the war, didn't it Our Mam?'

She looked up to the heavens. 'Cruel, very cruel. But we sailed through it and your Daddy thought, if he survived all that ... mud, he wasn't going to be beat by a bug you couldn't even see. The trams couldn't run properly; your school sent you home some days because there weren't enough teachers.' She chuckled, 'that was after Miss Pilkington - remember her? After she had tried to look after the whole school all on her own, well her and that daft caretaker? What a pair. Never again. Headmistress made a rule you all had to be sent home if they got down to only two teachers!'

She went on, 'the 1919 derby was a like a beam of light the Lord sent shining down on Sheffield at that time. First season after the war was greatly anticipated by the men - and the boys.

'The derby was at the start of the season - and it was to be two weeks running. The first game was at Hillsborough, Wednesday's home ground and they won. There's an advantage playing at home, you know that our Eric. Your own crowd shouts for you and you get a lift.'

We were both nodding.

'Your Daddy's wheezing was a good deal better - it was much worse back then, after he got back from the war. I think the gas must be clearing out of him slowly. It was summer and his wound hadn't given him much jip so he was winding himself up to give the Blades some home support. It meant a lot to him you see. When he had last been, he said it was the last time he was a whole man.'

She swung her head away and back and I saw one hand sweep away a tear.

'We made you after that match.' She blushed, but I knew she knew I was a man now, and would not be shocked.

I'd worked it out with my pal - if I was born in June 1915, then I was made in September 1914. We still didn't know *how* we were made though.

'And the next week he signed up for the Pals Brigade.' She let go of my hands, stood up, went over to the fireplace and put on a log. She lingered, looking down at Dad for a bit, her hand on her cheek. I couldn't see her face. When she turned back she was radiant - almost. She took my hands again and got back to telling me about Uncle not being my uncle.

'That game. 1919. I didn't want him taking you into that crowd breathing all those flu germs, but he was so positive, so strong.' She looked across at him again and he let out a relaxed sigh in his dream.

'He wasn't the only one who had that idea, and there was a good crowd. Your Daddy got you up on his shoulders and you saw the first goal. Unfortunately, you were in the way of a man behind you who happened to miss it. One nil to the Blades and he had missed it.

'He gave your Dad a prod in the back. "Eyup pal!" he starts. Well that was it.

'"Pal?" he says, "Pal? Call me Pal? My Pals are out there in the mud. In the Somme. I 'a'n't got no Pals here." And then he just says "Pal" over and over and over - and he was wilting.

'The bloke sees your Daddy's grey face ... and clutching at his throat ... and beginning to keel over. The bloke lifts you - more or less catches you, actually - and puts you up on his own shoulders. He sees your Daddy is looking out at the game, the rest of the crowd is roaring the Blades on, but Daddy is crying. The bloke doesn't know what to do. Shall he go or shall he stay? Your Daddy isn't going, so the bloke ... this total stranger, who just two minutes before was having a go at your Dad...' She stopped. She blinked away the tears. 'He put his arm around your Dad for the rest of the game ... like two old pals.'

I looked across at my Daddy and dragged a sleeve across my nose.

'Uncle Frank?'

23μ
Christmas 1943

Well that was a dismal affair, I'm sorry to say. It's a compliment to you though Pina - I was half hoping to maybe meet you at last. Mummy agreed to meet me. It was a civil cup of tea we had in Cole's restaurant, untouched by the Blitz which practically flattened The Moor just down the road ...and Bramall Lane. Poor Blades.

I didn't dare touch upon your health and progress. I had a dread that Grandmama would have you under a spell. Mummy is so bonny. If you have a mix of her and my Mam, wow what a dreamboat you will be. Yes Mummy looks beautiful. Blooming beautiful?

Mam made a fuss of me over Christmas, of course. I had a couple of days. I'm not sure if I am allowed from my exile, but I didn't ask as refusal can be a bit embarrassing. Dad was ... beatific? Kind of saintly - a Christmas card sort. Like Father Christmas. No. He's grown a beard which has filled his face out a bit, but it's not like Old Bug Whiskers. (Ooh mustn't call him that else he might leave cinders in my stocking.) He sat and smiled a lot. Enjoyed Christmas dinner and in his few words he did make me feel good. He knows what I am doing and patted Mam on the hand when she fretted about my Strangeways experience.

He patted me on the head, too. Very fatherly. It fair choked me up.

Warmed Mam too, seeing that.

While in town I met up with three other COs from the medical experiment days. We all seem to have survived the itchy scratchy scabies.

One of them has been conscripted - and he really cannot get out of it. He is now to be a Bevin Boy. He had volunteered to work in the coal mines as an alternative to any work related to the military. We COs have a soft spot for Ernest Bevin the Minister of Labour. There was some reluctance by men being conscripted and then not sent into the forces, but down the pit. They didn't want people to think them Conchies, so old Bevin spoke up for us, Gawd Bless him. Though we may have refused to take up arms, thousands 'have shown as much courage as anyone else in Civil Defence,' he said.

The other two have moved into medical service - helping out with stretcher bearing/hospital orderly activity. Their interest in 'my POW' garnered some feint praise, but swiftly moved to one of the lads who actually helped-out bringing some wounded POWs off the boat.

'Straight from North Africa?' I asked, perhaps too enthusiastically. We aren't supposed to be taking a serious interest in the war. We did share the hope that Alamein actually was a turning point in the war, but the same troops seem to be stuck in southern Italy now.

Oh dear. I'm fraternising with a still very deadly enemy, albeit one whose homeland was bombed by the Nazis just a few weeks ago. Palmiro was worried about the gas at Bari - not far from home apparently. Was that our gas? I do hope not. It's not been mentioned on the news, but Palmiro has picked up on the grapevine - not in Il Corriere del Sabato either! - that Fritz made a right mess, killed lots of men and civilians, and filled the harbour with sunken ships (one of which was carrying mustard gas!!!!! How horrible. Who the hell is still thinking of using that - and getting their own back?) I couldn't console Palmiro about how far it can drift. Like everything else sent up in the air, it disperses. If you can read that...

Cousin Queenie managed to snatch an hour for a cuppa with me in Doncaster. What is it about women meeting with me in cafes? Away from prying eyes? I should be glad that Queenie is still willing to be seen with me - her sisters and mother ... her family won't be. Queenie is beside herself. Of course she knows her Jack is in the thick of it - the Eighth Army and Royal Tank Regiment have followed up huge losses in North Africa with what is appearing to be a war of attrition in Italy. At least he is not *in* tanks, but *with* them on his motorbike.

I wonder if he's got a Matchless too?

He gave her a consolation: 'I've been trained by the best,' he said. 'Fred Rist and Jackie Wood were in the National six day trial team - basically kicked out of Austria in 1939'. She treasures a photo of her Jack with them outside a pub in Ringwood. (Near their training camp down south.) They're on Nortons I think, though one is not so clear - it might be a Matchless.

The six day trial thing is like the Le Mans twenty four hour car race, but for motorbikes - they ride their bikes for lots of time trials to see which can keep going the longest, easiest and fastest. They had BSA motorbikes, but I don't want one of them because ... well simply that name and their symbol - it stands for Birmingham Small Arms and the symbol is three rifles. There I go again.

It was heart-warming to see Queenie lay her hand on the picture and ...

Back at Portland Farm (that's where I live with the Fox family) the lovely Mrs Sally Fox had put up a stocking for Palmiro and me. Palmiro had awaited my return to look in his - not a tradition he was familiar with. She had managed to get an Italian sausage for him. I think he maybe cried. He ran out of the room. He soon returned beaming and buried his head in her shoulder.

He had a great story for me too: The non-co-operators are still at Nether Headon camp. When Mussolini was sacked, remember, some of the POWs were still on Mussolini's side. He has set up a Fascist state with the Germans who had sprung him from Jail. They are not allowed to billet out like Palmiro whom they regard as a traitor. It doesn't stop them being good Catholics does it?

They are fully supervised and guarded, escorted wherever they go and of course locked in at night.

On Christmas Eve some of them escaped - went missing anyway. Of course there was a hue and cry, all were dragged out of bed and counted, and yes some were missing. Eventually some smiling lads told the guards. (They were a skeleton crew of single men, letting the family men be at home - at least for a few special hours, anyway). Apparently the missing had gone to Midnight mass.

There are not many Catholics round here - it's Wesley and Pilgrim Father country - but there is a Catholic Church in a Tin Tabernacle in Retford. When a team of Screws arrived at the church, the Irish priest, a Father Finneran apparently, (I wonder what he was feeling about the British army on Easter Sunday in 1916?) would not let them interrupt his service, or take their charges. 'They have sanctuary here, and you can wait until they have got what they came for.'

He made them wait. Palmiro was tickled that the old Padre swung more smoke, rang extra bells and sang the wonderful German carol Silent Night one more time with gusto, (bit of Italian there I think), so the guards could hear it out in their cold, cold lorry.

Not a white Christmas this year thank goodness. Strange that I am glad I won't be penned up in a warm house for weeks like the last couple of years. I can get out and work...

24μ
January 1944

This time last year Alec and his family had the daily task of clearing snow - for weeks on end. Bringing the animals out for even a short break was impossible.

It's still pretty cold this year, so he says we aren't leaving them out.

Short days make for a long time to get bored. Stir-crazy. Great term Palmiro taught me. Apparently quite a lot of the Italians in camps were sent from North Africa to India, America and Canada - out of the way of being released to fight again. They've now been brought back to join 'our' lads to help on the farms - and to save the Allies having to find their keep.

When the POWs kick off, make a fuss, get grumpy and cause trouble the GIs - that's American soldiers - called them stir-crazy. Stir is prison or jail. Gaol? I think I was in gaol. I was in prison. But now we might be getting a bit stir crazy. I would really like to take Palmiro somewhere, but I'm a fairly shifty looking character by myself, without drawing more attention traipsing about with a 'foreigner'.

I caught the library in Retford before it closed the other evening. Pleasant. A place of peace, if there can be such a thing. It was fairly busy with many people like me, out of the house, but also with a purpose - either looking for a good book to distract them, or reading ALL the newspapers to find details ... some doubtless about their boys.

Not quite sure where to look for an atlas, a very pleasant young woman (not like that Mummy), was obviously a little intrigued with my query: would they have a map which would show Italian villages? I could have demurred from her inquisitiveness and say it was to check up progress in villages we had honeymooned in, but I think there was something more about me that she recognised. Am I paranoid? She drew out a very detailed and quite old map book and we found Latronico. It is a mountain village. Perhaps it was my obvious relief.

She hovered. I didn't need her to continue helping me. She looked around, tidied a shelf and came back. She hinted 'family?'

I shook my head. 'Friend.'

'At war?'

Not any more.

'Oh dear,' she was so sorry.

I simply told her that he's okay, but worried about his home and family.

She guessed.

It poured out of me. A POW was billeted with us on our farm. Not so local - Egmanton, near Tuxford. She supervises Tuxford Library - and several other villages, where she is obviously proud to have started a little lending library, but realised that they may not keep a very detailed atlas. Maybe they should.

Us. I'm a farmer. Protected occupation.

She mentioned seeing the Italians out and about - coming in from Headon - to the cinema, she asked. She knew of course. They are escorted in groups with one of the Home Guard; maybe the non-co-operators have a real Tommy. Not only Headon, I proffered and I was snared. I told her about my quest: trying to record the camps and the background experiences of the captives.

She looked at my hands. Reminded me of a teacher. I thought she might look for spuds behind my ears too. My hands were in hers. She was shaking her head. Not used to the work, she thought. I was damned sure I was by now. I had to nail my segs - calluses on my leathered hands - to show they weren't blisters.

No one has held my hands for a while now. I pulled them away.

She felt it and stepped back, protesting a little too much I thought. But yes she also is a little intrigued, not a bit sure about this war; this fighting; all this killing. Hadn't 'they' learnt enough in the not so great war?

Then she spelt it out. I was an Objector - so - good for me.

I am. It was good to not be judged and condemned.

Her colleague came up to switch off the lights and found Miss Husbands covering up her fluster.

Yes, she told me her name, her *formal* name, Mummy - Miss Husbands. I think I was daydreaming about her name and wondering what to do next. She grabbed her coat, hailed farewell over her shoulder and more-or-less steered me out into the dark, total dark, with her.

She shook my hand as she closed the door with her other. She told me her name on the stairs down. One of the 'Profs', would call 'Miss Husbands' an oxy moron - two opposite words in one phrase - a woman can't be a man; a single woman can't be a married person. A husband's 'Miss' would more likely be a Mistress, or Mrs. Hm.

It was my turn to be flustered. I was thinking of going to the Criterion off Carolgate for a game of Billiards, but who with? (*With whom*, Mummy?) Miss Husbands may have also corrected it, had I said it. She is *freightfully jolly*. (That means posh, Pina - not funny.) I *had* mentioned my honeymoon, hadn't I?

She made me promise to keep her updated on the progress of my research, and patting me on my arm, she called me her Conchie and strode off ... towards the Criterion.

I looked around and rather sheepishly crossed into the graveyard of the church opposite. When I got to the gate I glanced back and she had disappeared. She must have turned off, or else she should still be visible as a silhouette on the almost deserted, moonlit Market Square.

In the Criterion bar there was a gaggle of girls, all of a giggle. On my own, I happened to earwig on their conversation - snatching at phrases. They were nurses. At Rampton. Now there's a different sort of prison again, Pina. It's a Criminal Lunatic Asylum and it's not a mile from Headon Camp. It's where they lock up people who are dangerous - and not only when there is a full moon.

I was more than snatching at phrases now. I was locked on to their conversation.

I surreptitiously picked up my pint, took a circuitous route to the bar, turned to look for a seat and chose one just along from the girls. The bar was not exactly packed in this early evening, so the girl did not need to hutch up for me. She turned, smiled and tucked her skirt under her.

They were on about the 'Ities'. They really liked them. Ah, only some of them really like the Italian POWs. Still killing our lads some of them, let's not forget. Only dented the conversation of a few. One of them showed off a really ornate hand-bag, to the obvious mystification of most. Even I know it is not any sort of fashion. A 'carpet bag' someone called it. Classic, the girl in possession hazarded. She said 'her' Itie gave it her. That did stop the conversation. All eyes on her, but she did not blush, she shook her hair in that - is it coquettish - way. Smiling.

'Threw over the fence, more like!' was the sour grape comment.

That broke the ice and they set off all at once. Apparently, in fine weather, and to save a bob or two, they walk up the hill to Rampton. Passing the camp, along with the ubiquitous 'Bella, 'Bella, Bella!' and snatches of 'O Solo Mio' etcetera, they get all sorts of little love tokens thrown over the fence - like bangles, beads and ... rings.

The smiler, leaned on my arm and whispered 'Betty Jones'. She showed me hers: it appears to be a circle of Perspex with the tiniest of glass beads pressed in around its perimeter. Against a black-out shaded gas light it still twinkled - like little stars. How did they make that in a prison camp?

The bag girl was protesting rather too much and getting a real ribbing. No it hadn't been thrown over the fence, she doesn't walk that way any road. It had been given to her by one of the lads billeted on their farm. Well not one of *them*, actually.

'Aahh!' and much finger wagging.

Much more fluster. No, one of their friends, billeted out at Rufford.

Rufford! Another new place.

Rufford Abbey, they asked.

The village idiot was watching me, mouth agape. I knew he could play snooker, so I stood, nodded to Betty, indicated 'my friend' and went upstairs. He's not actually an idiot, just not quite on the ticket, that's why he's not at war, that and a bit of a gammy leg. Also known as a bar-fly - hangs around hoping for a free beer - and gets some teasing. He got a beer off me, but I got a challenging game. They might not want him in the army, but his aim with a cue is true. He talked non-stop and I didn't hear a word he said.

25μ

What to do on these winter evenings? The boys in the camps have a full-ish life. That or go crazy, stir crazy I suppose. They seem to do lots of arts and crafts with whatever they can find. Many are learning English, they can be embarrassingly ingratiating, rather too willing to please much of the time. Want to make us understand them.

They are also desperate for female company. Mummy knows how I feel. I hope. Old Tom Collis's daughter - Jane or June, was it? - might say she doesn't like the attention over in Langwith. She may not actually - such a young lass. Some of the girls in the pub were also not so comfortable with the whistling, singing and ringing from the other side of the fence. There was more than one quiet girl in the group looking uncomfortable. It takes all sorts my Mam says, Pina. Remember that, when someone tells you that a person is or is not very nice. There is someone who loves them, and you, even if it is only their daddy.

I told Palmiro about the bag and the rings. I wasn't surprised at the rings - though I thought cutting slices off and polishing up copper pipe might look more like gold - and Palmiro was more interested in my cut lip.

I asked if he knew about Rufford.

Abbey, he thought. Camp there too. Like Langwith.

They know all about it. They could, but won't, tell the Corriere a few things.

He was scratching his head and smiling to himself.

In the end he hitched up his belt and pulled the inside of his pocket out - turned it inside out. Not something a man would normally do in mixed company. What would they unearth in there?

Palmiro's was actually beautiful. It almost twinkled like the ring. The lining was covered in shiny threads. It was like a miniature treasure chest. Almost surreal in our candle light.

He was revealing something of himself in doing this. Cautious. Checking my response. I was frowning. Deeply. Head shaking. I just could not fathom it.

'I see fred, I pick him up,' he said.

That didn't explain anything.

'Make picture'.

Ah - the hand bag. That's what has triggered it.

'You say tappery?'

'Yes, tapestry,' I said.

'I make tapestry,' he said pointing at himself.

I thought of the Bayeux Tapestry - and the girl in the pub's handbag of course - a picture made of cloth. To be truthful I could also think of a comic version made of it called Ye Berlyn Tapestrie, which showed the invasion of Belgium by the Germans in the last bash. Not so comical, but ironic. Either way, it was a man-sort of sewing.

'You?' I said. 'Where ... when?'

He took a little pack of cards and papers from his top pocket, sorted through and passed me a coloured picture. An old saint, I've seen lots of them - holy pictures. Come to think of it, yes lots of the boys have them as a sort of talisman, a good luck charm. Sometimes they get them out and kiss them and look to the heavens.

'My saint.'

S. EGIDIO ABATE
PROTETTORE DI LATRONICO (Potenza)

I read out 'Sant Egidio Abate.'

'Exact.' He pointed at the picture of a giant bishop with a town and mountain behind him. Nodding and looking back to me he said the rather obvious, 'My town.'

I read 'Protector of Latronico in Potenza' below the saint's name.

'Si. Me. Yes. Make tapestry Sant Egidio.'

'You?' I said, 'tapestry?'

'Yeah. One thread, one prayer, get me home ... please?'

I smiled. I might have even shed a tear. I coughed. 'Where is it?'

He double-checked me, and then went across to his room. (Cell?)

It is beautiful. I do hope you get to see the finished work one day. Work of Art? Bayeux Tapestry? That really is comic with its funny horses - you'll be able to draw better when you are five. This is ... I'm stuck for words. To think he has scavenged these threads, found them on the floor (he has washed them all of course) and he's sewing them in to a piece of ... I don't know what that is either, but a good strong piece of buff cloth. He's got it between sheets of paper

- remarkably clean paper - and there's at least four needles dangling from different colours of thread. He's got his own system going here. He's 'drawn' on the figure with fine black cotton, exactly like the card and he's filling in the colours.

'Sally help.'

Of course.

'Only more needles - I find fred.'

Amazing. Maybe it shouldn't be. I know the men in the camps have to keep themselves occupied, in fact the guards and Prisoner of War system have realised. They have to keep up morale, avoid more death. They find poor boys dead in the camps ... and outside ... quite a lot. Nothing suspicious, just very sad.

Mustn't get morbid - it's all too easy during these long evenings.

Palmiro let me take a photograph - of the card, not the tapestry - 'not fini' - I'll slot it in here when it's finished. You won't see the colour but if I tell you he has the face done - looks a bit like Father Christmas, sweet and gentle. He's found a pink that's just right for the face, and he's obviously found three common colours, red, blue and yellow to make the old Abbot's costume. Not finished, like he says, but coming along beautifully.

What was I doing to keep me occupied? His story of course, but I'm not telling him.

I do have another project I haven't mentioned to you, but he knows: I'm a plasher. What do you think of that? I don't think there will be another one in the whole of Sheffield. I'm learning to lay hedges. Townies will not realise how much work goes into keeping the beasts in the fields, then not having hedges turning into trees and hiding them all.

Of course Alec has had to grub up all of his scrub - dig up all the bushes and the self-set copses on poor land - to sew food crops. We did that mostly with the new tractor and plough. Thank goodness - brambles and nettles are almost intelligent - they get you before you can get them. But we plash the hedges.

I have got a secret other reason for being a plasher...

Palmiro wasn't going. He had told of his little secret. I had to tell of my lip.

'Well you know, you *do* know about men in the town. *You* go in a large group, protect each other and a guard to protect people from you.'

He was smiling.

'That's all really. Alone. Finish my game of billiards. Finish my second pint. Shake my opponent's hand and set off down stairs. Followed...'

He was nodding.

'Shoved across behind the town hall yard and given a bit of a pasting.' I pulled my souvenir feather from my pocket and twirled it.

He patted me on the shoulder - ouch - 'Sorry, Eric,' and we went to bed.

*Picture has come out well. I'll have to try some shots of the camps - if I don't get shot in the process. I've inserted the snap of Palmiro that was on the same roll of film. The Greyhound folding camera that my Mam got from cigarette coupons ten years ago is surprisingly good.

26μ

Alec knows I refuse to read the paper, but that I will consider Italian, Sheffield, POW and metal related items. He fingered the Express, raised his eyebrows and he slid it across the breakfast table towards me.

I saw Sally give him a frown. She looks after me, does Sally.

I couldn't help seeing a strange graphic - was it even a photo?

'Lufwaffe raiders drop them,' was the little headline for a long black strip down the centre of the front page leading to crinkles at the bottom.

'These "flutterers" fell again last night', is the caption. The description says they are up to two feet long and a quarter inch wide, tin foil sandwiched between black paper.

I shivered when I read it.

It's one of my early realisations that I was developing a weapon. We were asked to develop lots of different alloys - iron mixed with other metals - and make the thinnest possible strips. Basically like variations of shiny confetti. The first clue was that we were not told what it was for. They called it 'window' but our name 'chaff' stuck. (You know why tanks are so called don't you? When they were developing them in Lincoln it had to be a secret, so even the workers making separate parts were told they were simply parts for tanks for Mesopotamia - water tanks for a very dry country. The name 'tanks' stuck.)

I'm now working with real chaff for half the year - it's the husks from the wheat - the air is full of it over the summer and autumn.

The Express is explaining that they were used by raiders over the south east last night and people woke up to find the 'flutterers' 'probably used to confuse our radio location.'

So they've caught up with our 'chaff' have they? Ours ended up as mostly aluminium and despite it being ready in '42, as far as I can make out, were not used until only this year. It's pretty simple really, so as soon as Germans woke up to find our chaff, their boffins could make their own very quickly, so game over.

The Express explains that the 'flutterers' are similar to wrapping of cigarettes before the war. That's what I was told I was working on.

They are used by bombers to throw the Hun's radar off their scent. The 'chaff' is dropped out of the bomb bay; it forms a cloud which really does bounce the radar off. I am OK with it saving our aircrews' lives, of course, but I didn't want to help them to bomb thousands of women and children in their beds.

That was the thin end of the wedge of my demise in the steel industry.

On a funnier note, Alec also tells me about food and farming stuff - of course.

I'll take you to a Pantomime one day. You'll love the custard pie scene - they always have one. The clowns always find themselves in a kitchen and start messing about. It inevitably ends up in fight - a silly one, where they don't shoot or bayonet each other, but slap custard pies in each others' faces (and sometimes down their trousers!)

Eric says that last Christmas they were told to stop using real flour.

'Too right,' we laughed. 'Here's us growing wheat in swamps and bramble patches, only for you to go throwing it about.'

Anyway, now they're using a chalky mixture.

(Maybe we shouldn't tell the children, it'll spoil the fun.)

27µ

Now that many more of the lads are billeted out with farmers, Palmiro does have his own 'social life'. I hope the story so far does not give the wrong impression that we lived in each other's pocket. (Hmm - I would be getting pieces of cotton up my nose, wouldn't I Pina?)

Not everybody ... not by a long shot ... likes the POWs, as you can imagine, but the Italians have not proved to be ardent fascists or whatever, like we think of Nazis, so they are not in secure camps - *prison* camps - any more. Mostly.

The Italians are fervently learning English, mostly with the intention of getting a smile or a song from the girls - and they succeed, I can tell you. They police themselves, and we hear little about them getting into trouble. They don't drink much and are not used to our beer drinking culture - or the Germans' for that matter. They know they are not really welcomed by the locals in their local public house so they simply do not go. They do however seem to hang about on corners and crossroads, where there is also often a pub.

Such is the case at Edwinstowe. There is a pub at the end of the lane from the camp, and that is only a hundred yards from the crossroads where there's another pub, where I have stopped off to make my researches. Ahem.

I hoped I might meet Joe Bennett again so asked. They told me he lived only two doors down, so I had the cheek to go and knock. He is a local lad, a collier - coal miner - at that coal mine - Thoresby. (The Duke's remember - of Hull - not so posh, so they give him a proper name I hadn't heard of. Apparently that fishy city's name is actually Kingston-upon-Hull).

Joe is in the Royal Navy. Having a tough time of it, by all accounts - but not his. The famous British stiff-upper-lip is not only the resort of the upper classes, as we might believe. You would think Joe was having fun cruising round, where in fact it is obvious that he has personally known hundreds, maybe thousands of men, who have been sent to the bottom of the Atlantic, in ships that sailed alongside his destroyer HMS Keppel. Apparently it was also the chief ship - he carried the Commodore of the fleet.

It's in dock in Hull for repair. 'Bit of a bump.'

He can't give me detail of course, but we all know of the convoys bringing in food - much reduced by U-Boat submarine attacks. That's what I am doing out here - replacing a quarter of the food we normally import. No, I am not doing it all by myself - Palmiro is helping me.

By this time their most important task is not bringing in food, but escorting troop ships fetching reinforcement forces from all over the empire, and across the Atlantic from Canada and America. Joe has had a few convoys on the Murmansk Run to Northern Russia, famous for its bitter cold, as much as for its fighting and sinking of U-Boats.

he joined me in the pub looking very smart in his uniform.

I nudged him.

He looked down at himself, then leaned in to me singing, 'Ship ahoy, Ship ahoy!'

To which I added in my sweet dulcet tones, 'All the nice girls love a sailor'.
'She's from round here y'know?'

I looked around. No young women in sight.

'Naah,' he said, 'Ella - the singer - Ella Retford!'

'Oh,' says I, frowning a bit. 'But you? Busy?'

'Not 'alf!'

(That means very busy).

''lantic convoy. Quick shore leave. Buy us a pint!'

I did. It's difficult to know what to say to that. Busy is not a proper word, and I don't like to ask how many ships they safely escorted to wherever, because there is always going to be how many they also lost.

Fortunately, he sensed it himself and told me funny thing instead. 'I'm not a gunner or owt, I'm a stoker, shovelling coal into a white hot furnace when we are full steam ahead - and that's most of the time. We don't want Fritz to catch us dawdling. Y'know it's that cold up by Russia that we got the world record for an icicle in our boiler room.'

He exaggerated the 'world record' bit so I know he only meant it was big. How big?

'It was ten foot long!'

I frowned in suspicion.

'Honestly - ten foot long.'

'But in a boiler room, Joe?'

He laughed. 'Does seem wrong doesn't it. But the Keppler, she's got these great big fans drawing in air for ramming the boiler, and they are in the top - outside of course. We're ten feet below stoking, and the freezing air meets our fug and much of it freezes instantly. So cold it stretched all the way from the deck to our floor.'

He took a swig, nodding proudly.

'Us stokers only get up top now and again, and the captain - Commodore - invited a couple of us up one day, just to sense the occasion. Think he said it were thirty below.'

That's very cold, Pina. Polar bears live in it, but we don't.

'We got wrapped up in all the clobber we could find,' (that's clothes, Pina,) 'me comms, two ganseys, jacket, greatcoat, hat, gloves and scarf, then one of the lads says to me "eyup, wrap this round yer face", and threw another pair of comms to me.'

I was chuckling, because though I got the sense, I could hardly understand him. 'Comms? Gansey?' I said.

'Sorry, combination - vest and under-trousers.'

'Oh, yes,' I said. 'Us Steelers don't need them so much, next to the furnaces.'

'Nor do us stokers - but up top. Wow! I thought the lad was joking to wrap his pants round my head, but just going up the ladder I found out and backed down to sort myself a turban. Lucky too. We looked around the stern - that's the back to you land-lubbers - there was no land, and the sea was calm, but we were pushing some flume out from our turbines. Very Pretty. The convoy was keeping up aft of us, all steaming safely. Right proud I were. But the picture soon froze over and we climbed back below. Where I had been breathing through the comms and scarf was a layer of ice built up in just those few minutes and my eyes were prickling with hoarfrost on my lashes.'

His reverie continued, his eyes looking straight through me to the freezing fiord of Murmansk.

We both took a long draught of our ale.

He licked his lips and swiped his cuff across them. 'Aye,' he sighed.

'Gansey?' I said.

He pulled the end of his pullover. 'What do you call this?'

'Cardigan? Jumper? Jersey?'

'Aye, lad. What's next to Jersey?'

'Guernsey? Oh Gansey!' I said. 'Not heard that.'

'Sailor talk. It's a very tight knit Jersey - waterproof even, especially from raw wool with some lanolin left in it. Super.'

He looked out of the door as it swung open. 'Ities,' he said, 'alright lads.'

I smiled. Dare I tell him. 'Speak to them do you?'

He looked across at the barman and whispered, 'He let me bring a couple in for a pint. Got a bit of a chum - Philippo they call him - ret long surname - keeps an eye out for me when I'm home.' He had a slurp and laughed. 'They hated the beer, but pretended to love it as I was being so nice. Nearly choking they were. Just lads like us. Glad to be out of it I reckon.'

'We have them working with us on the farm. They're billeting them, you know?'

'How d'you mean?'

'Letting them off the camp,' I said. 'Live on the farms. We've got one with us. Palmiro.'

He told me there were plenty here. They aren't strictly guarded. 'They're no problem. You seen their soccer pitch?'

I said I hadn't, how could I?

He told me to just wander up the lane. Nobody would stop me. They had cleared some awful bramble scrub at the top end, levelled it and sewed some grass seed. Being mostly peasant stock, they know how to make stuff grow.

'Not bad at footie, neither,' he said. The locals have quite taken to them, so much so they've given them a proper set of goalposts and now they play a scratch team from able bodied men and lads from the villages round about.

I agreed with him about them being 'lads like us' and told him about Palmiro and the barns full of billets, and one even maybe at Rufford Hall now.

'Oh very posh' he said.

We exchanged addresses and I told him I'd buy him a pint and a chaser if I let me know when he's back again.

'Phil might be out there. I'll call you to meet him if I see him,' and with a cheery wave and a 'Ship Ahoy!' to all in the pub, he marched towards the door, taking all eyes with him.

I do hope I see him again.

As the door closed behind him, my smiling eyes met with others. A man beckoned me over and asked if he heard me mention the Ities at Rufford. I laughed and told him I was making my way down to have a decko for myself.

He laughed and asked if I had heard that the Ities have been getting into the old house - 'a proper palace,' he said - and cutting strips off the tapestries hanging from every posh wall, then using it to make handbags for their girls ... and a few bob.

'Old palace?' I said, 'I thought it was an abbey.'

Apparently it's a long, long time since it was an abbey - Henry VIII dissolved it, and gave the estate to a henchman, yet another of these dukes - of Scarborough again - before one of his scions went bust and couldn't afford to keep it up.

It was only down the road, he told me, past the Rufford Arms - not in Rufford, but Edwinstowe - and less than two miles from The Royal (yes) Oak that I had been in at Edwinstowe. The chap said that if I wanted a bag for you Mummy, ask at the bar at the Rufford. I was probably shaking my head as I stepped out into a gloomy late afternoon.

Decision time - look for the pitch, or now I know, come back another day, but check out Rufford?

The, er, Abbey, not: wonderful great stone gate posts with an odd assortment of buildings - including a group of about twenty pretty typical camp huts of the Laing steel framed timber sort, but unpainted. They will easily sleep five hundred, but there were just a few POWs milling about as the light was fading rapidly, so I had to get back here.

I told Palmiro of his friends living like lords, amusingly engaged in a similar craft to himself, but out to impress the girls and not the Lord.

28μ

Palmiro was tight lipped about the handbaggers. I sensed his disapproval and possibly his resentment about his noble art of creating a tapestry being compared to people destroying a probably ancient piece of artwork.

He obviously didn't want to speak badly of them so I had to say it for him.

He simply commented, 'some good seed falls on stony ground'.

Biblical I do believe.

Anyhow, that was last week, today I had a piece of real excitement. The Foxes have been talking at dinner (that's the family here Pina, not the feral creatures catching the rabbits for us. That sort don't talk, despite what you might read in the fairy tales). Americans are crawling all over the place. Crawling is more Alec's than the ladies' sentiment. They obviously find the smart, healthy looking and smiley men - more men than boys, so well built I have to say and head taller than your average Italian - attractive.

That does not warm Alec to the notion of them coming over here, though he is really grateful that they may just be able to help 'us' out of the hole Churchill seems to be digging 'us' into.

This Sunday I thought I had better have a proper shufty at Carlton-in-Lindrick.

I took the road through Ollerton and ... well if I was nearly knocked off my bike once, I was nearly knocked off a hundred times. I was so glad I had put the Teledraulic forks on Maisie Matchless as I travelled most of the way on the roadside and even a short stretch along a very shallow dike.

Why?

Huge American lorries - trucks, they call them. They are head to toe in what I soon discovered was a convoy - two convoys, actually: one going in and one going out of Boughton Camp. That is just before Ollerton. Working on a Sunday too. There were a few last week, but there are always munitions lorries taking a constant supply from dumps hidden in these dukes estates - there's a Proteus army camp by Thoresby coal mine. I get the impression that is a big one. Like I said Thoresby is a Duke's house - of Kingston, apparently; that is next to Clumber - Newcastle's; Welbeck Abbey is the Duke of Portland's (I don't know where that is, but it's not round here - Isle of Wight I reckon); and Worksop's is the Duke of Norfolk's little cottage. Apparently Rufford Abbey - poor little place - is not a Ducal seat. (That is a very big chair, Pina.) It only belonged to a couple of Earls - of Scarborough and Shrewsbury.

Their grounds are pitted with bunkers full of hundreds and thousands of shells of every shape and size and Joe told me that two trains a day collect the munitions from each of the stations at Ollerton, Worksop, Edwinstowe and Retford. I told you about the ******** munitions factory near Retford. There must be a more hidden in Sher**** ***est too.

You will know about Robin Hood and his merry men hiding in Sherwood Forest. Well there are lots of merry Americans there now.

66

It was like Joe said - I needed to ride up from Ollerton, through the Dukeries on to Worksop to get to Carlton, and that was an eye-opener - mine nearly popped out, lucky they didn't as I would likely have been shot if I'd stopped to pick them up. All along the roadside there were random sizes of shells - fallen out of boxes I imagine, so the whole length of all the roads is in sight of a one guard after another - and 'don't you stop, Buster!' (That's a funny name the Americans called me.)

29μ

So how does Palmiro feel after several months with us? What are the differences?

No grape ... no snake.

Of course no grapes, but there are snakes.

He looked a little worried about that.

He made a biting face. Fangs with his fingers.

I smiled a reassuring smile. 'Not many,' I said.

Not reassuring enough.

We have adders I told him. 'Why didn't the viper vipe 'er nose, Pina? Because the adder 'ad 'er handkerchief.'

Did I hear Mummy groan?

We do have adders, and they are poisonous, but...

I asked him how common in his country. He told of an uncle visiting the house one day and telling him to sit still up on the bed. He then suddenly reached under the bed, grabbed a snake and swung it out of the window. Palmiro shivered.

No, I told him, we have only the adder as a poisonous snake, and ... I pointed at him, widened my eyes and acted the vampire.

He cringed.

'No! *You*,' I said. 'The adder is scared, frightened of *you*. Only bite you if you try to catch it. Does not come in the house.'

We had a little smile about all this. I then realised that I had better tell him about grass snakes. If he does see a snake, and he will in the fields or woods, and it doesn't slither away, it will be a grass snake or even just a worm - a slow worm.

I wasn't so sure I had him convinced so I moved on. Of course no grapes - not so warm here, either and that's why no grapes. He had a think about that and mentioned a greenhouse. I was not sure that the family would see it as a priority in wartime, not to mention the War Ag man checking up.

What was his impression of the British?

He started about Bardia again, yes they had a good few fights with each other, but I cut him a bit short. I don't want to know about that.

Alessandro and Swiss again. Then South Africa. He was totally fair about his treatment, in temporary camps in Alexandria and Suez despite the harshness. He's lucky to be alive. But not Durban camp. 'Terrible,' he repeated, several times shaking his head, but lifted it up and gave me a watery smile. 'There's always a way, Eric.'

Snakes in the desert of South Africa 'The worst thing on this earth is that thing that's meant to crawl on its belly.'

I suppose that's a very Catholic thing - the Devil is consistently a serpent. Consigned to crawl the earth and tempt us. Well, not me.

'Craps!' he exclaimed. 'And donkeys. Asses?'

'Crabs?' I said.

'Yeah we have crabs in the walls.'

I didn't remember this from our trip to Italy. I mimed nipping.

He nodded.

I shook my head. 'Donkeys,' I said. 'Alec used to call me his donkey - until we got the tractor, that is.'

No car or tractor in his village. Many donkeys. 'Eeyore wake you up every day - and chickens in the kitchen.'

Sally wouldn't put up with that would she?

He said the kitchen table was a little cage. Wire wrapped around the legs to keep babies in. No, not you Pina - 'chicks', I told him.

'You like Sally? Treating you well?'

Of course. How else? He was teaching her a thing or two in her kitchen garden. Growing for England. But no garlic.

Not very English I told him. Takes some getting used to. Mummy and I did, but people were generally very suspicious of this 'foreign muck.' I didn't tell him that, but mentioned onions, spring onions, leeks and chives. That not enough to be getting on with?

He says that Sally is trying to find him some garlic - maybe Retford market or even Lincoln. She does like him. Who wouldn't?

Ghosts.

Ghosts?

Witches.

Witches? Curiouser and curiouser. I could see he was unsure whether to go ahead, but I assured him we did have ghosts, but not witches. I didn't tell him we have burnt them all at the stake, well that's only if they survived the ducking stool.

I got the impression that was not quite it - more like a mystic woman. He really believed in her magic powers though: the mystic woman in the village was not to be crossed: Palmiro's sister Maria had crossed her and the 'family saw her lifted up a foot above her bed' - it was the witch that did it.

'Not Sally,' I assured him.

He stood, not completely sure whether or not to set off across the dark creaky boards to his room. Cell.

I hadn't gleaned much on his impression of the British, but I think that will be it. I haven't heard him say a bad word against anybody - ever.

I shooed him away laughing, and made a quiet 'woo-oo-oogh' as his door groaned to.

30μ

You could ask me if Palmiro is my friend. Though a fair question it is a little tricky to answer. I look at, I watch, these boys who have 'fought together'. I put that in quotes because it is a saying, and it does not mean quite what it says. They did not actually go into battle together. Not like my Daddy did with his pals.

The army learnt from what it did to the Pals - the ones still alive let their pals back home, and their wives, mothers and children too, know just how horrible war is. That pals actually do die. And lots of them. It brought it home to them, to their house and the homes of neighbours - many of them. Whole streets of people suddenly know not just one, but several men - boys - who had cheerfully set off to war as Pals and died together. Thousands in one day. They were going to be home for Christmas, the family feast, not left behind, disappeared, in some foreign field.

It was a lesson that all the world's armies learnt.

So these Italians are not pals. They might say they are now - they are all in this together - and with me too.

Cautious is what we are. All these boys know people who died. This will be difficult for you Pina. It is difficult for Palmiro.

I told you that 130,000 Italians were captured in one day, who 'didn't fire a shot', because they had run out of bullets. What I did not tell you was that they had used up the ones they started with. They had shot them all. At British soldiers. And killed some. Lots of them.

Lots of Queenie's Jack's friends.

But they are not really his friends. Pals.

In armies they know it is best to not make friends, because many will die. So might Jack.

Queenie loves Jack. If he dies, she will be very sad. I love Mummy and I will love you. I really hope that you won't be killed. So when you wonder what I did in the war, I hope you will be happy that I made a big effort to not kill anybody, because that would make Mummy and you sad.

While I am writing this Mummy is very sad about *how* I am trying to not make her sad. What I am doing does make her sad at the moment.

It is a dilemma. Mummy and Grandpapa want me to be like all the young people they know and join up and kill some other wives' and mothers' husbands and sons, or even fly bomber planes over the houses of people I cannot even see and blow them up.

Is Palmiro - or Alec for that matter - my friend?

We are probably comrades. Some would say colleagues. I can't think of any better words. We worry that anytime soon one of us is going to disappear, or die, so we avoid getting close to each other. Are we points of a triangle? Palmiro and Alec are enemies, still. Alec does not agree with my war. Palmiro may not be my friend. I love Alec and his family for their understanding of both Palmiro and me. Palmiro certainly feels good that I am friendly towards him - certainly much nicer than I am allowed to be. We are all very caring towards each other.

Good friends help each other but comrades help each other. People do things for the best of each other. Team mates do it. Blades at Sheffield play hard together so that United will win. But they do not need to be friends.

Palmiro and I work together most of the time - most of the daylight hours together, out in the fields.

We also do some things in our free time together.

But alone together.

We cannot be seen together in public.

It makes me feel ashamed that I have the Matchless which, like most motorbikes, has a pillion - a seat for a passenger. But I can't take Palmiro. I could, but both of us could get into trouble.

He is supposed to be my enemy. In fact some of his comrades, other Italians who have not been captured yet, are still fighting against British and other Allied troops. Troopers like Queenie's Jack.

If we manage to survive this horror, I hope we will all laugh and hug and be the very best of friends.

Will Palmiro and Jack?

Maybe Palmiro will do me the honour of being your Godfather.

31μ
Summer 1944

What a turn-up that was. I came out of the pub at Carlton-in-Lindrick on Sunday afternoon - blinded on a sunny Sunday that let my Matchless almost gleam, but it wasn't my bike that caught my eye, but an immaculately dressed GI looking at it. GI might as well have stood for Ghostly Individual not General Inscript or whatever it really means - except that it means an American Soldier. Everybody calls all the Americans 'GIs'.

I stood and watched him, enjoying his wonder. Of course all military bikes are painted in 'uniform' to suit the place they are being used. Jack is a dispatch rider - he carries messages around for the officers, dashing on his motorbike. I don't know if he's got a Matchless, or maybe a Norton. Whatever, in North Africa (hush, hush, of course we don't know where he is) his bike will have been a sandy colour, to hide in the desert. When he was learning over here it will have been army green. If he's in Italy I don't know what colour it would be. Green like the grass or grey like the mountains? If he's in the jungle in Burma, will it be stripy like a tiger?

He caught me smiling at him. I pulled a straight face in case he thought I was laughing at him. We don't know what they do. They are foreigners too.

He was fine. Admiring the shiny black paintwork, the coloured flying 'M' sign on the petrol tank. (I have been stopped by an Air Raid Warden who asked if my shiny paintwork is legal. I shrugged and distracted him by showing him my lights hooded for the blackout.)

'Matchless, London?'

That was funny - as if he knew about the firm that made it. It doesn't say it on the tank or the engine. I pulled a face. He pointed to the transfer of the M on the leg-guard toolbox. It's a lovely victorious M - in races, not wars - wrapped in a laurel wreath.

I was looking at his Jeep. It too was a nice clean *not* shiny one - out in its Sunday best, though. I had seen plenty. Up too close for comfort, charging down the lanes all around us - especially down into Boughton - many times having to swerve to avoid being ditched by one. All muddy.

He offered me a ride

I didn't feel I needed to reciprocate, so accepted.

He said I could maybe show him around.

Turn him around on a sixpence more like.

We drew whistles from a gaggle outside the pub, and not a few rubber-neckers. And he set off towards Worksop. Jeeps have windshields which can be dropped down. It was down. The wind was in our hair. At the village edge he squealed to a halt, turned off the engine and turned to me.

He gave me a chance to wipe my hair lashed eyes.

Did I know where the Prisoner of War Camp was?

I was probably opening and closing my mouth - rather foolishly. Catching flies your Grandma would say.

72

Why me?

Why not?

Guys (Guys! Now that's speaking American!) Guys in the pub said it was down Church Lane. We were sitting opposite it.

I suddenly got scared.

Why is an American soldier (Ally) looking for a Prisoner of War Camp for Axis Prisoners?

Revenge?

Murder?

He looked quite excited - but in a nice way.

It's easy to get out of a Jeep - you don't even need the door.

Should I jump out?

I nearly twisted my head off my neck looking around for options.

That's Church Lane.

He told me.

I knew.

I found it myself.

By myself.

On my bike.

In civvies.

I didn't want to go down there in a military vehicle.

Calm down.

I smiled. What is an American soldier a) doing here; and b) looking for a POW camp for?

He told me to relax.

I didn't look relaxed?

He is looking for his uncle.

His uncle?

His uncle is an Italian.

Ah! I see the likeness.

His uncle Luca Ritucci is an Italian POW. He is supposed to be at *Caroltone in Linderick Camp.* That's here isn't it?

I didn't correct his pronunciation.

I nodded.

I told him that I too was looking for the POW camp, and that yes I thought it was down Church Lane. But maybe we shouldn't go down in a military vehicle?

What better, he thought, starting up and skidding across into the lane.

'Joe', he said offering me his hand.

I suddenly realised I was in the wrong seat and he was on the wrong side of the road. I went to pull the wheel, but pulled myself up short.

Calm down Eric.

We were promptly at a gate house. A typical Estate gatehouse. With a rather untypical boom across its gate and a guard pointing a rifle appearing out of our cloud of dust.

Joe jumped out - actually sprung out - saluted the guard, then offered his hand. 'Joe Santacroce, US Army.'

The guard was disarmed. He looked at his gun, shouldered it and offered his hand to Joe.

He asked him inside, checked me sitting in the Jeep, and left me waiting. Blocking the gate.

What if a truckload of men turned up? Soldiers. POWs.

It was a wait, but not a long one.

Joe vaulted back in, slung the car into reverse and me at his dashboard, turned onto the lane - continuing along to a corner, another gate opposite the church and this time broadsided to a halt.

'Luca's out,' he said, looking at his watch. 'You garda get me to him.'

He had the address of a farm at Mattersey Thorpe. I haven't been there. I hadn't heard of it. But I did have my map. About five miles north of Retford, east of Carlton. So I became his navigator.

Tinkers Hill then Hundred Acre Lane - didn't see Winnie the Pooh in his wood.

We were looking for a big farm in a tiny village. Got to the village and the first person we asked, pointed us to Mr Leslie Marshal's and disappeared in another cloud of dust.

For the first time Joe stopped. He sucked in his lips looking at a barn side. He steadily clambered out of the Jeep. Somewhat bone-shaken, I gingerly scrambled after him. We both stretched our backs as if we had been travelling since dawn.

Joe straightened his side cap, or should I say sided his GI cap smartly? Pulled down his shirt. Brushed it. Pinched the pleats in his bags.

At the point of arrival, he seemed reluctant to complete the journey.

He about-turned and marched.

Rounding the barn we came upon a big old tractor wheel, not like the little donkey War Ag had given us, and two guys (it's catching - if you could hear me you'd think I was a Yank)... two guys were deep in conversation. One looked up and took out his pipe.

The other...

The other...

...the other, a really tanned man, looked at Joe and ... went pale. It was a very strange sight, but lasted only seconds, before both men ran round the tractor and into each other's arms and ... wept.

Yes - big boys can and do cry.

Even Daddy. It's bringing a tear to my eyes as I write this now.

Back at Portland Farm I told Palmiro about the encounter. I was still breathless. Or maybe just speechless. What is war about? On my way home, by myself after Joe dropped me of at my bike, I had time to register that sometimes it's a step beyond Pals - this bit of war is about close family. Joe is Luca's sister's son. He is here preparing to go into battle against his own cousins.

But then I thought of that first war, my Daddy's war. It was in one way of looking at it a war between first cousins - our King, Kaiser Bill of Germany and Czar Nicholas of Russia - but not in a real way. Those royals didn't fight each other - they had other people who they didn't even know, kill and die for them, with no gain for themselves.

Am I making sense?

Palmiro listened attentively. I didn't rant about Kaisers and Czars to him. (I think Kaiser is the German and Czar is the Russian word for Caesar - he was the most famous Emperor - but of Italy long ago.)

Luca is older than Palmiro. I talk of these 'boys'. I have included Palmiro in that but Palmiro is 24 now to some of their 18, (or less, though they deny it), but Luca could be a Daddy to these children.

I couldn't tell much about him, because Mr Marshall, 'call me Leslie', brought us all in for tea. Joe had to laugh about English tea. Leslie then led me into another room to let them jabber away to each other in very excited Italian.

Leslie is very impressed with Luca.

In the few minutes we had, he told me just how much he depends on Luca. Leslie had inherited the farm, with no farming experience of his own. Luca, not to put to fine a point on it, is running his farm for him.

He told how when they were bringing in the hay, Luca had been pitching the hay off a cart up to two men in the loft. Despite there being the two of them, and him pitching over his own head, he was working too fast for them.

They objected - shouted him to slow down.

He ignored them.

They let the stooks fall back down.

What did Luca do?

He kept on pitching.

What were they to do?

Embarrassed they upped their own work rates and brought the hay in.

'Good man.'

Luca soon called us back in as Joe had only a short leave from base and had to get off. More tears and neither had touched their tea.

32μ

I'm a Duke!

Portland Farm. I don't think I told you that is the name Alec Fox's farm.

I've just learnt that it's called Portland because it is the Duke's Farm.

I have been cynical about all the big country houses round here belonging to dukes and I live in one.

Actually it isn't his house but one of his many farms. Maybe I am one of his pigs? Oh no - I'm Alec's donkey aren't I?

The Duke's house is Welbeck Abbey, but like Rufford, it's not an Abbey any longer. Henry VIII took it off the Abbot and gave it to his friend for getting lots of men to fight wars for him.

33µ

Where do I stand now? Am I doubting myself? Mankind?

We are at war. It's the middle of 1944 - over four years. I am not at war, nor is Palmiro, nor are thousands of his comrades from the Italian Army. I say thousands because there are ... how many camps in this area alone? There must be an equivalent across the country. Their agricultural deployment is handled by the War Ag and there's one of these in each county. I believe there are camps across England, Wales and Scotland and can only assume there are some in rural Northern Ireland. Isn't it *all* farming besides Belfast?

Very strangely for us out here in the countryside, it feels a bit like the phoney war, as the early months were called. War was going on and the German army was doing terrible things to the Polish. The Russians are fighting the Finnish, though the Allies had not committed any forces to the war.

The Polish stuff goes on ... and on. The word in the unwelcome headlines I caught site of most last year was Kharkov, and that's near Tarnopil. So far away. In Ukraine. Part of Poland. Near Stalingrad. The horrors there do not bear thinking about. So I try not to.

In the skies around here we have got so used to the constant coming and going of planes, but the villagers tell me that they have had their war - as we had in Sheffield, our Blitz was two years ago - and many of the villages round here had a few bombs and they could see the fireworks from aerodromes all over this region - especially over Lincolnshire and to the east.

Phoney because it is not real. To us.

We can still have a real sense that the Nazis could overrun us. Will you be forced to speak German at school? I could say the fear is palpable, but that's not the British way. We shall not be beaten. They do say 'with no help from you Eric.'

But I am at least feeding you. So are the other prisoners. I say that because I am serving a sentence just like them, but I am not your enemy. Now, nor are they.

So what have I found out?

Around Sheffield there are several 'camps': Lodge Moor, is a huge camp. I think it was an original as it was used in the last war, and of course it was also an army base where Dad did his trench warfare training. I reckon it is a transit camp: the POWs are brought into the country in huge numbers and then sorted there. The ardent Nazis were shipped out to Canada and other dominions away from escaping and getting back to help their own war effort. Some were kept over here - but I think more likely in places like Grisedale.

If I do a rough calculation of our area, then match that across the country, there are likely to be 150,000 Italians - yes one hundred and fifty thousand - around this country. There are bound to be a few really substantial camps, and the ardent fascists will need to separated out. By 1943 when I started to notice and Palmiro had only just been brought over from South Africa, this had already been sorted. Lodge Moor must be the filter for this region.

From there they were then sent out to smaller camps, nearer to the places their services would be in demand - the rural areas mostly.

Sheffield seems to have had POWs working on buildings - like Parsons Cross and the pre-fabs for Blitz victims at Potter Hill in High Green, and Bracken Hill at Burncross on the Barnes Hall estate. There was talk in our factory of one in Ecclesfield, too. These are all only a mile or so apart. I think maybe the Potter Hill pre-fabs had low risk Italian - co-operators like Palmiro moved in as families went to preferred houses as soon as they could.

Then at the other side of the city is Norton Camp where the POWs have been seen working in the nearby quarry.

Turning my attention to the rural area: all those I know of round here in Notts are working for the War Ag.

The few camps that existed at the beginning of the war seemed to have been only for Germans - Luftwaffe pilots and U-Boat sailors. These few included Lodge Moor and Grisedale, and Doncaster racecourse. For the Italians these became dispersal camps to other local ones. More were required for the rapid import of Italian labour and they were strictly guarded in barb-wired encampments, mostly specially built to a standard pattern - that's Nether Headon style and there's one up at Malton, with a similar sounding name - Eden Camp. I've been told that there were around forty of these started supposedly using contractors, but in fact the majority built by Italians with professional oversight. They were first put up in tents - a great encouragement to put up huts before the British Winter comes howling in.

They had to exercise these men, and a local field is not always available. They route marched them with a platoon of infantry, all with rifles, bayonets mounted, on several days per week. This lasted only about six weeks, then the number of men on guard began to shrink, bayonets were removed, and finally the rifles disappeared. The Italians did not want to escape and would sing their way along the roads, waving to all the girls.

As Palmiro found, in the end they would be helping their elderly Look-Duck-and-Vanish, Home Guard chap with his walking stick. (Cheeky that, Pina. They are cynically called after their original initials Local Defence Volunteers" or LDV.)

Other camps appear to have been on commandeered property, like the country houses the dukes cannot afford to maintain any longer. Places like Bracken Hill Camp on Barnes Hall Estate in High Green; then Serlby Hall and Carlton-in-Lindrick Hall. I can't find out how secure these are, but Rufford Abbey is not at all - and none are barbed enclosures. I told you about them using the tapestries for handbags. I've just heard of another camp at Ravenfield Hall, on the other side of Sheffield. The Duke's not too chuffed with his guests who have killed the deer roaming in the park and been poaching fish from his lordship's lakes. Dastardly chaps!

Finally there are the small camps of hutments, built to 'billet' co-operating Italians, mostly on some sort of military establishment and comprising Nissen, Laing and precast concrete huts. Edwinstowe is just such, where there are about six concrete ones, and Langwith has a few Nissens. Cousin Queenie tells of one near Thorne at Crowle - just three huts for about a hundred men and a some others for the guards, cookhouse, admin, etc.

There are apparently some near Newark - at Caunton and Little Carlton. There is a big park in Newark called Sconce. I am told there are some there.

I'm surprised there don't seem to be many near Mansfield. With several coal mines in the area and lots of industry, I wonder if it's all a bit strategic?

Nottingham itself, I haven't gone into.

Am I wearying of it all now, Pina?

In prison, one has a sentence and if you behave yourself you know you will serve no longer. I behaved, too well perhaps, so my three months was reduced. Not really: my conviction remained but my sentence to prison was 'commuted' to exile a long way from home.

Joining the forces, even in conscription, one is called up for a specific period - usually in multiples of three years or 'for the duration of the war.'

However, the POWs and I are on indeterminate sentences.

Many of the Italians thought that at a point soon after becoming 'co-operators' and their comrades in the Royal (not fascist Mussolini) forces, fighting with the Allies - 'Co-Belligerent' they call them - they would be sent home. So they are now with me in *this* phoney war.

My tribunal sentenced me to perform specified civilian work - farming or forestry. That was after I had already served my prison sentence. I might tell you about that another day.

I might not.

The fate of the Fascist supporters, is to be kept in fenced and guarded camps, I think. Palmiro doesn't know. One of Alec's farmer friends, Gordon Tasker up at Wheatley, the other side of Retford, had two fascist POWs one from Milan and the other from Sicily. The family really liked them and they worked hard. They put them up in the house. They sought permission to live on the farm when this was becoming acceptable to the authorities at the end of '43.

Mr Tasker told them they would have to accept that they would be 'Co-Operators' and cease to have any fascist inclinations.

They had obviously heard about this in the camp - like Palmiro told me about the commandant separating them out.

'What?' they said, 'You mean have "Co-operator" marked on our sleeves?'

'Yes and remove your patches. You will have more liberty to go about, too.'

They could not accept this. They were Fascist Idealists - and here's the strangest reason - *because fascism had saved Italy from the corruption of being completely run by the Mafia.* During the rise of Mussolini and the Fascist era of the 1930s the Mafia had lost its control, they felt. If that is true, Old Duchy can't be all bad, for me.

I don't know what to think about this. Palmiro expressed no ideas either. He knew no Mafia. he was in two minds about Mussolini. He did wonder about his experience in the Sardinian salt 'mines.' This had been one of Mussolini's initiatives to improve the income of poor peasant farmers. I think in Palmiro's case, the fascists shot themselves in the foot, sort of - not really, because as I told you, he was only twelve. Wading in and raking salt? I'm shaking my head now. That put pay to any good impression Palmiro may have got about the benefits of fascism.

Apparently the Fascists, accepting their fate like the Category A 'Black' Nazis, they were moved from Headon to a secure camp, far up north. Perhaps only to Lodge Moor, more likely Scotland, I believe.

Taskers had some Land Army girls, until some more of the Italians realised what they were missing out on by not co-operating and came over.

One of these was a giant of a lad, really only a lad - 18 when captured. They called him 'Fatty' - in a nice way - but it had not been the case during his captivity in South Africa. Palmiro has given plenty of detail about his poor diet there, but even so I could tell he was saving us from more gruesome elements when he said it was 28 months of agony.

Poor Fatty said he had so little food, that at one stretch he hadn't needed the toilet for 13 days.

Palmiro did say 'The life it was really misery ... terrible.'

I might be doubting mankind.

34μ
August 1944

What a strange experience.

Stuck in the doldrums as I seem to be ... When will I get home and when will I see you? ... it suddenly dawned on me that there must be no POWs left in the standard camps like Headon, so I took a ride up.

It would have been great to take Palmiro with me to see the old place ... but I dare not.

Harvesting is upon us, so I won't have many days off for a while - not even Sundays.

As I approached the camp on the Rampton road, I started up the rolling hills which separate the river Trent from the Idle that runs through Retford, and realised I was on the winding lane where the Italian boy crashed his bike into the bus. I shook my head, tightened my grip on the handlebars, and rode on, down a dip, then into a very nasty bend and it was upon me.

The camp is well hidden there.

I pulled up at the corner of the site. The camp was on my left with a couple of concrete huts behind a bigger - much bigger - three section brick building. Still single storey, so I could see the water tower over the top of it. No guard-towers, though, and no fence just here.

It was a pleasant summer afternoon and there was no movement except for birds. I removed the helmet Mummy had bought me ... and listened. Peace.

I decided to leave Maisie Matchless on her stand and walk up. The nurses told me they walk past up to the asylum. I left the helmet with the bike and slipped the camera into my pocket. You never know?

I walked past the main entrance.

Slowly.

A dog barked.

I walked on.

The lane rises up immediately and I could look back down on the camp. It appears to be in two sections. Probably the prisoners' section away from the road and the guard buildings nearer. But no fences - not guard fences anyway.

I was being watched.

A soldier with an Alsatian dog was at the entrance. His rifle was shouldered.

We watched each other. I saw him look back into the camp.

Guards coming running?

No. He waved me over.

I walked quickly up to him. He was smiling, cigarette in the corner of his mouth. So I don't look so threatening, then?

I told him who I was and what I was doing and he shook my hand. Not a kid. Probably in his fifties. Three stripes though. Scots Guard? Did I want to take a look around?

Did I?

Look at this:

Can you see anybody?

We walked into the site and he pointed to his guard room immediately to the right. He's doing the duty - no family at home, so letting the family lads have a day off. 'Ities' all off womanising, no doubt. Just a handful kept on to look after the place.

I told him how I had followed the fortunes of the Italians and the camps, and knowing there were lots of them out, billeted on farms and other hutments, I did wonder what was happening here.

Mothballing.

Well not quite.

He hopes it won't be too long before they'll throw the fences back up - and electrify them! - for the whole ******* German Army. He fingered the side of his nose. We know what he means, don't we?

He set off walking into the camp. Not marching, more like dawdling.

Commandant's office is next on right, then four huts of stores and tools etc.

On the left a few huts - guard room, a wave - and finally 'Jankers' - the detention block. That *has* got a fence round it. He chuckled.

Taking a look back, I suspect to see he wasn't being watched, he pointed to the big building at the front by the road: 'Regimental Institute'. Posh words for cinema, Palais de Danse, theatre, showing off to the locals.

'Dance?' I asked.

'Och Aye,' he said. Apparently it is a great disciplinary measure - bait for good behaviour. Locals - specially selected - are invited along to dances, preferably with their own boyfriends, and particularly uniformed. Locals appreciate coming in to see the films too. Saves a traipse into town. Guards like it too. Yes POWs do get to dance with a girl.

Establishing it was all clear, he indicated my camera: but only the Prison Camp like, not the barracks.

I was OK with that, thank you very much.

As you can tell he let me take some *particular* photographs. He didn't want to be on them himself - official secrets and all. The nose-touch again. He asked if I wanted to be on them, but immediately demured. I wouldnay gi' 'em to the press or oot? Anyway, better not.

He whistled - boy, could he whistle. He shouted and waved at a POW who obviously knew to make himself scarce.

So to the pictures: you can tell just how much the camp is cared for. Look at those flowerbeds. And no fences. These are nicely painted concrete huts, but there are some to the sides that are the Laing steel-framed corrugated-iron and timber type.

Fancy lamp standards - POWs made them in their workshops. Very inventive chappies. No trouble. Look after themselves. Not saying they *didn't* have some trouble.

I mentioned the fascists.

He nodded.

These are a nice lot. Some say they don't want to fight. Cowards. Not him. He pointed to his stripes. Last kerfuffle. Ha! Not quite your Grandad's sentiment. Great word. A jock word I suspect. I think that, like me, he didn't quite hold with press-ganging men to fight for ... what? He had seen it all and by some fluke survived. He shook his head.

But take a look at this chapel.
Their pride and joy.
Faith and hope, too.
Religious fanatics, don't I know?
I do.
Lovely though.
Focal point of the camp - dead central.
Pride of place.

And inside:

A carved altar

On the right there, that's a church organ - well a pedal-harmonium.

It's a Sunday and I've been to church. I prayed for you Pina, I really did. I hope this terrible war is all over before you get to school and this time it really is the war to end all wars.

Back at Portland, I didn't tell Palmiro where I had been. I wanted to wait until I had the photos developed and I could tell and show.

His eyes welled up.

35μ
October 1944

Oh God, how awful this is getting. I don't believe in your God, Mummy, sorry. I don't know why I called upon him. Maybe I just *called* him. It was definitely in vain.

Reality is biting me. Of course I don't blame a spirit for causing all this outpouring of human blood. I blame men.

Sunday: Alec was biting his lip and frowning. He stabbed the paper with his forefinger. He peered at me under his brows. He shoved the Express at me throwing himself back in his chair. He looked at the ceiling, gasped and drew his hands firmly across his now shaking head.

I had to look. The headline should have been enough: 'HISTORY'S GREATEST HORROR.' What could cap our own forces firebombing cities of thousands? I must read on.

Hopefully you won't see this until you are older, my children, but I have to tell how I feel just now. There is nothing phoney or remotely funny about this war ... any war.

Under the headline it says 'Hitler is now exterminating 30 million Russians.' That is incomprehensible. There are less than fifty million in our whole country. Is it journalistic exaggeration?

Maybe not: it goes on to describe the previously indescribable 'appalling story of Rzhev,' 'only 137 left alive out of 65,000.'

It continues to tell the wider picture, followed by one excruciating example of cruelty: all the able bodied men that have survived the onslaught have been marched west to slavery, and death en route; then one houseful of women and children brutally ... not simply killed ... but mutilated and murdered.

Alec had leant back over the sideboard and down a small pile found a newspaper, looked at it then threw it at me. Hard. In the face.

He stormed out.

That hurt. I had to wipe my eyes and nose before I could find what irked him so. Alec? Me?

I went to stand as Sally went out after him, but sat to regroup my thoughts.

Picking the hurled paper up, I could immediately see why.

'STALINGRAD 330,000 WIPED OUT.'

Date?

First of Feb 1943 - Last year! Not today's, but last year. Alec is trying to wake me up. Wake me to his reality?

Gallons of blood - tankers ... swimming pools ... rivers of human lifeblood.

If I had stayed in steel, I would be making the guns and bombs to stop all this. All? How much can I do? Are all the people making them, my people and the people in Essen...?

God, God, God! Right next to this GREATEST HORROR is the report of *our* 'Shattering 1000 tons attack' on Germany's Sheffield - Essen. How many boys like me have been incinerated in that 800 acre Krupp site?

If I met one of them walking along the lane here in Egmanton I'd ... run him through with my razor sharp plasher ... well wouldn't I?

If I knew he had done it, I really would. He could well have landed in Hull and already advanced through Sheffield, fired my Mam's house and powered on down here in his Opel Blitz truck, behind Panzer tanks...

My nose is bleeding.

Corner of that paper at great force.

I bang my head down on the table. Idiot.

A quake strikes up from my gut.

I sob.

I stand.

I sit back down.

Bloodstained tears dripping on Alec's new and old paper, and Sally and Barbara haven't seen today's yet. Nor seen me bloodstained from the fray.

Blood.

Blitz truck.

I did mention the Jeeps, and being pushed off the roads round Boughton, but what I have just imagined is a translation: within weeks of now, thousands of huge American six-wheel-drive GMC trucks, not Opel Blitzes that are made by GM in Germany, will be leaving Boughton, just over the hill from me. They will hopefully carry good men. They will liberate poor people from the tyranny and horror being meted out by the Nazis, on civilian families, all the way across Europe - even to far flung places, with unpronounceable names like Rzhev and Kharkov.

Can I help? Can I fight? If I did, would these boys, from a whole other continent, which has not been bombed, which is not at risk of invasion from the Nazis, need to come over here ... and certainly die in thousands, for me and for you Pina.

I am feeding them. Palmiro is feeding his Italian American 'cousin'. They say they march on their stomachs. If they can't march...

Really it does not bear thinking about. Really.

36μ

Gentleman as he is, Alec soon apologised, but felt he needed to remind me that, (he kept a lookout over his shoulder) though I might feel sympathetic to the 130,000 Italians like Palmiro being caught 'without firing a shot,' but (gritted teeth) 'Rommel hadn't captured 80,000 British in '42 single-handed, y'know. Half his men and 250 of his tanks were fucking Ities.'

I was contrite.

He cares for Palmiro, too, but he would exclude him from his disdain for the Hun and those 'bloody Blackshirts.'

He offered me some bacca, and then remembered.

He went on to ask me about the plashing. I had done a short stretch of hedging myself, but it was slow work with the tools he gave me.

Yes I know - a bad workman...

He revealed that he had used a contracting gang last time and that his men had never done the hedge-laying themselves. He had overlooked the fencework since the outbreak of war (priorities, y' know). so appreciated my interest.

That reveals the state of the billhook and plasher. They were ones Noah brought back with his ark. It means I can discuss how poor they are without hurting his pride - he's got no idea himself.

Jim Lister the farrier had been to shoe up the horses for the new season. Nice bloke - comes a good way. He's the best farrier according to Alec.

He tidied up the scythes too. He has a 'portable-furnace' - gas fired furnace thing. Very swift - and he's meticulous with red hot steel.

I've got an idea. A notion.

37μ

Sewing - everything. Everywhere. Everybody. Gangs of men. Some Land Army girls.

Policing!

Men without women.

We've got drilling machines for seeds, but taters are being put in by hand. There we have the Italians and girls in the same field. Sally and Barbara keeping up refreshments., trying to keep the work going.

P.C Eric Chapman on duty separating not wheat from chaff.

The poor Italian boys arrive with the hair slicked back and the girls have their turbans clean, neat and mostly colourful. Specially for the occasion ... and the opportunity.

I miss Mummy. Has Papa got you going into the office, or is he letting you off a bit lightly, sewing a few herbs in the garden; tomatoes and carrots; feet up over a light lunch, then back to peas and beets? Take care.

They are chasing each other round barns, stacks, sacks and hedges. Home Guard don't stay at all these days.

They are brought out on lorries by civilians. Out regular guy is a Clarrie Mumby from Treswell. It's a village right next to Headon. I shared with him about Headon being almost empty now. He concurred but pointed out five of today's chaps who were still at the camp. 'Reluctant Co-Operators' apparently. A skeleton crew maintaining the camp with a few Labour Corps soldiers.

I mentioned my Scot.

He laughed.

Clarrie has a proper traipse round several billets to pick up a full team. There are apparently three lots in Tuxford - a couple of huts on Lincoln Road and some on the Army camp - not twenty in that barn I mentioned, more like a hundred or so. It's not a barn, it's an old works of some sort - great big three storey place. It's not fenced or guarded. See to themselves apparently.

'No 'arm in 'em is thee?' He spits. Nicely.

For shorter and smaller jobs, he's in and out of farms all day long, five here, a dozen there. Waved a little order book at me.

I asked him about Boughton.

What about it?

Not a POW camp?

It is.

It's what? Not another. Not all those huts.

What did I want to know for?

Uh - oh. Keep Mum. Spies about. And me - an able bodied young man. I had to go and check on Palmiro and his help in the kitchen garden.

Palmiro's got real green fingers. The Fox family having him running their Black Market for them. That's a little joke. Many true words are spoken in jest...

He's got that garlic. Sally found some and it's already sprouting nicely. Next he's asked her to find him a grapevine. Now that's a greater challenge. She says she will perhaps try one of the Duke's gardeners at Welbeck. She's heard that they have a huge hothouse and must surely have been tempted to grow grapes there.

Palmiro hadn't thought that they didn't grow grapes everywhere. Everyone he knows has a vine of some sort, even if they have no land, it'll be growing up the side of the house.

Sally had to reveal to him that grapes just will not ripen over here.

He has his own notion. You didn't know Italians had them did you? I've caught him sizing things up in and out of one of the greenhouses. The one on the end nearest the sun. The tomato house, Sally calls it.

Steady as she goes, Palmiro.

Drop me a line, please Mummy?

38μ

Leslie Marshall dropped me a line. He invited me to bring Palmiro over for tea with him and Luca.

I was a bit scared at first because of the non-fraternisation thing. What if we were stopped?

I needn't have worried. The whole Fox family thought it a super idea and rallied to make it run smoothly. The idea of us sitting down to 'tea' tickled me bit too.

They easily found some civvies that fitted Palmiro, remarkably well as it happens, and excitedly waved us off. Palmiro really needed the greatcoat and leather gauntlets as there was a fair old nip in the air, and I gave the bike plenty of throttle. Mustn't get caught.

Mr Marshall is a Quaker - they are Christian people who care a lot for people in misfortune. They are also mostly COs like me and he knows several who have gone through the same traumas as I have. Though he asked about my own reasons, hinting at some religious principle or other, he seemed even perked by my simple humanitarian stance. Pat on the shoulder. No attempt at conversion.

He knew I wanted to know Luca's story. He was also sensitive to the fact that he was also introducing 'my' POW to his as a means of ongoing mutual support for each other.

I hope I was not too eager on my own account. I needn't have worried: he sent the boys off, telling Luca to show Palmiro round his domain, then took me in for a snifter. Very generous. It was how he revealed his Quakerism: he gave me a whisky and a lovely dash of ginger, but had only the ginger ale himself. 'TT y'know.'

Of course - and not forcing Tee Totalling on others.

He had got Luca's story himself and shared basic information with me. Won't need to take too much bonding time off the boys.

As I suspected, it wasn't just the hardships of war and his moustache that make Luca look older - he is. Older than me too - born 1912. He comes from a mountain village called Volturara Appula in Apulia and he's married to - you'll never guess ... Giuseppina! They also have a daughter Nina (Giovannina) who is a good bit older than you Pina - she'll be ten next July - and Luca really hopes to be able to see her before then.

Mr 'do call me Leslie' Marshall, told me of the hopes dashed when the Italians weren't let home after the capitulation. 'Dashed cruel, really', but we can understand that there is a whole bunch of fascists still playing merry hell with our chaps in Italy. And of course there are tens of thousands of Brits held in who knows what conditions by Germany and Japan.

However, Leslie is keeping his ears to the wind via contacts, to let Luca see his family at the earliest opportunity.

Luca had thought he had done with soldiering when he completed his national service back in 1934, but he was called back up in August 1939. He

91

thought he would be let off as he had a growth on his nose which he hoped the forces might think contagious - but no such luck. They gave him some cream and three weeks to use it up.

Straight off to Libya, then. No war of course - but rumblings.

The Grand Old Duce soon had his men marching up the coast and marched them down again.

I mentioned Queenie's Jack.

'Tobruk?' said Leslie.

'Tank Regiment,' I said. 'Not absolutely sure where he is, but it seems very likely. Dispatch rider. Not exactly in a tank, but certainly in among them.'

'Got a bit of a dispatch yourself, today, Eric,' he said, throwing a nod in Palmiro's direction.

We laughed, but it's not funny, is it?

'Maybe rounded up our boys, eh?'

That is a very strong possibility and not one lost on Queenie.

'It's all very well,' he went on, 'that Palmiro's division were caught without a shot being fired, but in another battle for Tobruk the Nazis, (he says it like Churchill - 'nah-zie', no 't' sound in his nat-sy) with just as many Italians, y'know, (I don't want to) took in 30,000 of our boys.'

Tobruk. That's where Luca's battling finished.

Leslie shook his head. 'But his war's not over is it?' he said. 'Nor yours?'

I thanked him for his awareness. I asked if he knew what kind of a camp it is at Carlton-in-Lindrick.

He hadn't thought of it. Isn't a camp a camp - tents?

I told him it was at one of the Manor houses - from across a lake it looks like a big farm estate - lots of barns and buildings.

'Come to think of it,' he said, 'Luca actually had a bunk in a barn. But I thought that might be because of his seniority.' (Luca is one of the older ones.)

The boys came back in then, so Leslie had a real treat - wine! Palmiro doesn't understand our liking for beer, but they have a good vineyard at home. He calls it his, not his family's. He hopes they are looking after it for him.

Apparently Luca was doing quite well for himself before the war. As a young man his father had gone to seek his fortune in North and South America - Brazil - and did make enough to buy a decent farm back home. He and his wife had just a daughter beside Luca. She had been jilted, and heartbroken went to America never to be seen again.

Palmiro didn't let on that he had got as far as the salt 'mines' as a mere child, and that he was the eldest of ten - only the small vineyard was his bit of farm.

Leaving they hugged, then Palmiro bowed saying 'Zio Luca.'

Luca shooed him shouting 'Calabrese' and they laughed.

39μ

Uplifted by the connection between Palmiro La Banca and Luca Ritucci, I decided to try to tie up the camp situation across the two counties of Yorkshire and Nottinghamshire. I won't be able to get to North Yorkshire, but Sheffield area and now Notts. Something to occupy my mind a bit more positively. A quest?

Alec had very kindly taken a note of some for me at the last farmers meeting with Notts War Ag, asking casually - mustn't give out too much information, hush-hush, Keep Mum and all - but he's got me a list.

Sally and Barbara joined the scheming and made me a good pack-up - almost a picnic actually, with a large flask of tea (not my favourite - it gets a bit stewed as the day goes on, but I didn't show anything other than excited gratitude) and ... a bottle of beer.

I set off early on Sunday to do a tour of what might be out there.

The Matchless's Teledraulic suspension did save me a huge amount of stress on the arms, but in the end I didn't do it any favours so it bucked me off. Don't worry!

The Great North Road is one of the nation's finest and most historic roads, so I set off down towards Newark. I made real headway with only churchgoers out at the start of a Sunday morning.

Traffic in the sky was a different story - busy, buzzy. There are bomber airfields all over the area between that road and the sea. Herr Hitler's boys are not great church goers so our chaps are on their mettle.

Sadly some are off their metal: I was excited, yet saddened to be waved past a huge convoy of lorries. It's more exciting for boys than girls - but impressive, nevertheless. The first lorry (actually at the back, because I was overtaking the steady stream) had several engines on it and I realised they were plane engines all with twisted propellers - then I saw the plane - one section at a time, on five more Queen Mary's. Now that's more for you girls!

I'm teasing - that is the nickname of the huge lorries they are using to carry the planes and, on this occasion, a crashed one. Apparently they set out every day to collect pieces of planes for repair and recycling; plus research of German Planes shot down. We have to keep up with Nazi Boffins scheming technology don't we?

The next lorry had tail pieces, then a lorry for each wing, part of the fuselage, and the cockpit lorry was just turning into an aerodrome as I finished overtaking.

I pulled up just afterwards to check my map. Winthorpe. (Don't tell Lord Haw Haw.)

CAUNTON

LITTLE
CARLTON

WINTHORPE

NEWARK

SCONCE

BULWELL

SYERSTON

ARNOLD
WOODBOROUGH

NOTTINGHAM

WOLLATON
HALL

SAXONDALE

TOLLERTON

LANGAR

Looking up, I could have slapped myself. There at the side of the road was small collection of huts and a more substantial building - and out of an old cottage, were streaming - Prisoners of War! No patches, but the same uniform as Palmiro's - dyed battledress. Was that the mess room, then?

Before I could take a breath, some of the chaps ran over to look at my bike. I shook a few hands and accepted a few compliments - I hope that's what they were.

I also got insistence for attention from a little chap: 'Me, Benelli!' he pointed away. 'House ... me ... Benelli ... brum, brum,' nodding for my understanding. Then he pointed at me - 'You TT, Si?'

'Yes, Ja, Si!' I said, laughing and slapping Maisie Matchless on the tank.

However, I didn't actually get it until I had set off with a cheer from my crowd. I got it! He has a Benelli at home. A Brit won the Isle of Man TT on an Italian Benelli 250cc in '39.

Got to get on, if I'm to get back before dark.

Wow - what next, just down the road a very big - finger-to-nose - factory. Guarded. I was waved on. I reckon the Wellington with clipped wings will end up there.

I checked the map. Should I nip up to Little Carlton and Caunton on the other side of the river? No, I could get there easily from Egmanton - maybe on a lighter evening in Summer. Allington? Oops - that's over the border. People think it's Newark, but it's the other way from Caunton into Lincolnshire. Keep Calm Eric - you've got enough to carry on with your story so far...

Sconce is a huge park - don't know whereabouts the camp is, so won't see from the road.

Off down the old Fosse Way - past another airfield just next to the straight Roman Road, there are apparently a few little camps at the end of that.

When I got there - well the bit that's in Notts, because the Romans didn't stop at Bingham, but continued on down to Leicester - I happened upon a very interesting scene. It appeared to be an altercation between a local bobby and a POW, but they were having great fun. The policeman was playing the Plod, arms on hips, then wagging his truncheon and the Italian was waving, gesticulating; so between them it was a live Punch and Judy show, and I expected them to break into the laughing policeman song. (I'll sing that with you, Pina.)

Stopped, I got my map out and with the pretence of asking my way, sidled up to them. Catching me in his peripheral vision, the policeman wiped the smile off his face, then realised he had his hand on the tiny Italian's shoulder. He tightened his grip and shook him. 'Just apprehending this ... cheeky chappy.'

The POW just looked at him quizzically - so much so that they both burst out laughing again.

I was of course fully OK with that. 'Great to see you having fun together - seriously,' I said. 'Got my own Italian POW back at the farm.'

Not scared to fraternise the tiniest bit, I first offered the little fellow my hand.

I saw the Policeman frown, but then it was his turn. 'Michael here is one of my regulars aren't you?'

Michael didn't follow, but smiled an assent.

'Still not got any lights, for the umpteenth time.'

I looked to the bright blue sky.

'Ah, yes sir - doesn't need them now, but he will when he comes back to Saxondale tonight, but I'll be off duty, as long as there's no raiders about.'

Seizing the opportunity I said, 'Where are you off to?' And realising Michael might not understand, I asked Plod where he was going?'

'Long Bennington?' said the policeman to Michael.

'Yes sir.' Then stepping on the pedal he said 'Long ride!' and set off.

PC Plod, hands back on hips, watched Michael disappear with a look of real affection on his face. 'Not his fault,' he said, turning to me, 'ruddy farmer has to provide the bike, and he really should give him a road worthy one. Now sir, how can I help?'

I waved the map, had a little think, and then decided to tell the truth about my research. He couldn't be more obliging.

They have a little camp just up the road for co-operator Ities - I nodded my understanding - a few huts for lads working in farms all round here. Supposed to be nearer than Bennington - ten or twelve miles - but they're allowed if the farmer provides transport. 'Poor lad, Shanks's pony would be more comfortable than that old cronk with its creaky crank!'

He thought most of these lads were billeted out from the big camp at Willerton Hall across town.

I wrote that down.

He assumed I had just come from Langar - 'some on the airfield just five miles straight down there.' I could easily nip, but asked if there is anything to see. Not really - huts!

Then he added, waving his arm the opposite way towards the city, 'With that machine you can take in Tollerton Hall on your way to see ... you've spelt that wrong it's Woolerton, no not Woolerton, Woolerton with one 'o'.'

I pulled a funny face at him, scrutinised the map and he pointed at Wollaton. 'Yes, well...'

I mentioned the thing about the old Halls and country houses, Dukeries and all.

He laughed. 'Buggers can't afford to keep 'em up can they?' and he rubbed his hands. 'Anyway, I don't know about Tollerton, much, I think they are using the old squire's Manor, but somebody said it was the GIs over here. Plenty of land for a few tents, and the GIs won't stand for any nonsense from these lads. See to their own policing you know?'

I do.

'Except for lights on bikes!' He went on to give me a few hints of how to get to Wollaton - definitely worth a look - one of the finest parks in the country, if they haven't wrecked it with ... he hears it's a big camp ... or maybe a few camps.

I rode past Tollerton Hall - a veritable castle - Jeeps and a couple of those great big American trucks, with much business of round helmeted soldiers, but no sign of tents or huts. I didn't have time for a good look, so went straight up to what I think must be Notts' equivalent of Lodge Moor. It is a huge camp on the north corner of real piece of baronial land - a deer park, if the POWs haven't been enjoying the venison.

Plod had given me a great tip - 'Remember Eton and Harrow,' he said and pointed at the junction of the two streets off Wollaton Road. If I could get into the park from there I should be able to see the camp for myself.

He was right and I could. Not all of it of course, but I could get a feel that there were lots of huts - more than Headon, and also different looking because they are all Nissen huts. Not all I could see were fenced, but there did appear to be a fenced section. Fascists, I wonder?

By the time I got to Bulwell I had missed closing time - in fact it was nearly opening time again. I found a couple of pubs near the Bulwell Hall Park where I do believe there is a POW camp. The Apollo looked a bit rough so I stood the bike outside the Forest. It looked a classier establishment altogether. I'm not sure how my choice would affect how I would find out about our Italian friends.

I was in for a different education.

I had to duck immediately as a squadron of planes roared over. I exaggerate, but I did shrivel at the sudden roar as several fighter planes took off close enough to blow my helmet off.

When I took it off for myself I realised I was being laughed at by a couple of airmen. Polish airmen. I didn't need to be Sherlock Holmes - they had 'Polish' underneath their wings badge. They ambled over and one of them took hold of the handlebars. I waved him to take a seat. His chum smiled paternally.

I pointed to my shoulder and nodded at his badge. He told me he was Polish. Yes. We laughed. He then pointed in the direction the planes came from - 'Hucknall.'

I haven't heard of it. Polish squadron based there. Good lads.

The Forest is a hotel. I noticed a door was open. I popped my nose in and was hailed a welcome. I gave the lads the thumbs up and went in.

They followed me up to a receptionist who told me the bar was closed but we could have a drink - a real drink. All three of us may as well have been Poles because we stood in a row frowning at her - the three stupid monkeys.

'Water,' she blurted and laughed at herself - and at us. She waved us to sit down and brought three tumblers of orange squash poured from a great jug.

The boys stuck up their thumbs and burst out laughing. I was a little uncomfortable because they were obviously laughing at me. I checked my fly buttons and wiped my face - have I a mud-mask - all but where my goggles have been?

Chez shook his head, put out his hand and introduced himself and Antoni.

They then stuck up all their thumbs ... and wiggled them.

There's a story there I thought. I wasn't wrong.

Chez got out a little notebook which had seen much better days. He opened a page and pointed to a thumbs up sign he had drawn. It was against an entry '24th June 1940 Arandora Star. Liverpool.'

Aha - safely arrived in England - presumably from Poland?

No - France.

I shook my head and got out my own notebook. Last entry - Bulwell. I pointed to the floor. They nodded. We had a dumb-show going. I pointed in the planes' direction - Hucknall. Chez flapped some wings and pointed to Antoni and himself.

'English?' I asked.

'Leedle,' and the shakey hand.

I took a proper look at his book, which he simply handed over and encouraged me to read it. I flicked a few pages.

I showed him mine - a list of places with a sentence or two next to each. (You've just read it yourself, so you know what I mean.)

While he looked at mine I read more of his, seeing if I could get back to the start of a trip. Too much. I smiled at him.

Chez said 'Same,' meaning our journey. 'Escape - you?'

I had to do some explaining but they caught on when they realised that I had arrived to find the Prisoner of War Camp supposedly just here. The barmaid shouted across that yes it is on the Hall estate, 'over there - full of lovely Ities,' she said '...but these lads are lovely too.'

She realised that they did know what she was saying and she blushed.

They also got what my list was saying and eventually gave a whistle at the numbers of camps. Everybody is beginning to do that. Jiminy Cricket will tell you to give a little whistle, Pina, and always let your conscience be your guide.

They wondered about me. I'm a farmer of course - no lie.

I went back to the book. When I realised what it was telling I asked if I could take some notes.

The barmaid brought three brimming pints to us. It was still a bit before opening time so that eased our paths.

This may be a bit much, but I must tell you as an example - just how one man with a few friends did what hundreds of thousands did - escape from their home country, Poland, and aimed for Britain whichever way they could. They are now an Army and Air Force in exile. We know that they were the aces of the Battle of Britain ... but the extent and ... extreme!

We tend to assume that they will have sailed or flown their planes and been at most a few days from the North, or a few weeks if they had to get out of the south and come through the Mediterranean.

Chez and Antoni's 9 month journey to join friendly forces.

After they had given me some idea of the zig-zag route they took dodging bombers all the way, and for nine long months, I felt the need to record the detail. I hope you agree that this is interesting, and shows the complexity of war and the risks people take. There is a little map below to help you follow. On the one hand I know they are escaping to save their lives, yet on the other, I am taken with the anonymity of defending ourselves from mechanised war. Take note of any point over the nine months when Chez and Antoni actually see their enemy.

1ˢᵗ September 1939 near Lvov in far eastern Poland when the Germans invaded from the West and North and the War started. That day the Germans bombed Lvov.

By 7ᵗʰ Lvov station was ruined. In the evening his group marched to a little aerodrome 15km west of Lvov

9ᵗʰ was a terrible day. At 5am the first round of bombing. After 7am there was a second round of bombing all around lasting all day. Many aircraft and buildings were destroyed. Scrambled behind a hangar and hid. Lucky to escape alive.

10ᵗʰ Marched from the ruined station. Reached Busk (east of Lwow) before dinner when German planes appeared again.

13th Arrived beautiful Sniatyn (heading south-easterly to the Romanian border) - a place by the river where they had a swim.

17th Sniatyn's railway station bombed by Germans.

17 days into the war they saw some defence - *they saw Russian planes for the first time.*

18th Crossed Romanian border, gave up weapons and transport at Radolcze. A tribunal gave them status of interned Polish Forces in a friendly-at–the-time Romania. Slept on bare floorboards.

19th Comfortable passenger train to Turdy north-west Romania.

23rd Marched 12 km to quarters in a large house belonging to a Bulgarian. Cooked own meals, comfortable and happy in the hope that they were a little nearer to their goal.

That's three solid weeks on the run from bombers. It's funny for us to think of this - to avoid catching dysentery they ate lots of garlic with onions, cabbage and bread, and drank home-produced vodka.

October
7th Moved to living quarters in a Romanian woman's home near Constanta, the Bucharest Black Sea Port. Very friendly lady - a reasonable Christmas.

1940 January - after a three month break from the heat of battle, life was good, but not happy because they knew they were at war and needed to fight.

16th Decided to travel to Constanta, to catch a ship. They met many like-minded Poles.

25th Paid for passage out of the Black Sea to Istanbul in Turkey, then on to Piraeus in Greece. After leaving port an earthquake shook the area. Another narrow escape.

Onwards down Mediterranean they stopped at Haifa, Palestine.

30th Back north to Beirut, Syria. For two weeks.

Chez's Grandpapa had eaten a pear one time, the skin of which had clung to the lining of his stomach. He recovered after vodka (strong Polish whisky) and garlic for medicinal purposes. Now Chez had to do the same for his friend and saved his life by buying him a bottle of rum!

So the pear was an enemy he *could* see.

February
15th left Beirut across the sea to Alexandria, Egypt.

17th Alexandria 5 days through dangerous storm right across the Mediterranean to France.

22nd Marseilles. Very happy.

25th Crossing France passed the Septfonds 'Les Judes' Internment Camp, which was a terrible sight. ('Les Judes' means 'The Jews'. Chez and Antoni saw something bad there. I didn't ask for detail.)

Continued west.

March
12th Last leg to Bordeaux.
16th Given French Air Force uniforms and equipment.

April
8th Practical examinations for
17th work in a munitions factory for 2 months.

June
18th Night-time bombardment Bordeaux, so left to retrace our journey back towards the south-east coast of France.

(21st Chez travelled through Lourdes, half-way to Toulouse.)

Aiming for Port-Vendres, south East France, close to the Spanish border, but failed only to have to make a hazardous journey back to
20th South-west coast of France.

24th Bayonne lucky to find passage to an unknown destination on the English ship The Arandora Star.

After nine months avoiding the Germans, their destination turned out to be the port of Liverpool.

(Chez wrote their proper names for me - Czezlaw Kowalczyk and Antoni Parylak. I'll stick with Chez and Antoni.)

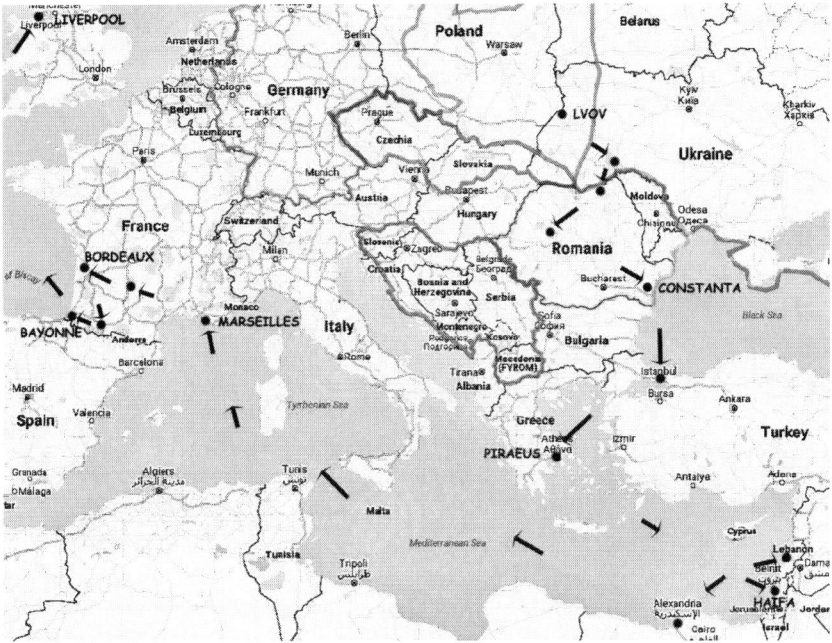

So that was Chez and Antoni. Here is a map with arrows to show just how they travelled right round Europe - and a bit of the Middle East - to get here. I felt very humble in such company. Paid for our drinks and another for each of my new friends and set off towards home.

I foolishly decided while I was down there, to find one final camp at Arnold. Except it wasn't at Arnold, it was at yet another old Hall at Woodborough and then not quite, but up the lane. Another fairly small camp of about ten huts - that should still hold around three hundred men, though.

Fortunately it was almost in a direct line back to Egmanton. In the near darkness I strode my trusty steed for the final leg somewhat wearily.

Too wearily, I have to report. I fell asleep riding along. I awoke in a ditch. A dry one luckily. Or not lucky to have fallen off? I must have ground to a halt and met the ground. I was not hurt in the least and the bike's telematic suspension will have saved the front forks, giving it some bounce. We had scooped up a little bit of mud on knees and axles, and my shoulder does ache a bit. No harm done.

Only when I came to write up that story, did mention of the Arandora Star stir a memory. I didn't tell Chez, but I seemed to recall that the Arandora was the ship carrying those Internees to Canada.

I have checked the date against Chez's story: the Arandora Star was sunk on 2nd July 1940 - it must have been the Star's very next voyage.

40μ

I wasn't expecting the other letter. Mummy could not reply, so Grandmama sent news.

Middlewood mental hospital was not where I next expected to meet Mummy.

Though Grandmama undoubtedly wished to head me off to explain Mummy's situation, in other words to vent her spleen on me with a 'Look what you have done to my daughter', I decided to bide my time. I had spied Grandpapa's Rover and decided to spy on her departure.

What she no doubt did fume about, would be how heartless I am to not even turn up.

A nurse took my elbow and sat me down. Yes I am her husband; is she not Mrs Chapman?

I had to explain my difficulty in arriving and, surprisingly, I received a lot of sympathy - a cousin is a CO, and a very brave chap too.

I therefore had the chance to explain that I had not been informed what my wife was doing in the mental hospital. I had to bite my quivering tongue to not say 'Lunatic Asylum', which Grandpapa would undoubtedly call it.

Nurse revealed that more than one 'Conchie ... sorry,' had been admitted after collapsing under the strain and ... hatred, heaped upon him. How was I bearing up?

Better, if I only had the support of my wife's family. I believe, and hope, that Mummy did have a huge choice to make too - her parents or me.

I had to 'go into exile', and I thought it unfair, even if it were not forbidden, to take my wife with me.

She did not choose it anyway.

She is very poorly. She may not speak.

What is wrong with her?

That is not what I said.

I said nothing. More than my tongue now quivered and Nurse fetched me a 'nice cuppa.' She restrained me from going anywhere - from pacing the corridor peering into wards and rooms.

It is not the forbidding place I was expecting after my observations of Rampton 'Hospital' during my rides around Nether Headon and its neighbouring villages.

Oh my darling, what have we done?

I had the chance to hold your hand.

You did not want to do ... that ... to yourself, did you?

Did I do that to you?

You could not tell me.

You could not tell it was me who was holding your hand.

And how sad you looked ... as you looked at me. My pretty, tragic, love.

I am doing this for you and for our children.
Oh, Pina I did not ask after you.

I took the risk of calling back past the house and my own mother; I didn't care if one of my old 'friends' reported me to the tribunal, but nevertheless I did leave the bike in the next street. The crater from the blitz has been levelled out. They said they could fit two buses in it. Keep calm and carry on, Eric.

My Mam of course knows that Mummy could not be with me. She does not know the condition of our relationship. Mummy is my wife and that's it. That is how it should be.

Mam was desperate to know what is wrong. I could only say that my wife has had some sort of breakdown.

'Oh poor Eric.'

I accept her misplaced sympathy, because it is an understandable response of a loving mother to her own devastated child.

I visited Mummy again this Sunday. Some improvement - some colour and mobility. Not out and about. Not happy. Not talking - not to me anyway.

I kept up a cheery face and spoke of gardening, planting, my plashing project and how the Fox family and Palmiro look after me. I did not mention the war.

Nurse told me that my wife had made a full recovery - of her body - but they were keeping her under observation for a little while longer. She's been talking and is very nervous about the war, biting her nails - she never did that before, and I hadn't noticed the change. Men!

She thought they may let her go home during the week and asked me if everything would be safe for her.

What a question, and to me of all people. Of course I would like to keep her safe, but what are Herr Hitler's plans?

And where is home?

When she noticed my reticence, she took my hand and apologised. With the other hand over her mouth, she wondered...

I assured her that Grandmama and Grandpapa would wrap her up in cotton wool - maybe even send her to America 'for the duration'. My little laugh was also hollow.

They are to notify me on Alec's phone and I will take Mummy home.

I did not inform her that I will take her on my motorbike. Getting that mush petrol remains a problem. I will get a taxi. I haven't exactly had a lot to spend my farm labourer's £3/10/- a week on. The Foxes will accept nothing for my keep despite it being a condition - for Palmiro and for me.

41μ
The last μ - the micron that broke a metallurgist's back.

Mummy was ready and waiting for me. Dressed. Very smart, but sombre clothes. Was it her funeral attire? We hadn't been to a funeral together. I pecked her on the cheek. She accepted but did not reciprocate. She looked at me ... a look that froze my heart. Her eyes, welled up, but did not shed the tears. Fortunately I was able to command my body to carry out my duty.

She accepted the steer I gave her elbow through her sumptuous mink overcoat, stepped easily into the taxi and we set off for Dore.

Grandmama and Grandpapa were on the doorstep waiting for us, evidently watching through the windows for our arrival - they were not in outdoor clothes this blustery afternoon.

I went up the steps with Mummy, Grandpapa stepped between us and elbowed me back down the steps, my bottom to the gravel. I glanced up to see the door close behind them.

I looked around.

The taxi driver wiped a smile off his face. He was still there though. Was he waiting for me?

I can't go on.

42μ
January 1945

I have not written during the lead-up to Christmas. All hope went out of me - of peace *as I see it* and of the wish, 'Peace on earth and goodwill to all men,' just as the slaughter intensifies all across Europe ... the Middle East ... the Far East ... *world* war.

However, I am not so churlish as to resist the prayers for peace, so I accepted all invitations to church services in the village. My own cynicism against the Governments who led their people into battle with padres and prayers, was tempered by the palpable sense of hope of the ordinary people, evident in the Christmas church services.

Young Barbara could not be resisted in her exhortations to attend a carol service at the Anglican church before Christmas; the Christmas Day service at Egmanton Chapel next door; and today at the Anglican's again, I had my own Epiphany at a Crib.

Two funny words - Epiphany and Crib. The first seems to mean 'realisation' and I thought the second meant to cheat. I probably mean that I must build up a realisation of myself so that I can move on in this New Year and to grasp some hope from...

At the Crib - a scene of a cave, beautifully created from heavy brown paper by Barbara and her school friends, floored with hay that I had scythed and stooked. There were statues of Mary and Joseph, the baby in a trough, a cow, a donkey, with sheep and lambs milling about. Today, Twelfth Night, the Minister blessed three toddlers as they added The Kings bringing gifts to the stable.

It was these gifts I was most taken with - ones given to a refugee family.

There are refugees all over the world at present. Where there is war, there are always refugees and this is of course a world war. I have met some myself, for what are Chez and Antoni from Poland, or the evacuee children?

Down at Eaton Hall, just outside Retford, there are mothers just like Mary, giving birth away from home, solely seeking safety from being bombed in Hull.

Looking at the scene I imagined, say, Alec, Palmiro and I as the three kings. Alec's the man with the money, so of course there he is giving his gold to the family from Hull. Dad a docker given a day off from loading munitions onto warships, to visit his newborn, and his young - too young - war wife. Despite looking frightened, she is nevertheless smiling radiantly down on the babe in her arms.

Palmiro with his strange hair, curls brushed up and outwards, radiant against the light, would surely looked crowned. His gift would have to be, no not garlic, but Myrrh - scented olive oil.

That leaves me scratching for something to give of my own. I would and I can give of myself - I am giving myself, my all, to feed this sainted family. What do you need Mary? How can I help? I somehow doubt if my Tribunal or

War Ag would give me time off. Do I have anything personal to give, work of my own hands?

Palmiro actually does have his tapestry - very pretty *and* picturing a Saint.

I have my hedging tools, my plasher and billhook, and lots of prunings! A bundle of sticks! Everybody's struggling for fuel - even Good King Wenceslas gathering winter fu-u-el.

I was taken back to last summer in Alec's stand of pine trees. A ray of sunlight broke though the canopy and fell onto jewels on a tree trunk. I looked closely - drips on a dry sunny day? I brushed some. Pine perspiration. Sticky. Scented. Nice Pina. I saw some drops had dried, paler. I picked at them - hard, well tough really. I gathered a few pieces and back at the farm after tea, I showed Alec.

He popped one into his mouth. 'Ah, gum, Eric,' he said chomping for a minute.

I looked at a piece and licked it. Not nice.

Alec laughed at me and spat his out onto his hand. 'Not quite what the Yanks call gum, but watch.'

He fashioned a blob onto the end of a matchstick and held it over a gas mantle.

We waited, Sally, Barbara and I. Palmiro was nodding and smiling.

'He's seen this trick before,' I thought.

After a long minute Alec said, 'See?'

No.

'Smell!' he said.

Ah, yes. The room had become scented with the pine smoke.

'Incense!' I cried.

'Exactly.'

I wondered if that should be my gift - air freshener? But young Mary might think that I assume the houses of the poor of Hull would need freshening up, and slap me round the chops for my efforts. She would be incensed.

Smiling as I was at the whole notion, young Barbara saw me, smiled back across the twelfth night crib and mouthed 'Happy Christmas, Eric.'

43μ

Queenie's Married!
    Here's her invitation card.

Am I?

Part Three - Autumn 1944

The Germans arrive

44μ

I leant my head, my forehead, against the brick, my helmet hanging in my hand. There was no light, no chink of Christmas cheer emanating from my mother's door. Sunday lunchtime and I'm thinking about light. There is no lighting my life. Mam is probably bringing light to some homeless families in a church hall somewhere. YMCA van, perhaps.

It was dawn when I left Egmanton, not early at this time of year. It was foggy, too - quite a decision whether to go or not, but the fog had prevailed since 19th December, generally lifting in the middle of the day for a bit of sun. I had to visit Mam at Christmas ... if no one else.

Sally had packed me up some snap, and I had packed the panniers with the gifts only farmers could give ... 'for your mother Eric, and...' She couldn't say it.

Maisie Matchless fair sparkled on Saturday. I had spent the eve of Christmas Eve scraping off autumn's mud. I hadn't loved her.

I hadn't loved.

So with water, paraffin, oil, grease and a final polish, her true beauty now shone through. Alec had helped me build up a supply of petrol, a little at a time. Before I fired her up, young Barbara gave me a hug then stood back. As I nodded to Sally, she put her arm around her daughter, now kneading her hands and biting her lips.

I had to go.

Where had I been? I had been avoiding all built up areas in case I found them blown down.

Equipment and materials would yet be pouring out of Boughton and into France, to be restocked promptly with munitions and machines, arriving on trains from all over the country ... the empire. The soldiers were gone, but the worker bees - and prisoners of war - would be swarming from Nissen hives over trucks and lorries ... and me if I got in the way. I skirted round that and took minor roads through the villages. It is tiring peering through fog endlessly, and gripping tight as I dipped into the murk at the bottom of valleys and the roads were full of military vehicles - a menace to bikers. I pulled into Retford where I took the train through to Sheffield. - saved some fuel, too.

The cold brick door pillar sent an ache into my brain so I turned and looked into the street. Luckily I couldn't see much, so I had my thoughts to myself, but they turned to you Pina. Oh little child of Dore on the Moor, how sweet I see thee lie.

I stamped my feet and shook myself out. A couple walked past arm in arm, eyes only for each other.

Should I get back on Maisie Matchless and trundle over to Grandpapa's Hall on the Hill? I knew I was totally unwanted; did I need to have it shoved in my face? I could take a ride past, Mummy might just be alone in the house and ...

I did.

Scotland for Christmas and Hogmanay! I met a neighbour along the lane who told me. She had seen Mummy out with a dog, but she didn't look a well woman, 'Sorry sir.'

I took the moor-line route back past Lodge Moor and down Redmires Lane. There were lots of guards and a couple of them followed me with their guns, so my slowing was, well, speeding up. I considered popping into the Three Merry Lads, the guards' local; however, even at Christmas, merry was not quite how I felt. Though I could hear the singing over the engine as I passed and an open door let out a billow of smoke, it did not cheer me.

Like a ghost, a memory appeared to me - my quest. I pulled up and stood beside my bike for a moment, helmet off. Icy blast to the brain. Yes, I might find out something about the changes at the camp - guards with guns was a contrast to sleepy Nether Headon.

In the fug at the pub, I took a seat with a pint and a forced smile. Someone recognised it and steered round 'cheer up mate, it might never happen,' sitting himself down beside me. It was the last remaining space.

When a little Dutch courage enabled me to proffer him a greeting, his stripes told me he was a sergeant,

'Not local, then?' he said.

Funny question - it is of course a local pub. Aha - but not near any houses. It's the 'camp pub', though there were some civilians in there.

'I know everyone else in civvies,' he said, 'work at the camp, see?'

'By your accent, you're not local either,' I said.

'Welsh. Wales isn't it, boyo!'

I had to scratch my head to realise that, despite having people from all over the Britain and the world working in Steel City, I hadn't personally met any Welsh folk. I told him.

He put out his hand. 'Here's a first then - Willy Constant'.

I'm so glad to say I immediately warmed to Willy. I needed warming. He had already told me basically, that everyone in the room worked at the POW camp, so I had no problem slipping back into my mission. I explained my reason for passing - on my way between my wife and my mother, and needing a break from the cold and fog.

'No heater in the car then?' he said.

I laughed. 'No, not on my Matchless motorbike either.'

Keeping Mum, I knew I couldn't quiz him, but told him of my trip to Headon and it being almost deserted.

'Not any more it's not - packed and maybe even with some tentage,' he said. 'We've been bringing Germans in from France, by the tens of thousands, daily.'

I whistled.

He went on. 'That must have been around September/October time?'

I nodded.

'Heard of the Falaise Gap?'

I had. The first major success of D-Day with a round up of tens of thousands of Germans.

'We've gone on from there. We had handfuls of Germans, some French, until October; and quite a lot of Italians working on farms and throwing up prefabs - houses you know?'

I do,

'We don't even guard them.' He chuckled.

I told him about Palmiro.

'Farmer, then?'

I didn't lie. 'Lovely bloke. They all seem to be pretty happy - and willing workers,' I said 'Not quite happy, but fairly content.' Could I steer him to get a bit more info?

'Oh, yes,' Willy said, 'some say they didn't want to fight, cowards, even. Not me. Called up, I went willingly, but didn't fancy a fight - who does?'

'My sentiments entirely,' I said. 'We haven't had any Germans sent to us, though?'

'No! Not yet. Gotta sort them out.'

'Black, grey, white?'

'All pretty black so far - straight from the battlefield, and until a few months ago, masters of Europe. Not giving up yet.' He coughed. 'Some of them in a pretty bad way actually.' He tapped his temple; shook his hand. 'Half-starved, too, poor buggers.'

I thought that was about as much info as I could hope for, so I told how I noticed more fencework and guard towers, from when I last passed.

He told me it had been a massive building site with concrete pouring and corrugated iron deliveries and erections constantly. He proffered just a few words behind his hand, 'three separate enclosures - camps within the camp. Need to separate out real Nazis as a first.' He pretended to finish wiping his mouth.

I got my exercise book out and tore off a strip, adding my address. 'Within the law, of course, will you keep me informed of ... developments, of the camp system and the like, please?' I said.

He turned on his seat and squared up to give me a real scrutiny. He seemed satisfied. He took my slip and rustling in his breast pocket, swapped it, looked around to see only merry makers, oblivious to us, and passed me his own slip. I slotted it straight into my notes.

I wished him happy Christmas saying, 'what's that in Welsh?'

He shook my hand, and with a somewhat enigmatic smile said, 'Merry Christmas,' stood up, pulled down his tunic and marched out.

Mam was all over me when I got back home. (Home? Where is my home, now?)

Enough negativity.

The smell of cooking, of baking. Decorations - homemade crepe ones. Not new, but not faded. A little tree - a holly branch actually - prettily decorated with trinkets accumulated during my childhood and perhaps Mam's, too.

She had several beers in and had sourced a small bottle of whisky for me. The drink and the heat in the nice warm house, the nurture of a mother's arms. I drifted off.

Mummy, me and you up by a lakeside up on the moors. You with your little frock tucked into your nappy, holding my finger as you paddle in the water's edge...

But Pina, how can I write about you now? You never will paddle in the lake.

I woke with a jolt.

'Oh Eric,' said Mam, cradling my head in her bosom as my tears soaked into her sleeve. The sobs shook and rattled out of me.

I had to tell her that there was to be no baby. I couldn't tell her how or why - mothers lost babies all the time. No need to explain.

But Pina, the thought of you - the reality of you - has sustained me, alone, away from Mummy, outcast from the people I love, because of my love for people.

Perhaps your spirit lives, lives on, at least it does so in me, inside of me.

I think I depend, continue to depend, on a love for you. You will come to be. You will carry my story forward to ... in you ... to children.

My future. Our future. All our futures.

45μ

I was turning my plasher over and over in my hand. The last light coming through the cobwebbed window was not showing me the beautiful pattern weld marking on weapon. Through the rust I could just see a glint of real steel - on the break.

'You won't find it there.'

I jumped. Had Alec been watching me?

I held the nasty blade out to him. 'Broken,' I said.

He fended the blade with his forearm whilst looking only into my eyes.

I let the blade fall, resting the point - ex-point - on the byre floor.

'Is it all lost, Eric?' he said.

I shook my head slowly.

'The Missis,' he said,' you didn't see her at Christmas did you?'

'Mam...'

'Come on Eric, not your mother. I thought your wife was expecting.'

I was limp, looking into Alec's eyes and seeing ... smoke. Fog? He has grey eyes.

Alec stood forward; I jumped and dropped the plasher. He picked it up and left it on my workbench. He took hold of my shoulders. I looked at his. He went to lift me, shake me, by my shirt. I was an almost empty sack. He shook it.

'What happened, Eric?'

I tightened my lips across my teeth. Bit my cheek. 'Falaise', I said. 'Pocket.'

'Gap,' he said.

'Yes.'

'Well I've got something for you, there,' he said, letting go of me and taking a letter out of his pocket. He didn't pass it me. He looked down at it, unfolding and re-folding it before putting it back in his pocket.

'We'll come to that, but Eric. Sally is worried about you ... we're all worried about you. Me, Sally ... Palmiro, for fuck's sake.'

I pulled my neck in. Alec doesn't swear. 'Palmiro,' I said, 'worried about me?'

Alec lowered his head and looked at me through his substantial brows.

I dragged my hand across my chin. Slowly. 'Palmiro. Yeah, not good when a prisoner of war gets to worrying about me. What's wrong with me?'

Eric looked towards the door as if someone might be coming to answer. 'Look, I'm not one for...'

'Swearing,' I said. 'It must be serious.'

He cocked his head and smiled a little. 'Mm.'

I shook my hand as if it were cut. I don't know why.

We both looked at it, so I hid it in my other hand.

'Queenie's married,' I said.

'Si' down,' he said, sweeping the bench and hopping onto it.

I did as I was told. I could feel my brain start to think, like the Fordson on these winter mornings, starting, but reluctantly.

'Queenie? Who's Queenie?

'Cousin Queenie.'

A real look of consternation swept over his face.

'*Cousin* Queenie?'

'Sort of,' I said, 'Mam's cousin ten times removed or something.'

He looked at the door again. No cavalry coming to rescue him. Or me.

'Eric. Falaise pocket I know something about. What's your cousin got to do with it ... or more importantly, what's your cousin got to do with ... with you? Not...?'

I suddenly realised that I was sad about Queenie getting married, but Alec got a totally different idea. 'Ha! I'm not sad about Queenie, well not like that, but I am sad about the whole D-Day, Normandy ... what colour is that sea ... the blood? The land ... mud, but not through falling rain, but blood of the fallen?' I shook my head. I shook it again, like a dog with a flea in its ear, a real good shake this time with a whistling intake of breath through gritted teeth.

My index finger was writing on my other palm. Here's the story I told Alec:

My wife lives with my in-laws. They've got plenty of money. I married the boss's daughter. She's lovely, she's not like them. Well she wasn't. Not all about money. He's what they call a steel magnate. I almost got jokey about steel *magnet*, but the brain, beginning to get going, told me that it would not be appropriate. Steel and war, I told him. Krupps, Ruhr Valley - Essen and Sheffield. Weapons.

I'm a grinder, I told him, a cutler, maker of fine kitchenware, and the best in the world. It seems that every good invention gets better when a warmonger wants it for his battle. Kitchen knife to bayonet. Stay sharp. Don't get rusty. Manganese steel. That's my job. Silver Plate. I mentioned my old hero, Thomas Boulsover who accidentally made plate from fusing copper and silver. What could I discover in our laboratory? All the boss wanted was better shell cases for bullets; stronger barrels to shoot them out of.; lighter, sharper, easier to store and fix bayonets, perhaps?

Eventually my brain was producing a bit more sense. I apologised to Alec and told of my wife's problems ... with me. How she was originally completely supportive of my stand on peace. Who does prefer war, or even want it? However, after poor old Chamberlain waved his stupid - *not stupid, Alec* - peace paper, reality bit. Where I was proud of Boulsover the cutler who invented silver plate, wanted in peace *and* war, her Papa wanted the quick money to be made from munitions. He envied Hadfield's invention of manganese steel, now turning out 18 inch armour piercing shells, and Vickers (THE machine gun maker) turning Spitfire engine cranks. Couldn't we do something like that? We didn't have Vickers huge drop hammer, or an oil pit for tempering gun barrels - so deep they have a lift to get in to clean them - but couldn't we make the specialised small parts? Firing pins, Eric?

But I didn't want to.

115

Okay, I did work on the chaff - I saw it as protecting our planes - even if they were bombers. That was a thin edge of a wedge, and I saw it.

It was easy to turn the factory over to any number of pieces wanted for the war machine, but he didn't have the capacity of Hadfield's making huge cannons - you should see that pit, I told Alec, almost with a sense of pride.

Stop it Eric.

So, could I tell, let alone explain to Alec what had happened to my wife?

'You thought my wife was expecting,' I said. 'The girls have been quite excited but have not mentioned it for a few ... well, months actually. She is expecting no longer, apparently. We could say...' But I didn't.

Eventually Alec turned the conversation and my concentration around. 'It's winter, Eric, short days and long nights turning us to dark thoughts. But look here,' he swept up my plasher, 'you're a steel man and you've set yourself a project of that hedge, haven't you?' He waved the plasher - not too dangerously in my little pig-sty workshop. 'Can't you fix this?'

Can't I? Yes I can, but not without heat. I asked about a local smithy - I hadn't noticed one. Alec doesn't really have a need for one, because Jim Lister, a mobile farrier comes to shoe the horses, and he has a gas forge in a lorry.

My eyebrows rose.

Alec nodded. 'I'll have him round soon - we need the horses sorting before spring. Jim Lister comes a long way, but spends a day or two in each village with all the farmers then moves on. Have a word.' He stopped and took a deep breath. He shoved his hands deep into his trouser pockets and looked at me.

Trouble, I thought. Had somebody seen me in Sheffield and reported me to the Tribunal? Surely not at Christmas.

Alec pulled the envelope out of his pocket - bit crumpled now. He tapped it on his hand. Yes, a letter from the tribunal. 'Now then Eric - we're not entirely eye-to-eye on the POWs, but we don't get to hear or read much about them, and your story could well be as good a record as us civilians will ever get to see. I like what you're doing. I like Palmiro ... in fact, other than one or two who gave young Barbara a bit too much attention, I haven't had any kind of bad feeling about our purported enemies.'

I shook my head. 'Good phrase, Alec. Not one of them has given any indication to me that they ever were up for a fight with us. There must be some fascists among them, but Gordon Tasker really liked his two, didn't he? Even wanted them to billet with the family?'

He held out the envelope. 'Here's the next stage for you.'

I took it and looked at him.

'I need you to start looking *up*, Eric. Chin *up*! We are hopeful that Overlord is at last turning the Bosch back home. Join us. That envelope is an introduction to Charlie Gregory in South Leverton. He's got a few of the Germans on a trial with him - first co-operative lads from the new intake at Headon Camp. You can use the phone. Go and get his story and share it with us.'

Gruff farmer types. Heart of gold. I was smiling and nodding. 'Thanks a lot for thinking that way, Alec.' I put my hand out.

'Get away with you!' he said and gave me a bear hug.

46μ

Cousin Queenie is married. I couldn't face writing anything about it, but before I return to my quest, I had better get it off my chest ... or own up.

I had got a nice pile of Christmas cards - somebody out there loves me - but I didn't discern from the writing, the one I really wanted to open. So I didn't open any. Not until I got back from Mam's, the day after Boxing Day. I needn't have come back, there's not much to do on the farm, but Mam, not really thinking I could stay, had made herself busy, out helping with people bombed out, moving in - to the new pre-fabricated houses they slung up - mostly away from the city, up Chapeltown way. I recalled the women at work saying Italians were building them. Palmiro's Pals?

Gone off again, haven't I?

I think I was probably Queenie's little secret. Similar to her Jack in some ways, but totally different - he a professional soldier since 1936, me a pacifist; him away at war, me safely at home.

Queenie Thomas wasn't supposed to fall in love with Jack Saunders, he is her first cousin - their mothers are Tomlinson sisters. I suspect she has written to Jack actually daily, though I reckon he wouldn't get all of them. She has shared with me what she could glean about his whereabouts and his state. Of course the War Office will have kept the former from her and Jack will have saved her from the latter. So they spoke of love and life other than war.

He would see films, which of course she would make very effort to catch in order to share with him. He loves Robert Donat, and of course so does every girl, but Queenie loves Jack more. Mr Chips gets more than a mention in their letters apparently - I suspect something special happened when they saw 'Goodbye' in 1939 - possibly on one of his breaks from Bovington Camp, even embarkation leave before Dunkirk. (I am allowed to mention that - the Royal Tank Regiment training base on Salisbury Plain. And Jack's first sortie was to relieve the pressure from Gerry attacking the beach head. They failed, left all their new kit burnt-out on the dock-side in Cherbourg.)

Sealed their relationship that day? She's been going to marry him since then. '"If"* just hasn't crept into her letters to me, and nor to him I am sure. *"When"* he returns, they will be married and will have two children, a boy John, and a girl Diane. And live happily...

Oh, Pina, I *will* get to name you - Josephine, rather than Giuseppina Chapman, but always Pina to me. You are my promise in this war.

Queenie is now married. I am so glad for her, but I strongly suspect that that means the end of our special friendship. I have seen her through, I hope. She couldn't share her hopes with her family as they don't approve of the cousins marrying, so she has shared her dreams with me, and some of her fears.

I have broad shoulders. (I haven't really, as you know, but it means I can carry a lot. Yes I am tough, but last autumn was too heavy for me.) She has lambasted me in one of her letters about me *shirking the war, coward...* but she hid that page, the one smudged, she said by her tears, under another explaining her 'outburst' and apologising, but thought I could handle what I must get all the time, even from friends...

I do.

I am fairly sure I can. Now. Spring is round the corner.

...but she says it has taken a lot of courage on my part, especially the way I took my punishment at Strangeways, and the Scabies. *'Don't mention the little bugs, makes me itch!'* (I'm nearly crying myself now. Look away Pina.)

...she knows what I want all my children to know - what I did in the war was for all of them, too. You must not have to do what Jack has had to do. Or Queenie.

Queenie wrote:

> *"On the morning of November 5th 1944 I came home from working night-shift in Leeds. As usual on Tuesday I cleaned the sitting room for mum and had a bath. I usually then went to bed for a few hours but not that day. As I was almost in my pyjamas a man walked past the bathroom window, so I ran into my room.*
>
> *Something made me realise it was Jack and his dad. Jack home fit and well.*
>
> *My prayers had been answered. When he went away I was 19 and he was 20. Now I was 24 and Jack was almost 26; almost five years and hundreds of letters that kept us loving each other. Mum and Dad, bless them, gave us a wedding fit for a queen."*

She did invite me. I didn't open the letter until after I had opened the Christmas cards - and her letter - I realised that I had put it by...

So there was me moping, and cousin Queenie had the best news I could possibly hope for, except...

Despite their reservations, their families had come round. We all need good news, and what a love story, against all odds.

So on December 16th - just 5 weeks later, they got married in Thorne.

But not happy ever after quite, yet. Like me, he can't stop, until it's stopped for everybody else. Amazingly, nor can Queenie. I know that her shells will be required until that madman is wiped off the face of the earth - I don't think Hitler will ever give in. They had a week off, and then Jack went back to Bovington Camp and Queenie to her digs in Leeds.

Jack had been pulled out of the advance up Italy. Very thoughtful of the army - men are not expected to be away from home for more than five years, so they've brought him back just in time. Five years away from home - completely. Abroad.

I count my blessings.

47μ
February 1945

Sunday lunch with the Gregory family in South Leverton. Now there's a rare winter's treat! February the eighteenth. Snow a couple of weeks ago has melted away, now we have heat pushing up from the Azores putting a real spring in our heels.

A whole family outing - Alec and Sally up front, with young Barbara and me sitting in the back of Alec's pride and joy - his Wolseley Wasp. Rightly proud - very comfy.

I don't need my 'Letter of Introduction' - Alec does it in person.

Charlie manages what was supposed to be a Market Garden, for Hopkinsons - quite a big concern, with farms across South Yorks and North Notts - very near Headon Camp. I say supposed to be, because they grow what the War Ag tells them to as they *are* 'the market.'

The Germans are the reason for my 'Letter of Introduction'. Charlie still has some Italians *and* some Land Army girls, but pressure to grow more ... and on every piece of land, allied with his supply of casual labour being away at war, means he has decided to have two POWs regularly.

Before we sat down to lunch, Sally joined Charlie's wife Emma in the kitchen; Barbara disappeared with Charlie's daughter Betty, leaving Alec, Charlie and me 'inspecting the estate', while the POWs mooched around an orchard.

Charlie was obviously letting the boys feel a little freedom. He said it was not usual to have Germans out, but he had the Italians, so the Camp Commandant let him try a couple of real trusties. Lieutenant Ferguson feels that he needs 'bait' to get the men to feel both that good behaviour gets rewards and makes them less depressed.

We didn't bring Palmiro. He was keener to use his real freedom looking for girls.

Charlie enjoys talking politics and even engaged the Italian POWs. (He hasn't started on the Germans yet!)

He said he was trying to persuade an Italian that surely he would like to decide from a choice of candidates - to not have a dictator. The Italians could not even grasp the notion of democracy. In the end Charlie burst out, 'That's it - the buggers don't know what they want!' and kicked a somewhat rotten apple, spraying us all with ... cider? Is that called getting your own back?

I was intrigued to see how Alec would engage, but he didn't rise at all, simply smiled along with the much more garrulous Charlie. He did say we had a couple of Italians, but simply said 'nice enough chaps.'

Charlie was on a roll and laughed his way through telling us how he had asked the gang of four Italians to help with the plum harvest. '"Do *not* shake them off the tree," I told 'em, "they are not olives," - even got one of them to understand and translate it, to be sure - "non sono olive a!" I shouts at 'em, "Si? Si?"'

He nudged Alec and smiling round at me breathed and polished his nails, 'Italian that! See?'

We both chuckled at him.

'Seen olives, haven't you?' he went on. 'Hard as bullets - wouldn't surprise me if that's what they used, not pea-shooters, olive poppers, ha!'

We all looked at the Gerries - just lads chatting, but in their chocolate uniforms and orange patches, in Sunday best condition. They can't work the farms in those.

'Course they did shake, them?' said Alec.

'Sacked the buggers,' Charlie said. 'Told old Fergy to not send 'em back to me. Well I told them, didn't I, and I saw them listen to their companio, didn't I? Stressed it myself, well, didn't I? But they knew best o' course - or were too bloody lazy to do it properly.' He coughed, looked round and then spat. 'Poor Sal and Betty had to help me sort through for obvious bruising. Course it doesn't show immediately. Just hoped they got straight to market and eaten!'

We were hailed from the farmhouse.

'Talking of eating,' said Charlie, 'got a nice big chicken we hid from War Ag. Come on.' He hailed the boys over and introduced Karl and Bernard, 'no, Bernard and Karl?'

I could hardly picture poor Bernard as a soldier. Thin, weak, shy, specs - utterly dejected, but obviously making an effort. I patted him on the back and he looked up from the floor and smiled weakly at me.

The girls didn't join us at table, and Charlie explained, (after checking the boys first, then moving into a bit of dialect to more confuse them), he said 'yon lass not so enamoured of us sitting down with the less than friendly,' he smiled at the lads, 'so I tells her she can ruddy well starve then ... 'scuse me Sal...'

But she butted in with a laugh, 'she'll not starve, m' lad. We've sent the kids up a plate a piece.' She gesticulated to the Germans to get stuck in. They did.

After a massive roly-poly - 'our raspberries' - and custard - 'fresh eggs' - I needed a stretch. Charlie elbowed me into Bernard and told me to, 'get on with what you've come for.' I hadn't needed the Letter of Introduction. I wondered why not Karl, but assumed Charlie had worked out that one would tell, or be able to tell, more than the other.

There's a church almost next door, so I thought we'd set off for a bit of a walk round the village, and keep it for shelter if the day kept to its threat to rain, maybe even snow.

'Bern-hard Per-nicker,' said the young man, taking my notebook and pencil, and writing 'Bernhard Pönicke.' He pointed to the two dots on the ö and said 'umlaut' then made a circle of lips - 'er.' He nodded me to try, 'Guten tag Herr Pönicke.'

I parroted.

'Ah! Sehr gut,' he said. 'Hardy!' he said. 'Me - freund - Hardy.'

I speak German now, Pina! Me and mine freund Hardy, sprechen ze deutch.

Actually in my now fairly well developed sign language, gesticulation and good old British shouting, I managed to piece together a bit of his war story.

'Me, Eric. Sheffield. You?'

He laughed and snatched the notebook again. 'Mühlhausen/Thüringen,' he wrote in very ornate script. Sounds like a donkey shed - a mule-house.

Anyway, a Danish girl, taught him some English. (He's a bit like a girl himself, he said this in such a coy way, and pointed at himself, then looped his arm as if holding hers. I get it.) Apparently Danes and Germans can understand each other, and despite fraternising with their occupiers in a pretty big way, she wanted to talk the language of the big Hollywood romances.

Mühlhausen is a pretty medieval city in the centre of Germany apparently. He pointed to the church and mimed piano playing - ah, organ - he pointed at himself Johann Sebastian Bach. The man himself was their church organist, I think.

He's the youngest of eight, mostly girls, but with a cheeky big brother who... 'Kristalnacht?' he asked, shaking his head.

I nodded with a raised brow.

Hardy threw a stone and shook his head. 'Me not. Brudder, Ja. Me, nein. No. Hitler Youth, Ja, must. Not good. Sorry!'

I patted his sleeve and walked on.

Enough of the silly talk, then: His big brother loves the Wehrmacht, army stuff, but dad was ashamed at needing the army. Dad's a locksmith or doormaker and, just like here, work was scarce in the 1930s. The Fuhrer built a large barracks and that gave the town plenty of work. There are lots of doors in barracks.

Kristalnacht was the night all Germany 'spontaneously' decided to wreck Jewish property, so there were a lot of bricks thrown through shop windows, and next morning the pavements were covered in 'crystals.' The Germans have really taken Jew bashing to a new level, a sight more than over here, so we are told ... a lot more, really. I just hope it's only propaganda. I say spontaneously, because Bernhard indicated that Hitler Youth were *encouraged* to turn out in support. He wasn't supporting, but still had to turn out. Some Synagogues were burnt down, but not in Mühlhausen - it's only a small one, anyway.

Come the war, Hardy wasn't old enough so joined a labour corps in Lodge in Poland, however, by December 1941 at just eighteen he was thrown into the thick of Barbarossa - the German offensive against Russia. He wrapped his arms round himself.

I knew about this - Stalingrad especially.

'Kalt und shnee,' he said. Even you can guess that. He shivered.

We were on a track going round South Leverton passing the road to North Leverton and we heard, then saw, a train pass over the crossing a couple of hundred yards away. I gestured towards it. He nodded so we took a little walk towards the Station Hotel. Not sure it's a hotel - like a big house really. I did think we might step in for a beer, but no. A few looks from people, and Hardy's uniform, told me that was not a good idea.

122

We looked up and down the line and a goods train was steaming towards us. We stood at the gate to watch it pass, full of ... vehicles.

'Oy!' I heard and looked round to see a man, point to Hardy, then say 'push off, or else!'

We did.

He told me a story of just how cold it had been in Russia:

He was a telefunken - we know what that is, don't we?

We can't imagine it.

He was billeted, so Bernhard said. In a house. On the frozen waste of the eastern front. Just how many were billeted in Operation Barbarossa, the Nazi's attempt to succeed where Napoleon failed - to take Russia?

My Gentles, I don't *want* you to imagine.

I have to write this down, maybe Mummy will skip this for you, but it shook me.

Gentle Bernhard. His mates may call him Hardy, you couldn't imagine a more ironic epithet. Perhaps that's why they put him in a billet. Who else got a billet that wasn't a hole in the snow? The officers, surely.

When he looks me in the eye, it's only when I'm *not* looking at him. If I catch him, he demures and smiles, at the floor, like a girl.

Though Bernhard was there in that carnage, I think even he had to imagine it, building an image from the signals pouring in his ears. His comrades' blood pouring through his headphones, the staccato of gunfire, flowing down the canal of his ear, cannon blasts, into this brain, into his dreams, his waking nightmares.

He heard the crunch, crunch, crunch of his comrades marching to the front - in their thousands, hundreds of thousands. Hear swoosh, swoosh, returning. Some of them. Stepping out for air, he would be knee-deep in pink slush.

He didn't tell me about that.

He told me about his hostess. He was staying with a young mother and baby. He was not a welcome guest. She fed him. At breakfast he saw her, babe in arms, take a big swig from her frosted water jug and swill, swill, swill it round her mouth. (He swirled his head, musing.) Then she sprayed it right over the baby's face. He took a sharp breath remembering it. Again.

He glanced at me. 'No hot water, Eric.'

I was looking.

He smiled at the floor but I also saw a tear drop. 'I write Mutti - *what has this madman got us into*?' he said.

He bucked up then, and told me that after Russia, he had been sent to Denmark. Showed me a picture. He looked OK. Wasn't starved or emaciated or anything. He got himself a stripe - not quite a Corporal?

Funny to remember that little country was in the war. Well it isn't really I don't think. The Germans invaded it and just occupied it, didn't they? Hardy had a nice time there, even had a girlfriend. He looked at the floor and smiled. He's not even the sort of chap I could give a "Woo, Bernhard!" to. I did point smart young man in the photo he was still holding. I nodded at it and raised an eyebrow.

He frowned - looked me in the eye! - then smiled and shook his head.

I think I brought him out of the war ... to some sort of comfort zone.

We walked on quietly until we came to the back of the church. I led him in. Pensive, he held back, but then joined me holding back the large door. Mid afternoon, with a little heat left in the place after Sunday worship; no people.

He liked it, looking round and nodding to himself and to me.

He sat, then knelt, obviously praying.

I found the organ and when he looked up, I waved him over.

'Johann Sebastian Bach,' he muttered.

I lifted the lid and wiped my hand along the keys, then offered it to him.

He smiled and turned to walk away.

Time to head back.

'Prisoner, you taken prisoner?' I said as we shut the church door.

'Mm, Frank reich,' he said. We took a few more strides, him shaking his head.

'Girls,' he said. He's got lots of sisters. Smiling now. One big brother - frowns and mime slapping and kicking. Not so good. No. He rolled up his sleeve - quite a nasty burn.

'Bomb?' I said.

'Nine, shvester, sister,' he laughed. He mimed ironing. Good sister, accident. He rubbed it gently, as if thinking of the last place he was kissed.

I thought of the girl in Denmark and asked.

No, finished.

I looked at the scar again: it is the shape of a smoothing iron. Him and his sister just pace-egging about, as Grandma would say.

Wife?

Laugh. No wife. He looked towards the house as we approached and smiled. Home. No home.

As we were about to set off, the family were in the Wasp. Charlie shaking my hand pulled me in close and whispered 'Conchie?' in my ear.

I pulled back, but he still had my hand. I didn't know how to respond.

'Not a coward?' he said, gritted teeth very near my nose. 'Shot in the last shebang. Could be a Medic, y'know. I had a few with me - Wipers, Somme...'

'My Dad was gassed,' I butted in. 'Took him twenty years ... of a living death. My city makes guns.'

He bit his lip; looked deep into me. He squeezed my hand and shoved me into my seat.

Bernhard Pönicke is a very shy man.
Charlie let me snap his ID card while Bernhard wasn't looking.

48μ

That was a bit of a scare, Charlie whispering in my ear. I should be used to hearing it through clenched teeth and I tense-up to avoid the inevitable head-butt to follow. Had a few sore cheeks, but not the broken nose or teeth some COs have suffered.

I got a letter from one of the chaps at 'Kreb's Empire', as the locals are now calling the Medical Research place in Sheffield, where I did the scabies trial. He was apologising to me that some of the COs who had gone into the Non Combatant Corps (NCC), were renouncing their CO status and joining in combat. Some in the Royal Army Medical Corps. Almost home after being quiet most of the way, Alec *happened* to say that Charlie had been in the RAMC.

How did I feel hearing about what Bernhard was hinting at, and what is coming through on Newsreels. German atrocities?

Yes, how do I feel?

I don't know quite why he felt the need to apologise to me, poor lad. It is so hard. Would I rather risk being shot, blown up, or gassed like Dad, if I knew back then what I am now finding out? Probably not - my Mam has had enough, and so has all Sheffield. I am doing my bit, and I have suffered for my country, men and women. You may well ask how, so I had better tell you.

At the moment nobody wants to know.

Funny I didn't even think of such things in 1940, but back then, I'm told, half a dozen chaps were prosecuted for publishing a poster reading "War will cease when men refuse to fight. What are YOU going to do about it?" They were accused of encouraging disaffection among troops. So not having any other way of expressing my horror, I've kept it to myself.

Most think it is sheer cowardice, and only a few appreciate how hard it is: so many buckle under the pressure, peer pressure mainly from other men, but surprisingly, from women too. Though they tend to go for the white feather rather than the knuckle-duster.

Why 'surprisingly'?

It genuinely shocks me how little was learnt from the war to end all wars. It really should have ended war, especially for the ordinary man. I say ordinary because, though I know that the rich, the powerful, and the masters did lose many sons among the almost forty million casualties, they still had something after the war. Ordinary folk didn't even have jobs after the munitions factories cut back. Ordinary women didn't have fathers, brothers and sons - lots of them. Queenie's Grandma lost 3 sons - her mother's 3 brothers and her own 3 uncles.

The women also didn't have the jobs they did for the men who had gone to war.

But Grandpapa and his cronies made fortunes from selling arms.

The casualties were not all deaths and they weren't all British of course, but I am more concerned about *basic humanity*, rather than nationality - Nationalism.

I am also concerned about perceived benefits - who gains from war? Who wins what? What are the real principles?

On Pathe news we see the destruction of whole cities which are being fought over by opposing forces. But ... children ... just look at our Sheffield Blitz: Over half of all Sheffield's houses were damaged - over 80,000. Two thirds of all the schools. These buildings not in any firing line. They are occupied by people who are *not* shooting shells, *not* raining bombs down from a black sky.

So yes, Cousin Queenie and most of Sheffield workers are making guns, shells and bombs.

Some say we started the terror bombing of non-military targets, that Herr Hitler didn't want to do this, but joined in as tit-for-tat. V1 stands for Vengeance weapon - in both English and German. Doodlebug sounds funny. It's not.

We thought those V1 rockets couldn't reach this far north. But news is leaking out that Hitler had a special surprise for some of us this Christmas - they carried some up the North Sea on planes and let them go towards Manchester. Not very accurate, but spread some terror: one up near Retford at Sturton-le-Steeple; one just below Doncaster at Bawtry, and another in Beighton, Sheffield. Luckily all landed in fields. Still they are big bombs and blew out lots of windows. We haven't picked up what happened further west. Some must have been bad for Manchester - a large area of houses not so easy to miss. I might ask Miss Husbands next time I'm at the library if she can find some Manchester reports for me. Retford Times tells us nothing - hasn't mentioned POWs or local bombings - not that we suffer much, other than our own planes crashing, including a fully loaded Lancaster with all on board killed at Milton across the hill.

It was the early hours of Christmas Eve - 1944

I was a weapon maker. I didn't sign up for it, but I became one.

I knew Dad had not only lost loads of Pals, and Mam and me were affected because though he didn't die out there, he lost his life - the one he had - and was never able to get it back. This was because someone somewhere made a shell with poison gas in it. Every weapon is made by somebody, and of course each military organisation tries to get a weapon which is more effective than the enemy's.

I'm a Grinder, a Steeler, come on the Blades! I don't want my blades to cut down people, though. I want people to live in peace with each other - I am a pacifist. That is a dirty word at the moment, well since poor old Mr Chamberlain was hoodwinked by Herr Hitler.

When Grandpapa wanted our factory to move into making munitions, I had to continue helping to test, develop, mix and shape our metals. After a little while I hinted that I didn't like doing this. Managers got to hear of it. They of course fear that a Conscientious Objector might make weapons not work -

sabotage them. They put me out of the lab and onto a lathe, turning barrels for guns. Big mistake - I might make them square not round!

Weeks from hint to boot. I was kicked out, now no job and no chance of getting one. 'Why did you leave your last job, Mr Chapman?' did not need to be asked. The whisper of 'Conchie!' was deafening in Sheffield.

Mummy cried. 'How could you do that to my Papa, Eric?'

One man.

Many victims.

What could I do?

Firstly I joined about thirty students who were purposely getting Scabies - little bugs under our skin. This was at Kreb's that I mentioned. Before I got there in late '41 they couldn't work out how to put the scabies in - inject them? That didn't work.

Now look away, Pina - this is not for the ears of nice girls!

Scabies is a nasty catching thing, it itches like mad - yes, makes you nearly screaming mad. We scratched until we bled ... except when we caught each other and helped.

Why were we doing this? Lots of poor people and people living in poor conditions - including soldiers and sailors who were trying to bring food into the country - would have scabies and no one knew why or how they caught it. Old Mellanby was the professor trying to find out - and he couldn't get us infected. Mad, eh?

Then he had a really mad idea. He got us to wear the unwashed underpants of people who had scabies. Yes we caught it!

At that point all of us were volunteers; most were students and some were still working, but ... with scabies being infectious, that had to change, so they put us up at Fairholme - a big house in Broomhill.

I was neither a student nor still working, but we were all Conscientious Objectors, doing something 'for the good of humanity'.

Poor Mummy - did I think of her? This was our first time apart since our marriage as, of course, I now had an infectious disease and so couldn't stay with her. The underpants bit did not entirely enthral her. She did think it terribly brave of me, but, needless to say, her father thought it simply stupid, and that I couldn't love his daughter if I was willing to put her at such risk.

(How come munitions manufacturers never think they will maybe get their own back ... yes, get their own bombs on their family?)

At work I was in a protected occupation, serving the war effort, and now I was ... nobody. I was however potential Cannon Fodder - that is food for the guns. That was what my Daddy was, and all those Pals: if they simply walked out in their thousands the machine guns chewing them up would eventually run out of ammunition, and hopefully there would be some left to follow on and take over Germany. Or vice versa, of course - the German and Italian lads were just as dispensable. How long have we got to carry on not learning from history?

Mummy taught me a bit of Shakespeare. Funny fat old Falstaff told the future king off for criticising his rag-bag group of soldiers, saying "good enough to toss; food for powder, food for powder; they'll fill a pit as well as better [men]..." - food for gunpowder and good enough to toss into mass graves.

Some consolation that is - me in good company with the Bard himself in his attitude to the futility of war.

Mellanby did find out and my effort solved a lot of itching and scratching across the high seas.

Next was the ships biscuits - and torpedoes. With the U-Boat wolf-packs sinking so many ships, men were spending sometimes days in lifeboats waiting to be rescued. How long could they survive without water?

I can tell you - three and a half days. I did it. Horrible. We had to survive on typical emergency food stored in lifeboats - dried food like sea biscuits and chocolate - nothing to drink. (No you can't drink sea water, it drives you mad. I tell you what - thirst would make you try it.)

Now there's two things I did in the war, laying down my life, the Christians would say. They did. Say it and do it. None of us died doing it because the doctors were watching over us, but several were pulled up early because of fear they might die. They were willing for God's sake.

Good people.

Why not for people's sake is what I ask. I didn't say it. Dying of thirst is enough to be getting on with.

Then the military caught up with me. I was no longer in a protected occupation. I wasn't even a Conscientious Objector as far as Mr Churchill could tell. I didn't tell. I hadn't told anyone. I just heard about these lads doing their bit for the welfare of the people and ... nobody wanted me for a grinder any more. Didn't trust me with their knives... or their wives ... mothers ... children.

'Prefers Nazi kids,' I heard someone say.

That wounded me.

The COs told me to just report to the Tribunal and tell my reasoning.

I felt no need to tell why men shouldn't kill babies, let along other men. There's not so many men being killed in England. Lots of children.

Mam enjoyed me being around and helping out. I joined her on soup runs and serving tea. People were nice to me. I didn't say much so they thought me retarded or, though they couldn't see it, perhaps wounded. The older ones knew about wounds you couldn't see. They knew men like Dad.

His wounds killed him. Eventually. The new war did for him. He realised it had not been worth it.

The house was not the same, that's why Mam spent less time in it now.

I really wanted to help my wife, but her Papa said I wasn't helping her. Being married to a coward does not make a woman feel good. He was worried she would relapse - get sad again.

I was worried too.

She laughed when I left to take on scabies, kissed me and said how brave I was. 'My Eric.'

What to do? I was not going to take up arms.

One of the CO's mothers took me in, but only for a few weeks, if that.

The Tribunal smelt blood. Threatened prison if I didn't get to the third appointment for me to have a medical. You don't have to go in the army if you aren't fit. But even if you are not running and jumping fit, they find you a job you can do. Sitting at a desk and ordering more bullets and shells is an important job for them.

Then came the knock. On the door. A policeman. Another Policeman. And another Policeman. I almost thought Alec Fox had come for me sitting at the wheel of the Wolseley model.

Nice chaps. Took me up the hill, Manchester Road - the 'Strange way', cajoling me to 'just turn up for your medical, son,' 'you might not be A1, lad,' 'couldn't you do an office job?' They were just so nice. No hand-cuffs, no rough stuff at all. We even stopped for a 'blind bacon butty', one of them called it.

The other two Bobbies and I all gave him a queer look.

'Bread and Butter,' he bellowed. 'Bacon butty without bacon!'

We of course did get a fried Spam sandwich. Thanks goodness for America after all.

I would like to say that among the three of them there was a balance of opinion - and support or otherwise for me - but it would not be true. Two were Great War veterans and the other served in the twenties. Though they couldn't say it, I felt they all actually supported me. I of course told them about Dad - they all nodded. I told them about our city - they were all Steelers, but actually supported The Owls - Sheffield Wednesday Footie club. That was the only jip they gave me at all.

But they really did not want me to go into Strangeways Prison. 'I fear for you son.'

As we wound our way down the other side of the Pennines into Manchester, I have to say I feared for myself. However, I simply brought to mind how Dad's Pals (the ones who had survived so far), must have felt once the horrific reality of war had set in. The knot in my stomach felt like one in the Queen Mary's anchor chain. When the fancy tower of the prison was pointed out to me I thought my weight would crush through the bottom of the car.

The Bobbies pulled up some way off and stood me overlooking the site and trying one more time to change my mind, but stupid as I might be, I couldn't think how I could refuse my right to choose not to kill. The whole vista was one of destroyed buildings, with one or two fingers pointing to the sky - blaming bombers, or defiant ... or blaming God?

Strangeways Prison has a very fancy chimney; in fact the whole place is well designed with stripy bricks. Apparently the other tower is of the court house, and that was gutted in the Christmas Blitz in 1940. The prison had a near miss.

I felt gutted for that hour. I knew about gutting - hasn't Sheffield had its own?

49μ
March 1945

I fell asleep writing that last section, Pina, I hope you didn't. Woke up with no covers on, and freezing. I will have to tell you about my experience in Strangeways Prison another time.

Looking for something in my pockets the other day, I found Alec's letter of introduction and was about to throw it away, when I thought I'd see what he said about me. Nice things. But - there were two letters - with the one to Charlie was another to a Mr Harold Hardy at Gringley-on-the-Hill. Sounds like a chocolate box village. It is.

When I apologised to Alec, he tapped the side of his nose. Didn't say anything, but smiled.

Intrigue.

Rightly.

The weather has continued exceptionally warm - warmest in March since the 1880s - so I took advantage of it for the quite long ride out, past Tuxford and Retford to Gringley. It is famous (sort of) because it is on a hill that stands above the surrounding area and it has a beacon, a fire on a pole, from the time before telephones, when England was afraid that the Spanish would invade with their Armada of ships. If they were seen near the coast, a beacon would be lit and the next hill would see it, and light theirs, and so on up the country, so even as far north as Newcastle, people would know within the hour if the Armada was seen off Land's End. It wouldn't help with bombers.

Mr Hardy's farm is overlooked by the beacon - and it nearly wasn't.

I arrived at a village pond, so I thought it, and a young lad was drawn out by the approach of Maisie Matchless. Not being too forward in his admiration for the machine, he told me he nearly drowned in the pond. He laughed and said he didn't really remember it, but was told that when he was three, he went in after the dog, but it obviously swam out itself and left him stuck in the mud.

This was the right place - Pond Farm - with a building either side of the gate - the one on the right looked as if the roof was blown off.

'Top half was blown right off the dovecote,' said young Les Hardy, for that is his name.

'What, by the gales?' I said.

'No, by the bomber,' he said with pride.

I laughed and looked, even to a child, incredulous.

'Was, sir! A screamer,' he whistled. 'I saw it myself.'

I nodded and looked into the yard. A proper farmstead with a house to the right, but straight ahead a lot of rubble. The house was looking as if it had been recently spruced up.

Dad hove into view and proper introductions were exchanged. He didn't need the letter. 'Any friend of Alec Fox's...' We wandered around the farm a bit while Harold, the man of few words, confirmed with constant extra detail from young Les, that in May 1941 the village had had a Blitz.

I did not tell him that he had no idea what he was talking about, lucky for me as it happens, because he has.

Les was too excited to restrain, so Harold let his son tell the tale.

'I saw this Heinkel 111 fly over and down the by-pass...'

'New road, just there,' said Harold, 'finished in thirty nine but not opened. Got all sorts of stuff stored up on it - wagons and that.'

'Yeah, it were bright moonlight so I could see it clearly,' Les went on. 'It flies off towards Bawtry, then I hears it coming back. Gets over our covered yard and lets it go.' He whistled again. 'Me ears are ringing and it's all I can hear. I peeps up after a bit, and all that there,' he waved across the upper side of the farm yard, 'it were gone except that bit o'wall.' He started laughing, looking at his hands. It was still gone of course.

His dad smiled at him and swung a friendly swipe across the ears.

'Missed! Ah ha! He's laughing at me diving in the stingers,' said Les, pointing to a nettlebed at the other side of the house. He rubbed his hands together. 'I had a rash all over.'

'Still had your 'ead on ... and that tongue in it,' said Harold, and turning to me added, 'he were very lucky.' He shook his head. 'We all were. Took off all the roofs, blew out all the windows, and pushed the doors in.'

'Where were you?' I said.

'In the house. Me and Missis. Not a scratch. Course we were all of a stitherum,' he said. 'Had to move out across theear.' He nodded at the rather grand house at the other side of the pond. 'Go tell yer Mam to get kettle on, lad.'

Les skittered off into the house and Harold gave me more sober details.

Apparently the boy fancied he heard some whumps roundabouts and thought maybe Gainsborough was getting a bit of a pounding. He ran out and saw that Fox Covert Wood, the other side of the by-pass was on fire. The plane roared over his head, really exciting him. Not fearing in any way - nothing to fear out there in the countryside - he ran out to the farm gate by the dovecote to see it fly onwards. But it returned.

Sensibly Les ran back into the yard and behind the house, watching for the plane all the while - not a long while.

He heard the whistle and dived.

The bomb had taken out all their cattle area. Luckily for them, the annual discussion as to whether to let the cows out takes place on May 8th, and 'with Mr Walker, we agreed we'd be reight. Lucky for us, else they would have been pulped. It fell right in the covered yard and took out the whole lot - sheds, walls and barn - except for that wall.'

I could see it had a lean on it. I looked at the nice house. 'When was this Mr Hardy?'

'Oh - yes, sorry, nearly four year ago - May the eighth, nineteen forty one.' he shook his head. 'No sign of a crater, though.'

They had called Les inside and all hid under the stairs. The roof-tiles were off, but the woodwork and brickwork were okay. The raiders were buzzing around for about four hours, but luckily for the Hardys, Fritz did not follow up the high explosive with incendiaries or else they would have lost the whole farm.

I commented how it looked ... not so bad now.

'Make do and mend,' said Harold. They had to, it is all they've got and they still had all the cattle - in fact all the beasts and birds, except for one pig, which just squealed and squealed, though it did not have any visible injuries.

'Frightened out of its skin we reckoned ... so we made cracklin' out of it.' He cackled.

Apparently his mother has married Mr Walker at Homestead farm, up the road, and there's another story.

Mrs Hardy called us in for tea and I could smell the new paint - cream, brown and green of course.

50μ
Strange Ways

Prison is not nice, but I am proud that I did it. I hope I can instil in all my children that there are some things that we just have to do, so if we have to do it, then make it fun. I can't think of a better word. You still aren't going to 'enjoy' it, and you are also not actually 'happy' doing it. It'll do for me.

I was convicted 'in absentia' - in my absence as I refused to turn up to the Tribunal. Three months, but they warned me it could easily be a year ... and I can always change my mind.

'We don't want to keep good men locked up,' said the Police Sergeant.

It pains only a little to remember it. Spring '45 has come early. War Ag man has told Alec to get some earlies in - taters, peas, carrots, more chickens to feed the men coming home from the war. Got to get rid of the rationing ... soon as. We need the Horn of Plenty after all this warring. Got to make it all worth it.

I have to admire his optimism. You know if I think it was worth it.

We put up an extra greenhouse and Palmiro's green fingers got more fingers sprouting out of his compost - so we are ready and we've got our backs stuck into it. Not much energy left for thinking of bad times, and writing it all up. Sorry Pina.

So ... quickly then, just so you know what Daddy did in the war.

At Strangeways Prison in Manchester, the screws doubted I was a baddy; some knew in their hearts I was a goody. I really wanted to show the former that I was the latter. 'Screws' is what we call the prison guards.

It took a little time, and most of the baddies in that strange place act like baddies and know everyone's a baddy, so they all treat everyone bad - except if they want something from them, and of course if they are scared of them.

In that locked-in society, it's like 1939 again. Constantly like a war is about to break out and it's too hard to stop it happening.

But all of the men have got family outside, and many have someone buried in rubble. But though they all make out that they are innocent, many are here for robbing from the rubble. Looting houses of the dead and injured. Nobody likes them. Selling stuff onto the Black Market. The intense shortage welcomes the chance to get anything you need - at any cost. Spivs are the new businessmen, and most are well liked for finding that special thing, just when you need it - nice wedding present for the rushed bride, say. They are well liked by too many women, too: unfortunately part of their allure is that they aim to be spick and span - always smart in suits and coloured shirts no-one else can afford, even if they could find them.

But some are grave robbers.

Got to give the spiv a shiv.

That's where I came in.

The screws knew I was willing and assumed my good will, so they soon found I could be useful. Steel keeps us all in here - bars, locks, bolts, hinges, knives and forks... knives. Not knives - we don't have them. Spoons. Knives are too easily sharpened. Shivs are made out of spoons - or any sort of metal left lying around. Shiv - the prisoner's weapon.

Don't leave any tools around Chapman. Don't even put them down.

They gave me my own tool belt and I spent all my time helping out the many workmen needed to keep us locked in safely.

The cons - as we are all now, unfortunately not all CONscientious Objectors, but CONvicts - find out I'm a Grinder. I can make them shivs - stabbing knives, but mine won't be home made from a bit of soft lead pipe, parts of razor with wooden handles, or even a sharpened bone toothbrush. A real blade from perhaps a hinge-plate - or 'get me a chisel Chapman, or else!'

It took a couple weeks of me being just one of the men. Not much to eat, no privies and too much privacy. We had a potty in our room - our cell that's locked up every night, but my first shock was that the eating was not so kind to my stomach, so it threw it out too quickly ... and there was not much to wipe with. The screw on my landing the first week of lock-up, 'didn't like the cut of my jib'. He would give me one single piece of toilet paper.

The only other paper in my cell was in my library book and the good book, to some - the bible. I haven't got anything against it, but I had to see it like the Quakers - as a gift from God. There was a Religious CO in there with me, but the Tribunal didn't believe him, because the other courts had sent him in here twice in the 1930s - he was a convicted brawler - always fighting and even hit a woman. Not so good, and likes to fight. The Quakers are lovely Christian folk - come visiting prisoners, too, bless them. And when he got the call up papers, he remembered they refused to fight.

Tribunal laughed him out.

The library book would have to be handed back - and checked. The bible however ... a better class of paper. So I made a deal with their God. I thanked him, and read a bit of verse from his book before I made the only use for it that I had.

The next thing you have to do is empty your potty - it's called slopping out - and we all troop along the landing to pour it down a sluice. I have to say that, other than constant fear of a shiv in the back, slopping out was the worst thing about prison. Toilets are not very nice; horrible ones make you feel sick; and slopping out...

The worst thing about prison ... was actually worse. Sorry, but I cannot tell. Prison is a terrible experience - clanging of cold steel doors, grating of keys in the lock, a final peep in the spy hole by the screw - sometimes lingered over, I could not resist trying to stare him out, holding my gaze, his gaze - a black hole, the leer imagined... then fourteen hours alone with a library book, the bible (edited version!) and mail bags to sew.

I day-dreamed in my sleep, or slept through my day-dreams - we weren't tired enough to sleep properly, so prison was mostly a waking nightmare.

I dreamed of Italy and the first Pina; of Mummy's love and the Amalfi coast - the love of total strangers to us funny pair from another world. Sunshine through my darkest hours. All quiet on the western front of my Pennines.

After only a few days, a week maybe, I was given promotion from mailbags to sweeping up. One evening after lock-down, I was taken out. That was scary.

The Senior Officer who took down my particulars when I was in the reception cell, with another screw (my guard) took me on a trek off the wing. Took me into a maintenance workshop and leant on the locked door smoking while I ... cleaned ... a nod ... and tidied up the tools ... another nod, plus one to each other ... so I looked around and organised bits and pieces stored there, inspecting and blowing dust off some to discern their appropriate shelf.

They marched me back to my cell without a word.

Next day, after slopping out and my bread and porridge, still hungry, a screw grabbed my elbow and took me back the way I remembered from the night before.

The workshop was now a hive of activity, and though all the civilians at least looked up at my arrival, none lingered, but I did notice a hostile glare from the only other con in the room. I nodded and smiled, humbly I hoped.

'Grinder, eh?' said one of the workmen. And that, as they say, was the beginning of the rest of my life.

I spent my time, mostly in the workshop, sharpening chisels, saws (that's a skill even most chippies don't understand, but appreciate,) screwdrivers (not a joke), fixing new handles on hammers, axes, tools and even a few doors. I was given the toolbelt with every tool counted in and out and signed for, when I spent the latter days of my stay as a chippy's mate (carpenter), or sparky's mate (electrician).

Until late one afternoon I went out of the other door - the one that did not lead onto the wings.

'Look here, Chapman...' It was that Senior Officer again, waving me into the first comfy chair I had seen in six weeks, 'you are a waste of money...'

I thought he might add 'and space', and perhaps send me out to be shot, but the mouth sucking on the pipe was not an ugly one.

'Ought to be some way to let you,' he referred to his notes, 'keep - your - right - not - to - kill, what?'

Those were my words. I nodded and probably frowned.

He slid a packet of cigarettes towards me. I declined, with a huge smile I reckon.

'Good worker. Proud of your work, what?'

'Yes sir, if a jobs worth doing...'

'...it's worth doing well, what? Even in prison, eh?'

'In life, sir,' I said. I don't know where that came from, but it worked.

He stood up and looked out over his wrecked city.

'But what about these fucking bombers, son? Sheffield, too. You?'

'Sir.'

'Well?'

'Mam, the wife and me, couldn't do much in our blitz. Crater to hide a bus in the next street to my mother.'

'Your steel works vital to the war effort. You had exemption.'

'Making guns isn't what I signed up for, sir.'

He sucked his teeth and hummed.

'Cutting down trees, offend you, does it?' He jutted his chin. 'Growing taters for all the Mams and Gra'mas?'

'Tribunal didn't give me that option, sir.'

He grumbled something about do-gooding magistrates wasting his time. 'Look,' he said, 'we've even had our cells cleared out of real badduns, dashed rapists and every sort of fiddler, sent orf to fight the Hun ... and locking up good chaps like you ... could be doing *some* good.'

I was probably looking hopefully at him. I told him that I had only ever worked in a factory since leaving school. When I was a kid we had only a cobbled yard, and the front door gave onto the street. I'm sorry Mummy, but I did not say how you had shown me, or rather Papa's gardener had really shown me, how to grow our own, up at Dore.

'Well?' I jumped when he shouted.

'Well, yes sir...' Was I weakening? 'Reckon I could pick up a bit of horticulture...'

'Horticulture?' he harrumphed, 'Horticulture, bless my soul. How about digging taters? That shouldn't be beyond a man of your, your... well, what have you, Chapman?'

'No sir.'

'No sir, or Yes sir?'

'I am willing to do agricultural work sir. Even I can't see how that is killing.'

His eyes narrowed. Had I erred into facetiousness?

'Well why the hell did you not say, man?'

'I didn't get the chance.'

'What? Whadidya say, Chapman? How the heck you ended up here - without a say?'

The Officer was obviously as unfamiliar with the Tribunal system as I was inexperienced. 'Just didn't turn up, sir, so the Bobbies came for me.'

He sat down, put his elbows on the desk, one hand over his mouth, the other holding his pipe and gazed long into my eyes.

They may have welled up.

He flicked back a few pages of what was obviously 'my file'. He mumbled about me not turning up for my medical and not paying my fine. He hummed.

'Convicted! For courage?' He continued to stare at me. He bit his lip. He clacked his dentures. He shook his head - eyes not leaving me.

He slapped the file shut, stood up, and pointing at the door shouted 'Get - Out!'

It was a good job a screw had hold of my elbow. My knees were knocking so hard he may have needed a mate to help carry me back to my cell. What happened?

Three days solitary - shocked at the sudden turn of events, and on my own in my cell, only let out for slopping. Three days with an air raid on the second night. Locked in during an air raid! Each round of Ack-Ack like a slap on the ears, each bomb a kick in the guts. Hide in the corner. Which one - outside wall or inside wall? Lie on the floor under the bed. Hands over ears. Mummy.

Out on the street, blinded by the full sun, but warmed; smell of cordite, taste of brick dust, roar of a trolleybus faster than a bomber buzzing over me. The speed.

The reception officer had it wrong - not six weeks, more like six years.

I had been dressed in my civvies, all my bits thrown in my little case, handed a few slips of paper and shoved, hand in my back, out of the main gate. 'Now fuck off!'

I staggered to adjust to even standing out in the 'fresh' air. What was happening?

I squeezed my eyes shut and open again and awoke to the bits I had been handed. A travel pass and a letter.

I unfolded the letter.

'Mr Alec Fox, Portland Farm, Egmanton, Newark, Nottinghamshire.'

51μ
Spring 1945

That is how I found myself here and I've told you a bit about my place of exile, for that is what it is. Now I'll tell you how Gringley-on-the-Hill really gets my POW story off to a proper start. What, you ask, after all I've said already?

I started to write this after hearing Palmiro's sad story about the lad on the bike, but the actual start of the Prisoner of War system was soon after the war began and enemy fighters were captured.

After the German Internees, the first 'proper' POWs were seagoing men, mostly U-Boat crew who had survived being Depth Charged - that's a bomb dropped into the sea and down onto submarines in the depths below. I did mention how the King's cousin Louis Mountbatten's flotilla caught a U-Boat crew. Apparently they damaged it, but rescued the whole crew. I like that. There weren't any proper camps for Prisoners of War then - the war had only been going for three months and we even called it a 'phoney war,' because nothing had happened in England yet... yet.

They sent Louis' captives to a proper prison, though - the one fit for kings, the Tower of London.

I've now heard what actually happened to the sub-mariners: their captain was a cheeky chappy, he wouldn't surrender to anyone of his own rank or below, and went on hunger strike until someone came for him to surrender to. When Mountbatten heard about it, he went along himself.

Then we see the class system at work - the Von Fritzes recognise it just like our Dukes do: from the Tower, the Officers were sent to a stately home in the Lake District - Grisedale Hall - and the crew were sent to an old mill in Oldham, near Manchester. (I went past there on my way to my posh prison.)

But it was all a temporary affair. The country was afraid of invasion, and the Nazis setting their men free, so the captives were sent all over the Empire. I'm not allowed to say if it was Canada ... or India or Australia, but well out of the way.

The other group of POWs were aircrew shot down over England. Thousands and thousands of planes flew over, especially during the big blitzes, and some of them were shot down. I am glad to say that many of the crew - ours and theirs - did manage to survive by parachuting out.

Now that's where Gringley played its part:

While we were having our cup of tea and a very respectable cake, (Les's mum had put in an extra egg in honour of her visitor, that's me - very honoured) she announced that there was no answer from the Homestead's neighbour's telephone. 'Les, you can show Mr Chapman up to your Gran's, can't you?'

'Can he have a ride on my bike, Ma'am?' I said.

Of course he leapt up and pleaded.

'I'll manage to milk the cows without you,' smiled Harold, 'just this once mind.'

Les rode pillion the short distance.

He leapt off and disappeared into the farmyard. I stowed the helmet and gloves and followed slowly.

As I rounded the corner towards the house, I bumped into him. He was standing looking across what they call 'the crew yard' - the partly covered yard where they keep the cattle over winter. It's also where Hardy's bomb struck. I stepped back. I had an odd feeling about him, so I took his shoulders and looked into his face. He was ghostly pale.

'What is it son?'

His eyes welled up.

'Is it a reminder of your near miss?' I said.

He shook himself loose. 'Gran's not here. She's not in.' He looked around the yard like he was expecting her to materialise. 'She's gone out. I don't know where she is.' All this as if it were his fault.

I nudged him to bring him round and move him to do as he wished. He didn't. So I walked up to the door of the farmhouse, turned and surveyed the scene.

'It were 'ere,' said Les. 'Their bomb were 'ere.' He was looking all around.

There was no sign of a crater or even damage, actually. Bit of fresh paint on windows and doors, only like a spring clean.

I wandered across to the other side and out of a gap towards fields. Les came with me, standing very close as if I were to protect him. I rested a hand on his shoulder by way of reassurance. 'You don't have to talk about it, Les.'

'What sir?'

'The ... bomb?'

He looked at me 'gone out' as my Mam would say.

'Come on,' I said steering back to the bike. He followed.

Beside Maisie he stopped and looked down the road - farms to left and right. 'Gina,' he said. He pulled himself together. 'Georgina Christmas knows. She'll tell you.'

I looked back the other way, across a turning where the road winds up a hill. No sign of any girls. In a doorway several houses along, two women stood chatting.

'She's at the camp. She might be there, 'cept if she's gone home. Sunday and all.'

Apparently Gina was the maid at The Homestead when the big raid was on, and is now with the Land Army in a camp at the end of the village. I stepped back into the crew yard to make a mental note of the state of it, then handed Les the helmet.

I thought the chances of catching any of the Land Army girls was a bit slim, but got Les to show me the huts, then ran him back home.

His passing shot was 'I saw the doodlebugs Mister!'

Quite something. I frowned. I wasn't sure I even believed the story. 'Doodlebug zzz,' I said, making the buzzing noise.

He didn't laugh, but said, 'Yeah. Saw three on 'em fly over here on Christmas day.'

I offered my hand by way of congratulations and a grown up farewell.

'Say one of 'em landed by Scaftworth By-Pass.' his arm swept west and towards Doncaster.

My smile was patronising, but I don't think the kid could tell. Doodlebugs can't reach this far north.

I returned to the huts to make further enquiries.

Gringley's Hill is a beacon hill as I told you. The village is built along a hill from which you can see in all directions and north of it is a big flat valley called 'The Carrs', with Doncaster the other side. The Carrs are the flood plain of the river Idle. The camp is actually just a few wooden huts at the end of the village looking over the Carrs. Coincidentally, they were drained by Prisoners of War from the last war. Now the Government - War Ag - has taken on the land to farm, to feed the nation.

It's continuing an exceptionally warm March - there even appeared to be a heat haze over the Carrs. Perhaps the girls may be sunning themselves on well earned Sunday rest. I was a little surprised that these huts were actually for accommodation - not even as nice as Headon POW camp.

All quiet. I rounded the back calling quietly. Two youngsters were indeed lounging, hats over faces.

'And you can clear off,' one mumbled.

I decided on a deep throaty cough.

She peered out then jumped up. 'I beg your pardon, sir,' she said, grabbing her hat over her bosom, 'thought it was the local lads sneaking up ... for a kiss,' she giggled.

I assured her I wasn't local, but wasn't averse to a peck of welcome. I told her I was looking for Georgina Christmas and she kicked the other girl's chair. 'Your dad's here Gina.'

Waking rather suddenly Gina fell off her chair and stumbled to her feet clambering the hut wall.

We were all laughing. I offered my hand and some explanation. She shoved 'Peg' whom I steadied from falling too.

I then explained my quest: that the Hardys had told me their story and I had called by Homestead Farm. She grimaced slightly and I feared I wasn't going to get anywhere with her side of the story. Saying that young Les had suggested she might help, set the girls going - 'he's her boyfriend,' 'not,' 'is so,' etc, and more jostling.

With my hand over my face, shaking my head, they remembered their age. 'Just a tease, Mister. The little lads come up begging for kisses - well why not, I ask you?' (Gina later told me she was 19. Les is about 12.)

I needn't have worried: the Walker's ex-maid was more than willing to tell of her near escape from the Nazi Bombers. I'm not sure Peg believed half of it, but here goes, Pina. I think she's a bit mixed up, poor lass, but I'll check her details another time.

Before she got going I reminded her that I had been to Mr Hardy's and did have the story of their bomb.

'It damaged their house pretty badly,' she said. 'Mr. Hardy is the son of Mrs. Walker,'

'A stepson of Mr. Walker?'

'Yes, a family link. The second bomb dropped on our farm at an angle.'

'My Hardy told me that there was another big one?'

'A third one dropped in the field at the top of the road, at the top of Finkle Street, in the field, made a crater and buried a cow all but her neck.' She took a breath.

'They fetched the cows next morning and the farm labourer said to me, because Mr & Mrs Walker were in such shock they took them away to a safer place and let them rest, and the farm labourer and I were left to cope and he said, "Can you fetch the cows while I sort something out where I can milk them?" Because the buildings were just dropped.' She gasped and Peg was shaking her head.

Gina went on 'When I came back he said to me, "Well, it was a shock for me to come to work this morning, but you must have been shocked, you can't count!"

'I said "I can count."'

'"You're missing the blue roan, yes?" he said. "Why?"

'"Why?" I said. "You, me and a gang of Irish navvies need shovels and we'll get her dug out. There's a hole enough to bury the farm and the whole of its contents in the field, and she's up to her neck in clay."

'So I said, "She's alive, because she's warm and she chewed her cud when I touched her."

Almost puffed out, Gina bent down and back up. 'Anyway she didn't give any milk that day.'

Aren't they funny these farmer types? No, the poor old cow had a day off, bless her!

Harold - and Alec Fox for that matter - had not sent me up here to get the story of a Blitz, I didn't think. Both heard how I had come from Sheffield. No news to me. However, I let Gina get her traumatic experience off her chest before I steered her to my quest for Prisoners of War.

She looked at me blankly at first. Eyes shrank. She looked over the Carrs and started telling me about getting a few POWs coming from Nether Headon Camp ... Germans. She was not at ease, so I told her about Palmiro and the peace we had, sharing life, he was once supposed to be our enemy, now my really good friend.

Gina liked that, so I felt I could go on and mention that I had met one of the 'new lot', Bernhard.

That opened a door.

'The pilot, I found him - dead in the potato field,' she said.

I frowned at that. I told her how there were lots of our poor lads crashing all round the place.

Her turn to frown. 'What happened was, on May 7th, a German plane was shot down somewhere in the vicinity.'

'This last May?'

I could see how she was thinking me a bit slow. She reminded me that I had just come up from Hardy's and wasn't I talking about her bombs - same day in 1941.

'Three German prisoners were later captured. One gave himself up. The fifth one, the pilot, was found dead in the potato field on the 8th May.' (So maybe not by her? Well she is a young lass.) 'Then, of course, on the 8th May my boss said could we get the animals out. Because it was the 8th May, and he was a stickler for putting the animals out on the 8th May. May Day, you know. So we put them out and that's what happened.'

'Ah, I see now,' I said, 'Mr Hardy told me they had the same discussion and said if they hadn't, then his herd would have been "pulped". You had the bomb in your crew yard. I didn't know about a bomber crew.'

She had needed the toilet in the night. I think most of us are light sleepers in these times.

'There was this toilet and it had, like a concrete facing step. To get in you stepped like that onto it and my heel must have caught the edge of the step and the bomb started ticking and, you see, there was no sound before and then this ticking noise and I assumed it was someone's pocket watch. But it wasn't.'

So she scarpered sharpish back to bed. All a little bit childlike and confused. She heard the Air Raid siren and the bomb ticking ... decided it was a watch. She was sixteen and had been a worker for two years, not actually still a kid.

'And then I heard this big bang and it was obvious that the bomb was at Mr Hardy's place. And I got out of bed and went to my own bathroom where I could see the village and that end and saw this big blaze.'

'Actual fire, or lighting up the sky?' I said.

She ignored me. 'And I went and woke Mr Walker and I said, "Mr Walker, I believe Gainsborough's on fire. Do you think we should get up?"

I didn't understand why she said that - she had just told me that it was obviously at Hardy's place, and not 5 miles away. I thought it would perhaps come clear.

'And he came to my landing and said. "That's not Gainsborough, that's the Fox Covert at Gringley. Just near the Beacon Hill". And he said "Yes, we'd better get up."

'When we were back on the landing he stopped me and said "Was I dreaming or was there a shattering, a bang?"

'I said "Yes there was a thud, a really big thud."

'"Oh," he said "it could have been that."'

Her eyes were ... glazed over, like she was in a dream. I expect on that hillside in Gringley, she was reliving that moment, that awful moment four years ago.

'We had no idea, you see, that it had dropped on his stepson's farm.'

(But she said it was obvious!)

'"Well," he said, "I think we'd better get up, so I'll wake Agnes up and do come downstairs and we're going to go under the staircase."'

I'm giving you all this detail Pina, because of the life changing moment I am about to reveal - not just bombing, war, death, but change of life for those of us left behind, those not physically affected, but ... mentally. Bit like Dad, though it was his lungs that were damaged.

Gina was blinking fiercely as she continued, '"And don't get dressed because if they're still around we may have to get out. But don't get dressed, just put your dressing gown on and your slippers."

'I could not find my slippers because they had gone right under my bed.'

I thought she meant because of the bomb, but perhaps not, or she confused the slipper hunt until after the bomb.

'So I opened the drawer and got out a new pair of slippers that had been bought for my birthday and I always kept them in that drawer for something special and put them on.

'As I was going under the door of the staircase the clock fell off the wall and gave me a sort of a push. I just got under the staircase and, you know, thinking it won't be long before it's over, and there was a bump and that was our bomb. And she said "Oh, that was near".

Her head was spinning, almost like an owl can turn it right round, but more the way we are when on alert, looking swiftly all around for menace or danger.

'Dare I tell her that the house door wasn't fastened? Mrs. Walker was fastidious about the door being fastened. "The door's come off", she said, "Was that glass breaking?"

'"Yes, I think it was, I hope it wasn't the mirror, which means seven years bad luck."

'"I don't think so". And I was there shaking like anything.'

Her head stopped. Her voice stopped. Her eyes stopped and stared - at me. They welled up and a tear fell.

Her hand swept up, she looked at the wetness and back to me, her mouth now open, and still. What on earth was she thinking?

I looked at Peg - switched off and dozing - she had no doubt heard the story one too many times. She jumped up as Gina burst out crying noisily. I took a quick check that no one would come rushing and accuse me of ... something inappropriate. No one, so I took the poor girl in my arms.

Her crying subsided into a long loud sighing, like groaning.

She stepped away from me, re-evaluating the complete stranger holding her in his arms.

'Mister...'

'Eric,' I said, 'Eric Chapman dear,' and in the absence of anything more reassuring to say I added, 'I'm a friend of Harold's - Mr Hardy.'

It worked. She stood nodding. 'You know what she said, you know what Mrs Walker said? She said, she told me,' she took a breath, sucked in a sob. She looked at Peg who nodded. 'She said, she told me "That's the last you've seen of your mother."' Her whole face was agape - mouth and eyes fully wide.

She stood and cried gently. Peg had her arm round her.

While she settled I had to dig deep to find something appropriate to say. 'That was not fair of her, Georgina,' I said, giving her the full name her mother doubtless calls her. I bit my lip.

She swept her hair off her face, rubbed her eyes with the heels of her hands and dried them on her smock. She took a deep, very deep breath and went back to her story.

'Anyway. I'd go and try and shut the door but I knew it was off. And I went back and I screamed "There's no water there to the crew yard and the crew yard trough is in the middle of the crew yard and it was just behind the wall originally. I thought, Oh dear, and I do so want to go to the toilet. And that's how it came about.'

That lost me completely. She had seemingly told me a whole story, but now seemed to be adding the beginning. And she was so affected by what happened that she did say 'crew yard' so often.

I had seen Hardy's and then their crew yard - both now open spaces, where I knew they had once been covered, and will have had troughs and feeders, and I don't know what. She had mentioned three bombs, and I hadn't seen a crater. What had bumped her under the stairs, knocked the door off?

I reminded her about the toilet episode

'That was funny. But I was only a girl,' she said. Four years ago - she was only a girl! It was all too exciting for her, what with a new audience - me.

'It dropped right in the crew yard. What happened was that they decided they were going to lead the manure out. They realised that the horse and cart, when the cart was full in the crew yard, the horse would have to pull up a slope, a good slide. The surface of the yard was such that a horse pulling a heavy load would slide and scrape its shoes. So they piled their manure up and as near to the big gates as they could to give the horses a better chance of getting the carts out without straining the horses and this bomb dropped and did throw all this dirt on to buildings yards and yards away and sent the house front in and the doors and windows in. It didn't floor them completely but damaged buildings so they were beyond repair.'

Blurted out without breathing in!

So when I went back in the house. Mr.Walker said to me "Well, did you manage to get where you were going.?" I said "Yes, thank you". I didn't tell him about the ticking noise. Mrs. Walker was hysterical. It was their home and they had worked hard. They were old people. She said "Was there any damage out there?"

"Yes, the crew yard wall has gone", I said.

"What about anything else?"

"I think there's a few bricks come down".

Anyway, she said she was going upstairs for something. She was going to get her shawl and she was cold. While she was upstairs I said to Mr. Walker, "The buildings are badly damaged, no wash-house, the cow house and the stables just half size and it is a mess out there. The crew yard, there's no manure in the crew yard. It's on the buildings all around. The floor of the crew yard is like a big cobbled area. The trough is in the middle of the crew yard".

'He said "She is going to go out of her mind, I know these things happen and they can happen anywhere. What will have happened is, I bet our planes were chasing that plane and he's got rid of them to get height and go."

'I said to him "You don't think it's because that man's in the Blue Bell, do you? That dead German is in the Blue Bell?"'

Hooray! She got back round to it without me interfering too much. I didn't correct her in that Mr Hardy said it was the White Hart - in the upstairs room where the Home Guard meet.

'He said he didn't think so. And he kept calm and all at once she started on about the damage and the cash box had gone in that short time. He tried to calm her and it upset him. When the doctor came in he said that they had to be moved to somewhere safer, and would be sedated and given some rest, and was I alright. So I said "Yes, I was frightened, but I shall be alright." So I went next door to some people that we knew. They said did I want to go to bed again. I said "No, I don't want to go to bed". "You can have Sheila's bed".

'"No, I don't want to go to bed. I will just sit in the chair till it's time I suppose I shall have to help Sam." I said "Where are Mr. and Mrs. Walker?" She said "We don't know, they have just gone to a safe place to have some rest." Where they took them away I never did know.'

I have written this all out as best as I recall - which was all in a bit of jumble. The poor lass had obviously been traumatised by her near death experience, and not least by the strangely unsympathetic thing she felt Mrs Walker had said about her mother. Gladly it was not true. Her mother is alive and well. She had heard the thuds from the next village, Clayworth, but like everybody in the rural villages, she assumed Sheffield, Doncaster or Gainsborough or other big cities were taking yet another pounding - not us.

But I am pleased to add this sorry tale of widespread war and terror bombing. This *must* be the war to end all wars and I *must* do more than the last generation did to ensure it.

Alec had sent me out here to get a story of the Prisoners of War. The first ones like U-Boat and bomber crews, and Gringley's part in the story.

52μ

Just to let you know that there is a war still going on outside of my war - no I have not, I cannot, forget. But it is another story, one that you will be able to read about in the history books. Fortunately, I know I am fortunate, but I am not sure we - any of us on the planet in this world war, should talk this way - but it is looking like the war will be over soon.

After the British 1000 ton bombing of Essen - at least it was supposedly against Krupp's munitions factories - the American's have fire bombed Tokyo and killed over 100,000 people living in the wooden houses.

Yes the poorer people.

How *just* can this warring be? All sides are engaged in terror: we need the people to be terrorised into demanding that their masters give up the fight.

Those Doodlebugs over ... Manchester? Over Gringley on their way. A Christmas present from a Christian nation?

The papers covered demobbing almost as soon as our troops cleared the coast last September. I didn't dare think of my sentence. Reading it, I compare myself to conscripts - to everyone! Under 36 it will be four years. I will be thirty in June. Will anybody send me the present I most crave - peace? I will not get my liberty.

I daren't ask. I still have never communicated with the CO Tribunals, except for signing my Certificate of Exemption. I have assiduously ignored all calls to battle.

Re-reading the application sent by Strangeways on my behalf (their behalf really - they wanted rid of me!) they said I was of extremely good character, a willing worker, always pleasant. The chairman was a county court judge. He would have a couple of others such as a trade union Steward. Respectable. The exemption is dated 31st May 1946. Three years. Is that how long the conscripts get - or 'for the duration'? It is pleasant enough here. The Foxes have made me - and Palmiro - part of their family.

It is not my family.

Oh God.

Why do I say that?

53μ

The Land Army Girls were calmer now and offered me 'a brew'. How could I refuse? Besides, I still needed to find out about the rest of the bomber crew - the ones that weren't buried. The sun was lower in the sky, and hiding behind a cloud every now and again. It may be the warmest March on record, but that doesn't make it summer. 'Ne'er cast a clout 'til May is out,' Mam says.

So I had discovered that on May 8th 1941, a bomber had been shot down and the pilot found dead. The next night, the Gringley area had had a 'mini blitz lasting several hours.' The big fire Gina saw was not the high explosive which flattened Hardy's, but the rain of incendiaries which had caught the wood at Fox Covert, just near Hardy's.

The bomber Les had seen had followed the white concrete of the Gringley by-pass, clear in the bright moonlight, there and back, and decided that the building at the end of it must be an important factory.

Other 'nuisance raiders', as the press call them, probably saw the fire and decided to try their luck in the neighbourhood: they shot out the searchlight on the Beckingham to Gringley road; they bombed the railway line in Beckingham, the next village - and missed; they blew the church windows out; they gave a couple of woods a good firing thinking they maybe hid another works; a whole stick of bombs peppered a field at Saundby - a mile from Hardy's; they buzzed around for over four hours.

That is quite a long air raid even for the likes of my big city.

'My little village' of Egmanton has had no such experience, except for almost constant crashing of our allied planes, mostly training it would seem.

Then the poor crew of the Lancaster at Milton.

We're on the Laxton Road - and Laxton did have a stick of bombs one night in 1940 before I got here. Locals are sad that the daughter of a much loved teaching 'dynasty' Barbara Willis, was killed in the doorway of the old school house where she had retired. That was the time of the real Blitz all over Britain.

They are all real to the people caught up in them, Eric.

I got my map out in the 'orrible 'ut as Gina called it, and looking for Scaftworth, the girls said they were pretty sure a Doodlebug didn't land there, but one did land up near the big aerodrome at Finningley - beside the Doncaster road from Bawtry. Well, Les's arm sweep was over that direction.

They didn't hear them. 'Middle of the night wasn't it?

I think Les was up for the milking perhaps - 5.30 about right.

'You told me that there was a dead German,' I prompted, hoping to find as much detail as I could.

'I had to go down there for the farmer. He was in the potato field.

I saw Peg's eyebrows flick. 'They didn't believe you when you came back?'

'No. It was known that there was another German somewhere because one gave himself up, three were captured and the...'

'Five crew, yes?'

'Yes. And, of course, some of them spoke enough English to say that they weren't the pilot and this airman that came he just looked. I don't even know the German's name now. I didn't want to know it. He just said, "This b*****, I trained him at Finningley before and he knew his way to Finningley and that's where he was going." Of course, we all said that because he was lying in state in the Blue Bell on the 9th May, we ... er...'

'They thought it could be retaliation - the blitz?' I said.

'I don't think it could have been. It just wasn't real. I mean they couldn't possibly have known where ... He was only a young man but he has the best of graves, and it is cared for.'

'What?' He is buried at Gringley?'

'Oh yes. He's got a lovely plot to himself and it's cared for. Someone keeps that grave in immaculate condition the whole time. There is always some flowers on it.'

I had to stop and pretend to be exploring my map. I took a deep breath. I coughed and smacked my lips. No nice cake in the 'orrible 'ut. But they did apologise. The tea was passable - they do have fresh milk.

I looked out over the Carrs. 'Where did the plane crash?'

'It crashed some distance away,' Gina said. 'Whether they baled out and.... of course, since then I've heard the joke about the air force. Where the sergeant will tell you to go to the store and get a parachute and when you jump, if you parachute doesn't open, go to the store and get another one.'

One of the other girls had returned from a home visit, and there was a collective gasp at such a story - from me included.

The new girl broke the tension with 'Cake anybody? Mum's eggless sponge, but...'

'Cake is cake,' was the general consensus. It was remarkably good. I didn't collect the recipe. Sally's is never eggless.

I did collect the final details on the airmen. Scaftworth did get a mention again. Apparently three of the men were found walking on the by-pass there - I think it must be the new road which also leads through Gringley - finished in 1939, but not opened to traffic. The squire's gamekeeper rounded them up at gunpoint and marched them to Bawtry Police station. Another gave himself up on the Carrs somewhere.

Last anybody heard they were sent to Ranby Camp at Retford. Point noted for the record. Not a POW camp I don't believe. There was some discussion among the girls that it would surely be Headon POW camp, but I told them that back then, 1941, I didn't think the camp had been built. I wondered about Lodge Moor...

I exchanged addresses with Gina - her family's home is in Clayworth. (If it's only the next village, how come she hadn't gone home for tea? I didn't ask. I might have to take her out to tea at Bawtry or somewhere nice another day. Poor lass, I felt quite sorry for her.) I hoped she might update me with tales of the new Germans joining them on the Government farms at some point.

Bernhard did not strike me as a typical Nazi Wehrmacht fighter.

On my way home and in the fading light, I called by the cemetery. There it was, a simple wooden cross with fresh flowers - it's Sunday - and a tag 'Emil Kölmel, HPTM 4.5.12 +8.5.41'. Three years older than me, but 15 (maybe more!) than some of the lads being captured. Many queries in the press about some of the men being rounded up being kids in uniforms too big for them. That Pathe news thing about Italian lads and the Scots Guards bringing home the garlic?

I wonder what HPTM means?

54μ

Two letters in one day - Panic!

Cousin Queenie insists I come to Leeds to 'clear things up'. I know what she means, I think. She also asks if anything is wrong with me. Why didn't I even send a card for her wedding?

The other is a poor sad thing - a 'Dear Mister' Gina wrote in a very unsteady hand. She says I wanted to know about the Germans, 'but I carnt writ it all hear, how horrible and what they done to poor Peg.' She also insists I call back up there as soon as possible - after 4 o'clock, because she's going home to Mam Sundays from now on.

I wondered about two birds with one stone - but train to Leeds from Retford would be best, and not leave time to bike up to Gringley on my one day (afternoon) off.

Queenie first - duty bound.

My hedge is budding up already and I've only laid about twenty yards of it. Next autumn?

55μ
April 1945

We had been hearing about the liberation of what are called Concentration Camps - huge areas where the Nazis 'concentrated' their enemies and undesirables - perhaps in the tens of thousands. Reports had come in since January of the Russians finding death camps where people were worked or starved to death. But we were already mistrusting the propaganda and bragging of our supposed ally in the east.

After the finding of Buchenwald by our trusted ally, America, reported at the weekend, though we had missed most of the broadcast, a stunned silence descended on our little family at Portland farm, for that day and a couple days following.

What can you say? It is unspeakable.

Then the confirmation of what we had decided not to believe: the village got hold of several copies of yesterday's London Times and today - a weekday - Thursday 19th April 1945 - Alec Fox gathered us round his rather grand radio gramophone in anticipation of a report from our own trusted BBC. His wife and daughter, Sally and Barbara, along with Palmiro and I, had first to absorb the ghastly enormity of a photograph, a picture which speaks more of the ghastly Nazi regime than a stack of bibles.

Palmiro was obviously concerned about the wisdom of allowing teenage Barbara to suffer this, but who are Palmiro and me to question?

A group of half a dozen American soldiers have confronted a group of citizens of Weimar with a lorry trailer, one side dropped to reveal a stack of corpses - head-feet-head-feet. Only one had any semblance of hair.

I later calculated that there were around fifty or sixty corpses.

One of the soldiers with what appears to be a Military Police stripe round his helmet, has hand on hip, the other on a whip-thin stick, head cocked at a mixed crowd of immaculately dressed citizens. They are looking at him and he is presumably seeking their explanation of the awful sight revealed to them.

All are looking at the officer, except for two who are looking at the floor and a woman at the back who has a hand to her forehead. None appear to be looking at the corpses.

Pina, my children, great as my reluctance will certainly be, I will want you to see this, when you are big, but before you are grown up. You must not grow up to have hearts as hard as that crowd appears to have.

The radio had been quietly crackling in the background, when Alec suddenly turned up the volume on a BBC announcer seriously intoning.

What followed is the worst report I ever hope to hear. The impact of the spoken words over a newspaper report immeasurably greater:

A Richard Dimbleby started by assuring us that he had waited a day, so that he could be absolutely sure of the facts now available. Like him, I couldn't take it all in at once, and I do not wish to record here all that was said. It will become the core of much history yet to be written.

A few of the things that struck me, were the expressions of the reporter rather than the facts, which even he says, convey nothing of themselves:

He wishes that everyone fighting, 'those directing this war,' could come with him into the inner compound where 10,000 people had been clubbed and fed alive into a furnace in reprisal for the death of 2 SS guards.

He says that 'what is ghastly, is the breakdown of civilisation,' where professional folk have ceased to care about the conventions of normal life.

Kept to the end is witness to the fact that people had been reduced to cannibalisation.

Mr Fox did not wait for any further commentary. He switched off the radio. Palmiro was looking at him for some explanation - had his Italian ears understood the horror of what we just heard?

I too was looking to the Man of the House, until I heard a sniff and saw young Barbara lift her head to catch her breath and spilling tears; her mother Sally, head-kept-in-hands, glanced and gaped at her husband.

His lips were tightly pursed over a rippled chin. He was nodding. 'It's what we've been fighting... what we've been fighting for... isn't it Eric?'

I recoiled. I looked around as if to check that there was not another Eric in the room. I coughed. Put my hand over my mouth.

'Makes you *proud,*' he added.

Sally looked up, stood up, and bustled her daughter out of the room.

Palmiro, no doubt familiar with Vesuvius, glanced from Alec, to me, to Alec, pointed a finger up, as if he'd just remembered something and slipped out.

I felt duty bound to stay ... to face my host of the last two years. I knew he didn't hold totally with my position, but in fact I still had no idea if he felt any sympathy at all.

He had loaded that word 'proud'.

He could have said the same words several ways: 'Makes *you* proud'; perhaps most heavily as a question 'Makes you proud?' It was this that I felt compelled to answer ... at least address.

I stood as I believe a soldier stands at ease - still upright, but feet apart, facing the Sgt Major squarely, with my hands behind my back. Not speaking until I am spoken to - again.

Was Alec thinking that all the bloodshed had been worth it, and therefore makes the nation proud?

I am proud of what we have achieved together. I have misgivings about the way we have gone about it, and I know Alec has been very dubious about the morality of blanket bombing cities - civilians - and of the tit-for-tat to Hitler's terror tactics. So not whole-hearted ... and not proud of everything.

'You didn't want to run up that beach...' he said.

I didn't respond.

'How would you be feeling if you were one of the chaps walking into Buchenwald ... or Belsen?'

The newspaper said the British soldiers machine-gunned - summarily executed - the SS Guards. I would have thrown up if my comrade had done that. I simply shook my head.

Alec tutted, turned to the fireplace and kicked the fire-guard. Gently, but enough to throw sparks onto the tatty-rug. As he patiently squeezed them underfoot he said, 'Can you ... how can you ... be proud?'

'Come on Alec,' I began. I waved a hand across the farm. 'Me? You?' I sucked my teeth. 'What's the difference?'

He threw his head back.

Of course ... we're the same, but I am not saying that. I am not reminding him that rather than shoot a steeler like me, but one from Essen, I had twice laid my life on the line for the betterment of society - accepting scabies and vitamin deprivation - and not just for British society, but the people of the world. It so happened that I did this with a *German* professor Hans Adolf Krebs.

Now don't get petty, Eric. I looked out of the window. Grey.

In the war effort, we have not done the same - I have done more. I'm not saying it though. I am not going to assert that I have done more. We have both done our best - differently. Does it take courage to continue your normal work inb a protected occupation?

Don't get petty Eric.

We have both worked dawn to dusk. 'An army marches on its stomach,' I said eventually. 'Sounds silly, but without the food *we* have provided ... not just for our own women and children, but for our soldiers *and* our enemies - the prisoners of war.'

Alec is a man of few words, me of a few more, but I bit my tongue.

'Palmiro wasn't proud...' he started, completely throwing me off scent. 'He wasn't proud to be marching up and down that North Africa coast...'

I shook my head, not in disagreement, but to shake out my thoughts and make room for Alec's. I jutted my chin, raised my brows.

'...the Krauts, fucking Hun ... proud. The product...' he pointed at the newspaper, the truck full of corpses, '...left on *display.'* He hawked up and spat on the fire. 'Starved people ... left to rot where they simply fell. "Look vot ve haf done!"'

We both looked at the wireless - it made no comment.

'If War Ag send me any of these bastards, I'd be at risk of taking my shotgun to them ... Eric?'

I again looked over my shoulder.

Was he asking for my support - my blessing? 'If you feel that way, Alec.' It just came out as I took a small step towards him.

'I do, I do, Eric.' He coughed, ran a sleeve along his nose. 'But would you be proud of me?'

'Alec,' I said.

'Would I be proud of myself?'

'I am proud of you asking me that question Alec,' I said, offering him my hand.

56μ

So I had better keep poor Bernhard out of his way.

Before I get swept up with the Germans, I think I had better get my facts straight about what's happening to the Italians. It did seem as if they were cleared out of Headon Camp before the Germans came, but perhaps not all of them are billeted out; perhaps they have been organised, grouped together. I can't see it being easy to control docile Italians mixing with recently captured, very recently fanatical Nazi fighters.

Bernhard was not so fanatical.

Palmiro is a bit cut off from whoever is left at Headon. He associates with those like him - there are hundreds of them billeted out round here - some on almost every farm.

I don't know whether to take a ride west towards Edwinstowe and Langwith or up North to check out Lesley Marshall and Luca.

I thought about Willy Constant - where is his slip?

I had it in my notebook and not looked at it after he passed it me in the Three Merry Lads up at Lodge Moor. I thought he had a funny accent! Look at this - his name is not Constant, but Willy Kohnstamm. Got to be German. I wonder if he's a Jew? Address is c/o - care of - his family in Wales. Curiouser and curiouser as Alice would say. It's a bit round about to have to send it via Wales. I don't think I can ring up the camp and ask to meet him...? No, I will drop him a line - no rush.

57μ

The journey up to Leeds on Sunday morning April 22nd, was filled with anticipation. What exactly needed to be 'cleared up?' I had no idea why Cousin Queenie had called me in so urgently. I still hadn't even congratulated her/them on their marriage. I don't really know why. I was delighted and, as I said, it was really good news.

Giving up my usual reluctance, I had called into Tuxford library to swat up on the recent progress of her Jack's Royal Tank Regiment.

Early evening and 'Josie' had gone back to Retford. Yes she's happy - busy, helping people, including some POWs doing everything to pick up more English. So it's *Josie* Husbands.

The RTR are part of the 8th Army still fighting their way up Italy. It's looking fairly hopeful that they will finally sweep the Germans out of Italy, maybe this week. There is a civil war there with partisans and Co-Belligerent royalist Italian Regiments alongside the Allies, pitted against the Italian fascist forces press-ganged by the Nazis, (I hope not volunteered) in Mussolini's puppet state. There's a Battle for Bologna imminent.

It was the first thing I asked Queenie over tea in Leeds station cafe: she told me Jack was pulled out at the Po Valley. (That's on the furthest north east coast.) Apparently, if he had continued the War Office will have 'broken their contract' with Jack, keeping him on the war front for over five years. It's been a terrible trek for the RTR up the east coast of Italy, a fresh battle every hundred miles. Jack - is - out - of - it!

She was holding her hand flat on the table all the while, but typical insensitive man me, I didn't realise until her smile became so extreme and she glanced from rings to me and nodded. I half stood, took the hand, admired the wedding ring now nestled against the engagement ring, and kissed it.

Her eyes welled up. Perhaps mine did.

She took the hand back into the other and added a kiss to mine.

Jack's still at Bovington camp on Salisbury Plain. Light duties: mechanics, fixing, cleaning.

Cleaning ... she had to laugh. She told me the tale:

The regiment's Officers were planning their annual steeplechase, so Jack and other old Desert Rats were marched off to build the fences. After putting in a little effort, they sat down for a crafty fag when a sparkling new lieutenant trotted across and told them to stop lazing about and get the job finished.

After a little more work, they stopped for another fag. This time the lieutenant galloped across to them and started raging.

Jack was not happy about this and tried to respond politely: 'Sir, we have done quite a lot of work and only...' Not allowing Jack to finish, the lieutenant flew off the handle and put them on a charge for insubordination and failure to follow commands. They were to report to the Colonel's office at sixteen hundred hours. (No, that doesn't mean in 66 days - just army talk for 4 o'clock this afternoon.)

The Desert Rats showed up and stood to attention while the lieutenant read out the charge. The Colonel looked across at Jack and shook his head. Jack read his expression and tried to keep a straight face. Jack had been the Colonel's driver in Egypt and Italy.

The Colonel shifted his eyes to the spick and span lieutenant. 'Have you any idea what these men have done,' he said, 'what they are, where they fought, their war record? Rather than charging them, you should be thanking them.

'Without them there would no regiment, no England and probably be no bloody you! Dismiss!'

Queenie was smiling, lost, caressing her ring finger again. 'My Jack.'

She heard me clink my cup back onto the saucer. She gradually withdrew from her reverie and sat back.

'Sorry Eric. Worked nights last night. Tired and emotional.'

I smiled and nodded. 'You want to ... clear things up?'

She sat up and took a sip of her tea, looked at it and grimaced. 'Mm. Not sure where we stand, Eric. I don't want Jack to get any funny ideas, so...'

'You writing to another man?' I laughed.

'Yes. Sort of.'

I rushed to assure her, but she cut across me.

'You are my cousin,' she said, 'but ... how *are* we cousins?' she chuckled. 'Dad's Grandad and your Mam's twice removed ... Sheffield?'

I reminded her how my mother had always spoken of Cousin Queenie and her dad Wilmoth Thomas with such affection. How she had taken me as a 'pen pal'. I hoped I had been some comfort to her with her boyfriend away at war and me, well, not.

She said she wasn't sure how Jack would take it, me being a Conchie and all. She was alright with it of course.

I wasn't so sure about that, but told how I also appreciated someone who was not judgemental. Everybody was judgemental...

We both knew that she had had her doubts - *'shirking the war, coward'.* She had written that.

'I know,' I said, 'you apologised back then. I understand how you feel. Don't you think I tell myself it sometimes?'

'I've wanted to say this to you from the start, Eric ... but I was not ... I am not...'

Her hand, back on the table, bunched into a fist. A fist? Queenie?

She saw me notice and pulled it under the cloth. She coughed and said, 'if Jack had died ... I would never have forgiven you.'

I stirred the dregs of my cold tea. What to say to that? I mumbled something like, 'I constantly have my doubts ... just what are my convictions?'

I looked up at her pulling a funny face and mouthing, 'Strange ways!'

I smiled. The tension was broken.

'Now look, Con-grat-u-la-tions!' I said. I bit my lip and sucked. 'I had stuff ... I didn't open your card ... any cards...'

She laid her shaking hand over now trembling one.

'It was not a merry Christmas. If only I had opened your letter and card, it might well have been. It was great news. The only good news in ... since last...' I couldn't go on. I couldn't tell her about you Pina. I couldn't...

'Look,' I said, ' sweeping my hands through my hair, literally pulling myself together. 'A bun? What about dinner?'

They had some kind of stew, with dumplings or cobbles. Not totally tasteless, and ravenous as we always tended to be, we licked the platter clean. She told me she would like me to meet up with Jack, as a distant cousin, but one who couldn't avoid missing the wedding, doing important work for the War Agricultural Ministry. Not sure about the Conchie stuff, but interested in the POWs.

Sounded like a plan to me, especially when she added that she had another contact for me, and very close to home. All the same, that was tricky too: apparently Jack's brother, Harold, is also a CO, but in the Pioneer Corps - non-combatant - and he has been assigned to ... wait for it ... POW camp guard duties.

Very interesting.

Tricky, because Jack almost certainly does not know and their own father had thrown Harold out. (He has relented a little after receiving a photo of Harold in normal army battledress.)

Queenie thought I could perhaps get Jack's North Africa experience out of him. Yes she had asked him about the Italians. He gave her no gory details at all. The big battle where they took 230,000 prisoners (Yes!) he had been delivering munitions. Walking round a sand dune - not carrying munitions on his back! - he came upon a Platoon of Italian soldiers with an officer. Alone on foot, Jack thought he'd had it, but the officer immediately surrendered. 'It wasn't difficult,' he said, 'they had "lost" their weapons.' The Officer had a pistol which he offered up - even that had no firing pin.

I told her that Palmiro had been one of those, but of course she realised from my letters - that's why she was telling me.

She added another funny story: apparently the best bit of beating the Italians was obtaining a huge supply of Nestlé chocolate, either by capture or trade. The POWs were particularly keen to trade it for British corned beef, which they found hugely preferable to their tinned meat which they called 'vechy homo'. (Old man). (Had I smelt Terry's chocolate factory on my way through York? No, I missed that - too much soot from the trains.)

We agreed that it looked likely that the war really would end soon, and that possibly - when would I be demobbed?

When would Jack, or Queenie?

What is my conviction, my sentence? She complimented me on the courage of my convictions.

'Yes, Eric, it has taken courage, I recognise that.' She smiled and went on, 'I know you have suffered and I do not mean only with the itchy old scabies.' She shuddered. 'How are things with...?'

I bit my lip and looked Queenie in the eye.

'I am so sorry Eric ... when this is all over ... is there hope?'

I don't think I moved.

'Conviction, eh, Eric? Funny old word. I had originally meant your penalty ... sentenced to so many years?'

'I don't think I can expect any less time *in service* than conscripted men,' I said. 'I've looked at the only sheet I have and it says three years.'

'You've served that by now haven't you?'

I laughed. 'Seems like it, but actually three years less than you already! It's from May 1943.'

She looked up at the ceiling, calculating. She pursed her lips, frowned and nodded. 'Yes well, Jack doesn't get demobbed until February 1946.'

'Another year! That really does not seem fair. How many times has that poor man laid down his life? How come it's so long?'

She smiled ruefully. 'Well there is it is Eric, he did volunteer,' she leaned into me a little and nodded again. 'Sorry...'

'No, no, no,' I interrupted, 'that's real courage. He has shown the true courage of his convictions - and never grumbled, I don't think?'

She smiled, shaking her head.

'I think you have willed him through the war. Fritz couldn't drive his Panzer through the barrier of your love - like Perseus' polished shield reflecting the many headed Wehrmacht...' She gave a little chuckle at my poetry.

I could come over to tea and meet Jack. A good idea, we agreed.

The ex-Canary Girl still has to produce shells. - the war is not over yet. I don't know if that bird can sing. She needs her sleep this afternoon, so it's Blue birds over the White Cliffs of Dover for now.

She laughed telling me that some of the girls who can cope with the colour even had yellow babies, but it's no harm to them.

I got back to Retford station about four o'clock (1600 hours!). Gina had said after four, so maybe I could nip up to Gringley and get back to Egmanton before dark.

Oh dear. It was a most strange experience. The Land Army Girls positively avoided me, excusing themselves, humming and aahing, don't knowing, but 'I think she's had an accident',

They were distinctly cautious, checking out my credentials, why I was asking, etc. I'm just a friend of Georgina - Gina? It was almost as if they didn't know her ... didn't want to know.

I told how Gina had written that *Peg* had had an accident. That was enough, everybody clammed up.

One girl, blood drained from her face, suggested behind her hand that I check out Gina's family: 'Dad works for Laycock in Clayworth doesn't he?' and walked out.

I don't remember my ride back to Portland farm; there was a lot to think about.

In an envelope postmarked Cardiff, was this cutting:

FOUR GERMAN P.O.W. CHARGED WITH MURDER

Non-Nazi's Death in a Sheffield Camp

Four German prisoners of war appeared before a military court at Kensington Palace Gardens, London, yesterday charged with the murder at Sheffield on March 24 of another prisoner, Unteroffizier Gerhardt Rettig.

The accused are Feldwebel Emil Schmittendorf, San Gefreiter Armin Kuehne, Unteroffizier Heinz Ditzler, and Soldat Juergen Kersting. They all pleaded not guilty. During the trial the name of German witnesses will be kept secret.

Major R. A. L. Hillard, prosecuting officer, said that Rettig and a friend in a barrack hut were non-Nazis. On the afternoon of March 24 Rettig communicated with the British guards through the wire and later, after being spoken to by the Lagerführer, they began to pack their kit. Later Rettig left the hut and almost immediately came running back, followed by a crowd of about twenty or thirty prisoners.

"Kuehne and Ditzler were among the first of that crowd to rush in after Rettig. They chased Rettig and beat him with their firsts," said Major Hillard. "Rettig was pushed out of the hut with his face covered with blood and his eyes nearly closed. The crowd chased him across the open ground outside the hut in the direction of the washhouse. The crowd cornered him outside the washhouse. There were probably at that time a hundred men collected around him. Some were shouting 'Beat him to death' and others 'Hang him.' Later Rettig was lying on the ground crumpled up, Schmittendorf dragged Rettig's head clear of his arms and kicked him with his boot on the head.

DIED IN AMBULANCE

"Water was poured over Rettig and he got to his feet, ran from the washhouse in the direction of the kitchen and up the passage. At that time the crowd was considerably larger—one witness puts it at between three hundred to five hundred men. In the passage between the dining-room and the kitchen there is a containing wall for a rubbish heap. Rettig was last seen standing at the place where the rubbish is shot."

A medical orderly found Rettig lying between the arms of the rubbish bin. He was taken by ambulance to hospital near Sheffield and he died in the ambulance. The cause of death was severe injuries to the head. The skull was not fractured, but the blows caused tearing of the covering of the brain which resulted in coma and death.

The first German witness told the Court that on March 24 an escape tunnel was discovered by the British guards, and that afternoon the witness and Rettig handed a note through the wire to the guards. Later the German camp leader told witness that he and Rettig would be transferred. Later Rettig came running back to the hut pursued by a crowd some of whom set on witness. Before being taken into protective custody by the British, a sentry had to draw his revolver to keep off some of the crowd and there were cries of "Hang him" and "Traitor." He added that he thought Schmittendorf might have incited the crowd against him.

"At Doncaster I said that if I were questioned by a British officer I would speak the truth—that Germany had lost the war," he said. "Schmittendorf then pointed me out as a scoundrel and a criminal. I have been threatened secretly.'

"KICKED ON THE HEAD"

Another witness said that after Schmittendorf had struck Rettig several times in the face Rettig crumpled up. Then Schmittendorf pulled his hair and kicked him on the head twice. He added that Kuehne spoke to him after the affair and said Rettig had "given away about the escape tunnel."

A later witness said that Schmittendorf accused Rettig of treason and he was "in for the high jump."

Another witness told the Court that Schmittendorf said, "The whole affair has been very successful." Schmittendorf also said, "The man has got so many blows from me that he will not think about treachery a second time, but we will have to take care because there are spies among us." He afterwards heard that Schmittendorf, with four others, had escaped from the camp.

A German Red Cross sergeant said that he went to render aid to Rettig but the crowd prevented him, shouting, "Knock him down. He is going to help the traitor." Rettig's upper lip was so badly split that his teeth showed through.

The trial was adjourned until to-day.

Part Four - May 1945

V E Day
The War is Over

59μ
V E Day 8th May 1945

It's over - somebody won a war. How many bodies lie in the mud?

We have won apparently. That's not Palmiro, Bernhard and me, just me. I've won with my Allies.

If it's anything like Dad winning the Great War ... yes, it has to be. Too many people have died and this time it's not only fighters and soldiers, who have died, but millions of civilians, women and children, cooking and at school, have been vapourised by my industrial friends - Grandpapa.

It wasn't him, but Vickers in Sheffield who made 'Ten-Ton Tess' - a twenty two thousand pound bomb.

I didn't tell you about my Dad, your Grandad. I think it's because I couldn't talk about it. He died. I had thought about it for too long - all my life he has been dying. As soon as I could think - that footie match maybe - I knew he couldn't play footie with me; couldn't play with me.

At his funeral, not long after Strangeways, soon after I'd settled in Egmanton with the Foxes during '43, Uncle Frank said it was not - my criminal conviction - that that did for him, 'He was proud of you Eric - he knew you were fighting for *him*.'

He took his hand off my shoulder, put it in his pocket, looked out of the window and I saw him blink away a tear. Dragging his nose along his sleeve he laughed and said 'he just woke up dead one morning.'

The war killed him. The other war. I'm thinking of him now and smiling. He can watch and cheer the Blades all he likes. And perhaps he hung on, hung around to hold me up on his shoulders.

And Mam - she let him go. She held other people up in this other war.

She did well. She still does. It's over, but it's not finished.

We've won, but there's no prize.

Did we win anything?

'We won the b-- war!' they say.

I'm holding my hands out - holding the prize.

There's nothing there.

I went to see Mam after Hiroshima and the Japanese - after someone decided the *World* war was finished.

She held me so tight. Her body quaked. She cried. So hard, it was almost like barking - and at the moon. 'Your Dad's in a better place,' is how she told it.

As the distress, perhaps release, ebbed out of her, Mam cupped my cheeks in her hands. She looked into my eyes. 'Are you Eric?'

My dry eyes didn't ... couldn't speak.

'You look after your boys, now.'

60μ
September 1945

I am now. In a better place. And my boys - how can I look after them? It's September 1945 now and the last big job - the potato harvest - is in. There's an Italian or two on every farm round here. Some have had German gangs ... but not Alec.

He's had Land Army and local women and children. A few older men - and farmers helping each other - we've leant a hand at Merryfields - that's Alec Fox's brother Charlie's place up the road at Marnham - and they've been across here.

It was a distraction for me. People, lots of them, every one wild with excitement and anticipation, of returning, returning to 'normal,' the returning of the men and women. De-mob. Palmiro and all the Prisoners of War, too. I think they will be disappointed in expecting to be going home straight away.

The nation has kicked out the War Prime Minister, Churchill, and Labour is going to bring in some great, much needed changes to the pre-war - Medieval - status quo, with us as serfs, and them as masters. They are the ones who really win any war - the Industrialists who do not volunteer their services, but do volunteer their workers to feed the guns.

It seems the new Prime Minister, Atlee, might want the enemies to pay for the damage they caused - reparations - and to be punished so they do not try again.

Palmiro agrees with him! So not expecting to go home soon. He showed me his tapestry - colourful, clean, and almost finished. Hmm? He kissed Saint Egidio, winked at me, and carefully packed him up again.

61μ

We all heard about a great escape from a POW camp in Bridgend, Wales. About seventy men got out through a tunnel, but the authorities bragged about capturing them all. I've just heard that the whole lot have been brought over here to yet another of these duke's estates, this one at Welbeck Abbey - yes where Sally got Palmiro's garlic seeds from. Apparently they are mostly officers, pretty staunch supporters of Hitler.

The Fuhrer is dead, but I don't suppose his ideology is. He killed himself; I don't suppose the same can be hoped for his ideology. It will have to be stamped out. Apparently the commandant at the camp - it's called Carburton - has done famously well with re-educating his first intake of Nazis on the benefits of democracy, and has actually *asked* to have the tough escapees sent to him in order to prove his ideas. They've given him all 1200 of the Bridgend lot!

I took a ride over - lovely area. The camp at Carburton (hardly even a village, though it does have a tiny church) is just off the Edwinstowe to Worksop road, so it is also in the Sherwood Forest, where Joe Bennett told me all the munitions are stored. Don't tell the Hun!

We can see the large style Nissen Huts from the corner, but because of the security risk of these captives, a close approach is not possible. I got it wrong - it's not the Commandant who has the big idea though, but his translator, a chap called Henry Faulk. The locals joke about that: they say Fritz thinks he is one of their Volk - (pronounced 'folk'). He is a very good German speaker and even taught in Germany before the war - knows a thing or two about the rise of Nazional Socialism too, then?

I wish him luck.

Strangely, there is another camp nearby with an entirely different clientele ... they hope so. Welbeck estate has a wonderful long lake and I was able to ride along the south side. Man made - not by the Duke's sweat of brow of course, but lovely to behold - and strictly from a distance. Carburton is at one end and about half way along (I'd say it is a mile long), and on the other side is Norton, also called Norton Cuckney, to distinguish it from Sheffield's Norton camp, I expect. This Norton is a tiny hamlet next to the bigger Cuckney. It is actually housing for estate workers, with fine and fancy houses which they call 'Wedding Cake', because the chimneys are ornate like the stands holding the layers of posh cakes.

At the end of the village is a 'welcome' area I *was* able to approach. Lining an estate road is a row of about twenty huts which are actually the national centre of the Young Men's Christian Association's Nazi re-education centre. An American millionaire has funded the YMCA to not only train captured Germans in democracy, but also in their own National School Leaving Certificate - the 'Abitur' - because so many were drafted into the forces by way of their own Hitler Youth, rather than after school, that they have missed 'normal' education. But especially, he is motivated to fund Christian education - to train up well meaning, good, non-Nazi POWs to become church Pastors and teachers.

I like this.

It has been difficult for me to get, and hold onto, my CO status purely on humanitarian grounds. CO friends had really been pressured to give evidence of religious attendance and conviction. That's partly why I didn't respond to the Tribunal. I knew I couldn't win, but did sort of hope they might forget about me!

Of course, the fact that Conscientious Objection has been recognised in such numbers, has at least saved me from being heavily punished, or even shot like in the last war. (Come to think of it, Strangeways was actually quite heavy.)

You have met my German and Italian friends along the way so far. They are just men (and boys) like me.

There will be people among them with very strong beliefs, just like me, but they think Hitler and Mussolini did a lot of good for them and their families. I'm sure they did - but they then did a lot of horrible things, and made their soldiers do as they were told, or else.

We are going to meet some more to get a full picture.

Norton and Carburton are both huge camps, and as yet very secure. Norton's POW encampment is accessed through the row of YMCA HQ huts. I am sure these will be more comfortably furnished for the guards and tutors than the billets in the *camp*, or as I am learning, what is sometimes referred to by the guards as *'the cage'*.

The closest I was going to get to it was the HQ but at least I got a hand waving description of a camp in three sections: on the left are students training to be teachers; on the right the theology students; and in between, the Abitur students. Nissen huts stand under the oak trees and grouped around a hill on the top of which is the focal point for the YMCA, yet not unlike Headon - the camp chapel. Way over to the left on level open ground I could see a good soccer pitch with a running track around it. Apparently a parade ground is beyond the sports ground, and mess huts are in taller Nissen huts. These are also used for lectures and teaching.

Proper. Treating the enemies like humans. I may come to be proud of being British if we can keep this up.

Not Buchenwald round here.

62μ

Lesley Marshall from Mattersey has been in touch - he says I will be interested in the variety of developments with the numbers of Italians billeted out in North Notts, and the Germans who are joining them in the fields. Luca has the stories and his English is 'coming on a treat'.

What happened to Gina? I'll have to scoot up to the Gringley/Clayworth area.

It offends my sensibilities to say I'll kill two birds with one stone, but I hope you will forgive me the figure of speech.

Luca first: 'his camp' is Carlton-in Lindrick, just outside Worksop. All of the billeted men are recognised as 'Co-operators', wear the uniform, patches removed, but are still POWs and have a base camp. He put me in touch with a recent Italian addition, one who speaks better French than English. He is billeted out in Notts' furthest northerly point at West Stockwith - where the local rivers and the Chesterfield Canal join the great tidal River Trent. He says that Umberto Ferrarelli has a different slant on POW status, but will tell me himself. And I might get a bit more for my story, as he is billeted with twenty five others at Harris's Mount Pleasant farm, a big concern with Market Gardens across North Notts and South Yorkshire.

Clayworth and Gringley are en route so I called in and asked around for the Christmas family. Yes well, I did have to put up with some corny stuff about Jesus, Mary and Joseph not being in the stable, but their boss might well be chasing a Land Army girl around one.

Mr Christmas confirmed that Georgina had had ... an accident on the Government farm and was in hospital - legs quite badly injured. I'm not so sure he believed it was an accident. Apparently she has some head injuries too and could be a while. I wish I could have got hold of a bunch of flowers for the poor lass.

And so to the aptly named Mount Pleasant: the Italian billet was easy to find. I pulled up Maisie Matchless in front of the big farmhouse and as soon as my ears adjusted from the motor, I could hear what could only be a rumpus of Italian exuberance for a Sunday-after-harvest-afternoon. There was singing - operatic and romantic of course - and shouting, from a large barn and its surroundings, and Umberto 'Bert' Ferrarelli was the man of the moment - he had just fed them well. Garlic - Si!

After I graciously accepted a glass of ersatz - pretending - grappa, Bert took me to a quieter area. Luca had told him about me. Grazie for showing an interest. I didn't tell him that I personally know how that feels.

He is not one of the North African, El Alamein captives. He was part of El Duce's other aim, to capture some more of Italy's Northern hinterland - the French Riviera and alps - for the new Roman Empire.

With lots of blowing of hands and arms bashing his sides, he told of the awful battles in the alpine crossings, how more men died of the cold than in battle, and only one town taken - Menton - along with a small strip of land around. I didn't know that they had a truce with the French and kept it. So for a couple of years Bert had what the Americans call a 'swell time' living on the Riviera. He picked up a lot of French there.

'Van rouge, tray bon, van blonk,' he kissed his fingers, then pointed at the 'grappa', and shook his head 'mared!' I guess he liked the French plonk - I had to agree as not much had gone from my own glass of grappa. (My Daddy told me about that when I was little - French white wine is called 'blanc', but the soldiers heard 'plonk'.)

The Italians were a more welcome enemy to the French than the Germans. A couple of years - until Mussolini capitulated in 1943, and the Germans took over and locked their turncoat old allies up. (Bert didn't say that).

We now know that Hitler had Mussolini sprung from prison and set him up in a puppet state - a bit like that other Italian Pinocchio, who had his strings pulled. Bert told of lots of cruelty by his old German allies.

It was the Americans who liberated the area from the Germans, and Umberto from their Prison of War Camp, sending him directly to England. Carlton was a holiday camp compared, and the Brits soon recognised a man happy to co-operate.

Harrises have got 25 POWs billeted here - a very big concern, and more a large Market Garden than a farm of beasts or corn. They've also recognised a man who could do more for them than farm labouring - he is a great cook. They let him do half duties and feed the men - a self sufficient Italian camp. Everybody's happy - but of course they want to go home, except ... he took a look around ... 'Ze Laydeez, si?'

West Stockwith is basically a suburb of what I later learnt is the 'longest village in England' - Misterton. It's got a lot of the Lavly Laydeez and they like the charming Italian lads ... a lot. With comic mime show and lots of laughter that drew the attention of a few of the other lads, and yes perhaps some bragging, he made it clear to me that he had to fight off the women.

While he sat back enjoying the moment, I took in the 'Viva!' sentiment in the songs. Mummy and I had picked up that this is the Italian of 'long live', or 'to life'. My own thoughts moved to the Laydeez, and to you lovely Mummy, our time on the Amalfi coast and the big hit 'Vivere!' The lads gave a rousing rendition, concluding with a kind of three cheers 'Viva Verdi! Viva Verdi! Viva Verdi'.

My frown spoke to Bert, 'Verdi?'

He laughed, pulled a pencil stub from behind his ear and a scrap of paper from his pocket and wrote 'Viva V.E.R.D.I. - Viva **V**ictor **E**mmanuele lll **R**egienti **D**e **I**talia'. He underlined the 'Regi' and sweeping a hand round the group added, 'Like you - Royal, non fascist'. The boys were all agreeing and nodding to me. 'Non-Fasci. Viva Verdi!' One made a gesture I've only seen

Italians do - flicked his thumb away from his tooth, said 'El Duce!' and spat on the floor; this drew another 'Viva Verdi! From the throng.

So ... 'Viva V.E.R.D.I.' translates as 'Long live Victor Emmanuele King of Italy.'

They aren't all fighting off the women of course. He took a look around and picked out an obviously embarrassed man. 'Antonio!' he called. After a little Italian banter and some jostling from the others, Tony Dalla Riva told his story in a dumb show. Not so dumb:

He held his heart; he kissed the sweet, sweet sky; he pointed to his ring finger; he nodded to me and my wedding ring; he laughed at big Bert's coquettish girlie pose, hands out from under the chin, bunching his blond - yes blond - curls; he sighed close to my ears, 'Steph-an-ie'.

A question swept across his face; he shrugged and cradled a baby in his arms.

A hush went over the group - measuring my response.

I jumped up and clapped him round the shoulders.

I translate: Tony is in love with a beautiful girl called Stephanie; they are married and expecting a baby. He is still a prisoner of war.

Bert put on his serious face when the hilarity had worn down, and quietly confused me about wife and not wife. I think he means that he, Umberto, has a wife. Stephanie is not yet married to Tony, though they want to be, and hope to be soon - as she is expecting a baby.

I've got a feeling old Atlee is going to be a bit mean about this...

A kind of hum built up from the boys - first one, joined by others, building into the crescendo of what I recognised as The March of the Hebrew Slaves. See Mummy, I have learnt a little from your high-brow ways. I blinked away a tear and turned back to my host.

Bert sipped the grappa and pulled a face. Pointing to himself then away across the sea saying 'vinyeto, me' which I took to be Venice. He indicated good wine.

I nodded. Famous for its wines.

I asked about the camp.

Good. Germans too.

'Carlton?' I said.

'Si. Yes'.

'France,' I said. 'German camp in France?'

He spluttered and sat up. 'Non. No - not good. German B------o! Food, bad.' He sat shaking his head. Was he trembling in fear or anger?

Pointing to him I said 'Soldier?' I pointed up. 'Air?'

'Primo air,' he pointed to the past. 'In war, Infanteria in mountains.'

'Alpine?'

'No Alpini. Brother...' He shook and scratched his head. 'Beau-frère...' He laughed at himself, now speaking french I think. 'Brother wife, wife brother ?' he pleaded.

'Brother-in-law,' I said.

'Ah, si, si. My brother-in-law, he Alpini in Al-ba-nia. He Fascisti.' More shaking of head. 'Me royal, want peace.'

I shook his hand. I then asked how he came to England.

Americans sent him on a boat to Liverpool, and then he came across to Carlton-in-Lindrick where there were Germans and Italians. All peaceable. Not like France.

I was about to go, when Tony rejoined us, so I asked about his war. He actually spoke pretty good English - I suppose his Stephanie and he have developed beyond dumb-show. He fought in a lot of the big battles in North Africa before being captured. He didn't want to fight, and the British eighth army actually had him driving support vehicles for them. He may have shared duties with Queenie's Jack?

In '43 he was brought into Liverpool on the Queen Mary and sent on to York. It's a racecourse with lots of bunking in the grandstand. He pointed to a milk churn in the corner and mimed that there were a lot of them - for toilets.

Fencework around the back gave them an area for exercise and fresh air.

Only rice to eat ... well a few bits. Everything smelt and tasted of chocolate - I had to laugh. Queenie asked me if I'd smelt Terry's on the way through York.

Not long - only a few years, er weeks! - before being sent to 'Nayder Highdon. Good camp.'

I mentioned Palmiro, and that he had been at Nether Headon, too.

Tony confirmed that there are many boys billeted out of the camp, all over the countryside. Not Germans. Only camp for them. I didn't argue with him. I know Bernhard is an exception, so far.

I took a last look around at the lads settling down to letter writing, card games and reading. Bert and Tony are quite noticeably the 'Godfathers' to this group of very young men. They must both be thirty years old.

The whole platoon came to admire Maisie and wave me off.

Lovely day.

63μ

Palmiro smiles. He is smiling constantly now. It is a shy smile and he brushes up his now very long curls when he catches me noticing him being so ... happy.

Bells are ringing. Church bells have been silent for the duration, but now the war is finished. Palmiro tells me, 'I tell Mama I go home.'

That was a kind of shock to me, but of course he will go home and of course it is something, it is a lot to smile about. Queenie's Jack was away for almost five years. The Army had to send him home to his mother ... to his new wife. Palmiro has been away for longer now. He had left home and was sent to Libya before Italy declared war. So at least five years. I'm not going to push him to think of it. Left as a boy - now very much a man.

He showed me a photograph a while ago of him and a friend with two girls. He is so shy of them ... but not. I think perhaps he tries too hard. He is always pulling some sort of funny face. Even around Sally and Barbara, if he becomes conscious of being looked at, it's a funny grin or he pumps up his bouffant. On the photo he is leaning in to the girl, but looking back at the camera. I asked him about her. The smile disappeared. He shook his head. Not a nice girl.

'Any nice girls?' I said.

The smile returned. 'Lot!'

We laughed together. Not quite peals of laughter, but bells are ringing all the time - the radio has them constantly. Big Ben laughs again on the hour, every hour.

Church bells - they haven't any on the chapel next door, but the 'Anglo Catholic' church of Our Lady of Egmanton (it used to be a place of pilgrimage before old Henry VIII trod on the Catholics, but apparently there was some interest in reviving it when ... the old rivalries subsided, I suppose. We've been to them all. Yes Mummy, I have also been to churches. I don't wish to be niggardly: there must be a God to make this entire wonderful world. He she, or it. (I don't suppose he needs sex, but 'it' doesn't seem to fit anything which has cares, and as a creator, I believe him to be nearer to female characteristics...)

Anyway, I can thank her wherever. I also love my fellow people and will certainly celebrate my reason for being - peace and love - with them.

Peace has not quite broken out all over. The horrors of war, previously thought to be fought among honourable men and not against civilians - and women ... and children ... are being revealed at every turn. The Japanese do not seem to respect life - not even their own. They had bomber pilots who actually volunteered to kill themselves in order to kill us, their enemies - rather than dropping bombs- and perhaps missing, they would steer straight at the targets - mostly ships. Death is a sure thing for some soldiers, but even their aim is to protect themselves from others trying to kill them ... and theirs. We are learning that the Japanese disrespect men who will not fight to the death, so much so that they kill themselves rather than become prisoners of war. That does seem to take courage.

I also get the impression that our allies throughout the whole war, the Ruskies, are now not to be trusted. Stuff about the Ivans raping their way to Berlin. I somehow suspect sour grapes - the British and Americans both wanted to be first to Berlin, to capture Hitler, but the Russians beat them to it. Stalin does certainly seem to be staking a claim for all of the Germany he has taken.

There has always been that fear of revolution - 'Commies!' and 'Reds!' and even of us Conchies too. Fear? That we want peace and they want war?

So 'my boys' on the other side of the world are not even fit to come home yet. 'Our POWs are *convalescing* from ill-treatment. Like the people Dimbleby told us about, only they weren't even POWs - just people. I actually do not understand what the Nazis were doing treating them so badly. It just does not make sense. Even if you hate people, if you've got them captured they must be some use to you, but the Germans seem to have spent so much on the killing of civilians that they perhaps ran out of munitions to win the war with.

I'm not sure I want to celebrate that aspect.

We have peace, and not much left to enjoy it with. Apparently about a third of the homes in the cities are now uninhabitable and we cannot import the food we need from abroad because the ships have been lost and sunk - and so have the sailors.

So I may be forced to stay here longer than my three years, or the duration. War Ag won't want their captive labour taken from them either. Old Atlee might force the unwilling Germans to work. Oh dear!

Anglo-Catholic has been alright for Palmiro for his time here so far, but he thinks it's not really Catholic, so I found him the genuine article down past Boughton Camp, in Ollerton. Straight away that smile was fixed for him. There were several POWs in uniform there. They've been coming in from all around - locally of course, from Boughton, but from Edwinstowe, Rufford and from billets on the farms, like Palmiro - and me.

There is a great camaraderie outside of church, much exchanging of information, talk of home, and the dreaded and reluctant raising of expectations of return there any time soon.

The local people are extremely nice to the chaps. Most surely know someone who has died at the hands of the Axis. However, the reality of the people, the actual men, is that they are ... people, just like them, who love and want peace with family - just like them.

My darling, are you at peace with your Mama and Papa in dear old Dore?

64μ

On the ride around the area, I pulled up alongside another motorbike at the bottom of the hill - a very steep one from here to Ollerton, where the huge Boughton camp is almost hidden under the hill.

Quite a clever move: the British broke the unwritten rule of not letting the enemy know where their POWs were being kept, lest upon invasion they set them free to rejoin the fray. They let it be known that that Boughton is a Prisoner of War camp. From the air the Heinkels and Dorniers will have it clearly marked to avoid bombing their own boys. Little did they know that the huge huts are not Nissens for personnel, but much larger ones called Romneys. It's not a secret any more that Boughton was actually an American munitions store in the centre of England in the build up to the invasion of Europe on D-Day. I guessed as much - what with all the massive American trucks Maisie and I had to avoid on the roads around here.

The chap on the bike introduced himself as Guy Reckin, an army sergeant - I saw his stripes. He was doing the same as me - sort of. He has been appointed to Boughton POW as quartermaster for his final year of service, but out of interest he is documenting the camp on film. He has promised to show it me when it's finished - it'll be after Christmas he supposes - he has got a proper job to do.

He was stopped also for the same reason as me - to glean a perspective on the camp. It is on both sides of the road and actually has three sections. I take it that this is for the same reason as firebreaks in forests - if one section goes up, it doesn't spread to another. Reckin nodded at my notion. While from the air the huts will look the same as Nissen's, from the road they are clearly bigger and higher - raised even, to enable easy loading onto lorries.

We had quite a chat that Sunday afternoon, sitting on our bikes at the side of the now tranquil road. Like Willy Kohnstamm, he's been sent here ostensibly as the Quartermaster Sergeant, but strategically ... he did check me out before proceeding ... because he speaks German. British Intelligence wants him to help identify any prisoners who are on the war crimes register. They also want him to ascertain how much they knew about the Holocaust, a new word to me. Apparently the bodies on the truck at Buchenwald were all Jews and it's thought the Nazis were actually trying to wipe all Jews off the face of the earth.

Is that war?

Reckin had a baleful chuckle as he told me that the POWs don't even have a hut at all - they are all under canvas in a small corner, and come out each day to work in the nearby 'munitions factory'. I can't see that - he must mean the huge huts in the camp proper. Could be munition *stores*.

He smiled as he noticed a small truck swing into the gate. 'POW,' he said, obviously referring to the driver.

I did the double take, and he explained.

'The driver - a Prisoner of War. Only a kid, but, phew has he had some war!'

'German?'

'Aye. Luftwaffe pilot, Parachute Regiment, then infantryman, blasted in the rear guard action defending Berlin. Patched up in London. Sent up North as a Nazi, and then proved he wasn't.' The sergeant smiled and went on. 'He's still only nineteen and what we call a Trusty, now. We have him on Dispatch, delivering, fetching and carrying, laundry, supplies; officers out to sort disputes with farmers.' He chuckled. 'Plenty of them.'

He put out his hand, 'nice to meet you...'

I told him my name and that I was a Conscientious Objector working over the hill.

He gave me a queer look, but then smiled, nodded, put his helmet back on and saying 'better get to work,' fired up his Norton and followed his trusty German prisoner into the camp.

65μ
Autumn 1945

Günter, Headon camp's 'chauffeur' and I were standing at the edge of the wood. A gang of POWs and I had been gathering, logging and stacking the timber coppiced a few weeks ago, mostly by the same gang, he had brought over.

'Mostly' was the problem apparently, and that was why I had the chance to meet up with one of the boys who most intrigued me - for boys is what many of them are.

I had been eating my snap watching a trail of ants. Günter held what I now recognised as a characteristic pose: leaning with arms and legs crossed, head cocked on one side musing about the state of the world.

'Luft, Aric!' He remembered my name - sort of.

I followed his look out across a field, a clear view down it to the Trent in the distance. It had been a balmy early Autumn day, until a few of the lads went barmy with one of the others.

He had told me last time, a very little about his capture. He had been asked to do 'just a couple of months, as a paratrooper in Belgium to help the rear guard action for Berlin. It was a transfer, and from the Luftwaffe, but he had seemed very cagey about me asking about that aspect. I was wondering if he was now going to own up to his flying experience. 'Luft, Günter?'

'Luft ... vind?' he spread his arms and threw his head back. He took a deep breath.

I smiled but said nothing to break what may prove a reverie.

'Ah - ha!' he laughed, gulping great lungs-full of air.

I joined him and spread my wings.

He saw my arms and looked disdainfully at me.

'Spread your wings and learn to fly,' I said. 'You?'

'Ja. I had my glider licence like, when I was only twelve.'

'Twelve?' I said.

'Ja - young as possible.'

'How come?'

'When I was only nine,' he said (that's nearly the same in German as English, Pina) 'I saw film of aeroplanes and knew right away that I must fly.' He spread his arms again, but this time winced and grabbed his left arm with his right.

'Wound, Günter?'

'Ja, bleddy tank.'

He turned and looked back at the camp captain still remonstrating with the gang.

I asked him what the problem was - between the men.

He told me that the majority of the men at the camp had been through the system - like he himself had - and had settled at Headon readying themselves to go home. They knew that the Brits were not going to let them go if they were not what we would call whiter-than-white. They were categorised from Black -

extreme Nazi - through to White - just blokes who wanted their families and, like Bernhard, really wondered 'what this mad-man has got us into.' (That was the impression they knew they had to convey.) Like the Italians before them, the men at Headon are hardly belligerent and are being trusted with ever increasing degrees of freedom.

I hoped he was going to elaborate what the system had done to or for him.

'Some new lads were brought over from camp in America, and they thought they were going straight home, so they are very angry about British. Teasing?'

'Yes, I suppose. What has that to do with this morning's trouble - I'm the only Brit here?'

'Ah Aric, you good man. You not like war. Some boys like war and want others to fight - still.' He made a winding gesture.

'Winding, stirring up trouble?' I said.

'Go now. Exact!' he said.

'And you? You don't want any trouble, Günter?'

'I had my trouble,' he said. 'Mitchell shot me down ... tank shot me up.' He gave me a funny look.

'In the camp, I meant.'

'No! Only been there three days.'

Now I knew he was being disingenuous, or maybe throwing me off the scent. He turned away again. I looked back at the group. There was some shaking of hands going on. 'Captain having some success by the look of it. Good old British fair play. I poshed it up - "come along now chaps?"'.

'Not Captain,' he put three fingers on his sleeve.

'Sergeant,' I said. 'Having some luck though. You drive him ... after only three days?'

He double checked me. 'Ah, sorry Aric, only in the cage - the *prison* camp three days.'

'But Günter, you've been coming out here for about three months.'

He had to think about this. Remember he is a German, I am not writing *all* the funny accents and mistakes for you, I am translating.

'A-ha!' he laughed again, 'Not here, not there.' He snorted and tried again.

'Were you at Boughton?' I said. I sensed some coincidence.

He looked really surprised at that. His head cocked on one side, he pointed at me with a real frown, and then put his finger to his lips. He'd clammed up.

So I added, 'and what's this about the Luft?'

He looked back across the clearing. 'Nice vind, like.' He flapped his arms. 'Just saying. No, see, I was only in *prisoners* part of the camp for three days ... after Boughton. Now I am out of cage and in the barracks section, in dispatch office. Nice building. Own bedroom, like.'

'What did you do to deserve that?'

'Tommies say "keep your nose clean, Günter,"' he laughed. 'At Oldwistle I was like these lads from America - show the British vot ve can do like, and second time, got three weeks what Tommy say "on Jankers". Enough!'

I laughed at him. I was dying to know what it took. I held my hands out.

He chuckled. 'De-bagging a pervert!' He bit his lip.

Prison was pretty awful for me - and of course 'I hadn't done anything.' What must it be like in a detention centre - Jankers - *inside* a prison (of war camp)? I had heard him say 'shot down' too, so I was still hoping 'Luft' would get a 'waffe' attached making the 'Luftwaffe' that he was really in...

'Oldwhistle ... Boughton ... where else?' I said.

'*Halt*-whistle,' he stressed, 'in York-shire - Tommy say "best place for you lot - middle o'nowhere." Trees, river ... an old castle. Not for us, castle - only tents - from the last war, too. Full of holes.'

I couldn't guess where that may be, and me a Yorkshire lad too. Big place the Ridings. 'How long were you there?'

'Got there Christmas Eve. Told me to take a blanket off a snow covered pile.' He looked at me and nodded. 'I'm first in, so I looks at the roof to find a spot that's *not* under a hole.'

I'm holding my hand over my mouth and shaking my head.

'No, see, they wanted me out of the hospital in Woolwich at Christmas.'

He's seen more of England than me. 'Last year? '45?' I said.

'No - '44. Brought me to Woolwich in October '44.' He checked out the progress of the gang, and decided we had time for a smoke and offered *me* one. That's a first - POW not cadging off me. I shook my head and he sparked up. 'Tommies good to me - after killing all me mates, like.'

He says 'like' all the time. I think whoever taught him most English - I supposed maybe a squaddie who guarded him at the hospital. He must have been a Brummy because Günter says it almost every sentence and pronounces it 'loyk'.

'Ja, they took me to a field hospital, like, and patched up my arm.' He grabbed it again. 'I escapes again and gets a kick up the bum.'

'Wounded *and* escaped?' I said laughing.

He laughed at himself. 'Well they didn't expect us to get up off our sick-beds and escape, so they only had old men guarding us.'

'Chelsea Pensioner?' I said, but of course that threw him.

He laughed though and nodded. 'Ja, old man sitting at tent door with a machine gun over his legs. I have arm in sling and see he is sleeping. I get up and lift gun off, hide it under bed and walk out of hospital camp.'

'Where *is* this, Günter?' I asked, sounding more and more incredulous with each extra instalment in his fantasy.

'In Ostend. They took me from Brussels to Ostend.'

'Günter...' I now took a look back at the group who seemed to have got more heated again, and the sergeant was waving his arms. 'Günter, you are a well travelled young man and your story fascinates me. But you started at the end - when you came here - and keep going back one step to try to explain, the next step. I tell you what, how about just telling me about the Mitchells that shot you down?' I saw him tense, but I went on. 'You did say "Luft".' (I didn't add the "Waffe" which I took to mean Army or force - like air force or Waffen SS, SS Army - I hoped that he might).

He stammered a bit and nodded before saying 'Ja, spent four hours in the sea before being rescued.'

'But Günter, not in Brussels.'

He didn't laugh and I could see that, though I felt he was no rat, he was still cornered and I needed to move on.

I was saved by the bell - the sergeant shouting 'Rahn, here please.'

We walked over to the gang; the officer cut one of the gang out and led him by the elbow - gently - away to their little Bedford truck, pointing Günter to the cab.

I had to divert the lads, flexed my muscles - such as they are - smiled an 'arbeit?' and they all set to, as if actually relieved. I know I was.

So I will definitely have to get some time with Günter Rahn. If he isn't confined to the prison section of Nether Headon Camp, I might be able to pitch up during one evening and take a walk with him.

Wounded by a tank ... Ostend ... Shot down ... hours in the sea ... in Brussels ... Woolwich (I'm assuming that is London) ... at least three POW camps over here. Maybe in America, too, like Palmiro was sent to far South Africa first ... but not to be drawn into discussion about whether he was in the Luftwaffe - their Airforce.

Later, I thought I might take his photograph, but when he saw me with a camera one time, Günter Rahn produced a comb and practically insisted I snap him.

66µ

Alec doesn't have Palmiro working alongside the Germans. He discussed it with me - was I happy to do so?

Of course - it's my hobby now, finding out about these fighters! There's a compare and contrast element - who actually wanted to fight; who thought about the point of war; who really didn't want to kill anybody? All the squaddies I have met along the way seem to have held disdain for me. What could I expect? They don't want to think ... to think beyond that I am simply a coward. Anything else doesn't bear thinking about.

Not for me either!

So, yes I am okay working with the Germans, and I think it only fair that Palmiro is not expected to. Anyway, Palmiro has got the greenhouses and kitchen garden flourishing now. Exotic! Tomatoes, well out of season and ... garlic of course. I've developed quite a taste for it - good job I'm not expecting Mummy to kiss me very soon! I am looking forward to it though.

I visited my Mam and she's enjoying life, yes she's happy now, helping all and sundry with getting their lives back, despite rationing, despite broken houses, despite queues at every shop. We kept calm and carried on ... and we still do. It was Mam suggested I don't visit Mummy in Dore yet, not raise expectations, as I don't really know when I may be allowed, or even if I really can, go home.

I sent you a letter Mummy. I think you understand. I'm not the only one who can't come home yet.

67µ

Peace. We had a phoney war, now a phoney peace.

At the start we set about protecting ourselves from the imminent invasion of the Germans, who inexplicably stopped on the other side of the channel having waved off the last of the Dunkirk flotilla of little ships.

We are now 'enjoying the peace', but sadly have nothing to enjoy it with, and many of us have the sad challenge of the missing ... to enjoy it with. Including me. *In some corner of a foreign field, there is a part that will be forever England.* Is that right, Dad?

Palmiro and the other Italians have a heavily restrained hope of repatriation; slim hope, perhaps. Where punishment focuses the minds of the marshals and the old order of politicians, *food* is the pre-occupation of the ordinary. The *new order* is made up of the ordinary, the working people, Labour for the first time ever. My hope is that the old order do not use their fusty money, enhanced by their war profits, to try to do us down.

Where the Prisoners of War, the Italians at least, have hopes of returning home, I am more like the Germans - afraid of what I'll find, even if I were to dare to hope.

Sally and Barbara have felt the need to sit me down and ask me why I do not simply go, not that they want rid of me of course. 'Who would be bothered?' Good question.

It might be me.

My official sentence finishes in seven months, May 1946. I am fairly sure that no one cares ... even that I live or die. I neither lived for my country, nor died for it, so...

Christmas is coming and a goose somewhere is getting fat. Here at Egmanton, and probably in most rural areas, secret meats will be being revealed, but not all, in case they have to be shared with the almost starving cities. War Ag has supposedly been stood down, but in fact has simply been re-badged as the CountyAg - Nottinghamshire Agricultural Executive Committee, NAEC for example, but no one calls it that, it would be phoney - so 'War Ag' it definitely still is.

The men are not home from the corners of the earth, and of course many, too many, will never be so, so we 'migrant workers' remain to feed the nation. Still. (My euphemism - most call POWs anything - and through gritted teeth. If they even remember me, 'Conchie' is hawked out,)

They don't reveal their figures, but my calculation is that most rural counties will have a similar set up to each other - a 'Standard Camp' which holds about 1500 men. (I say men, but I have heard of a female German POW in Liverpool who accepts it as her duty to help in clearing Unexploded Bombs: "They are ours, we should clear them," is her attitude. Fair enough.)

If there are about 50 counties with their Standard camp, that's at least 75,000 men. I know that a few have more than one 'Standard', as in Notts we have Nether Headon, and Wollaton Hall seems to have three within it.

Similarly Sheffield's Lodge Moor has separate camps within it and there will certainly be more Standards across the Ridings of Yorkshire. Are they 'Counties?'

I also know that after '43 when Italy capitulated, many men who were already deemed as no threat, were almost immediately billeted out. Demand for labour continued, so more men brought over from the Empire to fill the camps.

Billeting generally means living actually on a farm like Palmiro and I. However, many more are referred to as POW camps: actually hutting, left by the forces as they set off to Normandy to re-take Europe from the Axis. More were specifically built for the POWs: perhaps around 10 huts like at Rufford and Little Carlton; half a dozen at several others. These are being referred to as 'Satellite camps' or 'PWW' - Prisoner of War Working Companies - Edwinstowe, for instance.

War Ag is really not going to alarm the nation with just how many *enemies are in our midst,* so doing some reckoning for myself:

- there must be more than 50 camps in England,
- 30 in Scotland,
- 15 in Wales
- and famously 6 in Northern Ireland,

So rounding that up to a total of 100, each with satellites holding about 3,000, that's a total of 300,000.

Wow!

At Portland Farm we have had to continue like normal - war-normal, not returning to peace-normal. Will we ever? That means that as soon as the spuds are out of the ground, there was ploughing to be done and winter wheat to be sown. The family has been industrious in Palmiro's green houses. It is here that hope lies for a decent harvest of tasty items for the Christmas table, and we will have some to share.

Palmiro's greenhouses! Are we readying ourselves to take over sometime soon?

And who is 'we'? Should that be 'are'?

Phoney peace!

68μ
Christmas 1945

Oh Pina this is exciting - but I hope it's not 'Boy's stuff!' Anyway, let's hope there may be boys to tell it to, too.

Willy Kohnstamm invited me up to Sheffield for Christmas Drinkies - not quite Christmas, but there are plenty of people celebrating peace, well - no war, so pubs are pretty full.

All cloak and dagger stuff - not the Three Merry Lads, but a 'secret location', a non-descript local towards the city, but quite a big one, a hotel actually, *'where we might get a bit of peace (!) ... and come in civvies!'* He's forgotten I don't have a uniform.

I must have got a bit jittery, as Sally fussed over me, suggested I might wear a suit - yes I have one - brushed me down, and persuaded her husband to lend me his Wolseley ... *'and you must take your wife out.'*

Then I was jittery. I had such a grip on the steering wheel, that I found it more exhausting than holding on to Maisie Matchless the motorbike.

As I stepped into the saloon bar, I had some difficulty remembering what I was doing there, let alone finding Willy. He was also in a suit and had his hair fairly long and flopping over his face. The Master Spy in disguise, greeted me with a hug - the newly commonplace greeting for those returning from the war - long lost loved one.

I did go along with it. It might be the only one I get.

He got the drinks in. 'A snifter too?' he asked, but I declined - I'm not used to alcohol, and...

Willy was a different man from our first meeting, and not just his image. He blurted out his story, several stories actually, telling me I might like to take some notes. He looked around for the listeners, before straightening and acting naturally gay. He waved a hand around and took an exaggeratedly appreciative slurp of his beer. He coughed, wiped his sleeve across his mouth. Only then did he regale me with his scariest moment of the war:

One night on guard duty, he heard some rustling near the camp perimeter fence. He suspected he had stumbled across an escape.

'Halt!' he shouted.

No response.

He heard the rustling again.

'Halt! Who goes there?' (Rapid fire in English - Italian - German.)

A large shape loomed up in front of him ... and mooed.

He laughed and a local laughed with him raising his glass, too. He couldn't know what he was laughing about above the din. Christmas cheers.

'How's the...' he went on, but didn't wait for a reply, but put his hand to his mouth and looked around. 'You got my letter?' and flicked his brow.

I opened the page where I had inserted the cutting he had sent.

'Oh, you heard about the escape?' he said too loudly. 'I reckon it were at Lodge Moor. Papers can't say like, can they?'

I had to laugh at his attempt to blend in with a Yorkshire accent. He forgot as he continued in a much quieter welsh voice, and getting more news-cuttings out of his pocket. After wiping some drips off the table with his cuff - and swearing (was that German!) as he realised he, like me, was in his rarely worn best suit - we shuffled pieces round, him pointing to names and details.

It has been quite a sensation, a murder by Germans in a Prisoner of war camp, in England, so we were not conspicuous if we were discussing it aloud. The press variously referred to a camp in Yorkshire, near Sheffield, and even murder *in* Sheffield.

'So you followed the trial, too then Eric?' He coughed.

I smiled.

He pursed his lips. 'Bad lot, this lot. Shame for poor Rettig ... and his mate had a very lucky escape.'

'Escape! I thought you foiled it,' I whispered.

His head snapped around the bar.

I grimaced and said 'sorry' into my beer.

He raised his brows at me and took a pensive drink from his glass. 'Cockles?' he said.

I had no idea what he was talking about.

'My Treat - Christmas present!' He laughed and called the cockle seller over.

I had to shake my head and laugh. I hadn't seen the pedlar come in.

'Go on! Bet you don't get fresh fish out in the village.'

'Oh, yes! Yes please,' I had to say.

'Mussels. Whelks. No Prawns.'

'Just cockles would be lovely please.' It was a very pleasant change. Almost forgotten taste - and texture.

So it was obvious that Willy was letting me know that he was part of the whole murder thing. I had read the cutting he sent, over and over, and then watched the press for the rest of the story. The Foxes were a little taken aback that I did at last want to find out what was happening in the war - now it's over!

I was dying to know if Willy was THE GUARD who had been handed the note by the first witness and the murdered man, Rettig. I couldn't ask out straight. I wasn't sure I could ask it at all. Willy would be at huge risk from anyone with German sympathies, if ever he were identified.

Thinking about where his sympathies might really lie, but careful not to alienate my valued informant, I turned his own note of name and address to him and pointed to his surname - Kohnstamm. It seems pretty German to me.

He chewed his lips looking into my eyes. 'Mm?' he said, nodding. He squeezed his nose and took a look around. Sipped his beer. Crunched up his paper cockle-cup.

'Mum's from London you know. Came back...' he clutched his forehead as if to draw out a memory, '... in the thirties. Widow you know. Dad...'

'Yes,' I said.

'Mum had a tough time as an English woman in Germany during the last bash.'

'She will have, poor lass.'

'Married her beau 1920. Rabbi' (whispered) 'wanted her to convert, but they ignored that and married anyway. Love ... all's fair in love...'

'...and war,' I said. 'Bit it isn't is it?'

'Not for you, eh?' he said.

'She came back, your Mother,' I said. 'Not so good for...'

He looked at me to go on, but I didn't. He nodded. 'Rabbi! Mm? I felt better as a Jew in a German school, than I did as a German in the English public school she sent me to, I can tell you that.' He took a very deep breath. 'So I asked to leave and went to work in Uncle's leather factory in Wales.' He laughed and said, 'Love and War, Eric!'

I looked at my finger and twisted my wedding ring around. 'Love and War, Willy.' I didn't go into any detail, except to say I was meeting my wife for tea afterwards.

'Kathleen Evans. Met her whilst doing gas masks, drill, stirrup pumps etcetera. Then I got called up and she became a teacher in Devon.'

'Love letters?'

He pursed his lips.

'Not fair,' I said. I moved him on "You joined up.'

'Yes, funny that,' I only got as far as here. On the train to training, Ha! I saw a poster asking for native German speakers and the rest, as they say, is history.'

'You mean...'

'Yes, this is as far as I got. I've been at Lodge Moor as Interpreter ever since.' he pointed at one of the cuttings. 'They did escape you know.'

'But they were ... being tried in London!'

'You didn't keep up with it Eric! Schmittendorf and Kuehne were hung at Pentonville a fortnight ago - 16th November.'

I was shocked. I shouldn't have been - what else could I expect in war?

'They were a vicious pair, and with ardent Nazism, life seems meaningless - now there is.'

Most would obviously agree with Willy.

'So some did escape from the tunnel?'

'No, no! We knew all about it. There's always someone plotting escape, but we are almost always onto it, keeps them occupied - boredom is our real enemy. We didn't need the note Schmittendorf and Kuehne thought had given them away, sadly for poor Rettig. He was a good man, in the wrong place at the wrong time. I had already got what we needed,' he looked down and seemed to take something out of an inside pocket.

I couldn't see anything, perhaps he changed his mind.

He went on, 'We have three separate wired camps in there, you know, we have to keep the Blacks away from the Whites, not...'

'Yes, I know about the categories,' I said.

'I told their camp leader to get Rettig out, and we'd move him away from the Nazis, but ... well the Leader himself might feel safer keeping well in with, er, his Nazi fellows!'

'All's fair?' I got up to get another drink without asking Willy. I asked the barman if he had anything special to celebrate Christmas and returned to the smiling Willy with two glasses of pre-war Port. We cheered each other and warmth spread inside out. I asked him about his de-mob and he said he was needed more now that the fighting was over. The priority of the British Government, is to stamp out all notions of Nazism; we have to get them not only agreeing to, but understanding and accepting the benefits of democracy. They won't get home until they do. So there is a large camp-full of Nazis up there on Lodge Moor, who are going to be there a good while yet.

I mentioned Carburton Camp, and he was surprised I knew about it. He informed me that their translator, Henry Faulk was making a name for himself nationally.

We laughed about him daring to ask for the escapees from Bridgend, which is of course a location Willy is personally familiar with, but not since he had joined up.

My addition of Norton Cuckney to the mix led him to ask about my Objection - Christian?

'No, simply human,' I had to say.

He nodded and passed his hand across the table for me to shake. There was something in it: a tiny piece of paper.

I gave him a querulous look.

'Now see here,' he said, almost as a threat, 'That is a very personal Christmas present to you. But you must not know who it is from.'

I felt it might just flair up on my hand. It is a small piece of paper, folded over. Grubby too. This is it:

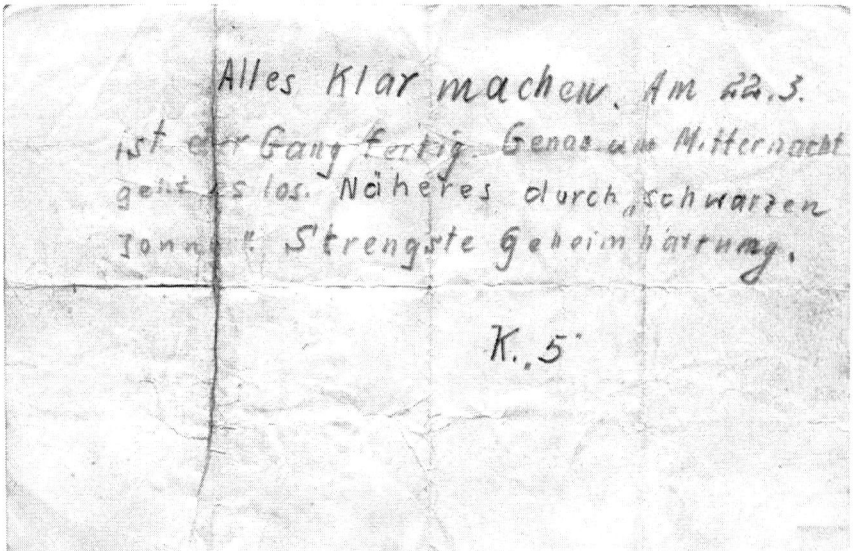

He then handed me another sheet on which he had written clearly what it said in German and in translation:

Alles klar machen. Am 22.3
ist der Gang fertig. Genau um Mitternacht
geht es los. Näheres zum „schwarzen
Jonne". Strengste Geheimhaltung K.5"

To make everything clear. On 22 March
ready to go. It begins exactly at midnight.
More details from "black
Jonne". Strictest secrecy. K. 5"

He told me "Black Jonne" and K."5" are code-names of two of the plotters.

'On their own,' Willy continued in his firmest voice, 'these are two pieces from a children's game. Put together with me, they could get me killed. However, they are also no use to me, but, am I right, pretty exciting for you?'

He could probably hear my heart beating over the hullabaloo in the bar. 'Thank you, thank you, Willy,' I said. 'You can trust me. It is a little piece of treasure which I will bury along with my memoir ... one which I am writing purely for ... my children, which of course we all hope will come along, eh? Kathleen is it?'

'Evans. Kathleen Evans, yes.'

'You write?'

His bitten lip, said not, so I stood, offered my hand and said, 'Then do so, Willy, before someone else snatches her up.' I spied a last drop of Port in the bottom of my glass, thanked him profusely, and after more Christmas greetings, promising to 'do this again', I dramatically lifted the glass and said 'now to *mia innamorata*!'

Bit of Italian for you there, Bella Mummy.

69μ

Yes I did go across to Dore, but as I was almost in town I decided I had better just pop in to see Mam.

Arriving at Dore Moor sooner than I expected, I was all of a tremble. I really did not know what to expect, though I had dropped Mummy a simple note to expect me.

It was a typical December early twilight. No lights were yet lit in the house. Had everyone gone out to avoid me? Helmet removed, a shiver of chill added to my quakes of fright. I was wuthering on the heights. I harkened to eventually hear movement within. The door creaked ajar. I suddenly was Cathy: 'Oh Mummy, let me in! I'm out on the moors. It's Eric!'

I did stumble in ... into Mummy's arms. I'm ashamed to admit it, but she did have to catch my fall.

I cried, didn't I?

We stumbled towards the parlour together, Mummy dragging a table lamp to the floor trying to find the switch with the hand she really needed to keep hold of me.

Once I was on an upright chair, she switched on a ceiling light, turned and stood with a hand over her mouth. 'Home from the war, Eric?' was barely audible.

She pulled herself together, thrust her hands towards me saying 'flannel', and disappeared out of the door, returning, I don't know when, to cover my face with a warm, wet cloth.

Shocked, I drew it gently down, catching a breath as the edge left my lip. I hadn't realised.

She looked out of the window. 'Have you fallen off your b...?' She had noticed the car. She drew another dining chair to sit facing and ministering to my wounds, shaking her head and tutting.

This was good. My trembling stopped. I could never have expected such a caring welcome. Mama and Papa were not in evidence.

She inspected my cheek. 'Women, Eric?' she said and almost laughed. She touched it. I jumped - it really did smart.

I started to speak and realised that a fat lip made me sound like an idiot. I did laugh. 'It's nothing.' I sat back and with both hands gave my face a proper wipe with the flannel and let out a huge sigh of relief. I shook my shoulders down and took a good look at my poor, frightened wife.

'I am alright,' I said. 'It really is nothing. This is not why I was such a wreck just then...' I stood and lifted her up to face me.

Didn't we both just smile for 25 hours?

She broke the spell. 'Tea!' and returned very shortly with a prepared tray. While she was out I noticed that the fire she must have only just lit, was managing to flicker unaided, as was a red candle on the mantelpiece. She hadn't been quite ready for my early arrival!

'Home from the war? War wounds, eh?' I said with my mouth full of a delicious ham and tomato sandwich. 'Who would not have guessed?'

It was time to explain myself.

Possibly out of habit, I parked Alec's car in a different, neighbouring street. (I'm not sure it mattered to the Tribunal any longer if I visited my Mother's house from my exile.) Rounding the corner I was lost in thought of the great escape, and my intrepid, now fearful, friend.

Bang. I saw stars. I had walked into a lamp post. But now it was flailing at me, caught my cheek, my lip. Now screaming 'What did you do in the war, you coward?' Her anger spent, she deflated onto my chest.

I blinked to catch up with the last few seconds, and took hold of the distraught lass, one from my class at school. I took a breath of her, expecting eau do Cologne, at least carbolic. It was not pleasant. Sweat, and perhaps stale beer. Had she been walking the streets?

It took a firm hand under her chin to look into her tear-stained face, but she would not look me in the eye. She mumbled to the pavement, I'm sure she said 'My Johnny's ... not coming marching home, *gasp*, again.'

I fell flat onto the road - she had head-butted me!

After a moment of recollection, I rolled onto my front, onto all-fours and crawled to the lamp post to drag myself up, just as the pilot set the mantel aglow.

Quarter of an hour drive to pull myself together seemed preferable to startling Mam. I didn't think of it startling my darling. I was more worried whether or not she would open the door to me, or worse - if it were her dragon.

Pina: after more than three years of 'she loves me, she loves me not' - she loves me.

I love her. I always have.

70μ

The war really is over, and my battle with Mummy and her family need continue no more. Those of us who remain, must pick up the pieces we do have. Many will count the cost, mostly those who have paid - with the life of a father, a husband, a son.

Not the war profiteers.

This Christmas I must make an effort of love and care, not wallow in the self-imposed oblivion of last year. I gained nothing from that.

Alec, Sally and Barbara, with Palmiro have been my family.

Cousin Queenie, cared about me. Still does, but she really will have a new life, a totally different life from now on.

Enemies become friends. Yes they are: Palmiro and Luca, with the wider Italian community are joined by Germans - Bernhard and Günter.

My Christmas list - 'Peace on earth'. We can hope. We must hope.

Joe Bennett - I just hope his destroyer has not hit any mines, and he can get back down his mine at Thoresby.

Mr and Mrs Queenie and Jack Saunders!

The farming community including Hardys and Walkers at Gringley, Taskers at Wheatley, Harrises at Misterton; and especially Lesley Marshall at Mattersey and Charlie Gregory and family at Leverton. How about Mr Tractor - young Duckie from Tuxford?

I dare send a card to the Governor's and staff at Strangeways - well they did do well for me, and seemed to appreciate my motives more than I expected the Conscientious Objector Tribunal to.

Prof Mellanby deserves hearty wishes up there in the Microbe research place in Broomhill. I nearly died for him ... for my country, actually. A few of the CO lads - and lasses.

And poor Gina Christmas. I haven't had a reply from my get well card, so I'll ... yes I'll take a hamper up to her family, I think. Quite touched me.

Josie, husband or not: the library staff do provide a port... I bet she's had some offers.

71μ

I decided to chance breaking through the fog we are having almost everyday and went over to Thorne. There I met Queenie basking in the love of her new husband. It was not a time for quizzing Jack over his war experience, but Queenie had set me up to meet his brother Harold, who was also home on a short leave break. He's a POW camp guard in Shropshire.

We took a stride out to sample some of south Yorkshire's fresher air, while he quizzed me about my experience as a CO. I had to tell him that I had had very little to do with the system, beside Strangeways - he whistled at that - and the occasional fat lip and white feather, at which he nodded.

I told him of Willy's recent update, at which his eyebrows shot up and he took a quick look around to see if there were any walls with ears. 'He told you that?' He shook his head.

It is a state secret, so writing this, I scratched my head wondering if I had let any cats out of bags. No, I had only told him that Willy was the translator at the camp where the murder was.

Harold was obviously keen to top that, and told me of an incident he got caught up in: after a couple of roll calls, a German POW was missing and of course that caused a hunt, but to no avail. One day the kitchen staff complained about the drains. The stench became unbearable around the camp. The drains were found to be blocked with raw meat and bones ... human. Poor bloke had been put among the wrong lot.

I didn't follow this at first - he had left out a lot of explanation in referring to a *wrong lot*. I thought of poor Rettig who was murdered at Lodge Moor.

Harold laughed and realised I probably wouldn't know anything about what he was saying. (He was wrong, but I didn't tell him that.)

This was similar to the Lodge Moor incident, but Harold was working at one of the huge 'cages' - Kempton Racecourse - sorting the POWs into the risk categories A,B,C - White, Grey and Black.

I wondered how he got that job and he held three fingers to his arm. 'Got made up to Sergeant because of my knowledge of the German language.'

'But you are a CO?' I said.

'Ah, yes. NCC.'

'Non Combatant Corps. I have a few friends who joined that and ... ended up on the battlefield?'

'Yes. A few did decide the Nazis were nasty enough to fight!' he said. 'There was a bit of pressure: help out with medical; then transport; to transporting munitions...' he chewed his lip. 'Anyway, I was put on a camp where we took new German prisoners in. We 'interview' them and split them into the categories. We can quickly tell who are Nazis and who are not.'

'A bit dangerous,' I said. 'There must have been mistakes made.'

Harold coughed. He nodded. 'That's where the *wrong lot* came in.'

'Put an appeaser in with the warmongers, eh?'

'Exactly. But in accordance with the correct procedure, a trial was held.' He twisted his mouth before continuing, 'Not knowing who the culprits were, we found a man guilty and he was punished.'

'How the heck did you find that out, with hundreds of blokes?'

He kicked a stone and said 'We picked the one who caused the most trouble.'

They say all's fair in love and war. It is not true. But it is what Harold means: the wrong chap was a recently captured enemy and he still liked to cause trouble, so deserves a punishment...

Harold moved quickly on to his current experience at Sherifhales in Shropshire, a Camp like Norton Cuckney or Carburton, perhaps - trying to re-educate the Nazional Socialists into democratic ways.

'D'ya like music?' he said. 'Bit of Beethoven?'

'Of course. Not averse to a bit of swing, too.'

'I play the German POWs recordings of Mendelssohn, to show them that Jews aren't all bad!' he said, lightening up. He rubbed his hands together, savouring the moment and leant in to tell me, 'We get out to neighbours' places for a bath and Sunday dinner sometimes (met a lovely girl). Dad's got a great collection of records. I like to let three or four of the prisoners dress in UK battle dress so they can go to listen to concerts in his cellar. We'd even listen to the Berlin Philharmonic Orchestra.'

I sucked my teeth and raised an eyebrow. 'Fraternising?'

'Aye - imprisonable offence, but I've got the keys to the gaol!' he laughed.

'Going back to Kempton,' I said, 'How do the cages work? A racecourse is a pretty big place to secure.'

'We don't use the whole place - buildings and a couple of hundred tents in a prisoners' compound, double perimeter fence, guard towers. Our Guards' compound had about 20 huts. It's only a reception camp - they don't stay long. You must know about Doncaster racecourse?'

I didn't, but I'd heard of York.

'Well - same thing there, too. Rush has died down now, of course. Think they've cleared the racecourses for peacetime racing to resume. The serious Blacks are held in the big standard camps like Lodge Moor...'

'And Nether Headon?' I said.

He frowned. 'I think that's more like our Shropshire camp, isn't it? Fairly peaceable whites, with perhaps a few greys open to democratic persuasion?'

I thought so, but it was good to get an insider's view.

We went on to agree that we can't have resentment left in these fellows, to be building up for another twenty years, when they return to try to thrash us again. We Conchies have got to 'do our bit.'

72µ

I stopped in on Charlie Gregory in South Leverton. He was surprised to see me, expecting me to go home as soon as the war finished.

Not the soldiers; not the POWs; not me.

As I might have expected, he told me one of his funny stories:

He said he had a group of Italians who came over to help in May. After his experience with the olive picking gang, he would rather have had Germans - he thinks. So he teased this lot: he showed them the picture of Mussolini and his mistress hanging.

He said they wouldn't believe it - it's only propaganda. 'No Boss,' they said, 'Strong Fasci!'

Over a cuppa, young Betty told me they have a famous pianist at the camp. She looked over at the instrument.

'Can you play it?' I said. I didn't ask how famous, because as you know, I'm no music aficionado.

She demured - she's only a kid.

'Go on,' I nudged, 'give us a tune?'

She didn't say she would. Instead she told me that the piano tuner had been taken ill when he came recently - Charlie had to run him back home in his car before the job was done.

Bernhard is now a regular worker for Charlie, who's provided him with a bike to get over every day. Bernhard heard of the piano problem and told of the shows the Prisoners put on - and Rudi the camp librarian who is also the musical director.

He might tune the piano.

I have found that POWs are ever keen to please.

Betty went bright red at the mention of the name Rudi and Charlie pointed at her, smiling.

All the POWs need something to do after work. Of course they do want to learn English and they also engage in as many arts and crafts as they possibly can. I told you about the lovely handbags made from Rufford Abbey tapestry.

The Germans are apparently keen on amateur dramatics, so indeed it came to pass - Rudi came to tune the piano.

Betty had wanted nothing to do with the Germans, you will recall she refused to sit at table with them?

Her resolve against the enemy within began to crumble when Bernhard brought Rudi Stenger from the camp. When it was done Charlie invited him to 'give us a tune'. Betty could hear the ivories tinkling - no, was that not a gramophone record?

It was not long before Rudi was showing Betty a few pieces on the piano, so I said 'come on then',

She protested, but Charlie nodded me to egg her on.

It is obviously a very tricky Chopin piece that's played on only the black keys. She made a great fist of the trilling right hand then said she could only play the hands separately.

I held up my one finger and no tunes it could play ... so 'go on then'.

The left plays a sort of dancing tune. Her finale was each run together left, right; left right; da-daaa! Worked beautifully.

Oh Pina, will you ever play, will you sing, will you dance for me?

Mention of camp activities makes me think back to Carburton and the Bridgend great escape: I haven't heard about any Italians trying to escape. I suppose they can simply walk off if they like ... but they don't.

Willy's horror story at Lodge Moor was all about an escape and there are regular titbits in the newspapers about German escapes now, and I've just remembered another!

It's before all this, before the shop floor, before Strangeways, and before Egmanton - 1941. That makes it before the proper camps and the Italians coming over. But there was a camp at Redmires as they called it: Dad's old training camp on Lodge Moor.

Someone brought in a cutting from the Express headed 'HEEL CLICK TRAPS NAZI', and then 'Staff reporter, Sheffield Monday'. That caused a buzz around the works, of course several people claimed to know the chap - after the fact.

A buzz about a bus, Pina.

It said a German Prisoner who had escaped from a North of England camp, (Ooh we did have fun guessing where exactly that was! Keep Mum Mr Express) had been successfully recaptured by the keen spy watching of a Bus Conductor.

The German was wearing a sports jacket and flannels, and I'm not sure if they mentioned a boater. (A little too British I think. Sheffield isn't quite Oxford!). He had an attaché case with him. They did say he spoke very good English when he handed over a florin for his ticket.

On receiving the ticket he clicked his heels sharply on force of habit.

The inscrutable Mr Spittle - I remember that was the Conductor's name - didn't react immediately, but casually went down to the driver and told him to stop when he saw a policeman.

The young German couldn't produce an identity card and tried to run away, but in the strong arm of the law, he eventually confessed.

The report had a footnote about the attaché case. Don't laugh, but guess what was in the case.

Microfilm?

Maps?

Documents with 'Top Secret' stamps?

No, the attaché case contained chocolate.

I missed out on the plashing project in my abject state last autumn. I'll have to finish laying a respectable strip of hedge - it's a war project after all - and the war is over.

73μ

Christmases at Christmas - Gina wouldn't see me, as her dad sensitively put it 'she's not a pretty sight.'

I said I thought it was her legs.

'Them too', he said. 'She can't come down stairs,' but she thanked me kindly. 'Me and her Mam do too. She's on t'mend, like. It's very nice of you to tek an interest in t'poor lass.'

He shut the door in my face.

I'm getting used to farming folk. I think.

74μ
January 1946

Christmas came and quickly moved into the New Year of 1946 and fresh hopes for the peace ... and home.

I'm not sure any of us dare speak the words peace and home, just in case they run away.

I had a really lucky near miss with my hedge. I've really got into the swing of it and in my enthusiasm to split a very thick hawthorn I swung the billhook back so fiercely and hooked the back of my head. It wasn't a helmet that saved me, but the very thick woollen hat my Mam had knitted for my first Christmas here. More accurately it was the Pompon Barbara topped it off with just this Christmas.

A little bump and a tinier cut. Lucky. A thirty yard strip of hedge done - and, though I say it myself, very respectable it is, too.

Now in the greenhouses daily with Palmiro - Mr Greenfingers.

75μ
February 1946

Oh my goodness - Palmiro has gone!

We did not speak the word 'home', but it looks like Palmiro is on his way back to all the LaBancas in Latronica, Potenza.

What will he find? Seven young men in his family - can all have survived?

Straight away panic hit the household.

Eric, will you see to the greenhouses?

Though it is obvious, I did not see it coming. Palmiro has been teaching me some of his 'Green Finger' tips.

Palmiro where are you?

He has been recalled to camp - not to Nether Headon, but to Little Carlton. I had heard of it, but that is all. Apparently it is one of Headon's 'Hostels', as they call them. It must be just to gather the men all together from their different billets - a few days. A week?

I can water the plants of course. Feed them? Mostly seedlings which will need planting out - but how far apart? Exactly when?

Panic over. Sorry about that. You will hear of somebody setting a cat among the pigeons. The cat in this case is a big fat question mark. We have all flown up in the air and no one can see the cat.

We had Palmiro back for Sunday Lunch. He is not quite sure what is happening except that they are being got ready to go home. Apparently they have to be sent home to their Regimental Headquarters, because they are in fact still soldiers in their own forces.

It's like Queenie's Jack - he still has to complete the nine years he signed up for.

...and me. Three years until May this year ... *somebody* signed me up for.

Alec Fox has really come to depend on us, and gangs of Italian Labour, as and when. Sally has come to depend on a constant flow of fresh and interesting vegetables and herbs from the greenhouses. She has also been trading them and putting the money by for Palmiro. She doesn't know how he can be given it, because the system is that what the POWs earn is banked for them in their own country. They get vouchers - Toy Town money - which they can spend in the camp Mess and on visiting mobile shops. Of course he is allowed - expected to be given - 'pocket money' to live day to day in billets.

I got him to walk me round the greenhouses with comments and tips as to how I can help the family with the new post-war produce. He pinched out weeds, pricked out a couple of dozen tomato plants, telling me how to pot on, etc. He must have picked up my sense of inadequacy, too. He looked me in the eye - a quite rare event for the shy man - and reiterated his byword: 'there's always a way, Eric.'

I am encouraged.

Then he wiped his hands on his new uniform! Shock and horror. Apparently he believes the Brits have called the lads back to camp to smarten and feed them up. They actually aren't routinely sending them out to work - and a complete set of new clothes. It's the same POW uniform, British battledress - less patches of course - but with the Italy Star on the collars. Ironic, that the best clothes he's had in almost six years a prisoner, he will rip off his back and burn as soon as he gets home.

Palmiro and I are both paid the Farmers' Union agreed rate for our work, less board and lodging. I can keep mine and with nothing much to spend it on beside Maisie Matchless, I've got a tidy sum put by. So officially has Palmiro, but...

Palmiro did a bit of hopping from one foot to the other and drew Sally's concern. 'Whatever is the matter, Palmiro?' she said, as if there wasn't a list of things that could be agitating the lad. He did his almost habitual combing of fingers up the sides of his head, fluffing up his now *very* substantial head of clown curls. He coughed. He searched the floor.

Eventually is spilled out - could he have a proper hot bath ... for his hair.

The girls really reined in the laughter that was bursting out of them ... but of course.

We have a tub in our converted hay loft, and we can have hot water, but we don't have a bath ... with taps.

Apparently the curls are like his trade mark, uniquely identifying him, and he wants to go home and be recognised as the same boy who disappeared from home six years ago. Hopefully his own regiment won't insist on a short-back-and-sides before they let him home.

I didn't let him see me shaking my head.

Anyway, I'm not sure I can meet the horticultural standard set by Palmiro. And what will happen when (if) I go ... in May?

Palmiro was actually quite anxious. They have not been given a date and more men are being brought in each day. It seems to him that the British are gathering together a 'full complement', whatever that may be - possibly a full train- or boat-load - before releasing any.

He is not the only one to be anxious: Alec needs to find out how he is fixed for staff on the farm, so he is determined to get together with some of his union friends as soon as possible to lobby War Ag - now NAEC - for some support.

I've told Mam so much about Palmiro that she wants to meet him before he goes. Alec is letting me borrow the car again to bring her over. Fingers crossed they don't send them home soon, then.

Oh dear, Eric - that is not what Palmiro wants now, is it?

Let's see - che sera, sera - Mummy?

77µ

Now I am interested in the war, or more precisely how our masters are organising the peace.

Here at Egmanton, the Fox family obviously do take a newspaper, but after I have actually rejected the offers to read it over the past two years, it is a little embarrassing to suddenly be an avid reader. So it's off to the library for me.

The records at Tuxford - only a village library after all - are not so great, so I headed to Retford.

Josie was there and seemed very pleased to see me. Perhaps she is like that with all the men ... people. She is a very nice woman.

While I pored over Nationals to find out what was going on with all the displacements across Europe (truly shocking), and how they are all being fed and sheltered (hardly at all, and that with great difficulty, Red Cross seeming to be doing a great job), she rooted through Retford Times records to see what it has to say about Headon, or any POWs. She, like me is appalled to discover that there is actually no mention of Camp 52, Nether Headon, at all - still not, even though the war is now over. Isn't that all very odd?

Not even incidents, such as the 'Heel Click Traps Nazi' report from Sheffield in the Express.

78μ

Mam and I (not Mummy) took Palmiro out and I took a photo:

You can probably guess that's Palmiro with Mam, Eric, Sally and Barbara. Don't they look nice?

They are.

I took the chance to do a recap on his experience: how was it for him?

He raised his eyebrows, bit his lip, tutted. 'What really happened there,' he shook his head, not really wanting to go on.

I selfishly said nothing, hoping he would.

He scratched the back of his head, looked at me studying him, raised a brow. 'We went so far into Egypt, but we couldn't go any further, because we didn't have any transport. We couldn't go any more on foot, because it's too far to go.' He held his hands out in a plea. His voice went up too. 'As I said, the Italian army decided to gather more lorry, more tank, more equipment, and make another push, but by then we had to push back because the British come for us. But we could not face them, shoot them, anything 'cos we had no ... just walking back to Libya, to Bardia, because more safer there. But British cut us out, 'cos Bardia's in a corner. Cut the road out to *Tob*-ruk *(gesticulates a chop)*, we didn't have one shot, we just got captured.'

That's all I was going to get.

'Africa not so good.' He cleared his throat. 'Wisbech,' he shrugged and we chuckled about throwing the dredgings back; Headon Camp good; and he was not about to criticise anybody: 'you win some you lose some'. (I took that to be about friends, not battles.)

He's a bit anxious about going home. News has been patchy, and none good. He suspects, as do we all, that his country and his town will be in a mess, trampled and fought over by Germans, Americans, Poles, Brits and men from all over the empire - not to mention Germany's and Italy's empires - that's what makes it 'World War', I suppose.

What of his brothers? Nobody has written of any deaths. Are they simply being kind as he is far away in prison?

We suspect most of the family will have little literacy, except perhaps his brother who is a Friar.

His parting gesture to Barbara, nay to us all, was a little nursery rhyme. Totally out of character for the Palmiro we all love, he mimicked a butterfly with his hands and sang:

> Farfallina, bella e bianco - butterfly beautiful and white - I understood;

> Fly, flies and never gets tired - I guess.

> Fly here - Barbara's left ear;

> Fly there - her right ear

> And goes to rest right here.

He touched his thumbs on her nose,
fluttered his fingers in front of her eyes,
then closed them on her cheeks,
parted his thumbs
and pecked her on the tip of her nose.

I didn't see what Alec and Sally did; I had to blow my nose.

Part Five - Spring 1946

The Italians go home

79μ
Spring 1946

It's early May 1946 and Palmiro has gone home now - but Alec hears from Lesley Marshal that he has kept Luca on for a year. He sent me over to get detail from Luca who told of the change of mind - a little too late for us to keep Palmiro.

When I told Alec he was a bit irritated. So was I. How come it wasn't general knowledge that a deal could be made, a contract could be offered to men who wanted and were wanted to stay on?

Looking into it a bit, we think Lesley Marshall would have pleaded a special case. He told me that he actually and really did depend on Luca Ritucci to run his farm on his behalf. His father had bought the farm for him - would you believe, it is yet another of the Portland Estate farms: at least thirty were sold off in 1941? Makes me spit. Dukes! Not their land to sell, I don't reckon.

Anyway, I think Lesley is what is perhaps known as a 'gentleman farmer' in some quarters - his Dad might well be a Landed Gent for all I know. Duke? I can't really see him getting his hands dirty.

He told me a great tale about why he wanted Luca:

Firstly he is really worried that he won't easily get labour from returning military men, and, not putting to fine a point on it, he was worried about the calibre of men who might be foisted on him.

That made me think of Alec's reluctance to accept Germans to replace the Italians.

Would they even have any farming experience?

That, of course, made me think of what I had to offer when I arrived!

Lesley was chuckling as he went on: 'this day we were bringing in the hay - '43, a great harvest?'

I nodded.

'Well Luca was pitching hay from the cart up to the loft over there...'

'Yes you were telling me.'

He frowned. 'Oh Hahaha, yes ... the dust clears and old Luca hove back into view still pitching.' He stopped, hand over his mouth and looked me full in the face.

'Not expecting anything of his men,' I said, 'that he couldn't or wouldn't do himself.'

'Precisely. Just the sort of mettle a chap needs for his farm manager.'

Luca looks the part: hard, slightly stern, and wiry. Apparently he knows his farming too. He is also more mature, the daddy of the lads around here. Carries the degree of authority Marshal seeks in his manager.

When I got back, Alec chuntered something about 'Deddy' probably sorting things for Marshal.

80μ
Secret Date

Sally cornered me, all of a fluster. She told me I was to ring Josie Husbands. She was most apologetic, it was not Alec being mean, or Sally, I could of course use their phone - which out of courtesy I normally would not - but Miss Husbands had insisted that I ring from the Public Callbox.

All a bit worrying or...

...not! Lots of fun.

Josie, *yes you may call me Josie*, has a secret contact through her organisation, who is willing to share the dirt on the inside system of a certain other organisation that I have been looking into for several years. We will refer to him as Hannay, Richard Hannay and whatever record I make must use this name, as it will easily be taken as a bit of playfulness if it falls into the wrong hands.

I am to be Paul Temple and refer to Josie simply as Stevie, and we can appear to be very friendly.

Mixing up our thrillers there - 'The 39 Steps' and a wireless detective serial. All good fun, though.

We are to dress up, because we are treating Mr Hannay to dinner at his Hotel, The Pheasant on Carolgate, Retford, one Friday in 1946 - the date of which I must not record in case the information can be traced back to our original informant.

It would be best if I could call for Josie/Stevie at her home on Bridgegate, and even come up and meet her Mother. We would walk the short distance to the Hotel where we would be shown to our table.

Though I was to be presentable, I was not to draw any attention. If I needed to travel in my motorcycle clothing, I could change into a suit at their house.

She was giggling the whole time she spoke - whispered - somewhat out of the character I had come to know. Warm, smiley, but not giggly.

The telephone call did end with me not really knowing what Josie actually meant. I did hope that the 'other organisation I have been looking into' means the POW camp system, but all the girly giggling, not to say dressing up, gave me a feeling she might be setting me up for a party in the blackout.

So it befell, that we were not even shown to a table at the Pheasant, which was more of a commercial hotel for travelling salesmen - not to say Spivs - who might stay over a night or two, expenses in these tightened times, not stretching to much luxury.

A happy chap waved us over to his table set for three, and very soon dropped the cheery demeanour in preference for a clipped military one. It was clear that Stevie had briefed him on my status as a colleague in her library service with a working brief on local history. The war is over and people do - and will more so - want to know detail of what we, the Bassetlaw and

Nottinghamshire people, did in the war. That Nether Headon is a Prisoner of War Camp is no longer a secret, so 'are its workings, Mr Hannay?'

His eyes did smile momentarily.

He assured himself with a guarded scan of the dining room, that a couple of loan travellers were engrossed in their day's accounts; a few spivs were noisily engaged with their Molls and each other; and a family of an older couple and perhaps their daughter and her beau, were far enough away - literally and metaphorically - for him to speak fairly openly, only ever referring to the places mentioned by pointing to a list.

He ordered us a drink. (On us, Josie had made it quite clear - on me, she hoped? But of course.) He then set off on the importance to the world that peace depended on democracy, and that these foreign chappies in our midst - *many of them just children, don't you know*, know nothing of our Mother of all Parliaments, or the benefits thereof.

Josie, nodding at me, assured him that we, in the library service after all Mr Hannay, are comparatively well informed.

'But it's the system, we are not so well up on,' I interjected. 'What is happening, now the war is over? I understand that Mr Attlee is pretty keen to ... punish?'

His tongue went into his cheek at the mention of our Prime Minister. He sort of changed the subject - to himself.

His role, (he looked around the room) is to assess the Re-education of the POWs, who will not be allowed home whilst still holding any views of a Nazi or Fascist inclination. His pronunciation of "Narzey" emulating the recently sacked War Prime Minister did indicate to me where his own political sympathies might lie.

He had a bottle of wine to Stevie's lemonade and my half pint of supposedly Best Bitter, and became relaxed, voluble and expansive very soon. This state was aided by the swift departure of most of the diners who had started well before our arrival.

The Prisoners have to be screened and 'carded' - 'and if I may round all figures up or down, Mr Temple?' he said there were up to 2000 held at (he points) Camp 52, almost a half are off site - at what are referred to as Hostels, plus 150 Billetees.

Only a very few have not been 'carded' at some point, but this week about half were unscreened, showing only about 25 Nazi and 130 whites. They do give them - on an index card I imagine - shades of grey from A to C, white to black, plus and minus. So that leaves over 800 B+, B, B- making the camp's 'present complexion grey.'

The Pheasant was not the sort of establishment where we might expect anything 'special' (that was not on ration), so neither Josie nor I fared as well as we might at our own tables, but Mr Hannay was not for losing out on his treat, making up in volume - 'never mind the quality, feel the width, eh?' as he shovelled a forkful of bullet-peas into his mouth.

He told me that the camp was founded on 13th October 1944 with 845 German POWs, which I noticed he wrote simply 'PW'. These were augmented by - I was able to ask for fairly accurate figures - during '45 by 320 from other camps; then in May and June '46 by 750 from America and Canada.

I coughed and pointed at my notes. 'Other camps? Please?' He chewed his cheek a second and showed me Haltwhistle, Warwickshire, Malton, and Leeds. I didn't want to push my luck, but felt the need to show knowledge of the rest of the Empire, asked about other territories, South Africa, for instance?

'Ities,' he said, 'gorn home. Thirty odd Germans have been let go, too.'

I told him of Palmiro. He nodded. And Bernhard - 'billetee eh?'

He coughed, to avoid choking on the latest mouthful I think, and then spluttered out, 'hundred and twenty odd been sent out to Carlton-in-Lindrick. No huts there you know, all put up in the Hall and farm buildings - but not one of my camps.'

The Re-education is apparently dependent for its success on having able white German leaders of some quality, decidedly lacking most of the time, causing the earliest attempt in May '45 to be dissolved: they had called themselves "the Anti-Fascist Front", and included a communist firebrand, whom the chaplain asked to be transferred out. That meant the end of communist influences at this camp.

Poor 'Stevie' laughed when the chap said that the Interpreter (an Englishman) is 'a quiet, efficient man *whose personality is nil*.'

He was to be demobbed anyway.

Another abortive attempt was made at Re-education before a few POWs took it on themselves and organised lectures which slowly caught on. That was before the two USA intakes arrived. This consisted of a large number of *young, discontented, lethargic men*, ('Stevie' hid in her hankie), a number of whom clung to Nazi ideas. It had a distinctly adverse effect on camp morale and its political complexion.

Hannay then surprised me with numbers: in the Main Camp at (points Nether Headon) there are 56 men in each hut - that's sixteen more than when Palmiro was there: he had said twenty each side. Of course needs must, and there has been a huge influx of Germans straight from the battlefield in 44/5. No wonder they sent the Italians home in the spring - plus the Americans and Canadians don't want to be feeding the Germans any longer than they need to.

And just last month (April) 'Hostelisation' was started.

He looked over to see that my notes were not too specific and told us about the ins and outs: at the time the 'Americans' arrived, ones who had been identified as properly white since their incarceration in late 44, were cleared out of the main camp and distributed to the other sites: 60 at Caunton Hostel, 130 at Little Carlton and 300 at Wigsley.

I tried very hard to not look surprised, but he was looking at his notes, so he didn't see. Wigsley! No one has mentioned it. It's apparently much bigger than even Little Carlton which I took Palmiro back to. That has upwards of 20 huts. I couldn't ask where the hell Wigsley is.

I did play a ruse clarifying 'Carlton-*in-Lindrick*?' which he pooh-poohed as 'belonging to Blyth.'

That threw me. As I was being careful to not show I knew too much. I would have to sort these out later with Josie.

He shoved his dinner plate away - and into mine - and sat back. He picked up the wine bottle and shook it. There was a glassful or so in it, so I sipped my flat awful glass-half-full and ignored his hint.

He stretched over to the next table and picked up a menu. 'Pudding Stevie?'

She smiled sweetly. 'Education, Mr Hannay? What's the book situation?'

He took a swig, smacked his lips, and looked at her. I could see her restraining herself expecting him to say something like *buggers can't read!* but in the end he parried by saying he would come to that - he would share his concerns as his recommendations.

Other outrageous remarks - particularly to Stevie's ears, included referring to the mature POWs as 'old stock' and 'infected by ex USA POWs with... lethargy'; 'communist tendencies lying dormant'; POWs 'prepared to support any party that offers the best immediate material benefits'; the under 25s are 'uncooperative and uninterested in re-education.'

Stevie did opt for a suet pudding with custard, and remarked how wonderful it would be to get bananas again. We all went with her choice. There is flour, and eggs, sugar and milk - what could go wrong?

She led on to what could reasonably be expected from the youngsters.

Hannay ran 39 steps onto the pitch, saying there are five sports clubs. The RC Padre has started a youth club. It attracts 50 members. They are expected to listen to lectures. Given by himself and two other white POWs.

He took a breath and nodded to himself. He turned to personalities in the camp, which is difficult for me to report on not being able to name names, but he did say that the camp leader is a 'typical German civil servant - not a great personality. Another pre-1933 Social Democrat holds strong anti-Nazi views.' But high praise was given to the RC Padre 'the most popular man among all the POWs in the camp ... a typical Bavarian' (Stevie pulled a long face - are we supposed to know what one of them is?) but redeemed by putting himself above denominational differences.

They also have a programme of talks given by touring lecturers.

Stevie broke into the soliloquy by asking if by Germans?

He had to think, but of course, there are not many of us English who can make them understand.

Stevie thought to snare him and asked how they could know that these weren't fomenting yet more Nazi sentiment ... especially in the light of the interpreter's *lack of personality.*

Hannay sniffed and licked his lips. He wiped them on his napkin. There are other whites who would object. He had mentioned some with strong anti-Nazi feelings.

So what sort of lectures? Stevie, like me, must be picturing these lethargic, unco-operative and young warriors even managing to sit in a 'lecture' for more than five minutes.

He coughed and suggested it is mostly the 'old stock' who take up the talks.

What about?

'"The Theory of the Totalitarian state." Erm ... "What can Germany learn from Swiss Democracy?" - very popular and well attended. And Yes, "The legend of the Prussian mission and Germany's mission in the world."'

Stevie and I looked at each other impressed.

'In spite of the higher level, and some of it not easy on German ears, the audience was impressed - a lively discussion followed.'

Stevie rubbed her hands. 'How's the reading material to back it up?'

'Ah, yes, we come to you, My Dear.' He leaned towards her. 'You see the library? We have around a thousand volumes, of which we have sent a couple of hundred to Wigsley and a hundred to Little Carlton. But what is wanted is more fiction, and political literature...' He stretched his lips out and sucked his teeth. '...but German?'

She tilted her head and nodded. I thought she might ask about the guards, but having met them, I think she decided to not bother.

'Paper?' he said.

'Would they welcome older issues of the dailies, we...'

'Sorry I meant paper for their own camp magazine. It has been discontinued because of paper shortage.'

'Oh dear,' said Stevie. 'Blank paper is not something a library has much call for.'

Hannay checked she was not teasing.

Inscrutable.

He went on that a few whites at the Main Camp were eager to resume the magazine, and the keenest contributor is a worryingly very dark grey at Wigsley persistently sending in material. The Padre does daily translations from the Catholic Herald and the German interpreter publishes daily translations from the British newspapers which he borrows from 'the sergeant i/c.'

I attempted to lighten the conversation, so mentioned Betty's Rudi and the theatricals.

He didn't recognise the name, but 'Oh yes, very keen if they can get their hands on the instruments. There's the makings of a classical orchestra and,' he laughed, 'and one they call "Shrammel Music" - polka/party group - oompah?'

We both mimed - Stevie a squeezebox and I a trombone.

'Exactly. Plays mostly at private parties in the barracks. Drama groups - there are three different ones: Classical; Variety and Cabaret; Musical performances. A programme in planning will include the "Light Cavalry" and some Rubenstein. Wigsley are planning their own - and they're hoping to form a Hostel orchestra if they can find instruments.' He shook his head. 'There're 2 violinists, an accordionist, a drummer and a guitarist! Er ... Miss: they could really do with some Music sheets?'

'Oh yes, we do have that. I'll see what I can do eh? Music - the international language, what?' I haven't mentioned that Josie is actually frightfully posh - she doesn't need to act up.

He looked from Stevie to me and raised and eyebrow. 'And of love?'

I didn't dare look at Josie, I could feel the heat of her blush. She did look around to see if anyone else was in the room.

Pleased with his effect, Hannay clapped his hands and stood up. I followed suit, but Stevie stayed put. 'So in the re-education report, may we ask ... in a rounded up way, of course, what you have concluded, please ... er, Mr Hannay?'

Enjoying the opportunity to talk down, he told us that the Re-education must be intensified. *Can't let any of the Nazi blighters loose again.* They need to watch over the influence of a B- they've let out to (pointed at Wigsley, despite only us there). Seeing my reaction he added, 'Walls ... ears, Mr Temple.'

I bowed.

He wants touring lecturers to make a point of visiting the Hostels as a matter of course and a real effort be made to support the re-start of the camp newspaper. More books as mentioned, and paper.

The US and Canada contingent make up almost half the camp and urgently need the Segregation Team to come and screen them.

His true colours shone when he said that though a Protestant Padre did visit every Sunday from Camp 174 - he wanted a resident appointed, one able to serve the hostels too. (He was really irritated when I asked where that was, so he snatched my note-pad and pencil and scribbled "Norton Cuckney". I am so glad I asked.)

Finally he wants the YMCA film units more often and to visit 'at least Wigsley'. He growled to himself when he let the word out. I think that must also be another reference to Norton, which I gather is the YMCA base.

On the threshold of the Pheasant. I pulled up the collar of my gaberdine, laughed at my Stevie and set off back to her mother's. We had a few minutes over a decent cuppa - I was (quietly) offered a 'small brandy', but for the road in blackout, I wasn't so sure it was the most sensible idea. We giggled together over our subterfuge - our spying activities.

Josie threatened to tell her father that mother thought Robert Donat was a very dishy Richard Hannay in '39 Steps', 'any film actually!' adding that her mother would run more than 39 steps from tonight's stuffy actor.

Josie turned to me and brushed my hair. 'How about Paul Temple, here?' and fanning her hands under her chin, 'or his Stevie?'

They were both giggling as they waived me off with my Maisie.

81μ

Wigsley - the biggest 'camp' in Headon's area, and no one has ever mentioned it. And the nearest! I had to find it.

So in late May '46, over the Trent at Dunham and straight on along the main road to Lincoln and across to the right.

Thorney has yet another 'old Hall' - bit sad looking, no POWs hanging around. Straight on to Wigsley village. There is an aerodrome just beyond. There are huts and possibly in use as a 'Hostel', but no one in the crisp evening air had the inclination to try to guess where POWs might be.

So it was a wild goose I brought home for Sally.

At Sunday lunch I barely mentioned my folly, but it was a mouthful of pork that Alec guffawed out. 'Where'd you turn off, Eric? Not Clifton way?'

'No, next turn - down a bit of a goat track.'

He wiped his mouth and apologised to the ladies (not me). 'Ha! Sorry if you'd gone up to next turn you'd have been at it. Found out after you asked, that it's in proper huts - the pre-fab concrete sort you said they have at Headon, at the prettily named Drinsey Nook.'

More profuse apologies, but I had to admit fault in peremptorily setting off after work.

A proper little camp then, and actually almost as near to Wigsley as Wigsley aerodrome is, but in the opposite direction.

That's all we need to know for the story.

And Hannay mentioned that they had a radio, and laughed, rather too gleefully I thought, that it didn't work. 'Italian property, y' know.'

Italian Standard Camp - now holding 300 Germans?

82μ

My de-mob - end of May 1946, beyond 'the duration': a long weekend 'at home' with Mummy ... Grandmama and Grandpapa ... very uncomfortable. There is no heart in it.

Mummy has put on a little weight and her colour is up. She talked to me - well to the dogs actually - as we went around feeding them and cleaning out the kennels. The business, if you could call it that (sorry Mummy, yes it is your little business) had not been strong as people had difficulty finding work during the thirties, despite the people in the area being the most well-off in Sheffield. But the real better-off had their own servants to look after the animals.

Lovely Mummy has filled the kennels up with strays - poor bombed out creatures that have lost their families. So it's a charity which Grandpapa can certainly afford to pay for.

Can our little family live off it?

I'm not going back to grinding. Even if they'll have me. I'd have to move. Word would still get out as to why I haven't worked through the war. And their men out fighting.

Alec, went around the houses, humming and hawing about getting staff and looking me up and down.

His reluctance to take on Germans.

I rescued him.

'Look Alec,' I said, 'I realise I don't know much, well didn't when I came out of ... came to you, but I've learnt a hell of a lot from Palmiro. I could carry on for the same money ... looking after your greenhouses.' I wasn't so sure of myself so added 'I think?'

He didn't actually snatch my hand off. He talked through Marshal's arrangement with Luca, and more importantly with War Ag ... NottsAg, 'whatever it's blimmin' called.'

Of course, he hasn't been paying me, the blimmin' Army has!

That was a bit of shock. Apparently War Ag pay the farmers to have the POWs, and also pays the men. However, the Conscientious Objector Tribunals are part of Army recruitment, so the army pays the farmer for me. Silly me. Fancy not even twigging. I've been in the employ of the army all along.

Nice as it is, was, with Mummy and the dogs, I really do not want to be around Grandpapa.

Sorry.

So ... in my somewhat penniless state, and rushed into ... no idea what to do next ... the only thing I know about besides grinding is ... well, farming, Alec.

I think I was begging really.

He clapped me on the shoulder, 'No, come on Eric, you're a wonder! I'm just wondering what I will do without you ... as well as Palmiro.'

That was a relief, but I am not so sure he really thinks I am a 'wonder'. I do work hard, I believe, and I haven't really committed many blunders. I'm alright with the Germans. My fingers are a little greener.

It's a lot of money to find - three men for a small farm like ours.

I asked what other farmers are doing. What the country's doing. The men aren't piling back from the war, keen to get stuck into farming. And of course War Ag made Alec plough up many new acres to bring into food production. Rationing isn't going to stop overnight.

He nodded. 'No. No, Eric. Of course you're right ... but you won't want stay on after May ... not with your family...'

Family?

I told him things were not so good. No job to go back too, remember where I came from?

He laughed recalling Strangeways Prison.

'If you want to stay on for a bit, however long, see me over to next season, of course I will pay *you*!' he said. He pointed out that it will be a crucial harvest: 'Pathe News has called it "the most momentous harvest of all time,"' he laughed behind his hand and, giving me a coy look, went on, 'Sally, Barbara, me brother and his lads, me ... and you ... are the "food commandos"...' he snorted, 'of 1946!'

I bit my lip, but took the joke.

'Old Marshal's got his Luca to stay on, but just for a year, given him a special contract, as a civilian. I missed out on getting that for Palmiro.' He grabbed his chin. 'Don't y'know Luca's got family back in Italy, wife and a daughter - Nina, apparently.'

Of course Palmiro does have family, a big one, but not wife and kids. I pursed my lips, shaking my head. Palmiro really wanted to go home.

I told Alec it would suit me just fine to stay on 'until I get back on my feet', wherever they are.

He clapped me in the shoulder and shook me. 'Come on Eric, you're a good man.'

He almost made me feel it.

Part Six - June 1946

My Sentence ends

83μ
June 1946

Now I am a farm labourer, no longer a convict, so I am entitled to holidays. It would be obvious to many how I should spend these, but it wasn't to me.

Were you expecting me, Mummy?

You did accept, and yes we did have a lovely week in the Lake. (I nearly left it there! The Lake District was like being in a lake that first week of June - twice the national average. I am so glad that Grandpapa did 'allow' Mummy to use 'her' little car - he of course had no problem 'finding' petrol. It would have been poor Maisie, poor us, in that downpour.)

Nice little Bed and Breakfast hotel - actually the only real break from pressure for the six war years. Doesn't compare to Queenie's Jack, being shot at for 5 whole years, away from home without a break.

We had to take it gently.

Mummy's nerves are not so good. I get the impression she is ground down by Grandpapa growling like a bear with a thorn in his paw the whole time. He has, rather obviously, had to lay off men - to be honest they are women he is laying off.

He is 'expected' to take on men returning from the war, at the same time as the government is not expecting him to produce more munitions. They aren't winding down, the forces have to restock. The press are hinting that the war has not quite finished for the Ruskies who are being made out as an enemy, after all we have been through together!

Surprise, surprise, the women are none too happy about that - being put back in the kitchen. Not going to happen, I don't think. Six years hard, but regular, factory work, with good pay. The women can decide for themselves how they use it, too. So Grandpapa is in a war of his own, being shot at from both sides.

With words, though. Something he is not used to.

Not Atom bombs either.

Straight back to work, and the word is, that it could be the worst harvest on record.

Reminds me that the year after the last war was the worst plague ever - flu killed more people than the war had.

Don't be so gloomy Eric, at least the war is over.

84μ

Queenie has written a note. She's obviously had some communication with her new brother-in-law Harold Saunders.

She asked if I had read of the great escape of POWs from a Welsh camp and... wait for it ... if I had heard that it was part of plan for a mass escape of prisoners, to arm themselves and rush on London. The start would be a landing of paratroops in the capital.

I think she has put 2 and 2 together and made a few thousand in a 'fifth column' which will rise up from within the country.

My reading of the newspapers tells me that this is very unlikely given the current state of mainland Europe and what is left of the Wehrmacht.

I told you about what the press called The Great Escape, from a camp in Wales, and the POWs being brought from there to Carburton, near here.

I decided to look back at the reporting and guess what I found: the papers blamed the guards for the escape, saying that they had full knowledge of the escape from *a note apparently thrown through the fence the very night of the escape* betraying the plot.

What of Willy's note, then?

I did two things - wrote to Willy telling what Queenie had cooked up; wrote to the address Queenie gave me for Harold to ask for his clarification.

In writing to Willy I was very careful to not even hint about a note. I simply told him how daft people get - as if there are any paratroops left under Wehrmacht command!

Now that the war is over, Willy is able to say that, ever since the outbreak, there had been a fear that upon any invasion, the POWs would be released to rejoin battle. That was why the Government had originally sent all those captured before 1942 to far-flung areas of the empire. But yes, after all the men were brought over from Normandy and corralled in huge cages, senior ranks in the camp management were always on the lookout for anything that looked like co-ordination of plotters in various camps. As it happened, the Welsh escape - from Bridgend apparently - took place on 10th March 1945, where the Lodge Moor escape was a fortnight later 22nd March 1945. Not exactly co-ordinated.

The authorities were more inclined to believe that the 'rush on London' was simple wishful thinking by the unbroken, category A "Black" Nazis in the camps.

That is not to say that the Doodlebug raid on Northern England, so late in the war, did not focus the minds on the potential for an airborne/paratroop landing from a similar location still within German held land. That would be the Christmas 1944 raid Les Hardy saw and heard. I never did look it up, but if, as Willy mentioned, the Luftwaffe can send over thirty or forty bombers with V1 Doodlebugs attached, they could also send over a thousand paratroopers. He said the Fallschirmjäger are the most elite and fanatically Nazi troops they have to handle in the camps. They really have to separate them out.

Harold said the note was almost a legend: lads in the camps were always looking for some softie to beat up for giving away their plots. You'd think there was a veritable snowstorm of notes flying over the fences. He reminded me of the body parts found ... enough of that.

However, when we consider the numbers - as I've guessed there must be 300,000 of them over here - if they could overpower munitions stores, they make a very big army within.

A formidable Fifth Column.

85μ
September 1946

Alec reluctantly accepted some German assistance for the '46 harvest. We had considerable help from local people, children again, too. Likewise we went round neighbouring farms, including Alec's brother at Merryfield.

I find that Charlie Gregory was very chuffed with a gang of fifteen who whipped his potato crop out in double quick time. No it's not all good/all bad Gina.

Young Les Hardy had helped out on a neighbour's farm at Saundby where the POWs had downed tools at knock off time, with some crop still left out. An officer had been brought out from the camp (by Günter, I shouldn't wonder) who negotiated with the men to carry on working ... so they did.

Remember the story of Luca tossing the hay up? This was very similar, except that Luca was pitching from the cart to the loft, where the Germans were pitching from the field onto the cart. They wouldn't stop - they simply built a huge haystack in the field ... with a cart buried within it.

You have to be careful what you wish for, Pina.

86μ

Spending more time in the library - both in Tuxford (very small) and Retford (quite grand) - I happened across Josie more often.

She gives me the queerest look, I think because she is intrigued about, firstly, my apparent reluctance to go home, and then my continuing interest in the POW situation.

'Well they haven't *gone* home,' I said, 'and our soldiers have still not *come* home.' This of course has a double meaning which Josie did not fail to miss - home, what home? She also has her own interest in the POWs because more and more trusties are coming in to swat up on English - and to try to get to the truth of the situation in their homelands. They cannot trust in a single news outlet, and they get nothing from their own ... whatever that may be. She seems very keen to be of help to one and all.

We also compare notes. I told her about the escape and the idea of a plot. She was surprised I wasn't more aware of the latter - or the 'obvious' risk, as she saw it: hundreds of thousands of Axis prisoners do really constitute a huge army of enemies on our home soil.

She chewed her pretty lip and smiled at my 300,000 estimate. 'I reckon you could easily double that, Eric!' she said.

I think someone might call my look at her a pensive one. I, we, can do little more than think. The War Office is not going to let that little ... big secret out.

She could be right.

She has to help these men, it's her job to help. But she may not be too friendly - the fraternisation that has been going on between the Foxes, Palmiro and I is illegal - punishable by imprisonment.

We discussed this in more than the usual hushed tones expected in a library. She thinks many of the men are 'lovely chaps', adding somewhat coyly, 'just like you Eric.'

I laughed and thanked her. I hope I did not blush.

Next time I was in, she made a bee-line straight for me, gifts in hand. Sort of: she didn't immediately reveal the print on what appeared to be tickets in her hand. She did a preamble from where we left off about fraternisation. Had I heard about men travelling between camps...

The Plot! Harold had said escapees from one camp had returned of their own free will, saying they couldn't find their way (all the signposts were removed at the start of the war). However, there was some suspicion that they had been to other camps to co-ordinate the planned escape and rush on London last Christmas.

Josie had her hand over her mouth while I ran with this. It took me a while to notice it was to restrain her laughter.

She had laid the tickets in front of me, and then had to point them out to me. Bringing me down to earth. They were simple invitations from the Commandant of Nether Headon Camp to Miss Joselyn Husbands and one friend, to attend a Cabaret show provided by a touring theatre troupe FROM PRISONER OF WAR CAMPS.

This was really something - I know that the German Prisoners love their musical and theatrical shows, Hannay, with Bernhard and the Gregory family attest to that, but to think that they - POWs - are allowed to travel around other camps - I am really surprised.

Surprised and delighted that Josie would think of me being that one friend. I had to go. I do hope I was not too enthusiastic as I grabbed her hand in gratitude and, by the looks and smiles from others in the library, I definitely broke the 'silence' rule.

So after a few nights at Headon, the troupe moves on to Norton, Cuckney on 13th October, then Carburton the following week, before continuing to other Notts camps I know about; after that, through Derbyshire, Leicestershire, Northamptonshire, Norfolk, Cambridgeshire and back to neighbouring Lincolnshire.

So that's how she gets a bigger estimate than me of the numbers - these camps cannot possibly be in the 'Black' category for ardent Nazis, or even slightly risky 'Greys', they must be the purely the friendly, already 'democratised' 'Whites'.

It shouldn't have surprised me that most-trusty Günter Rahn was at the main gate to the cage to welcome us special guests. Though we shared a smile of recognition, we each erred on the side of caution, and didn't let it show. Friendly but not fraternising.

Crammed as we were into what is the main mess hut in the 'cage' part of the camp, we invitees were actually joined by some more of the trusty POWs - all very smart and clean and every one of them smiling from ear to ear. These did not seem to be false. Sweet Josie's pretty face would drag a smile from a stone, and they so wanted to shake (hold) her hand, and welcome her, never casting a glance my way.

The show was all in German except for a translated verse or two of songs we guests might know such as Lily Marlene. Josie flicked a raised eyebrow at me. Well, whose song is it? I smiled with hands open. She nodded.

There were roars and whoops from the men at the gorgeous women in the sketches - fellow men, of course, extravagantly made up, and much pouting at us and swaying of hips.

All good, very good, clean fun. I don't think Betty's Rudi will have been MC as the touring troupe will surely have their own. However, though I didn't notice him, earlier, Bernhard had picked me out and ambled shyly up to me at the end when we were served drinkies and nibbles - I have totally forgotten about such things, and discovered a sort of cake or bread I really liked - it's got Marzipan inside it. It was a tiny piece - a real nibble - and I wonder if it was really marzipan, but I did seek out a second helping, to be sure...

There were photographs being taken. I hadn't dared to bring my camera in.

On the bus back to Retford (I'd left Maisie in Josie's Mother's safe alleyway) I was perhaps too strong in my profuse thanks - she only got the tickets, and for free, because she is one of the people who serve the camp - they take in books in a van and refresh them fortnightly. No great shakes.

But it is for me - to be inside one of 'my camps'.

She looked into my earnest eyes, biting her lip. 'Of course, Eric.' She patted my hand.

87μ

Having got a 'Dear Mister' letter from Gina, I headed up to Clayworth, sitting across the fields from Gringley's hill.

She has been decidedly buoyed up by unexpected responses from the Government farms on the Carrs - nothing in life is only black or white.

Her mum shooed a few little ones out into the back yard, snatched and waved my bunch of flowers into her 'parlour', where Gina sat smiling, turning a carved box in her hands. She didn't stand but offered up the box to me. 'They're not all bad,' she said.

It was an ornately carved trinket box with a close fitting lid. Well made.

'One of the German Prisoners of War gave it me,' she said with what appeared to be pride. It really threw me, because I was thinking I was coming to hear the story of something awful, something that had scarred her face ... and crippled her.

Her face was heavily made up and she was sitting apparently comfortably in the chair. Only her remaining sitting indicating that the legs were not fully functional.

I told her how lovely it was to see her - much better than I expected after what her dad told me at Christmas.

'My poor dad', she said with a wan smile. 'Yeah, I'm no weakling am I?'

I smiled, not wanting to infer anything about a lady's size.

'I weighed pretty heavy and my dad had to ... at night ... my legs were in plaster and irons. My dad had to put a bar like that,' she said, bending down to hold the imaginary bar, 'and hold my feet apart, because of me getting them together and getting the irons fast. So he had to unbolt feet and then carry me upstairs and then bolt my feet up again.'

I whistled, cocking my head.

'And he did that without a grumble and although I was such a big girl...'

We sat a moment taking it in.

She cleared her throat and went on, 'he still told me stories ... never grumbled ... strong as an ox - a farmer, y'know. Tried to tell me stories...' She stretched her face to the ceiling, perhaps blinking away a tear. 'Read to me.'

She straightened herself up in her chair and put her hands out for the box I still held. Looking at it she said,' they're not all bad,' then looking up to me, 'well they're not are they?'

I had to agree, but really I didn't know who she meant. I thought she would get round to it.

Mum then came in bearing tea - a lovely cuppa, of course - and cake, real cake. I bet the little ones didn't get much of that. Special for Gina's Mister.

Mum hovered a moment, but Gina gave her, then the door, a look.

I showed my appreciation of the cake with my mouthful, washed it down with too large a sup of the very hot tea.

We both laughed. Serves me right.

After I'd wiped my eyes and nose, I told her that I had called up to see her at the Land Army huts at Gringley, and the other girls were not very sure what happened to her, even where she was.

She frowned.

'Then I called by here at Christmas and your Dad told me you had ... an accident?'

She continued to simply look at me, so I thought I had better go around the horror that it must have been for her. 'So where did you get to in the Land Army after I met you ... when you left Walker's Farm?'

'I joined the Land Army to get away from Gringley!'

That was better. I knew why of course - I had had to console her, along with Peg, when she told me how Mrs Walker said it was the last she would see of her mother. As if the near miss of the bomb in the muck heap, three yards from the house weren't enough. 'So you went off to see the world!'

That misfired somewhat.

'No, I was put in the hostel. Stupid wooden hut. Gringley Carrs. That bleak place called Gringley Carrs.'

'But then they sent you to different places from there, didn't they?'

She pursed her lips. Was I being a bit slow?

'No. I worked for Gringley Carrs because it was Government farms, because I had to work on the same farm, and, of course, I worked with the horses eventually, until the Germans made a mess of me, the German prisoners.'

'Germans! They *attacked* you?' I could picture facial injuries, but smashing up her legs is another level of violence altogether.

'Yes, they was what they called leading carts. Four carts: one at the stack unloading; one had just left the stack empty going to the field; one had just left the field, going to the stack to pick that one up; and one in the field being filled - and two girls to do it.'

I didn't take that in immediately, and got her to talk it through before I left. She was now in full flood.

'And I knew that one of the horses was so flighty and it used to jump and run and I said to the other girl, "Don't come with Captain up the lane too quickly. When I meet you, I'll swap horses and you can go back to the field again and I'll go to the stack, because you'll never get him into the stackyard.

'So that was the arrangement.

'Well I go down the lane and, what do I do?' Her voice went up an octave. 'I meet this horse galloping up with the load and no girl with him. So, of course, I stopped it and asked one of the tractor drivers, who was ploughing in the field, if he could take him to the farm. I said "I can't manage him now he's got to this stage, I can't manage to get him into the stackyard. He'll shy and jump and, will you take him?"

'He said "Yes, but where's Peg?"

'I said "That is what I want to know."

'Peg was fastened to a gate post.' She stopped wide eyed.

I suppose I was too. Whatever next?

'They had held her against a gate post and run the cartwheel and crushed her pelvis, and she was unconscious and stuck to the gate post. That was the German prisoners.'

That was the German Prisoners. I shook my head. I closed my eyes. I was still shaking my head. Where were these German prisoners based? Surely 'Black' Nazis, securely locked up somewhere? In a farming camp on the Carrs?'

'No, Headon Camp.'

My turn to take a few breaths. I stood up. I looked out of the window and into the street. *This* is Peg. Has Gina moved the pain away from herself and transposed it onto another? But I've met Peg. She is a real person. Perhaps Gina has forgotten. I sat down again, hands on knees, looking into Gina's face.

She went on, now oblivious to me, sort of telling herself: 'And we ... she went to hospital and I don't know whether she's still alive, but she'd only three weeks before she got married and her boyfriend said, "Well, I shall marry her if she ever gets better".

'I know that she got married because they had the house made for her wheelchair, but she never walked again.'

That was Peg. So what, how, when, and even *did* the German's attack Gina?

She took a short breath and resumed: 'and a week later, I went and, of course, with it being a long way from the stack to the field, I usually stood in the cart with a long line and drove the horse and then got out of the cart.

'Well, they had what they call shells and gormers.'

She saw my face hadn't recognised a funny phrase. She held her hands open in front of her, 'extensions to the cart. We called them shells and gormers!'

The Fox's carts had the extensions, but I'd never heard of the term. I nodded.

'And the German prisoners jumped in the cart before I got out and pushed me through these spaces in the shells and gormers. The horse kicked my face and then they dropped my legs in the cart wheels.'

This is beyond horrific. I had no idea what to say ... or do.

Gina was sensitive to the extraordinary detail of her story, no doubt having told it, and perhaps been told not to tell it, as it is so incredible - literally unbelievable.

Do I believe it?

'They're not all bad, though, Mister, No.' She looked at her trinket box. 'Dad drives many of them all over the county, he says, even over into Gainsborough.'

'Perhaps to us,' I said, 'at Egmanton?'

She shook her head. Didn't know.

'Been in pot for nigh on two years years,' she said, 'just got it off.' She rubbed her legs fiercely then pulled her skirt down.

That makes a little sense. It will have been in the early rush of German POWs straight off the battlefield, in late '44, not screened carefully enough, bitter young ... thugs?

She now struggled with the arms of her chair and stood herself up. She laughed at the look of surprise on my face. Yes she can walk, but her mum doesn't want her to exert herself. Fair enough. She rejected my chivalrous offer of support.

'Yes, but, yes,' she said, 'They did come to fetch me for a day at the farm with the girls - just to be with them.

'Mind, I had a jolly good go ... and it took quite a few people to stop me running a hayfork into this German when I saw him.'

She laughed at herself and accepted the offer of my arm as she steered me to the door. My time was up.

The kids were angling for a gawp at Gina's Mister, fussing round me as she held herself at the doorpost - John twiddling Maisie's accelerator as I fired her up, and young Lydia pulling my hand back, to stop me putting on my skid-lid to gasp, eager to tell me, 'they brought our Gina home on the back of a lorry, they did, didn't they our Gina?'

Gina laughed and they all waved me off.

Part Seven - Christmas 1946

Enemies become Friends

88μ
Have a POW for Christmas 1946

People. Some People. People like other people. Most people. Some people like people they know. People are strange. People are even stranger when you're alone. People. Some people like strangers. I'm a stranger in my own country. I like people. I like strangers, like me. People don't like me because of it. Only some people.

The Prime Minister, Attlee, leads the people and he does not like the Germans. But it seems a lot of people like me are saying we need to show we like our enemies, or else they will remain our enemies, and maybe that's even what caused this war. So, be nice.

You may laugh, but you can go to prison for being nice to the Germans. Some nurses treated a German POW who had been injured in an accident. They were brought to court for being nice to him and ... I don't know *how* I can believe this, but I do ... one of them was sent to prison for being too nice.

The war finished and over a hundred thousand Italians were completely free to roam, go to cinemas, on our trains to the seaside, and to live in people's homes, but people were not supposed to 'fraternise' with them. That includes Alec, Sally, Barbara and me, with Palmiro. Most people do not understand this. Most people find that most other people are quite like them, and they get to like them. Tony Dalla Riva now has an English 'wife' and family here. (I don't know if Attlee has let them marry yet).

Poor Gina has good reason to hate some people, but finds it hard to not like some others who are like them.

There is a revolution among the people. Dangerous word. Part of the fear of the Ruskies is that the Russians had a big revolution which threw out the bosses and rulers and even killed their emperor, the Tsar, and his whole family.

The Labour Party has been elected. The Tories tried to frighten people that Labour are Communists, or Socialists, just like the Russian revolutionaries. But the people threw out the War 'Hero' Churchill and the Tories anyway. Now there are big promises for the health of ordinary people who won't have to pay for medical treatment. Attlee is the leader so I like him for that. But I do think he should be nice to the Germans now. I am glad to be part of a quiet revolution of people who agree with me, and some priests and vicars are asking their people to have a Prisoner of War for Christmas. No, Pina, not instead of a goose! As a guest - befriend him, break the Non-Fraternisation ban.

Alec was not amused. Sally was not going to be disloyal to her husband, nor Barbara to her father. He had 'let' me take charge of our German POW gangs over the harvest, but none had crossed the threshold into his kitchen yet.

The Government officially removed the fraternisation ban this autumn, and I believe hundreds of POWs did spend Christmas with families across North Notts. I'm sure Bernhard did.

A CO friend in Derby - Dennis Lovell - has sent me a photo of his wife and himself posing proudly with 'their' Christmas POW.

I was glad to be home, alone with Mummy in Dore. I would also have dearly loved to invite a couple of chaps over from Lodge Moor to join us - Willy Kohnstamm would surely have been able to recommend a couple of decent chaps. But Mummy and I had become strangers to ourselves, so it would not have been appropriate.

89μ
January 1947

Pathe News was not wrong - it was a crucial harvest for us, just to keep up our stocks, particularly of wheat for bread, but much of mainland Europe is devastated and short of men and machines. There is a fear of famine even. Of course there are those who hope the Germans... After the revelations of Buchenwald and Belsen, reports streamed in, particularly from the eastern areas they invaded - especially Poland. It seems they were trying to wipe out all the Jews - yes, all of them - from all the countries they invaded. They had taken them from towns all across Europe in cattle-trains and killed them.

I can't see that we will have much of our harvest to export for them even if the nation wanted to. It has been that crucial harvest in an awful summer: rain and wind flattening the corn, making it difficult to harvest with machines - many hands needed.

Whatever I could squeeze out of the greenhouses was so welcome, and fortunately, the storms some people had, didn't break any of my glass.

We've continued to work into autumn taking great care with clamping the root vegetables - spuds, carrots and beetroot for us. I'm glad to say we haven't got much greenstuff in the fields, so I won't be chapping my fingers picking sprouts at Christmas this year.

I spent a warm few days at Lyndhurst with Mummy - I'm glad to say, just Mummy. Grandmama and Grandpapa took their usual trip, lording it with Lairds and other war profiteers, with promising weather a late 'Hogmanay' in Scotland. Dore is a pretty village, but is a bit bleak where we are up on the Moors.

We brought my Mam up for Christmas Day itself, and, seeing Mummy still a bit shaky, Mam and I fussed around the kitchen with a small goose, courtesy of the Foxes. (I had fed it myself!)

90μ

One of the strange things about researching my quest in the newspapers is that they are restricted in what they can report. We are aware that our worst fears are allayed by not being told where air raids actually are - they say things like 'In a Northern town.'

I told you about the bus wrongly having the actual name of a munitions factory for its destination. The same applies to the camps and not letting on: to the locals that they sometimes have thousands of enemy personnel in their communities; or to the enemy where their lads are, to release them.

However, I joked about the people of Headon being the only ones who won't mention the camp round here.

The only reference to the Prisoner of War camps I found in all my searching of the Retford Times for the whole war, is a single one to Boughton Camp - and that's a good twelve miles south of the town.

Just before last Christmas a man was arraigned at Retford court because he was found with a child's toy under his seat on a bus. It is a funny place to have a toy, so you could forgive the bus conductor, or a nosy neighbour, from wondering why he hasn't got it wrapped, in a nice bag or something. And surely he would have had a reasonable explanation.

However, this war didn't make many people rich. Poor bloke was perhaps not very bright either.

He told the court that he had found it in a bin near Boughton Camp. We do have to ask ourselves what sort of person goes around looking in bins ... and near a POW camp of all places. Not many luxury goods being wasted there.

He said he went past and saw it, and didn't take it at first, but on his return he had another look, and saw it was still there. A German POW actually saw him.

You would think that would be enough to frighten him away, but no - the Prisoner smiled at him and said, 'Take. Take.' So he did.

A gift wrapping service was not included.

On the bus, he stowed the painted wooden toy under his seat. I suppose it had a flaw and was not perfect, not good enough to sell, so a reject. But it looked like new - not worn.

So what do you think about that whole affair?

Yes, the Judge was the same. He wondered at the state of our legal system if such a petty little case were brought all the way to court.

He threw the case out as a waste of time.

91μ

Thinking about all the excitement of escapes and murders, I wanted to find out what went on round here - surely must be something. Günter, despite his youth, is the most well travelled POW I've met so far, and the most willing to talk - except a bit shy about being in the Luftwaffe. Could it be shame? If I saw them, I chased out to see if Günter was dropping off Germans to the neighbours' farms, clearing up winter damage, and doing some sewing.

The watched pot never boils, and he came when I wasn't looking. The Quartermaster from Headon camp arrived to talk to Alec about his allocations and needs, perhaps to persuade him, I don't know, and I thought it was Günter standing by the cab smoking while he waited.

I told Alec where we were, got a very queer look from the Officer, and took Günter into the barn for a cuppa from the flask.

When I asked him about any escapes, he laughed and reminded me of his 'escape' from the field hospital.

'Was that true though, Günter?' I said.

He was wounded - not mortally, giving me a baby pout. 'Jawohl!'

(I've heard it for real, now! It's in all our war comic books.)

Laughing, he shook his head and went on, 'New Years Eve we wanted to give the guards summats to think about...'

'Where was this?'

'I told you - Haltwhistle. So we got some cats and tied some tins to their tails, and lifted the rolls and rolls of wire and let them out at various places round the camp.' He was really enjoying himself. 'And the army has come, and the police has come, and we are all out for roll call in the middle of the night, and they check and check again, and it's only flippin' cats got out.'

It was a bit stewed, but we supped some tea. Haltwhistle rang a bell.

'You didn't tell me how you were captured,' I said.

He frowned and massaged his arm, his wounded arm? 'They came and asked us to help out in the rearguard action to protect Berlin - just for a couple of months. They made us 7th Parachute Regiment and dropped us into Belgium.'

Something like the Boughton Quartermaster told me. 'Not Luftwaffe?' I said.

He gave me the 'don't be so stupid look' and went on, 'we were in this orchard, four of us. Tanks come in. One man gets shot straight away and the other shoots a panzershreck...' he shouldered a gun, 'yankee say bazooka ... at the first tank's tracks, disabling it. The other tanks pull back.

'Plane flies over and drops little bombs - to strip the leaves off the trees loyk, so they can see how many we are.

'Me and my mate are in a hole with a machine gun, me feeding, so we swaps round.

'Then they shouts "come on out", and we shouts "get lost."

239

'Then the disabled tank turret turns towards us, barrel drops ... bang. I wakes up and there's seven Tommies aiming at me "get out ye bastard!"' He rolled his sleeve up and showed me a livid scar under his bicep.

I gave a whistle. It really is nasty, but he didn't seem to think so.

'Got it all over me,' he said. 'Flack ... from the Mitchell bombers. Leg, too.' He rubbed it. 'Swimming,' he said. 'Very good.' He rotated his whole arm - as if it were a sport injury.

He lost me. I think he does like to brag. Apparently he loved sport at school, particularly swimming, and that saved his life - he spent four hours in the sea that time. He was lucky that it was in the nice warm Mediterranean. His squadron was flying supplies from Sicily to Rommel's lot in North Africa. Taking shells to shoot at Queenie's Jack, no doubt. It cast him in a somewhat darker light. He noticed and brightened it up.

'On the ship across to London, the Tommies said, "Get well quick son, and help us beat the Ruskies." That was nice, but we didn't really understand - the Russians are on *your* side?'

I was as mystified as he was.

'Well aren't they?'

I wanted to say 'not mine', but led him onwards. 'London, you said.'

'Yes they brought me to this big hospital in Woolwich.' He smiled at the reminiscence. 'It had these great big...' he gesticulated.

'Wards?'

'Yes - high wards - and this London smog came,' he lowered himself like Frankenstein's Egor, 'creeping round the buildings below us. You seen smog?'

I haven't but he didn't give me time to say.

He laughed out loud. 'We *knew* we were winning the war, because you British had so little grease, you even took it out of the bacon!' and he slapped me on the back.

Still full of himself, 'and you know...'

There was a shout from the house, so as we walked up the yard he finished, 'when they took us out for exercise, they were so scared of us, that for five wounded men, they escorted us with four Tommies - bayonets drawn; for nine, it was eight guards'. Heaving himself into the cab, he finished, 'just one less guard than the number of *wounded*.'

As his captain stood a minute giving Alec farewells, Günter took a surreptitious look and whispered back to me, 'Friday nights, Butchers' Arms, Laneham.'

92μ

Time flew at the start of 1947 as there was so much to do about everything - such immense changes just could not have been anticipated. Those walls of snow on top of frozen ground held back germination of crops, early flowering of daffodils - even snowdrops, but I had my own, my very own surprise blossom.

Easter Sunday was in the middle of a gale, but the floods had mostly subsided for a semblance of normality to resume. Barbara had inveigled her father to attend a cheering service at the church, and feeling a little sheepish in this rare occurrence, Alec literally dragged me along for moral or manly support, scuffing my freshly polished boot on the step as he bundled me out laughing.

The morning was calmer, some clouds scudding across an unusually blue sky, with air full of anticipation of things that could only get better. The service likewise - Barbara linking arms with father and me, squeezing and smiling to and fro during the Our Father.

As she skipped back home between us, I noticed for the first time that she is actually no longer a child, but a delightful young woman. Not scarred by the war ... we can hope.

As I entered the scullery and kicked off my boots, I didn't notice that they weren't following me, as I scanned the kitchen, mostly with my nose taking in the promise of a Sunday Roast, before moving on hailing Sally. No Sally but some giggling from the rarely used parlour. I halted on the threshold and all went silent. I pushed the door gently and was pounced upon with 'Surprise!' and push from behind into the arms of ... Mummy!

Three women now wrapped themselves around me, with the lord of the manor standing, arms folded, grinning. That is a momentary image fast in my mind now, because in a twinkling, My Darling and I were alone in each other's arms.

We tumbled into a heap on the settee. We laughed then breathed each other in.

Tea was laid on a crisp linen cloth. I'd never even seen Sally's best china before. The house was silent but for the quiet mumble and muted tune on the Home Service.

Neither of us knew where to begin, so the start was eventually with Mummy saying with a smile, 'So Papa has ... gone?'

My returning smile was doubtless quizzical. Is that simple, rather cold word 'gone' just as she sees it?

She took my hands and looked deeply into me.

I have no idea what she saw. I had nothing prepared nor anything hidden.

'I've been counting the days to the first of June 1947.'

I must surely have looked blank, as the date meant nothing to me at all.

Pina, is it you? I looked Mummy up and down. Lovely frock - couture I would guess from a starting point of complete ignorance of such a thing, except that she does love that one thing her Papa could spoil her with.

'Freedom. You're coming home!'

Am I? Where and what is home? Stupefied Eric - and looking it.

'Oh, Eric!' she said, again shaking my hands to awaken me. 'You've done it. You've served your time. It's over, you can come home.'

I felt a warmth spreading within me. Home. An image of Mam flashed into my head, and I squeezed it aside, shaking my head vigorously. 'But of course my dear,' I lied, probably unconvincingly. I stood and swung her up into my arms to compensate. I kissed her...

May and the end of my contract approaches. I have to seriously consider whether my home is with Mummy or Mam. Mummy is shocked that I should even conceive of such a notion. I had to explain how she and we have been with each other. It's like scales fell from her eyes - she didn't realise that it/she had been like that.

She has a long think about it, while I sip the now cold tea, then bite my lip.

'It's Papa, isn't it? A blindfold Eric, not scales. Have I blinded myself or did he blindfold me?'

There was no answer to either.

She looked out of the window. The skeleton of a tree quaked in the wind.

She took a very deep breath. Looking back I really think that was your primal scream, My Lovely. You moved out into a world which was not that of your parents.

I heard a distant call from Sally. She had our coats in her arms and ordered us to get out for a little walk round the village before she serves dinner in an hour. 'Perhaps call into the Plough for a ... what's your tipple, Dear? Now push off Eric.'

Sally still mothering me after all this time - could be forty years, not four.

A walk up and down the Main Street was all we could manage - battling up, blown back down. *Hold on to your hearts!* ... our own or each other's? I wanted to keep hold of you. I don't wish this war to have been the death of our love. It seemed that you wished the same, but you had not the strength to fight that wind, let alone fight for me.

I will take the fight to you. For you. For us.

Conscientiously Objecting no more, Eric.

93μ

It is cold. Coldest I remember in my life. The most snow anyway. Now the nation is grateful to the POWs. Rightly so. Thinking of the chaps pitching, pitching, pitching the hay at Saundby, at least they were welcome to do it in the snow. There were huge drifts all over the country from mid January 1947... and of course that cut many people off from the bare necessities - food and water; fuel - including electricity, because trains could not get the coal to the power stations. Then of course people had to resort to the woodpiles: they were buried deep and with the long freeze, they ran out. We do of course have plenty of wood and I had Germans helping me sort our supplies out. I first met Günter Rahn by the wood pile. Gentleman. I do hope someone extended Christmas cheer to him.

I don't suppose it was the cold, or even digging through snowdrifts that did it, but Grandpapa's heart gave out when they returned from Scotland in January 1947. The grave will have taken some hard digging into frozen soil. I stood with Mummy at the graveside, hankie at the ready.

She didn't shed a tear.

At the finest Dore's hoteliers could offer, Grandmama fussed around the host of dignitaries and Grandpapa's fellow steel magnates,.

Mummy stood alone and aloof to it all ... with me at her side warming a small glass of mild ale for the duration.

What to say? He was her Papa. What that meant to her, she had never...

I was lost for words. I didn't go back to the house. His house.

I returned to Egmanton by several replaced and re-routed trains to Tuxford, where Maisie Matchless stood frozen to the spot. I mean frozen. A slight thaw and melt had frozen her in a glaze that I had to chip off my seat and crack off the steering and pedals. I could lift off the stand, but she had a new one like that of a toy soldier - each wheel in a frozen puddle. I had to swap warmth from my hand to melt the accelerator, or else someone might have found a statue of man and bike there next morning.

German POWs from Headon had been out clearing drifts from the Great North Road. They were joined by Polish Forces, many based at Retford's Ranby Camp I believe, to clear the London to Edinburgh Railway. Both pass only 2 miles from here.

It didn't end there. Spring 1947 was a washout - not a spring clean. My green houses had survived wind and gales last year, but sheer weight of snow burst through one roof and flattened some good seedlings. A swift brushing round, burying myself several times in the process, saved the whole lot from toppling. In fact the inside of the green houses was the only green to be seen on this farm.

What then?

It all had to melt eventually. We are in the valley of the Trent - one of the largest rivers in Britain. It flows a long way from the Derbyshire Peaks before it gets to us. The richest folk in Nottingham at West Bridgford were not saved from waves of meltwater flooding homes and factories; nor were thousands of poor folk in Trentside villages downstream - those round here. We helped evacuate some on tractor and trailer. Our streets were streams, but some judicious and well anticipated (by Alec) sandbagging saved us from the worst. That can't be said for his brother's family at real Trentside Low (yes low) Marnham.

Stretches of railway and road became new tributaries.

What the nation would have done without the POWs does not bear thinking about, but there is plenty of thanking.

And the Poles. They have and haven't been de-mobbed. If they are actually to be released from their Polish Army, they should be from Poland - of course.

But no. It is now clear that we (not me!) went to war to save Poland from the invading German army. However, we also joined to help our ally, Russia, who apparently invaded Poland at the same time ... and though the Germans have now infamously mistreated lots of Jews, the Russians have been almost as cruel to the Polish. Poland in 1939 also included large areas which are now recognised as Ukraine and Belarus ... of but not their own country ... a United Socialist Soviet Republic, like the United Socialist Soviet Republic of Russia - USSR, but sneakily, exactly like it. 'Russia' now means everywhere they took off the Germans and more.

And the Poles do not want to live in that 'Russia'. In fact it is stated by some very important writers that Stalin is executing returning fighters who had joined SS Regiments that the Germans had formed of able and 'willing' men from invaded territories. That included tens of thousands of Georgian Cossacks.

Russia is clearing Poles from what it regards as its territory of Lithuania, Belarus and Ukraine - over a million is being mentioned. Of course it plants some of them in West Poland that Germany had snatched...

Oh dear, winners and losers.

We would not have won the Battle of Britain if it were not for Polish Airmen. They are afraid of returning home, so we must, yes we must, give them work and housing.

It seems the latter is going to require now vacant Army camps - like Ranby and huts at Tuxford, too.

94μ

Alec told me to get on up to Charlie Gregory as he has a story for me.

My invitation was not for Sunday lunch - they have other guests - so, perhaps for tea. I arrived around two and rode Maisie straight into the barn, surprising young Betty. As I took off my helmet she stood holding her hands to her chest in fright, but smiling broadly.

I returned her 'greeting' and she blurted out 'my barn of shocks!'

I shook my locks and cocked my head.

'Well Mr Chapman, I do seem to have had more shocks in here than anywhere else.'

I hoped it was not the sort of POW/Land Army encounter in the hay sort of shock. I didn't say that though.

She went right on, 'Poor Bernard...' but choked.

Poor Bernard, is it? I felt that perhaps I should hold her, but held back.

She took a deep breath, looked at me wondering if she should go on. She looked over towards a dark corner. She then continued as if talking to the corner, 'I came in here to tidy up for Dad - bailing twine, sacks and that. I'd done a few when I heard a snuffling over there. First, I thought a pig was out but in the gloom I saw it was Bernard on his knees and he was ... crying, I thought. He hadn't noticed me, so I stood silent. My heart started to pound - a man crying.' She turned to me. 'We've seen some sadness these years haven't we Mr Chapman? But something about poor Bernard struck me. I decided to tell Dad, so I tip-toed to find him.

'Bernard has the loveliest handwriting, Mr Chapman,' she said, leaving me thinking she wasn't going to tell what was wrong with the now *'Bernard'*. 'You should have seen the lovely card he sent me for my birthday. I panicked because my Birthday is Valentine's Day...' She then blushed very deeply. Sweetly. A tear in her eye. '...and y'know, I didn't ... well what might her Mum think? Anyway, I sneaked it up to my bedroom, only to find it was totally innocent, and the very prettiest Birthday card ... ever.' She held her hands against her throat, just as she did when I surprised her. She coughed. 'So I could show it to Mum. It's this fancy German script, y'know, like bibles and that at church?'

I nodded, finding myself smiling broadly. She seemed to have ground to a halt, so I said, more as a joke than anything, 'and that was here in the barn?'

She brought herself up, apologised and went back to the sad surprise. Well last September, Bernhard... ha! I said that - we call him Bernard now, English version is not so ... hard sounding?'

'Yes, I do see what you mean - *burn hard*. September,' I prompted.

'Well, yes. I thought he wanted me to be a bit like a spy and that, because he asked me if I would post a birthday card to his Mother - not have it opened and marked by the censor, you see. Special, clean and nice for his Mutti. Funny, he even showed the ... letter it was really, all coloured lettering and swirls,' she laughed, 'as if I would know if he was telling of an escape plan, or...' She carried on laughing and got her hankie out for a blow.

'It's not funny, though, it's very very sad. So, like his Mum's birthday was in September, then just before Christmas I came out here and there was Bernard - crying.

'Dad saw to him... well, I'm a bit,..'

'Yes,' was all I had to offer.

'Bernard had a got a letter back from his sister saying...' she sobbed, '...saying...' and she wept.

This time I couldn't help but take her in my arms.

She cried in my ear, 'she'd died. His Mutti and father had both died.' She took a huge breath and wailed into my ear, a wail of words I couldn't grasp.

Betty eventually calmed down, wiped her face, straightened her hair, blouse and skirt. She told how Bernhard's parents had *starved to death*. It has been hard for us to grow enough food and we are using the cream of Germany's youth to help us grow enough food - for us. I did not expect that consequence.

Betty qualified her description, saying that yes they had actually died from lack of food, but that did not help them having TB, that terrible disease of poverty and bad air, Tuberculosis.

She noticed some stray stooks of hay, and I joined her in tidying up a few bits and pieces, bridle on hook, tools in place, etc.

'Then a little while ago I was just here doing this - there's always something that needs seeing to, isn't there, Mr Chapman? - when I looked round and this big chap with a swathe of blond hair was leaning on the doorpost smiling at me. Gave me a proper fright, him being a German and all.'

'A German?'

'Yes. The Uniform. From the camp. He's the driver. I've seen him. But like you - just appearing. He did give me a fright. I didn't hear his lorry, see. Oh he is such a swaggerer.'

This sounded just like someone I know, but it was too much of a coincidence, so I said nothing.

'This barn,' she said, 'bit like it's haunted.' She picked up a length of twine and twisted it round and round her hand. 'And the ... and then, when we were sacking up beans, I found Bernard in here again, in a sorry sort of way. This time blood was pouring from his hand and he was clutching his elbow, just looking at it. I rushed over and got, well I got a sack actually, to wipe the blood. He looked at me such a sad look, but laughed - at the sack, y'know. Oh, Mr Chapman, my heart ... my heart did go out to poor Bernard. Poor Bernard.' She continued to twist the twine.

I told her that Mr Fox had sent me over, because there is a story here for me - I took the twine from her, 'and you've given me three already. I'm not sure that's what he meant?'

She frowned. Not her 'silly stories'.

A light came on and her father Charlie stood with his hand on the switch. 'Let - there - be - light!' he boomed. 'Good eh?'

I had to agree. We haven't even got light in my barn-loft bedroom. I suddenly noticed we were both freezing out there. Charlie brought us into the house.

I'm not so sure that Charlie had actually told Alec to send me across, but he always does have a story. He was most keen to tell me about the electricity. A supply has been brought out to the villages. I later found out that it had brought Josie Husbands to the area - her Dad had brought electricity to Retford, 'from Lincoln' (I laughed at that - as if he'd brought it over in a sack!) in 1926. It had been gradually fed out to the villages. I know that the Egmanton Parish Council has been shilly-shallying about whether they can afford to convert the street lights to electricity, and still haven't done it. They have had an 'it's not worth it during black-out' excuse, but that's no longer valid.

Charlie had wanted the wiring which had been installed to the house, spreading to other rooms, and out to the barn, but there aren't many men skilled up in electricity, and those that are, are in great demand. He saw this POW re-wiring a motor in Treswell Woods (the next village) and realised that took more skill than running a feed.

One thing led to another and he asked Günter to do it.

The coincidence was growing. 'Günter Rahn?' I said, nodding.

Yes, same Günter.

I shook my head.

'You know him?'

'Yes, he brings men to us - the few Mr Fox begrudgingly accepts.'

'He doesn't like the Germans?'

'I can't say that,' I said. 'He really liked the Italians, though.'

'Oh, this lot of Krauts can really see off a gang of Ities!'

I knew his sentiments about the olive pickers.

'Anyway, I gets young Günter to come over. I was getting desperate and had made a start. He arrives - they let him drive around in that five-hundredweight Bedford pick up, y'know?'

I do.

'I told him I'd buried a good earth. "What is it?" *Vot ist!* He said. 'Old copper kettle, I tells him. "Well dig it up again," he says, "it'll be wort' a few bop!" Well I had to laugh - ruddy Kraut kid telling me. Anyway he had it done in double quick time. Then he holds up two reels of cable he's been using and says, "not even a copper kettle's worth." Well not quite those words, but I knew what he meant.'

Charlie Gregory took off his cap, brushed his hair down and laughing at me, replaced the cap. 'Tea!'

I passed the lovely time of day with Emma and asked Betty about her piano playing. 'Rudi?' I said flicking my eyebrows. She tutted and went off. I heard her tinkling a few tunes while Charlie and I did an update on the POW situation.

Not billeted out like the Italians, he said, at which I mentioned Bernhard.

'Still biking it. It'll not be long for the likes of Bernard, though. You know they're graded C to A - black through grey to white - real Nazi SS through to

247

these ... well ordinary blokes?' No Officers. Ordinary ranks and a lot of young ones - not so bright either, he reckons. I don't know how he works that out. I do know the grading of course, but Charlie explained that he had worked out that Headon, Camp 52 Nether Headon, was a final stage. They are being repatriated from there.

'Already!' I was shocked. I thought old Attlee was having none of that.

Just a few so far, he said, but all the effort now is to re-educate them, away from Nazism. Democratise them. (I had heard about Carburton and Norton, Cuckney being mainly about that.) And to get rid of them. They are costing us, upkeep etc.

I thought of Bernhard's parents ... and the snow. 'Not so sure that they aren't actually serving us very well with so many men ... still away and, well, lost?'

He took an uncharacteristic break to think about that. 'But we can't keep them forever. They asked us to have one or two over for Christmas. We can be nice to them now, y'know. Get them to like us and they won't start another war. See that young Günter chappie. Doesn't know what's happened to his family. He's from East Prussia - and you've heard what's happened there.'

I hadn't, so he told me that the Russians - it's in the Russian sector - have taken it over completely, and they are not giving it back to the Germans, nor to Poland for that matter. I had heard that the British had bombed it pretty badly, it being a German state right on our ally's border. Charlie told me that the Russians are deporting all the Germans - those who dared remain after the Russians invaded - and they are having it as a Russian state. Even changed the name - capital Konigsburg ('King's Town' in German) is now Kaliningrad (*Kalinin's town* in Russian.) It gives them an ice free access to the North Sea.

I pictured Joe Bennett and his freezing convoys having to plough through ice in convoys, to take supplies round heavily guarded German East Prussia and its U-Boat submarines, on up to Murmansk. I understand why the Russians want to keep it. It doesn't make any less sense than leaving it there, like after the last war, cut off by Poland's Danzig Corridor to the North Sea. But all those people - a hundred percent proud German state for centuries.

And Günter doesn't know where his family are, or even if they have survived.

When they are captured, the POWs are given a card to send home to say they are safe. It's a Convention all sides agree to in war. It appears that Germany and now Russia are not keeping to it.

For that matter, nor are we - keeping POWs under canvas, through winter, too. But what can be expected when armies capture hundreds of thousands at once? It's a tricky one, no matter how nice you want to be Eric.

Finally he told me that after Bernard heard of the death of his parents, and the letter informing him, also told him to not come home yet, but make the best of what he can find in England, he had asked the Camp Commandant if he could be billeted out. 'Auntie Green', an elderly widow neighbour in South Leverton had offered to take Bernard in, especially after him trying so hard to get here in that awful snow, then lots of bits of road flooded. Poor Bernard.

And Poor Günter.

Some hope though.

After the leaders of the Nazi war were executed in Nuremberg last autumn, my old friends in I.G.Farben have been arraigned for their war crimes. Yes I was very taken with the young lab assistant like myself, taking inspiration leading to the founding a whole new colour and pharmaceutical industry.

I the grinder, the Blade, down to the finest micron - the greek µ *mew* - I have used as the measure of these chapters - with how much charcoal in the pig iron, copper in plate, chromium in stainless, tungsten for hardness; founding and forging. My chemicals and me in my lab-coat forging new ways. I had the courage of my convictions to not go too far. I wouldn't go where Grandpapa tried to lead.

Was I courageous? They convicted me of wrongdoing, for not wanting to make a better killing machine.

The bodies on that trailer at Buchenwald ... but worse was at Auschwitz and our own prisoners of war return to tell that they knew just from the smell, what was happening at the nearby I.G.Auschwitz. I.G.Farben is indicted on five counts, all implicating them in a complete absorption in the whole Nazi machine, and without whom there would really never have been such a war. The charge of slavery and mass murder is the one most crucial to our story here: innocent people were enslaved, imprisoned, held in camps and worked to death. They were also simply exterminated if they were not of use to the future German empire - their Third Reich.

Rat poison - we need such a chemical and prussic acid is very effective. Like many things - knives to swords and bayonets - it was used to a horrific end: under an I.G. trademark 'Zyclon B' it appears to have been used to gas six million unwanted human beings.

It must never happen again.

Betty told me that Bernard has the most awful scars on his back - as if he has been severely whipped, but in fact from louse-ridden straw in his bedding. His family rightly wonder what 'that madman got us into'. Not so mad - I.G.Farben *knew* what they were doing.

I am sad and sorry that Bernhard's parents may have starved to death; that Bernhard himself had a tough billet with a starving mother who had to feed him before, and in front of, her baby; that he like Palmiro had uncomfortable bedding? That I was convicted to endure punishment in one of our own high security prisons?

Must I now, in the peace, step up to the crease? Have I the courage? After all we are learning now, do I still hold the real conviction that war is not the way?

What have 'we' the people of Britain won from war?

What has Europe, Japan, the world won and lost from this Second World War?

How much courage flowed with the blood of ordinary men into the soil of another man's country?

95μ
June 1947

Alec allowed me to finish at the end of the month of May 1947, but I had a week of leave outstanding. Monday 26th being Whit weekend, the 31st being a Saturday, I tidied up the greenhouses on Tuesday and Wednesday and left a set of notes for the family to follow on (with perhaps a new man to follow me - though there has been no mention.)

During a horribly wet April, I did think Alec was going to beg me to stay and *will* the plants out of the sodden ground. However, things looked up in May - eastern England has had the driest month on record, and Mam says Sheffield has had it's hottest May day, too.

So before departing I took a few days to reconnoitre all my POW camp sites and say goodbye to my contacts, making sure I had their addresses and they mine.

Planning for any kind of Gala did seem a forlorn hope after such an awful winter and spring so far, but any excuse after years of war and rationing ... there were a few and they were enhanced by spontaneity and much goodwill. I wondered what Harrises had done about the sudden loss of 25 Italians - surely Tony Dalla Riva wasn't sent home. How about Gina and the Hardys and 'their' Government Farm POWs on the Carrs?

Misterton is the 'capital' village in north east Notts, with a couple of big factories as well as big farms. Newell's Social Club sponsored a gala mostly for their own, but it drew in from the surrounding villages. I had the chance to meet - albeit briefly - Tony Dalla Riva and - Yes! Yes! Yes! - his wife Stephanie. He was given leave to stay, and they to marry, just last month.

They were proudly swinging baby Susan round, bonny little lass. We laughed as she gambolled in 'imitation' of a couple of gymnasts.

Tony gave me a nudge and a wink that the strong men were 'Prigioniero tedesco'. Stephanie looked at me; we both looked at Tony; we all burst out laughing. She nudged him, 'Pigeon hair the nest oh, Tony?'

'Oh excuse me my little darling,' he said in poshest English. Not so dumb, any more. Really picked up the language - a steady relationship with an English girl (and maybe her family) would help. Putting his hand up to his mouth he whispered to me, 'German prisoner.'

I got him to write that in my book - never heard that word before. I decided to keep my eye on the Tedesco gymnasts, and double back to get their story before leaving.

Gina wasn't there, I don't suppose it could be expected, but a little girl and boy smiled shyly and said 'hello', before running off giggling. I'm pretty sure they were her siblings.

At that point I realised that there wasn't a uniform in sight. Everyone has thrown off the semblance of militarism, of being involved in war. Some men were looking uncomfortable in ill-fitting suits - I wasn't sure if they had lost weight in the forces or if they were the demobilisation, 'Demob', suits that the army was giving out. So no Land Army Girls to ask about Government farms, no 'Co-operators', even the Woman in the WVS tea van was in civvies... and a 'Kiss me quick' hat.

Young Les Hardy was there with a gang of lads; I mimed the pitch-forking and got a thumbs-up.

I sidled up to the gymnast, now in Sunday-Best - borrowed, I reckoned, though didn't ask. Georg Rasp smiled at my compliments, but looked to his silent and sullen pal for reassurance. I wasn't sure how to approach the subject in such a public arena, but felt compelled ... I had a pictorial advantage - no words required: as always I had my pocketbook with me, and my photo of the camp.

The pal's turn for reassurance. Georg smiled at him and pointed at the picture. 'Nedder Keedon - mine camp.'

I told him of my story - history - of the POW camps and my many German friends. I held back on the Italian bit.

They nodded.

Time for some tentative prodding. I said I had recently heard of repatriation - boys going home.

No smiles.

I said I thought that the 'old enemies' were becoming friends. How was Christmas for them?

Smiling again. Georg had been with a family. His friend not.

Georg mentioned turkey and 'Thanksgiving.'

I said yes and then realised what I might be hearing. 'American Bird - big - gobble, gobble, gobble - America?' I pointed to him.

He looked sheepishly at the floor grinning to himself. He pulled himself up and rubbed his tummy. 'Great food, better than here.'

His friend nudged him.

Not bad here, but rationing and he pointed at me. Of course. But not in America. And not for the Americans when they were over here in '43-4.

His friend nudged him and pointed to his watchless wrist.

They both looked around.

I started to panic. I showed him my book and notes within. 'Can I get your story, please? Were you in America?'

He nodded. 'And Canada.'

'And you came over here is '46? April?'

He was impressed that I seemed to know about *him.*

He shook his head and said in completely fluent American, 'I came here. Not home.'

I thought he was going to prod me in the chest.

'... and they...' His eyes welled up and he turned away for a moment.

'Georg Rasp - another Georg Rasp done bad things to people. Jews people. They think was that me.' A growl came up from within him.

His friend coughed and said 'Ranby' plus a sentence all in German. I think he thought I might know something I don't about Ranby - an Army camp at

Retford.

Georg turned back, his hand clapped across his mouth. He looked all around - quite a good crowd milling. He looked at me clamping his teeth together then a hissing intake of breath. He shook his head.

I clamped his arm, pursed my lips and nodded. I pulled an address slip from my notebook and slipped it into his hand, patted him on the chest, and nodding said and gesticulated 'later'.

He looked to his friend, back to me and he nodded. He stabbed a finger at my camp photo and gave a hollow laugh. 'We're at Lea Hall camp now...'

'Gainsborough!' I said with perhaps a little too much enthusiasm.

'Ja, but dat my camp real.'

In my physics night-school (thanks to Grandpapa) I learnt a bit more than apples falling on my head: Old Newton said that for every action, there is an equal and opposite reaction.

Mustn't push for what I need - especially a potentially raw enemy, not long from the battlefield.

Be patient Eric - somebody else said that good things come...

I crossed over the Trent - still very high with flood water - and returned on the Eastern side - the back road past Lea Hall. The Hall - yes, another faded landowner's place, is a biggish block in which many rooms with bunks would easily hold a hundred men. I see what Hannay meant. Plenty of them milling about, kicking a ball around and generally lounging this holiday evening - the first one of the year.

Part Eight - Summer 1947

Ukrainian POWs Arrive

Displaced Persons fill the camps

96μ

More news on the Prison of War camp status. Headon may well have been re-labelled NEAC - Nottinghamshire Agricultural Executive Camp - but the inmates remain Prisoners of War. Carburton and Norton are still most definitely Prison camps. I thought my story was almost complete, but I hear very interesting news about Carburton which has a new batch of POWs.

There has been a refugee support system for people displaced in Eastern Europe - mainly Ukraine, Poland and Latvia, but Czechoslovakia, Russia, Jugoslavia and other places which have felt the turmoil, and appear to suffer under the Russian hammer and sickle.

Not Germans, it seems, so Günter, though he may not be going back to East Prussia, could get sent back to another part. He'll hope it's the British or American sector.

The British have invited the East Europeans to various schemes under the banner 'European Voluntary Works' - EVWs. It includes many Poles who fought on our side. They are actually not being 'sent' back.

I did hear of them being housed in army camps, but the new development in my story is that a batch of men from an SS Brigade made up of Ukrainians, has been transferred from camps in Italy to here, and to Canada. A number of them have been brought to Carburton during this month - May. I suspected that secure Carburton has been used as a final filter out of greys and whites, holding on to the blacks.

Alec Fox is whole heartedly in support of that being carefully done: not usually a forthright man, he says, 'If having the Germans wasn't bad enough - we're having these bullies now.' (Word is out that Ukrainians worked the concentration camps.)

Carburton's real 'goodies' have been allowed across the lake to the religious training camp at Norton, on the Welbeck estate proper. I wonder if his Lordship invites them in for tea?

I will have to try to find out a bit more about them to properly finish off this story for you.

See how things go back 'home'.

I sent a *farewell, but keep in touch* card to all my contacts.

97μ

Not long after I had returned home, Willy Kohnstamm invited me to meet him and a 'special friend' in Sheffield to say goodbye. I had a guess who the special friend might be, and thought it might do Mummy good to meet someone else she may read about in my story.

Not so clandestine this time. I thought Willy might be with a girl and I was right. I was most surprised and delighted that the girl was Kathleen, the teacher with whom he had been close to before the serious matter of a war split them up. After a while, Kathleen got to thinking of Willy and contacted him to ask if they could meet up again. Romance blossomed from then, and they were married in Sheffield last year. 'Simple affair. Didn't invite anyone really. Sorry.'

Willy has had to continue in service until this year, and they will return to Cardiff, Willy to the family leather business.

With a fine early summer afternoon, we managed to sit in the hotel garden. Mummy and Kathleen hit it off well - good job, because I did want to get a bit of 'the boring war stuff' off Willy.

Nothing more dramatic like last time to report.

So to good news: Like a school certificate he was very proud of - a kind of leaving report, he showed us a fine watercolour of the camp presented to him. It had an inscription which brought a tear to four sets of eyes. It was in German, and Willy blushed as he read it to us:

"Dear Mr Kohnstamm, ... a memento - from one of the POWs who were in your care for years! ... a token of thanks for your sensitive and decent nature, your patience and your kindness towards the many thousands of German prisoners whose difficult conditions you certainly alleviated as much as possible ... *sniff, wipe* ... not only my own opinion but also the general verdict here in the camp. ... Fritz Zimmer."

We all admired the picture in silence before Mummy expressed surprise at the hotchpotch of huts - Nissens; concrete one with tin roof; tower and chimney. Willy explained to her that this was near the entrance to one of the three 'cages', which do each have twenty eight identical Nissen billet huts - sleeping huts - in a neat row, and a small set of administration buildings - dentist, ("Woo!") MO (doctor), library, etc.

'Twenty eight huts!' said Mummy. 'How many is that?'

Quick as a flash, Kathleen said 'twenty eight!' and they both fell about laughing.

'I get you, Dear,' said Willy, 'forty to a hut, twelve hundred to each cage.' He coughed and lowered his voice. 'Had to fit a lot more in some of the time.'

We were all four poring over the picture as he went on, 'The chimney is the boiler on a mess hut and,' turning to me, 'the house in the background there is the pub we first met in, Eric - the Three Merry Lads.'

'A real treasure,' I said, 'excellent artwork, colour and proportions.'

'And what a school report,' Mummy said.

258

He smiled and nodded a minute before telling how actually, far from punishing the enemy, he could truly say he had made many friends among the POWs he guarded and has a number of pictures given to him by them as gifts including this lovely one. He tapped my sleeve. 'The Italians, Eric? you wondered how they got on with the Tedesci?' He laughed.

I joined him, not knowing what he was going to say.

'Well though they were in separate sections - the cages I mentioned - generally they were all just men who wanted to get on with their lives, with each other and their families back home. One of my special friends is the tiniest/youngest German POW in the whole of Lodge Moor who's known by one and all as 'Bambino', as christened by his Italian colleagues also held at the camp.'

Peace.

I hope they all find peace at home soon, and knowing the value and rarity of a kind and considerate prison guard from personal experience, especially Willy and his new wife, Kathleen.

98μ
Sept 47

Alec Fox asked me go over during September for a week to help tidy up the greenhouses and ready them for a new season. They had found them a life-saver after the awful season out-doors, following *that* winter. I took a few of the evenings out to catch up with the POWs. There are still large numbers at Headon and the re-education continues at Norton Cuckney with the religious aspect in particular.

Carburton is still something of a transit camp, including for the time being some of the Ukrainians brought over in May and June. Apparently the powers that be, did not accept at face value that these chaps were all 'white' and willing workers.

Other than the actual Prisoners of War brought over from Italy, apparently many thousands of Ukrainian refugees have also been invited in to replace the depleting 'stock' of firstly the Italian POWs and now the rapidly depleting Germans.

Then there are the Poles who fought with the British - Anders' Army - and many flyers without whom the Battle of Britain would almost certainly have been some German phrase for 'The Great British Airforce Rout.' There are a couple of hundred thousand of them ... and the Ukrainians are not too happy that their actual citizenship is defined 'Polish' - as enforced at the end of the Great War.

Together therefore there are 3 types: Polish Free Fighters; Ukrainians displaced by Germany and Russia's invasion, and the oppression by Poland during the 1930s; The Ukrainian National Army - the renamed Galician Volunteer SS Regiment.

In the latter group, it is suspected that some were used by the Germans to 'work' the death camps we are hearing about, and as in the name, 'voluntarily.'

Josie Husbands has updated me in a couple of letters and said she could arrange for me to meet a few to get their stories of POW status under the British. I would need it to cap off my story wouldn't I? Yes, Josie, thank you.

What I am *still* doing in the war?

Mummy and I have been steadily, slowly, getting back on track. I have thrown myself into 'horticulture' on 'our' little estate in Dore. Grandpapa was probably there only to sleep and did not notice nature taking over his domain. Grandmama has kept up a tidy front garden, while Mummy ... Mummy has not been well enough for most of the war to upkeep her little kennel business. We had thought of reviving it, but can't really expect much demand in these continuing straightened times.

Palmiro has inspired me. If I can replicate the greenhouse setup at Egmanton, and extend it as I get into the rhythm of the seasons, we have enough land for a potentially handsome Market Garden. (I'm giving it Capital

Letters.) When I get back I will be ready to ask the council for the required Planning Permission.

Then I will need a little help.

There were far too many Ivans in the small group we managed to meet in their mess - a nissen hut. One of many at Carburton camp.

'Many hundred,' said one of the chaps at my wonderment.

'Men? Or Huts?'

He didn't get that.

'How many huts?' I asked.

'Many hundred camps ... houses...' he pointed at the huts.

I nodded.

Another chap queried him in Ukrainian and told me, 'More than a hundred huts - for prisoners. fifty or so for guards.'

I had seen no evidence of any guards.

No guards, now. All gone. They aren't Prisoners any more. EVWs. European Voluntary Workers.

It was the Friday night, and though they will all probably work every day, weekend days are usually shorter and ... Friday is Friday! I'll tell you about two Ivans and a Fedir Wacyk, who has already decided to use his second, more English sounding second name, Walter. So Ivan 'John' Pasaniuk leaving one Ivan - Andreculak, who arrived with his cousin Ivan Besjuk, who has a very similar story, anyway. Walter, John and Ivan.

It was Walter who had done the translating.

John is old enough to be the father of the other two, and has found himself less able to learn English, though that did not hinder him from telling me his story with wild gesticulations and explanations from Walter. Copious amounts of the 'vodka' from several stills on site may have helped.

The youngsters deferred respectfully to their drunken elder, so his story was 'allowed' to impress the pretty lady. Nobody's eye caught mine. I took notes and laughed.

Josie had the forethought to search out a decent enough map of the area of Europe which effectively was Germany's eastern front - basically all round Poland. I discover that Ukraine has its own alphabet, a bit like Russian, but *strictly* not Russian - don't *dare* call it that - and certainly not like English. I recognised some letters like Greek - for instance their 'P' is the same as the common Greek symbol used in Mathematics - Π, 'pie' - but the lower case is an 'n'; however, where M is the same as ours in Russian, Ukrainian uses a T shape. (They don't use my μ - that's a Greek m.)

So John showed me a photo of himself proudly sitting in a small group of much younger men. As I flipped it over, as you do, there was almost nothing I could read, and seeing my confusion, Walter gave me a quick lesson in Ukrainian. He says the inscription reads 'surviving the camps together in Italy' and he took me through the word 'Italy': Imanü. Enough said.

It wasn't only the writing that I needed a translator for - I understood almost nothing of John's story.

This is what I thought he told me: he was a 'good soldier', he was very proud of this and said it several times. Also he was in the Polish Cavalry, but changed to Infantry in the German army.

He was born in 1904 in Rusiliv - he showed this on a paper and Josie found it on the map - north of Lvov. He joined the Polish Army, as they all had to, when he was 21, in 1925. However, if you are not a good soldier, they give you a book. I took this to mean to be in reserves. But he was a good soldier and stayed on. 'Father die. Only sister, mother and me. Farm no good. Need money. Me good soldier.'

He then spoke a lot about horses, so I led him towards the legend which we had picked up, that Poland only had cavalry to fight against Hitler's Panzer Tanks. Yes. He waved a sword in the air and held onto the horse's reins. No good against machine-gun. One 'Germany Man' on motorbike with machine-gun captured all his group.

He was taken to Danzig and kept caged in a field with Russians and English - and no food.

'No food?'

'No food. Eat grass. Twelve days. Find some sugar beet. Eat raw sugar beet. Germans come and ask Ukrainian Man - "be soldier or arbeit?" Me know German arbeit, but me good soldier.'

I know German 'arbeit', too. They put it at the camp entrances - 'Arbeit macht frei', which means 'work makes free'. Apparently the Nazi's horrible slave labour machine promised their 'prisoners', who were not criminals at all, that working would make them free, whereas refusing to work meant they would be executed. What actually happened is that if they worked, they were not fed and so were worked to death. It seems that it may also have been just a simple trick to stop any kind of resistance to being simply exterminated - not work camps, simply death camps with huge cremation furnaces.

So only two weeks into this war, Poland was finished and John Pasaniuk became a German soldier who 'walk, walk, walk.' After several times him telling me this he said, 'no laugh you!' Slapped wrist, Eric. I looked at Walter. He was looking at Josie. She was looking at him. They caught me catching them and jumped to attention.

I asked Walter. 'Cavalry?'

They had a quick confab. 'Piehota' was reiterated with lots of nodding.

Another young man's ears pricked up, (horses do that don't they?) and he sidled onto the table with us. I smiled and lifted my glass.

'Not cavalry,' Walter said, 'infantry. He worked with the horses - supply horses - you say haulage.'

I nodded. More horses killed in the Great War than men. In this war too? I waved a sword like John had.

Another confab. Walter waves a sword. (Not a real one, Pina.) They laughed.

'Poland had a great army, good planes and tanks,' Walter said, but laughed, 'except that they didn't have many and they were all facing Russia. They were expecting the revolution to come from the east, not an invasion from the west.' He looked down at the table and swirled a finger in some spilt drink. 'But Russia came too, you know?'

I didn't. We went to war because Germany invaded Poland. I couldn't argue the case. Walter has picked up a great command of English, but not that great.

The younger man pointed to himself. 'Me horses, too,' he said - in his own way. He looked to 'Daddy John', to continue his story and sat back.

John walk, walk, walked into Austria and was caught by the Allies. Walter confirmed with a wave down the whole hut, that they were all in Austria.

'In camp in Italy Country,' said John. 'See San Marino ... see the stars.' He took a large swig of the vodka and looked down the hut for fresh supplies, which the youngster stretched over for him. 'Then Checky go home; Rusky go home; Dutchy go home. Me not know where me going. Captain come say goodbye, you good man, but me not know where me going. Me last man in camp...'

Walter smiled knowingly.

'... in big ship. Black Sea.' John waved his arms in a terrible storm. He swigged a full tumbler of the vodka, looked at the empty glass through watery eyes and rubbed a full sleeve across his mouth - face. 'Come ... English place ... come here.' He looked towards the cluster at the other end of the hut. Much noise and ribaldry. They were having a raw fish eating competition, and it was obvious that one braggart was taking odds on him eating a whole fish - head, fins and tail. We all stood to watch, but Josie sat back down, Walter with her.

John fell back on his stool, the youngster breaking his fall, but palming him onwards towards the boisterous end of the hut. He then sat rubbing his own leg very fiercely. I didn't see him catch it anywhere.

He turned and offered me his hand. 'Ivan Andreculak'. He wrote it down, slowly appreciating his own grasp of our lettering. His grasp of our language, though not up to Walter's, is also good.

Josie had her finger on the Black Sea and was looking at me with a frown. Walter also looked at the point and frowned too. The Black Sea is on the other side of ... well on the very far side of Josie's map, near Turkey. She told Walter what John had said - he had sailed from the Black Sea.

Walter and Ivan conferred for a moment before bursting into great guffaws of laughter, looking over to John, now head down on a table.

Walter explained that the 'black sea' was the storm at night. They were brought from camps in Rimini, which is in Italy, immediately below the beautiful independent state of San Marino.

Ivan cut in to reinforce just how bad the storm was. Everybody sea-sick.

We all pored over the map: Josie traced a route from north eastern Italy.

Walter pointed out 'Venice, from Venice we come.'

Josie whispered 'by canal' in my ear.

She slid down into the Med, to Gibraltar. The Ukrainians nodded, but as she got to north western Spain that both threw up their arms - as John had.

'The Bay of Biscay!' said Josie. 'Famous for its storms.'

Laughs all round.

Ivan went on to tell us that he and his cousin, yet another Ivan, had elected to be part of a very large group who had been made an offer by Canada, but after the storm in the Bay of Biscay, they feared that they wouldn't make it to Canada, and jumped ship with the contingent that Britain had accepted - about 8000 men.

The four of us then settled to a quiet discussion. Walter, assiduous to Josie's needs, whipped up a tray of teas to avoid the oblivion that the vodka was at risk of offering.

I was keen to clarify that the men were not actually war criminals escaping justice, but of course I could not ask this outright.

What I learnt was that Ukraine is a country, but none of the various empires will let them be. Prussia, Lithuania, Ottoman (Turkey), Austro-Hungary, Poland. Then Stalin had basically starved the Ukraine during the 1930s because it resisted his communist collectivisation.

Ivan told how his father had been in the Austro-Hungarian army, and the family owned a forestry business. His mother had been washed off a bridge and drowned when he was six, leaving just Ivan and his father Vasily. In 1936 the Russians came to his village to collect one male from each family to work in a collectivised forestry camp. 'Slave labour', he called it.

The first thing the Russians had done on arrival at their village was to drag out the parish priest and shoot him in the street. Resistance was futile. Ivan, only sixteen, offered to go in place of his widowed father, but the Russians took both of them, and their trees.

When Germany invaded 'Russia' in 1942, they liberated the Ukrainians. Then they made the Ukrainians an irresistible offer: help fight the Bolsheviks - and only the Bolsheviks - and Germany will give them their own country back if they win. They also offered to let them have their own Padres. This was what was called the Galician Volunteers Regiment. (They didn't use the term 'SS' - which I have already heard they were.) It did make me think of the Pals Brigade dad was in.

Swinging his thumb in John's direction, Ivan told how he did the same. The Germans had him foraging from farms along the way, especially horses. He rubbed his leg again. One day a pair of them took a horse from an old couple who begged them not to - it was all the Germans had left them of their farm. They took it anyway, but up the road, Ivan relented and slapped the horse on back home.

Arriving at camp horseless, the German Captain slapped his own horse and rode Ivan down, smashing his hip. He rubbed it yet again. Good now. He stood to show us, but Walter pointed out that it is shorter than the other, but almost certainly saved his life. The Regiment was marched straight onto the German guns at Brody and 50,000 of them were wiped out.

Ivan told of the white suits to camouflage them in the snow - but no guns. They were just to draw fire from the Russians to make them run out of ammunition before the Germans went in. I told you about cannon-fodder, didn't I, Pina? These poor lads were surely fed to the guns.

There's more: the Nazis wanted the men to keep their white uniforms clean, so wearing them, they hosed them down and made them dry them, sleeping straight up on their backs only. It beggars belief that some weren't frozen to the ground.

I asked Walter about his experiences. He looked at his watch. He looked at Josie. Time was getting on. So were they.

He told how he was from West Ukraine, near Delyatin, he pointed to the map. South of Lvov, towards Rumania.

Ivan took the opportunity to point to his house - almost in Rumania. Walter laughed at the name of his town - 'Big Village' he told me, 'its name means big village. Ha!'

They are the same age - born 1920, so John is 16 years their senior. Walter had had an extra year off the army draft because he was needed to work on the family farm, and joined the Volunteers directly - he said 1944, but though I challenged this, I wasn't happy that it was true. Who let him off - Nazis or Bolsheviks? And why draft at 21 and not 18 or even 16 like the Germans and Italians ended up doing?

I wanted to ask about Jews, but needed a context.

He didn't talk about fighting either. Did he miss Brody? I can't say *'liar!'* can I? Anyway he seems a nice enough chap.

He jumped straight to his POW time in Italy ... because it wasn't. I get it. He was hardly in the camp for five minutes, when he escaped for two years. It's a good story, but almost certainly contains some braggadocio. (Sounds Italian, that?)

I'm not sure he even glanced once at me - Josie was entranced. He teased her about being Italian. Says he's an Italian blacksmith. He proffered his hands to Josie, who scrutinised them against the single bulb hanging in the middle of the hut -black and calloused. She rubbed them. I thought she was going to kiss them for a minute. Black as coal and hard as iron. Ingrained black, there's not much to blacken them in these fields of golden corn and red clay.

'Italian, eh, er ... Walter?' I said, putting on my attentive and serious face.

He waved at all the lads, all in the same nice-ish uniform. 'We all from Italy, Jousie. You know dis?'

We played along, because time was pressing.

He whispered, now, surely so that 'Jousie' would lean in to hear him. Old trick.

Italy my darling. I know you will like this. It's a love story, too. Seaside as well. Rimini - not where we went, but up on the other side, top of the Adriatic coast. Of course you know. Daddy took you to San Marino - it overlooks Rimini. Well it overlooked Walter in his camp, too. But it was the stars he most looked up to.

He says he escaped from the camp -'Bleddy, Poles', he kept referring to, but I'll follow that up another day, 'Mebbe dey can't count'.

Just like here they were sent out on work parties, not sure if quite like here - starvation rations and forced labour more like, including bomb damage clearance and, yes even UXB clearance. Walter wasn't having any of that. He's done his warring for other people. Reckons he just hopped it when they were near some hedging, hid in a ditch and when the lads were rounded up, guard took a cursory glance around and the lorry set off back to camp leaving Walter a free man.

He didn't tell us how, yet, but he worked his way into the affections, ahem, of a blacksmith. Just like here, there is a shortage of men (and not of pretty women), in Italy and, probably 'her dad', took a bit of pity. Somewhat incongruous, because, though a handsome lad, he seems a hard man. (Maybe like you darling - I bet my move totally proved to Daddy that I'm your bit of rough. Grrrr!)

Reckons he stayed two years (yes two years! Bit of a romancer, don't you think?) on-the-run - actually staying with the blacksmith and he taught him all he knew. Treated him like a son. Walter didn't mention the daughter.

Times were hard in Italy but Walter enjoyed himself. Then he heard from fellow prisoners out on work detail, that Britain was recruiting land labourers and assumed this meant only Italians. He was told that it was Ukrainians who were being sent over so he reported back to camp - he just turned up for roll-call as if nothing had changed.

Josie needed to powder her nose - somewhat difficult in an all male POW camp hut, but Ivan hopped up to guard the door for her.

I noticed Walter open and shut his mouth as if he'd missed a trick. He had.

He swept his slicked hair back.

'Delyatin?' I said. 'Many Jews there?'

I looked over my shoulder as I was sure something behind me drew his attention. When I looked back he was on his feet attentive to the other end of the room. Quiet - but pretty drunk quiet. Maudlin is it? Quiet, sad singing.

He looked back to me and gave a rueful smile. 'No home,' he said. He sat down and confided in me very quickly. 'Some gotta go; nobody wants to. Guards made me translate. Some men very ...' he snarled and wriggled his head.

'Nasty? Angry ... rude?'

'Yes ... all things. I can't tell them to be nice or they will be sent to the Russians who will shoot them ... for fighting against them.'

He bared his teeth. Rubbed his hands. Shook his head. Cocked it at me.

Josie returned with her hand out to Walter. He straightened himself up with a fresh smile painted on. He took her hand in both of his.

Ivan shook his head at me. If it were in English he might have mouthed 'charmer!'

As ever I left my contact details and a nice group of smiley, mostly drunken chaps waved us off.

266

At the corners of various lanes of the vast camp, I could see how there may well be a hundred huts. On one stretch of our way past - an international community, not an English word heard, and not one disrespectful whistle from a single vagabond in this world of men. Passed three groupings of a dozen huts - handy for keeping nations apart. But on the other side of a drive just a mass. Wow. Room for four thousand men at least.

Where have all those staunch C- Nazi escapees gone?

Josie was a little pensive in the car on the way back. Funny old world, seemed to be her thinking. 'No home, eh, Eric?' she said.

'I know how they feel,' I did not say. 'Lot of homes gone for ever, and the people from them ... funny old world,' is what I did say.

After a couple of silent miles I added, 'I hope we can create a better new world.'

99µ

Later that same week I called in on the Gregorys at South Leverton.

Charlie and Emma were busy, but Betty was home from school and excited, getting ready for a date with Bernard. I was not totally surprised. Bernard is now a neighbour, properly billeted out with 'Auntie Green' - not a real aunt, but 'Auntie Green' to everybody - was widowed from her 'Dear Walter' who had brought a pickle helmet and Prussian boots home from the first war. She has taken Bernard in to save him from traipsing across from Headon now he was in regular employment on the farm. Betty wasn't in a rush to get ready, she even seemed to need me there for her. They are off to the Ritz Cinema in Retford. They cycle down together to see films - and shows at the Majestic - leaving their cycles with a woman for a penny each. Can't trust leaving them in the street - 'some Spiv would be selling it up Spital Hill next day, otherwise'.

In a kind of reverie for 'poor Bernard', she gave me some more snatches of his story.

He had got a good hiding on the Russian front - if only from the fleas - but I am sure in those arctic conditions, and terrible slaughter, he was still lucky to have survived.

I wasn't sure about how he got here - his capture. Betty still lingered so I asked if she knew.

Dying on their feet, almost starving after two weeks, living only on bitter cider apples, Bernard's remaining comrades under a Sergeant hid out in a barn in an orchard. It was on a T junction. French people were all around, but masses of Allied tanks and troop vehicles were simply rumbling by on the main road. Eventually an armoured car pulled off into the yard and the Feldwebel - that's his sergeant - hung a white handkerchief out of a window.

The Canadian soldier who took them in couldn't have been nicer. Seeing that Hardy just could not stop shaking , he pushed a cigarette into his mouth. Bernard wasn't a smoker, but did not wish to show ingratitude. Bernard was one of the 50,000 prisoners taken that now famous day of the Falaise Pocket.

Betty seemed pleased with her hair and make up and there was still an hour or more before the big moment. She laughed, looked at her watch for the umpteenth time and decided she had time to make me a cup of tea.

Bernard's captors sent him straight off the battlefield to, she thinks, Southampton where they were loaded onto trains - ordinary trains - and taken to a huge army barracks - The Marches or something in the south west. Devizes - Wiltshire is it?'

I nodded though I wasn't sure.

'Here they were checked over and sorted, kind of assessed for their Nazi fervour. Bernard had none. His father had written to him earlier in the war saying 'this madman has led us into damnation'. Bernard had told me something similar during our walk round the village.

At the Barracks five trainloads a day were bringing men in and then taking five trainloads out to camps across the country - Bernard straight to Nether Headon.

'He's not a bad man Mr Chapman.'

I know she thinks that - I can easily agree with her.

I had taken her down into sad thoughts so turned things around and asked, 'So - Courting?' Pretty obvious, but hardening the phrase.

She savoured the notion a moment before laughing her way through telling me of early 'erm ... dates.' First was secret. 'Dad loaned him a blue gabardine coat to cover his POW uniform to a concert at the Majestic. Then didn't trust us going out without him. Not that we would do anything ... you know! No, but in case anyone were to speak to the man, and discover, or even suspect his German accent.'

'He's pretty good, though,' I said, but it was taken almost as sarcasm.

She pursed her lips and frowned at me a moment before going on. 'So silly, I could hardly keep a straight face when anyone came near. Dad insisted we - him and me - we take one of Bernard's elbows each and not let go. Well we almost staggered along we held onto him so tight. It probably looked like we were smuggling a dummy ... a body even! We might have even tripped up over the thing - the coat was far too big for Bernard.'

Things are a little better now at Leverton Station - for just three bob they can get a train into the centre of Lincoln for the day.

She rubbed her ring finger - no ring on it. 'We're getting married.'

I didn't say anything - not even congratulating her. Some might call it a pregnant silence Mummy.

She bit her lip and looked at the ceiling. 'Daddy won't let me ...'

Oh dear I had turned things downwards again..

She shook her head. 'Oh no, it's not Bernard, it's that man, that awful man Attlee.'

Aha - the punishment angle. Prime Minister thinks they need punishing. Not happy about the fraternisation - still.

'Daddy's just protecting his only child, Mr Chapman', she was nodding but not convincing herself. 'It's that Bill. You know he's putting a Bill through Parliament saying that if English girls marry Germans they will have to take their nationality ... and if they are sent home ... have to go with them.'

I rested my hand on her arm a moment.

She had to get ready.

Bernard is also still unsure of his status. He has been released from POW status and seems to be covered by the EVW scheme now. He still answers to the NAEC at Nether Headon, and his 'leave to stay' is based on him remaining in the defined occupation - agriculture - for at least two years, and notifying the police of any changes to his address. More to the point, home has recently changed from America to Russia - his town of Muhlhausen in Thuringen has just been traded from the American sector by the Russians. And the Russians don't like any Germans who fought against them ... at all. Would Betty want to marry him and they both be sent home to an uncertain fate?

Betty is encouraged that several of her friends are 'seeing' German chaps, among them her cousin and two school friends. One of them, Mavis Mumby, was introduced because her Uncle Clarrie - yes Clarrie Mumby - drove the POWs out to the farms. A form of introduction agency?

Another lives in a pub which the POWs visit, The Butcher's Arms at Laneham.

I've heard that before.

It's too much of a coincidence.

The other's uncle drives the POWs to farms.

No.

After all that explaining, I thought another little map would show just how many camps there were: this is just 50 miles topt to bottom, and only 25 miles across. Nether Headon is Nottinghamshire's main rural Standard Camp. Lodge Moor in Sheffield and Wollaton Hall in Nottingham both have three full-sized camp enclosures. That's a capacity of over 4,000POWs.

Every dot is a camp:

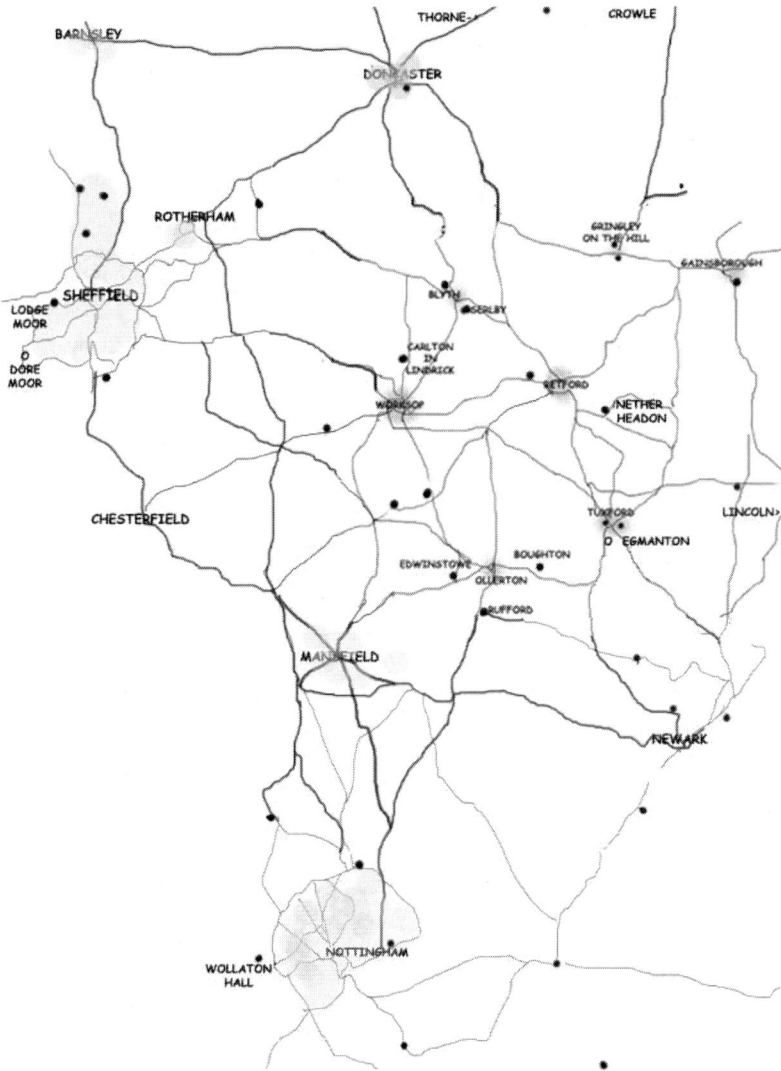

100μ
November 1947

Grandpapa has left us a substantial estate up on Dore Moor. It in no way compares to the grouse moors of the highlands that appealed to him, but inspired by Palmiro and all I have learnt from him, I have set about producing a fresh living for Mummy and me?

The decrepit kennels made a display that Guy Fawkes would have been proud of on bonfire night. Thinking of that spelling brought Carburton and the ardent Nazis to mind. How has Faulk got on with the Re-education? The other huts I saw were grouped - sectioned - perhaps there are some, many, Germans remaining there in their own compound. They can't all have 'found God' and gone over to the other side of the lake with the YMCA at Norton.

There was a distinct finality at Portland Farm after the poor harvest I helped with in the Summer. Alec 'presented me' with my billhook and plasher, and laughed heartily when I lifted the hook up to the light to find the engraving he said he had had done on it.

Good tease, and great to leave on a very happy note, though the smiles were a thin veneer over...

Anyway, both tools have been life savers, swathing through the years of scrub and brambles which had overtaken the site. I set small fires all across, raking embers to eat off the tops.

Now I have set half a dozen pigs on to 'plough' the plot, grub up as many old roots as possible and also provide a crackling Christmas for us.

The sheds were rotten, but the concrete floors have provided good standing for four greenhouses. It has been a delight to be quietly working alongside Mummy in them - she had hardly ever got her hands dirty before, and I warmed to see her looking in wonderment at them at the end of a day.

Green shoots. New life. Red cheeks. Health, even on rations. But a future for all. For you?

As we both stood 'looking over our estate,' stretching our aching backs, smiling at each other, I said 'we need a man.'

Who could I be thinking of?

Has Palmiro got plenty to do at home?

Does he need me, like I need him?

101μ

I need Palmiro. The hard grafting around the old Kennel site I have managed, but what I need now is the skills of a man with green fingers.

I have sent a parcel of little luxuries which I hope Palmiro and his large family will appreciate in the Christmas season.

My plans have been properly drawn up by an architect with agricultural experience, so he has included due consideration of any issues which may inhibit us getting permission.

I have therefore also enclosed a work permit for Palmiro that I have managed to secure from the 'Aliens' Office in London. It was not difficult - the country needs as many willing hands as it can get, and is recruiting directly in Italy, particularly men for hot work apparently - bricks in Peterborough, glass in St Helens and steel here in Sheffield.

The hottest thing out here is likely to be garlic.

I do hope Palmiro accepts and we can have a nice little Market Garden on site by the end of 1949.

102μ
Christmas 1947

I took Mummy down to give greetings to my wartime friends across north Notts - and to check out the status of 'my' camps. We drove directly to Nether Headon where a quick enquiry as to its status received a terse 'yeah, full up - re-education, still,' from one of the few guards. I asked after Günter Rahn and was shown to the hut next to reception. It is apparently his billet, but a squaddie on duty said he was 'ahem, at a family's place for Sunday lunch, kiss kiss.'

So on to the Foxes at Egmanton for lunch. Barbara has finished school and was out with 'her young man'.

I told them of my plans and the greenhouses, and Alec somewhat ruefully said 'you might as well have ours.' Sally gave him a very strange look, and he said no more on the subject. He told me that as far as he was aware, the proper camps were still working and were pretty much full. I told him how many had been sent home, but that others were brought from America and Canada to replace them.

The family knew several lasses Barbara's age who were seeing German chaps, to which Alec added - 'just glad our lass has herself a decent English chap,' but again Sally cut him short with a look. I mentioned Betty and Bernard. He remained tight-lipped and shook his head.

You won't need to remember the towns and villages where I did what I did in the war, but this little trip round with Mummy gives a flavour of just what could be found on a simple day-trip, probably anywhere in England - Britain maybe.

We then took a scenic route down to Newark to take in Palmiro's Nissens at Little Carlton and the concrete huts at Caunton, and then doubled back to Ollerton/Boughton - no camp to see but the huge number of large Nissen 'Romney' style storage huts, are still in military hands.

Just up the road, the collection of huts in Sherwood Forest - Edwinstowe Camp is not laid out like a Standard Camp - is now another Agricultural camp for the Displaced.

We rolled on past Clumber Park, still bristling with the military, to see Carburton on the hill across from the School but, simply regaling Mummy with the tales of the Ivans living in there.

I most wanted to show Mummy Norton camp. This is apparently still fairly full, with men voluntarily staying on to finish studies at what they have dubbed 'The University of Barbed Wire.' We spoke to one of the YMCA people for a little while with two Germans listening and nodding. All very proud of each other and their involvement with the local community.

Apparently many, not all, POWs who wish to be repatriated have already gone, but a good number are still to decide between a very uncertain future and seeking refugee status here. These have been joined by many Displaced Persons. The section of the younger ones, inculcated as Hitler Youth, now doing Abitur have still to satisfy the Re-Education inspectors of their enthusiasm for democracy.

The Worksop vicar encouraged his parishioners to invite Germans for Sunday dinner and this has now gone on for a couple of years. Chaps have studied at Mansfield College of Art and one has sculpted the Christmas crib for Cuckney Church, some Angel Candle sticks for Warsop and an altar front at another church. The vicar looked at his watch and said we might just catch one of the POWs playing the organ for Evensong at Cuckney church.

So we did.

In the car home, Mummy was quiet for a while. She had had a lot to take in.

She eventually burst out, 'There are lots of ... camps, POWs ... around here, Eric.'

I smiled and shook my head. 'I think ... in fact I am *positive* that it is like this over the whole country.'

'Oh, Eric,' she said, 'surely not.'

I smiled and nodded. 'Do you know, I think that what we have here will be mirrored right across the British Isles? Mr Fox is in a very broad network of farmers controlled by WarAg - yes *ordered* what to grow and where. They are to use whatever labour is available and that means women and children...'

'...women, yes, Eric,' she said, 'but not children?'

I raised my brows and drew my lips across my teeth. 'Afraid so. Not forced labour, of course, but you must have heard of the holiday camps?'

She pulled a face. '*POW* camps!'

I laughed and stroked her hand. 'I honestly reckon that there are hundreds of thousands of Germans and other Axis prisoners - you do know the hundred and fifty thousand or so Italians have been sent home - Palmiro with them?'

She frowned but gave a doubtful nod.

Yes, hundreds of thousands, along with a very welcome couple of hundred thousand Polish free Fighters are spread out across the whole of England and Wales, probably Scotland and Northern Ireland too. There could be around a couple of thousand camps - camps, hostels and billets.'

She looked at me, pulled another face, joined her hands in her lap and turned to watch the road home in silence.

103μ

By March 1948, I was getting desperate not having heard from Palmiro for 4 months. He had not replied to my offer - the work permit. I suspected two things might be at play: either he couldn't read or at least understand the implications of the formal document; or he thought perhaps I was simply being too kind.

I know his English - or his writing generally - is not good. I decided to visit Luca. It was time anyway, but I would ask him to write a really welcoming message to which I would attach a second permit.

I had telephoned Lesley Marshal to see how the land lies, so called to see him first out of courtesy. He is extremely pleased with himself - not to say relieved. He hinted that he really did not know if he could have even held onto the farm if he had to depend on whatever British labour might return from the war ... or none.

I told him about the Portland Farm connection with Hardy's in Gringley. He gave me a sideways glance before telling that 'he' had bought his farm off the Duke of Portland estates. Farms in Gringley and Egmanton had been sold off in 1941 - probably for death duties.

'Or gambling!' I said. He laughed and scratched his head.

Alec had told me that one of the old Welbeck Dukes - Harvey or Harley - had actually lost all of his fortune on the horses.

It's called Bleak House farm - not so bleak, and isn't a Dickens book called that? Wonder if he visited once upon a time? Lesley just laughed again.

During the war he had kept his POWs up in the converted attic. Nice and warm. However, he has gone one better. Like me Luca stayed the extra year until June '47, in fact a month longer than I did. By this point he was desperate to go home, whilst Lesley desperately needed him. 'Bring them here!' he said.

I imagined Luca picturing his wife and daughter up in the attic.

Though he did have some difficulty, as they are intended for city folk made homeless in the war, he managed to secure one of the Pre-fabs for the Ritucci family. Mattersey Thorpe is a very small hamlet. It did not lose any houses to bombs. It's in the rural farming community and Lesley needed a farm manager. These are small concrete houses built in sections in a factory and simply delivered and bolted together on site. There is a small estate of them in Mattersey Thorpe.

So Luca was 'at home' to me. His wife Giuseppina, with his daughter 'Nina'- from Giovannina - a young woman into her teens I would say, in a short few months have made a comfortable home for themselves. Apparently he stayed on in '46 and did not even go back home for them, some cousins brought them over.

Oh how he must have missed them,?

The ladies retired to the kitchen while we crafted a note to Palmiro. I had already written the basis of what I needed translating - and putting in suitably colloquial terms by Luca. We then had to decide in whose hand it should be. Is it from Luca or from me? We settled on him dictating - and spelling - to me, with him enclosing a little 'come on over' note in his handwriting.

Nina brought in a fresh pannacotta with the tea - English tea. Lovely.

Luca told how he had built up a small network of contacts from some others who had stayed behind like him. (I won't tell Alec there are more). He thought it useful to mention them - a Vincenzo Aversa and Filippo Bruccoleri.

Not names I knew so I asked if they were at Carlton-in-Lindrick with him. He was somewhat confused as to why I asked. I had to remind him how I first met him, bringing Joe his American cousin from there.

He got all smiley-tearful and brought Giovanna and Nina from the kitchen to regale them of Cousin Joe with much pointing and laughing at me.

104μ

July 48

The fresh Work Permit I sent for Palmiro was dated May 1948, and I was greatly relieved to get a note - which I suspect was written by a friend - to say thank you and that Palmiro would be arriving at Sheffield Station on 28th June 48.

Mummy had a room specially made up for him and I glanced away as I noticed his eyes well up in silence.

He was extremely tense and so obviously uncomfortable, that I took him to where I knew he would be at ease - the greenhouses. It was plain to see that I had modelled them on 'his' at Egmanton - what other example did I have? He nodded his way around, pricking out a couple of weeds, and settling seedlings and cuttings. I seemed to be getting his seal of approval.

We stood outside for a quiet time while he took in the 'estate'. He kicked up some soil in different places, and bit his lip. It is not the best soil, I said, but he waved that off and, patting Susanna the jolly good sow, said it would be much better next year, and it is much better than the soil of his sun bleached and exposed hilltop village.

By way of a kind of apology about ignoring my first work permit, he told us of his family: he is one of ten - most grown up now of course; how there is very little work and they are expected to live off what little land they do have - very little - and a donkey, by the sound of it.

The country - or rather the towns - in his district of Potenza are wrecked. His own town of Latronico is mountainous and at over 2400 feet above sea level, was tricky for armies to fight over. However, it is right in the middle, just at the top of the 'boot' of Italy where tens of thousand of allied troops landed to regain the south of Europe. The whole surrounding area is engaged in recovery and survival: and there is not enough for his family to survive on.

Palmiro refused to abandon them and come to me, but when the second permit arrived they persuaded him that he had an opportunity, and it would leave one less mouth to feed!

We had a laugh and moved to lighter things - at least we don't have snakes. I told you this before, but he had forgotten just how much he loathes them. Mummy shivered at the thought.

He showed us a family picture - most of them sitting on the front steps. How delightful - 3 brothers, 3 sisters, his parents and even grandma, plus three little nieces. A bearded monk is the only one who is not smiling. I pointed this out and he did a double take of it and laughed. His brother is a Franciscan Friar - not a monk, apparently. It was he who wrote to me.

I told him that from what little I do know of religions, that there is a Christian hero - that's a Saint - who does appeal to the Conscientious Objector in me - Francis of Assisi.

Palmiro nodded and pointed at his brother.

One of my religious fellow COs told me of the patron of the animals. How he had gone to the crusades to try to stop the Muslims and Christians fighting. He had been captured and became a Prisoner of War for a year. Undeterred by his earlier experience, a few years later he went along with another crusade. This time, in his raggedy old habit, he broke through his own lines and walked into the sultan's tent to try to convert him. The sultan had a carpet made of crosses, and pointed out to Francis that he was treading on the symbol of his faith. Unabashed, Francis simply pointed out that there was only one cross - the one his saviour had died on. The sultan was very impressed by the friar and this time kept him as a guest for a fortnight, to discuss God and faith with the sultan and his Muslim padre.

My CO friend said Francis could be my Patron Saint. I think he was trying to convert me.

Palmiro blessed himself as he said 'Si, si, San Francisco.'

I told him of Luca at Lesley Marshall's, how he had stayed on.

Palmiro cocked his head and thought for a minute. 'We went home?'

I raised an eyebrow and he laughed.

He got it: 'When they marched us to train - from Little Carlton ... to Newark and the ship home, yes?'

I nodded.

'Captain man stops us and asks us if we want to stay - as citizens. Take contract on farms. Well we all got new uniforms, thinking of home for two whole months. We too excited. No man wanted to stay.'

I wonder what the balance was. I actually don't know any others who stayed on farms besides Luca Ritucci.

I'll take Palmiro over to catch up with him when we get a free minute.

Pyrrhic victory, Mummy? I may have lasted out the war, fighting in my own way of *not* fighting in order to stop the fighting. But sometimes a victor doesn't win anything - or has nothing to show for his fight, even gets burnt up on a funeral pyre.

The council has refused us Planning Permission for the Market Garden.

I am perhaps being paranoid, but I cannot help feeling that I am being refused, because it is known hereabouts that I did not fight in the war. Also I have a conviction for it.

I have spent time in a high security prison.

I am an ex-convict.

They do not want the likes of me running a business - or making any success of one in the poshest part of the city that Dore considers itself.

Mummy is not speaking to me.

And Palmiro can't.

I hope you can listen to this one day. You may be the only one.

After a whole day out of the house, rummaging round the greenhouses and ruminating about my future, our future ... and poor Palmiro's future ... another fine mess I've got him into.

Palmiro is my responsibility - literally and legally.

What to do?

The only thing I could think of was to see if Alec could use Palmiro back at Portland Farm in Egmanton.

I couldn't get hold of him on the telephone, though. I rang daily for three days - morning, noon and night.

In the end I rang the Post Office. The Post Mistress told me that she thought the Foxes had left Portland. I couldn't believe this. How could they so soon, so suddenly?

She thought that she was perhaps mistaken, but would take my number and make some enquiries.

That evening Alec rang me.

I was devasted.

What else was going to go wrong? I could cope with myself - perhaps only myself. But what of Palmiro, here on the other side of the world from home and family?

Alec has given up the farm. He didn't like having to use German POWs - he didn't want people to hear that, by the way - so he had resolved to move into the new business of caravanning - to open a caravan park at a sea side.

So as the new season would need new sowing, the family decided to hand the farm over to someone who might sow for themselves. I didn't realise that he was only a tenant - he didn't own the old duke's farm.

He had an idea, a suggestion: his brother Charlie might take Palmiro on at Merryfields, in Marnham - a village a few miles away from Egmanton. He would put out some feelers with Charlie. No promises.

I couldn't build up Palmiro's hopes, but he brought the permit to me by way of exploring what his options might be.

Things just got worse.

Palmiro couldn't read the legal document with its jargon, and of course I was so happy to get it, and send it on to Palmiro that I had not read 'the small print.'

The permit - pretty legal document - states specifically that it is valid *'only for the particular employment for which it is issued'* - Horticulture - *'and not for employment of another kind or with another employer.'*

'Palmiero LA BANCA' is the above named *alien*, I am that employer. They have also given him an 'e' in his name.

How long is it going to take to change it, and are the authorities who have made things so difficult for me, going to turnabout and be nice to me?

Who is to know?

Who is to care?

Just before my head was about to explode, Charlie fox himself rang to tell me that of course Palmiro would be welcome to come and work for him. Bring him over as soon as I like.

Palmiro has an Identity card issued on his arrival in June and it states that he 'is the holder of an Alien's Registration certificate'. He sent the ID to the registration office with his new address at Merryfields and got it stamped on 16th Sept 48.

No questions asked.

He's helping the Merryfield Foxes to finish off the harvest.

My seedlings have grown out of their boxes and died, taking another piece of my heart with them.

Part Nine - Autumn 1948

Prisoner of War status ends

Thousands remain and some return

105μ
October 1948

Have I finished this story, now? What more will my children need to know about what Daddy did in the war? The war finished over three years ago, yet thousands, perhaps hundreds of thousands, of prisoners are still here. I have served my own sentence, but it appears that my conviction will remain on my record. As yet I do not know how this will affect my or our future.

What remains to tell of my story?

Many Germans remain, along with some of their Axis allies, like lots of Austrians who whole heartedly welcomed Hitler and his Nazi ideology. Now there are the Ukrainians and their 'fellow countrymen' the Polish free fighters.

Some POWs are struggling to stay here - particularly those who are with British families and with whom they are happy, especially if they have joined and even added to those families, such as Tony Dalla Riva!

Now others, like Palmiro, return.

I have returned home to Mummy.

Joe Bennett has survived being stalked by U-Boat Wolf Packs, only to go back into the bowels of the earth down the coal mine at Ollerton - Thoresby Pit. He tells of a pal he made among Germans - 'Freddie, a collier like me, but from Essen.' That jolted me - Germany's Sheffield - the essential centre of steel and munition factories, and the dams that were bombed and busted.

Joe is proud of the five U-Boat submarines that his ship sank, but seems to hold no enmity for his supposed enemy, even befriending Freddie - a survivor. Would he have survived the 1000 ton raid on Essen any better?

Joe asked Freddie why he was in a U-boat. He said, *'When they call you, you don't argue! They were going to shoot you. You don't stand and argue! I hated every minute.'*

Joe asserts that all the Germans at Edwinstowe had been sailors in U-boats - Under-sea Boats - submarines. They are let out at night and sit on the wall on the corner, opposite the Royal Oak. He laughed about them not being able to get away from the village as there was nowhere to go. They would come walking by and the village lads used to talk to them about where they had been and when had they been taken prisoner.

Joe has even researched and found the British ship that sank Freddie's boat as he wants to thank the Captain! They were depth charged, but managed to surface and everyone of the 52 crew were rescued - not a single casualty. Freddie and the majority of Edwinstowe's Germans have been repatriated, but Joe has written to say it was a Captain Walker of HMS Wren on 10th August 1944.

Most of those remaining billeted at the camp now are 'stateless', since their homelands are in Soviet Union territories, dominated by Stalin's Russia. They are East Europeans and speak a variety of languages from the Baltic North to

Southern Ukraine. I suspect that they will have been in SS brigades that helped Germany fight off Russia.

Joe says that some of them and a number of Polish Free Fighter chaps have been given work at the pit. I gave him Chez and Antoni's details and asked him to look out for them. I think a man who can work maintaining planes may seek mechanical work. It would be a coincidence if he came across them among so many.

He also mentions the Italian 'Phil' he took to the pub. Apparently he fell for a girl at the local Catholic Church, but though he wanted to stay with her, he didn't have a work permit and was sent home. He made his way back up to France where he did get a permit to work in a restaurant. His girlfriend eventually got a permit for him to work at Thoresby pit alongside Joe. She went over to France to get him and they married straight away.

That's love.

Willy has been demobbed, but Lodge Moor and Nether Headon are still working and holding a full complement of men. For Lodge Moor - effectively 3 standard camps and each capable of high security with electric fencing - could be holding over 4000 men.

I suspect that though Palmiro was called to Little Carlton satellite camp, the Standard camps - including Wollaton in Nottingham - will recall the Germans in to be 'carded' as Hannay had called it, assessed, and not being released or repatriated until they reach a white 'A' quality - thoroughly democratised.

Italians built the camps from 1942; the majority of the almost 170,000 were billeted out or in 'work camps' looking after themselves by late 1944. The camps were then extended after D-Day, June 1944, to contain much more belligerent Germans so that by the end of the war there were 400,000 of them. As the wounded and 'more innocent' were repatriated, by April 1946 they were replaced by others sent from the USA and Canada. These thought they were going home, but had not been 'carded' (assessed) for Nazi tendencies, so had to pass a successful re-education programme. That's why some are still here.

Some Ukrainians were brought over as POWs from camps in Italy, but joined many more refugees from Eastern Europe, plus perhaps 200,000 from the Free Polish forces, who are all afraid to return to their homelands which are in the hands of Soviet Russia.

Three years after the war has finished there are still perhaps 300,000 men housed in County Agricultural Executive Hostels - so Notts is NAEC - for Displaced Persons. Many of these are poor, most lacking any possessions at all. Some people are holding a dim view of them and 'DP' had become a rude name.

Not fair on such courageous people. We would not have won the war without them.

What did I do in the war and is my job done? I have been 'de-mobbed' but I suspect I have at least the equivalent of a Criminal Conviction. My conviction that war is wrong remains strong especially regarding industrial and even remote war - not hand-to-hand, but weapons from afar, from the sky.

There is now talk of a 'cold war'. A clever man called George Orwell has come up with the term and he may point me in a new direction, especially as my local rulers have taken away my first option of developing a Market Garden.

Orwell is a surprise to my Pacifist friends and me because he had said something awful about us in the earliest days of the war: "Since pacifists have more freedom of action in countries where traces of democracy survive, pacifism can act more effectively against democracy than for it. Objectively, the pacifist is pro-Nazi."

His new warnings arise out of the use of the Atomic bomb. He says that the history of civilisation is the history of weapons: that "ages in which the dominant weapon is expensive or difficult to make will tend to be ages of tyranny, dictatorship, totalitarianism and absolute rule; whereas when the dominant weapon is cheap and simple, the common people have a chance." Thus, for example, tanks, battleships and bombing planes and Doodlebugs are inherently tyrannical weapons, while rifles, swords, bayonets and hand-grenades are inherently democratic weapons. "A complex weapon makes the strong stronger, while a simple weapon - so long as there is no answer to it - gives claws to the weak."

I do not wish you to have claws.

It seems that the two great powers who think they won this second world war - Russia and America - are now in a war, or arms race at the very least, to make a total bomb - one bomb which can wipe out a nation.

The first and only of these 'Atomic' bombs to be used so far are those which wiped out two of Japans biggest cities - Hiroshima and Nagasaki. We can say 'wiped out', because the citizens simply evaporated and they can't tell how many there were - but it is somewhere between 130,000 and 230,000. Two bombs.

I would like to think that I could continue to help the Displaced Persons including the vast numbers of refugees who crossed whole countries to either get away from tyranny, destruction and hunger, or to get back home - what is left of it.

I told you about Bernard's parents starving in central Germany.

Günter still has not found his parents. He knows the Russians have flattened his city of Konigsberg and cleared all - every one - of the Germans out of his old state of East Prussia. I suspect that this number is a dreaded fear rather than reality, but the Germans are certainly unwelcome in this new Russian borderland.

106μ

As the nights started to close in towards the end of 1948, Mummy and I began to sit together by the fire listening to the radio. At peace. Together.

A first trip to the cinema since losing Palmiro was to see Oliver Twist. I found myself so profoundly moved by the poor boy's fate that for the first time, since our return from honeymoon I believe, Mummy felt the need to support me.

Discussing the effect on the couch, she tentatively approached the subject of these very words - what is it you are writing about, Eric?

One of my note books was on the arm of 'my' side chair and she looked across at it. I couldn't simply ignore her, or it. I leaned across for it, turned it over in my hand, and in my mind. What to say?

It has been my companion throughout the war ... you have been my companion ... and so has Mummy.

But really?

I took such a deep breath, followed by quaking exhale. I bit my lip and looked at her.

Just two days before, whilst Mummy was out shopping and I was mulling over the accounts, Grandmama came gently to me.

For the very first time. It was just as if I met a completely new person. She wanted me to understand that Mummy has changed. While I was away. It's not Mummy's fault.

Grandmama was reluctant to speak ill of her dead husband, but she did not wish to be implicated in his most dreadful deed.

I could think of a few, the worst of which to me was his profit making from the development and production of killing machines.

Now the greatest personal impact on me was drawing me into it, my objection and his rejection, which effectively sent me to prison. I chewed my lip thinking of these. My silence drew a supportive hand to my sleeve. I do believe that made me jump.

It was not the most dreadful deed.

She took a hankie out and wiped her nose. She took off her glasses and a first look at her eyes showed me that she was not weeping, she was crying.

I took hold of her hand. Warm. Dry. Soft. For a moment. Before she slipped it away to join the other hand in her lap. She recomposed herself.

I opened the notebook and flicked across the pages. It is nearing its end. It is a story for you Pina, my child. It is for Mummy to read. To read to you. We made you Pina. We did make you. Your spirit has led me through this war. The spirit of a child could not want this destruction, this carnage. You would want me to stop it. To not join in. To look after you. To look after your Mummy.

Grandpapa stopped me.

Grandmama told me that her husband had ... stopped you.

288

But you have continued to support me. Grandmama does not realise. The thought of you is more than that, more than a thought.

Mummy doesn't know either. She does not know what I know. I am sure she will be surprised to meet you in these pages.

The simple truth is best. Always. It is always the best truth, too.

From the moment I was sent to Strangeways Prison, I have been alone with my convictions. I believe I was right. Only my own mother believes it too. I dearly wish my child, my children, will believe in me.

Grandmama says there will be no children. *That is the most dreadful deed.*

The accounts, my lack of prospects, could not distract me from that searing assault. On my love. On my loves.

Mummy has not been strong since Middlewood Mental Hospital.

But she has recovered to a good strong woman. Beautiful. But we know the strength will always be fragile.

Somebody will want to know what I did in the war. I want them to. I want Mummy to and ... I want our children to.

My Daddy made me and went straight off to war. He lost. He came back alive but he had lost his life. He had Mam. He had me. He loved us until the day his body eventually died. He did not want war for me.

I made you Pina, and went straight off to prison.

The announcement of your imminent arrival came to Egmanton the day after my Tribunal's Sentence.

No news of your actual arrival was to follow.

I told Mummy that after Palmiro had told me of the boy on the bike, I felt the need to make a record of my experiences. I was doing what I was doing for our family, but like most of the adult males in the world, I was away from home, I was away at war. I had a different battle and even I would need to look back to see what I did in that war.

'It's a love letter,' I said, 'to you.' I flicked the pages again. I looked across at the drawer where I knew all the other notebooks lay. 'It isn't quite finished...'

'Because your war's not over is it, Eric?'

I stretched my lips across my teeth and bit the upper one. A strange image of Gina with her crazed face flashed before my eyes. I opened Mummy's hand and lay the book on her palm, with mine on top of it. I then lifted the book back off and put it on the floor at my heel.

She needed to know about you.

I took her back to the azure sea rolling onto the Amalfi coast. Then up into the hills, the green villages clinging to hills and valley sides. Olives, wine, laughter ... and garlic. Love all around. Black hair and olive skin, Mummy's red hair a rarity to behold and to stroke.

And that little girl. Black hair, but blue eyes. Giuseppina. Pina.

'Pina came with me to Egmanton,' I said.

Mummy laughed and grabbed my hand back. She lifted it to her mouth, kissed it and held it, breathing me in.

'I wanted to tell my story, but I didn't ... I still don't know, just who will ever read it, who will want to know. Future generations will hear all about "Our Finest Hour", "We will fight them on the beaches", "Never Surrender", but they will not be told about Palmiro and the peaceable Italians. Especially not about people like me ... who did not help.'

Mummy squeezed my hand so hard.

I looked down at the book. 'You are Pina's Mummy. I hoped it would be you who would tell her what I did in the war - in my words, sometimes.'

'But...'

I stopped her. 'I know now,' I said. 'I have probably known for a very long time. But hope is a wonderful thing. Hope ... and Pina and you ... yes you ... have carried me through.'

'But...'

I pointed out of the window. 'Out there. A real world full of people, a lot fewer people that ten years ago, all have hope. It is all that many of the people of Europe have. My prisoners of war yearned, hoped beyond hope, that their families were surviving, and they themselves would survive long enough to see them smile once more.'

'But Prisoners?'

'Yes Dear. My story is ... it is a love story.'

Mummy pulled a face.

'Love of you, of our children, of people, of people like us. Convicts like me.'

'You're not...'

'I am a convict. Yes I am playing on the word - but I am full of conviction that to kill is wrong. I have still not met anyone, man or woman, who disagrees with that. But they disagree with *me*. And they have convicted me of a crime. I have been sentenced, imprisoned and exiled.'

I'm sorry if I let out a self-pitying sob, there.

I went on, 'Palmiro told me of a boy from the camp, a prison of war camp, being killed whilst riding his bike.'

'Sniper?'

'No Dear. Near Retford. Free to ride into town. Perhaps a clandestine meeting with a forbidden love. Simply crashed into a bus.'

My hand dropped as hers clapped over her mouth. 'How awful.'

I bit my lip again and nodded a while. 'I had to record that.' I tilted my head. 'It wasn't in the Retford Times. But ... well here's the irony, I don't even know his name.'

We sat for a while. I picked the book back up, stood and walked over to my desk. I picked up the most dog-eared of the notebooks, flicked the pages and brought it over to Mummy. Before handing it over I told Mummy that of course I would want her to read it. I have, from page one, written it properly and clearly. It is a story and she will meet many of my friends, and here's the difficult bit, she will read about herself and our family.

My lip was held tight between teeth and the book between my fingers. I did not let go. 'You must assure me that you can ... are strong enough to carry this story. I will want your help to tell the children.'

The colour drained from her face. I plumped down beside her and took her arm firmly in mine. 'There will be a new generation of children, all around us. We - you and I - must adopt them and lead our neighbours, our Polish, English, comfortable people of Dore,' we laughed, 'Germans and Italians, Irish Navvies, Grinders, Blades and Owls - we must help lead them into safety...' I stopped to see if Mummy would catch up.

'The mushroom cloud hangs over us, Eric.'

We looked into each other's watery eyes. Nodding.

'We *will* have children.

I lifted the newspaper from the side table open at an advertisement for teachers.

You smiled at me.

107μ
November 1948

In the space of a week I had secured a conditional place in one of the new temporary Teacher Training Colleges set up last year. I cannot start yet, but they and I feel assured that I will show I have the basics in place for a full course of a year starting next September. Though I did pass my Matriculation, and they recognise my decade in a laboratory as of great value, they are worried that after a ten year career as a Grinder followed by four as a farm labourer - not even a 'farmer' - my brain may not be so sharp. Seriously I would start at night school after Christmas, swat up on English and maths ... and maybe take history a little more seriously. Now I have a history of my own to tell, eh?

We can live on my savings and Mummy's legacy for a while. There is enormous enthusiasm to get on with it. Of course I was learning all along the way.

I also made peace with the Peace Pledge Union (PPU).

Though I had little to do with them until I was in prison, they found me in Strangeways and I have nothing to show for it, though I imagine that the Governor must have been in touch with the Service Bureau - which I now know assists Conscientious Objectors in finding socially useful paid or voluntary work - to get me a place in agriculture.

Most, if not all of the COs on the Scabies trials were PPU people and tried to persuade me to 'come along'. However, because they were also almost all of some religious conviction, I felt myself somewhat set apart.

I also needed to express this to Mummy when she returned the first notebook to me, read in a few days.

Yes, what I did in the war was to be a 'Conscientious Objector'. I have a feeling that not only is the story of the Italians not going to be told, but also that of the hated 'Conchies'.

Mummy is concerned about the Atomic Bomb and for the first time, we did something together about world peace - she drove me to the PPU office in town and we signed up.

108μ
December 1948

Patience has paid off, hopefully with Mummy, but certainly with my 'Canadian' German POW Georg Rasp at least. I got a note from a 'Barbara' saying that she has a 'friend' in whom I had kindly showed an interest - 'George' (sic) Rasp. If I am still interested he would like to tell me his story. I telephoned a number she gave me and arranged to meet them in a Gainsborough Pub when I came over to pay visits at Christmas.

In the Horse and Jockey I found a handsome couple who appear very much in love, yet in the first flushes. It is Gainsborough because that's where Barbara White lives and also where they met.

I told them of my gratitude for getting in touch, as I am trying to get a full picture of how the POW camp system worked, and of course it has been secret for almost all the time. I asked if her family had had a POW for Christmas last year. She looked at and away from Georg and blushed. He grabbed her hand and said he had been at another family then.

I pointed out that to do similarly, say only in the summer of 1946, was an imprisonable offence. They both looked into their laps but did seem to know. But then the people - but *not* Mr Attlee's government - felt that we should show the Germans how good democracy is by being nice to them.

Georg was in full civvies, so I asked ... if he was ... well, a free man, now.

Oh yes. He had been at Lea Hall as a POW, but by the Summer of '47, so many men had been repatriated that they had shut that 'Camp'. 'Georgie' was now a farmer living and working at Barton's farm in Saundby - near Beckingham across the Trent bridge from Gainsborough.

I told them that I had pretty much the full story of the system, but not the bit that Georg, 'shall I call you George?' (a broad grin shot across both their faces), could tell me. I had a fair picture of the Italian situation, as 'we' had an Italian who had been in POW camp in South Africa, however I was short on detail of experiences in the USA and Canada - and hadn't George been to both?

Oh yes - and a very full story - with comparatively good English - in an American accent.

On what we called D-Day, George was 18 - his actual birthday June 6th 1944 - when hell arrived from the skies before dawn over the Cherbourg peninsula. George was with a much older man who said they may as well simply surrender. So they did. To American Paratroops who even let him drive for them for a little while before shipping over to America.

I imagine there were plenty of empty ships that brought those hundreds of thousands of men from across the Empire and the United States, that were not going to be taking them back very soon.

He was taken first to America to what sounds like a holiday camp - he loved it. He is a fine looking, very young man, and obviously took no delight in soldiering. He was given light duties and ate very well - he helped in the kitchens - had to try all the dishes! Something that obviously amused the young lady, he had to tell me: he was amazed by the guards' thirsts. I thought of them 'over here' drinking and carousing with the ladies. Not that sort of drinking: one of his jobs was to prepare their nightcap - a dustbin full of iced tea! I had heard how the 'Yanks' thought our putting milk in our tea to be strange, but having difficulty getting lemons during the U-Boat blockades, did not manage to persuade us of the error of our ways. Every evening George filled a bin - larger than our dustbins - with ice, then topped it up with tea and left it outside the mess. By morning the night guards would have emptied it. It was hot in America.

Just after the war actually ended, George was sent up to a camp in Canada. This was much cooler, but just as pleasant and comfortable. The move was because the British had to pay America to keep the German POWs, whereas they could expect their 'empire' friends to help themselves and guard their own enemies.

I understand that.

In June 1946 he was one of the many thinking he was on his way home. They shipped across the Atlantic and got a rougher reception at the English docks. Friends were split up and distributed around England.

George swept his hand across his face, clearing the colour from it, before he moved on to the next bit.

Barbara took his hand and squeezed it. He looked into her eyes and said 'I am going to tell this only once,' and throwing his hand away, added 'then I am going to forget it forever.'

This brought the attention of some of the locals, so the next bit was sotto voce. More Italian there?

They brought him to Nether Headon, but on almost the first roll call he was selected out and taken to a big army camp at Ranby and locked in a cell. After a few days some men from the Interrogation Department came and ... he didn't want to say how bad it was, but he did not understand why this was happening to him and they did not explain. 'Questions, questions, questions.'

He lifted Barbara's hand and kissed it, squeezed it, before moving on.

Next he was taken with a driver and guard in a car to a big house in Manchester where other high security...

Now he started to shake and his eyes welled up.

I broke the spell by telling of my experiences in Manchester. I think it eased his pain to realise that even 'a nice English man like me' can be imprisoned in a high security gaol. I had to explain my own true situation: the 'reserved occupation' in farming I had intimated, was not my first job.

I must have been almost as emotional as George - Barbara patted my hand.

'Soooo...' I said, 'I was sent into exile - like you in Canada. First to Egmanton...' I had to explain where that was even to my Lincolnshire neighbour. Also, about Palmiro and the start of my interest in the camps. I recalled that Georg when I first met him had said that Headon was his main camp, but he was at Lea Hall.

They told me that that was how they met. Before it closed a few months ago

- Summer 46.

My turn to tell Barbara about him.

She lives on Lea Road in Gainsborough, just over the river from Misterton and Beckingham. That road leads from the town to the Baronial Mansion of Lea - yet another of my 'ducal' estates, many old country houses being used as POW 'camps' - both proper, fenced in ones like Grisedale in the Lake District and Lea - not so secure.

No not secure, George assured. That's how he met Barbara.

Headon is the Standard Camp, possibly for the whole of Notts and it has 'Satellites', Lea Hall being one. I mentioned that Sconce in Newark and Little Carlton near me in Egmanton were also 'Satellites'. And there are many more.

Barbara told me how you can tell the Canadian POWs from the rest because instead of the patches they have 'PW' stencilled on the back and thigh of their uniforms.

George loves keep fit, walking on his hands along a bar, and on his friend's hands, flying somersaults, pretty clever stuff. Oh yes, I had seen this.

'Very impressive,' I said.

So he does swimming in the summer and has a bath in Winter - with keep fit on the covered pool - just across the road from Barbara's house on Lea Road.

Barbara told me that the raised expectations of repatriation ... stirred up considerable trouble when they found out that England was simply the next stop. But 'My Georgie' doesn't want to go home, doesn't really have a home, or family. He seems to have been brought up by begrudging wicked, fairytale, Godparents. He frowned at her for putting it so strongly. No 'Mom', only uncle and 'Aindy'. I thought the young lass would say that wouldn't she, but they do look so happy together.

His aunt has written to say that if he's got food, then stay here, because they have none - only milk from the cow.

Unlike Palmiro's treatment by the British in South Africa, Georg was very pleased with his treatment by the Americans and Canadians, and (Barbara stressed) especially the food. He rubbed his tummy and licked his lips. 'Chocolates - but not cigs or beer for me.' He flexed his muscles and she gave him an affectionate slap.

They looked at their watches in synchrony.

'Flicks!' she said. 'Georgie's taking me to see *Red Shoes* across the road at The State.'

Moira Shearer. Must take Mummy. Back row of the movies.

I do hope things work out for them.

We had crossed the dangerous bridge that was his trip to Manchester, but I was really intrigued what was going on. I thought a straight question might work. It did.

'Wrong Georg Rasp!'

His age saved him. Apparently there is a Hauptmann Georg Rasp - a notorious war criminal on the run.

(*Hauptmann*' 'Captain?' that's probably what HPTM stands for on Gina's

295

pilot's grave.)

George had one further problem - he is from Berchtesgarden, Hitler's hideout.

Fancy living there - or don't fancy - it got him into solitary confinement. In the end I think they managed to make two and two make four. Georgie is obviously young, very innocent seeming - hardly Captain material, particularly to my untrained eye, but in the Nazi War Machine?

Watches again. As my friends from the north east say a 'canny lass'. I have had my allotted hour. She's saving her Georgie from stress.

As for work finally, yes, he and his friends are spread out across every village for miles around Nether Headon, and he's living in a bungalow at Barton's in ... Saundby. I wonder if he was one of that cheeky gang. He certainly looks a cheeky chappy. Fit to pitch hay until morning. They have an Italian with them there, too. He cooks for them - a Mr Chimadoro - but his food is not as good as the Yanks'

'Or your mother's!' I said to Barbara, to shocked look from George. I dropped a clanger there. But Barbara was gracious. 'You weren't to know, Mr Chapman, but mother died of TB during the war.' She smiled at Georgie, too.

Time to go.

I slipped across the road with them. A very new Cinema, the State - not finished when war broke out, but they were given permission to complete.

We will see Red Shoes, Mummy - it looks very glamorous and despite Moira Shearer's co-stars sounding very German - Anton Walbrook, Marius Goring and Robert Helpmann - I do not think it is a war film.

I hope Georg Rasp doesn't either.

109μ
Christmas 48

I decided to introduce Mummy to Josie Husbands and needed an opportunity. I never did follow up that invitation to meet Günter at the pub in Laneham so a good time to kill two birds ... oh dear. I thought it had to be a Friday.

We called at Josie's place over the Sorting Office in Retford and took her with us to Laneham. I told her my reasoning and she had arranged for us to meet up with some of the Ukrainians we met at Carburton camp. It had to be early evening in order for us to get back to Sheffield, and a good job too: it got very busy later and we would not have had the marvellous opportunity to catch up.

I took the winding road from Retford past Headon and Rampton and for the first time I told the story of the 'boy' who rode into the bus on the bend. Not a merry start to Christmas.

Just as I had hoped, the smiling face of Günter greeted us across the smoky room. Josie nudged me laughing, and then pulled the 'he's a bit of alright' face to Mummy. They both settled to a merry start at last.

What I was not expecting was for Günter to serve the drinks - or was he such a regular that he can help himself? Oh he was enjoying himself. His swath of blond curls topped off what was decidedly a swagger. The 'barmaid' looked wistfully on until we were all settled - Günter with us at the table. Then he waved her over; she waved her mother from the next room, and Günter showed us her ring.

Rings. Günter has married Gwen Faulkner, the Landlord's daughter. I had my hand over my mouth in disbelief ... but calm down Eric. It's been a great year for the lad. After two and half years of not knowing, the British Red Cross have found his family. They are in western Germany at Bremervörde 1000 miles away from his birthplace, Sensburg in East Prussia. Sensburg is now in Poland and called Mrągowo.

Charlie Gregory had already told me of East Prussia's fate - wiped off the map - and off the world.

Miraculously his whole family has survived the trek, long distances before the advancing Russian army, mostly on foot, their only possessions being what they could carry. He can't get to see them yet - Attlee might not let him back in.

He was released from POW status in February, but stayed living at the NAEC camp at Headon until he was married on November 20th.

Gwen, a fine looking woman, looked around before telling how us that her father was dead against her courting a German, but Günter is such a 'gent' that he was won over. They do make a fine looking couple.

We all laughed at Günter who simply sat upright, inscrutable, absorbing her loving praise. She tried to crack his pastry, stretching to peck him on the cheek. No response, except perhaps for a gleam in the eye.

The Butchers Arms is Günter's new home. He's working on his electrical career with a sort of 'apprenticeship' with Newboult's - contractors in Retford.

We've seen the old lady's Lamp Shop on Bridgegate, just up from Josie.

A gang of Ukrainians burst in and one of them made a bee-line for Josie, attempting a resisted kiss ('Not in company!' Mummy heard her whisper.) Fedir 'Walter' Wacyk whom we met at Carburton.

Little Ivan Andreculak - he's already fed up with people asking how you spell that - came directly to me.

I'd like to say that Mummy was impressed by my 'circle of enemies'. So friendly. 'What did you do in the war?' she laughed.

Not funny, but I humoured you didn't I Mummy?

Walter rubbed his hands as he told us of his 'final' Christmas incident: he was with a gang of DPs picking the Christmas Sprouts for Farmer Proudley at Bole, I think that's near Georg in Saundby. It was knock off time. Mr Proudley wanted to finish the picking and asked Walter to translate the many languages to persuade the men to work later. He did and Mr Proudley gave them a (hushed voice and look around) 'Whole ham to take back to camp.'

Oh don't let us ration strapped populace hear of such luxury!

He then turned serious and warned of trouble ahead ... and his hand in it.

When we met them at Carburton last year, the Ukrainians wanted to be regarded as the Ukrainian First Army. Almost all had been recruited by the Nazis as the SS Galicia Volunteer Division to fight only Bolshies. Even the Pope had supported them being recognised as 'press-ganged' and not at all volunteers. Most - but strictly not all - were released from Prisoner of War status after only three months here. Walter and the friends we met were among these.

I said finally because he has got an 'apprenticeship' with Mr Lister, a blacksmith and farrier - shoes horses - at Scrooby. He 'knows' he can show Mr Lister he can do it - he was well taught by his blacksmith host in Italy. I smiled to myself - that's our Jim the farrier. I never did sort out my plasher.

He told us that he had been interpreting at Carburton. Some men were proud and angry, insisting on innocence, protesting so much as to raise suspicion that they were not. He did want to warn them of the fate of those sent 'home' into the Russian sector. But he also felt they were giving him and his fellows a bad name in a country who had offered them safety.

(I know that suspicion has been roused that war criminals have been hiding among the ranks of ordinary soldiers seeking to escape punishment - including many German SS, but also Galician volunteers who are suspected of cruelty in the ... extermination camps.)

Walter tells us that it is a good thing that we didn't agree to meet at Headon Camp - it is in turmoil. Atlee has decided to deport around 300 at the end of the month purportedly because of unsatisfactory behaviour as prisoners of war.

He was looking from Mummy to me, and pleading with Josie for support. The whole camp is threatening to strike. 'We are not bad men.'

She patted his hand and insisted in paying for a round of drinks for the whole group of almost a dozen of them. I had to get up and sort that - not at all reluctantly.

STOP PRESS: There was a General strike of the Ukrainian EVWs from December 28th 1948. It just goes to show how important these men are to our economy that just two days later the Home Office backed down - only 81 people were to leave, 45 choosing to go back to families, the remaining 36 with unsatisfactory behaviour would have to go.

110μ
Autumn 1950

Just as term started in September 1950, my colleagues from the training course were beginning their new teaching jobs without me.

But first let me tell you the good news:

I got a somewhat hurried note from Josie Husbands to say she was getting married - did I want to come. Not quite an invitation.

It turns out that Josie has been 'good friends' with the group of Ukrainians, more so with Fedir Walter Wacyk, who gave her an ultimatum: "Jousie, (sic) if you not marry it me this week, I marry it Pat next week." She accepted Walter's gallant offer, he told Mr. Knight, the one-eyed man with a flat cap at Nether Headon gate-house, who organised the Kommandos (work parties) for NAEC, that he wouldn't be back again. He packed his bags and stayed at a friend's on Sunday.

On Monday Walter Fedir Wacyk, married Joselyn Husbands at St Swithun's Church, across the road from her library and round the corner from her house. Not a very formal affair. Just a few of us and I got the wedding snap.

I can only think that Josie had not considered the notion of marriage, but was struck by it - totally.

At the wedding 'breakfast' slightly upmarket from the last hotel I had visited with Josie - as Stevie to my Paul Temple - Walter asked me what I 'did'.

He has continued with Mr Lister and is a fully fledged blacksmith now.

I sucked my lips before deciding to mention my metal work experience, but not going back to it because... No I didn't go there, but I laughed and said I needed him a while ago to sort out my plasher as it had broken trashing the brambles. I had to explain a 'plasher' but oh yes, bring it to him.

Not any more.

I did tell him that I had written up this story mentioning us Grinders and the folding and hammering of metal to make the finest blade, and how I have used the μ micron symbol of metal thicknesses for chapter headings. I had lost him a bit but he got it when I showed him it in my trusty notebook. I brought Josie and Mummy in as I told how it also became a comparison of how much I could take - what would really be the 'Last Straw' - for me the last micron.

Mummy and Josie stacked hands on mine, 'You made it, Eric.'

111μ
Christmas 1950

I completed my year of training in July with a thesis on my major in History.

It argued against Orwell, I have to accept very feebly, as he is after all a hero of literature. I realise that I was biased by him saying that the pacifist is pro-Nazi. He has warned about the Atom Bomb and a Cold War ... but I am a grinder, not an academic. The training year was hard - completely alien territory for me.

My thesis was the rant of a disappointed man - and a self pitying rant. I was told it was badly written, contained many factual errors, and is not acceptable as a premise on which to base a career as a History teacher. The tutor said 'What are you thinking? Poisoning the minds of our children!'

I could 'pass' my Certificate of Education - be recognised as a qualified teacher - but was pushed into accepting Metalwork and/or Chemistry as main subjects and deleting my History studies from the record.

Over the Summer I prevaricated and my half-hearted application for a job in the new term failed. *'What exactly do you wish to teach, Mr Chapman? And to whom?'*

At Christmas I studied, yes I did, Orwell's latest piece - '1984' - and can't help agreeing with his dystopian outlook for ... the world. He has taken our somewhat unvictorious state of affairs and cleverly turned round 1948 to 1984. Imagine this current dismal life stretching out for another ten years, let alone thirty four. I must do something about that.

With nothing else to do - no job and the greenhouses almost abandoned to nature - I read over your story.

How is *this* a plan for a history course, especially for the future leaders of our nation currently going though secondary schools?

I re-wrote my *History* thesis using samples and extracts from this and even used '1984' as support for my view: that our children must not be allowed to feel that war was worth it. Fighting the war. Gaping holes in ravaged streets. Rationing still ongoing. Big Brother watching us in a Cold War.

While I was at it, and with time on my hands, I decided that I would ask the thesis typist to type up my 'What I did in the War', for you, and got it bound, too.

I appealed to the university and did get a favourable hearing.

I was at last at a 'Tribunal' that I respect, and found a balance of respect in my favour.

In the new decade I secured a temporary post at Easter 1951. You are the only child I know really, so I was very tentative, perhaps a little too tentative.

I start a proper career as a History Teacher with my own class in September.
Definitely.
Positive.

112μ
Spring 1951

1950 had been a very tense year for Betty Gregory and her Bernard. They had a regular courtship becoming more intense, wishing to marry, but fearing for the future if they did. They would love to take tea with Betty's beloved Grandma, but not so much with Auntie Green who was getting senile and hygiene was not at its best.

Then when Parliament returned after the 1950 Christmas recess, Attlee abandoned the punitive Bill.

Betty heard the news and ran the two miles up to Treswell where Bernard was working to give him the news. She would be twenty one on Valentine's Day, so her father could hold her back no more and they married three days later at South Leverton Church.

I couldn't make that, but sent them the most heartfelt best wishes.

113μ
September 1951

Palmiro is not the best at letter writing, but I meet up with him a couple of times a year.

He found the irregular seasonal work on small farms provided an inconsistent income, so decided to follow many others down a coal mine. I'm sure it was a wrench for him, but in actual fact, he was also considering Charlie Fox, who would support him with a regular wage, despite not having work for him for some considerable periods. So he is yet another working at Thoresby Pit alongside Joe Bennett and many occupants of NAEC camp at Edwinstowe.

He knows Luca and a number of other Italians - both returned POWs and some of their friends and relations who have come to work here. Much flitting about to the fleshpots of Lincoln, Sheffield and Nottingham has not resulted in him finding that much sought after soul-mate. That was down to the friends who introduced Palmiro to Vincenza Fascia. She is one of many Italian women recruited to help in rebuilding British industry, particularly textiles. She had come to visit a friend in Hereford, almost in Wales. The friends set them up on a date. After a few dates Palmiro went all the way on his motorbike to propose and they were married at the beginning of September 1951, just three months after meeting.

We decided to stay over and I thought it a good wheeze to take Mummy to the scene of the Paul Temple and Stevie subterfuge. The Pheasant is not the most salubrious of Hotels, but it was clean ... and I can't live on Grandpapa's legacy for ever.

Of course we were there and I was so delighted to take this wonderful picture for them. 'My' POWs meeting up and forming a small community, seemingly based at the Tin Tabernacle which passes for a Catholic church in Retford.

Five of 'my' POWs on this one photograph: on the far left Is Filippo Bruccoleri who was at Edwinstowe; in the middle you can't miss the hair of Palmiro La Banca of Nether Headon; the new Mrs Vincenza La Banca is on his arm; the bridesmaid to the right is Nina almost hiding her father Luca Ritucci; on the right of her is Vincenzo Aversa, of Wigsley (see below) and his fiancée Giulia is on the far right; and the little man on the far right is...

I'll have to tell you about him: Mummy and I called in to the Coop on Retford's main street, Carolgate, to buy the lovely couple a present. We happened to overhear a receptionist who seemed to have an Italian accent. (Well noticed, Mummy.) We thought a bit of advice might come in handy. We joined a small queue. When the man in front stood forward, it wasn't to seek advice, but something rather odd and personal:

'You're Italian, Miss, yes?'

'Yes sir.'

He stroked his chin, looked round at us and leaned in. 'It's a funny thing but you remind me of ... a chap ... er, I was a policeman down the other side of the City ... cough ... and a ... er, camp, er ...'

The receptionist smiled and pointed at us and another couple standing behind us.

He looked around. 'Oh yes Miss, sorry but you do so remind me of an Italian chap I befriended.' He whispered, but we heard, 'a Prisoner of War at Bingham, Saxondale, called Michael?'

'He's over there behind you,' she said.

He looked. His jaw dropped - and so did mine - and Michael's. You could not make this sort of thing up, but the policeman from Bingham, and the cheeky POW with no lights on his bike, fell into each other's arms, slapping backs, laughing and, well, crying actually. I had to join in too, interloper though I was - I'm pretty sure neither of them remembered me.

That's Michele Gallucci, to give him his proper name, on the far right of the photograph.

I caught up with him at the very handsome wedding reception they threw - or their guests did, having pooled every ration card they could and begged quality food from the farms many of them work for. Their stories are very similar - he was actually caught at Tobruk, almost two years after Palmiro. He has a terrible wound by his bicep, and probably like Günter Rahn, he was patched up at a field hospital before being held in a camp there for a short time. He was brought on a big liner and the food was poor, until a friendly guard asked whereabouts he was from. He told him told him Apulia region.

Next time the guard was on duty, he saw Michael (I'll call him) and told him that one of the chefs at Top Table was from Apulia, so where in Apulia was Michael from?

Province of Foggia came the answer.

A couple more days passed and Michael was getting very hungry, when he saw the same guard make a bee-line for him. 'Where in Foggia?'

'San Marco, San Marco la Catola.'

It's a day of coincidences, but the chef was also from San Marco. Michael ate like the captain for the rest of the very long trip to Liverpool - in fact the leftovers from the Top Table.

And finally - it was he who introduced Palmiro to his cousin Vincenza.

And dare I mention another coincidence? Filippo is almost certainly Joe Bennett's 'Phil', though he's not sure he knows Joe. He was at Edwinstowe and the locals were very friendly. After the POWs cleared a patch of scrub and bramble to make a football pitch, the locals even made them a proper set of goal posts - and then regularly held matches with them.

I asked if they knew Umberto Ferrarelli and Tony Dalla Riva.

'Si, Si. Bert! Tony. Si!' Part of the burgeoning community, but unfortunately they couldn't make the wedding.

Wigsley? After Palmiro told me of the friend he had made while at Charlie Fox's, of course I asked if he had been a POW. He had to scratch his mop of curls. It wasn't because he didn't know: Vincenzo was a POW, but Palmiro was embarrassed to not be sure where - except that it was not at Headon, nor in South Africa.

Doing lots of networking at the reception, it was made known to me that the two tiny men had both been Prigioneri. I knew Michele/Michael Gallucci and was introduced to Vincenzo Aversa. I hope you will enjoy that at the very end of this story, this quest, this mission, I have found another missing link from the whole picture - a man held in one of the Indian POW camps. Vincenzo was captured at Tobruk - as was Michele, but they didn't know each other - in 1941. He was one of those sent to India - I've met one! I asked where and he was confused and said they got moved around - but he was there for three years and really enjoyed it. They were brought over to England in '44. He was one of around three hundred held in concrete huts at Wigsley camp. No it is not a village, just a farm with huts at Drinsey Nook next to a canal near Lincoln. He wasn't at the camp long as he was billeted on Barton Farm a couple of miles away. There he worked for farmer Sutton, who moved over the Trent to Marnham and took Vincenzo with him.

It was there in one of the many 'helping out a neighbour' days that Palmiro and Vincenzo met at Fox's Merryfields. When the Italians were repatriated in '46, Mr Sutton told him to come back if everything was not alright for him at home.

So the community builds.

As you can see, Luca Ritucci is on the photograph and I have mentioned his daughter. Luca was like 'the father of the bride' giving away Vincenza to be married. it was supposed to be her cousin Michael, who had introduced them, but he didn't get to wedding on time.

Luca and his wife are well settled here, and his daughter Nina (Maria Giovanna 'Giovannina' I was told to write down,) is the Bridesmaid along with Nina's neighbour and best friend from Mattersey.

Other men and women on the photo are almost all Italians who have been invited to work over here, some recruited by advertisements placed in Italian newspapers by agencies in London, to help with rebuilding after the war, and the women for the service and textile industries, too.

They are welcome.

I am so glad I took Mummy over to the wedding. She was able to see something of what I did in the war. On the way back on the train I overheard her musing, talking to herself I think, and she said something like 'you fought for a peace...

...and won, Eric.'

114μ
Autumn term 1951

At registration, I fixed my eye on one of the girls in my new form of thirteen year olds and smiled.

She reciprocated.

'Pina,' I said. She looked confused, so I rapidly looked to a girl in the back row. 'Children ... my children,' I looked round the class, 'each one of you will have had a father involved in the war.' There were mixed reactions which I had anticipated, so moved quickly on. 'Some will have been soldiers, airmen ... some not in the forces, some wounded and some sadly have ... died. All of us have had something to be sad about. Now all of us have had the chance to rejoice that the war is over and the baddies,' I chuckled as this was a 'childish' word to a class of teens, 'have been beaten - well and truly beaten. I nodded round the room, tough-chinned, to encourage more of the same.

'Your mothers and grandparents were also all affected by the war. Your grandparents will have hoped that the Great War of 1914-18 had been the war to end all wars, and saddened to find it was not. Is this second world war to be the end of all wars?'

There was some grumbling and the beginnings of responses, which petered out.

'My Dad was one of your Grandparents' generation and his Great War killed him ... but not until just a few years ago. You are ordinary kids of the City of Sheffield. A large city, not unlike cities all over the country, all over the world, in other countries ... yes there are cities just like Sheffield in Germany, in Japan. All these cities are mostly populated by ordinary people just like you, with Mams and Dads, Grampies and Nanas ... little brothers and sisters. They will all know someone who is sad about the war.'

At some risk of losing them, but seizing the quiet concentration of the moment, I went on, 'Many of your dads will not want to talk about the war,' (heads shaking ... and nodding), 'to forget it, but if we are to avoid another war, something has to be said about it, because there's always a lot more said than done, isn't there?'

That got nods and smiles.

'I've heard in the staff room that several of the teachers have already been asked "what did you do in the war?" so over the coming weeks, I am going to tell a story that you will probably never hear from anyone else, a little bit at a time, a bit about me, and a lot about many people I met in the war ... many of them the *enemies* of our people.'

That got them looking round and a few 'ooh's and 'aahs'.

The bell went for first lesson, but I was to take my own class for first lesson.

'I'll start at the beginning of lessons.'

I gave them the chance to stand, move around for five minutes ... and behave ... while I stepped out into the corridor to gather my thoughts.

When the second bell went, I stepped back in and the whole class sat down and looked up at me in anticipation. I looked around and gave a smile of appreciation. I started:

He cycled towards Retford. He felt freedom. He felt peace. He felt the wind in his hair.

As the lane from Rampton weaved down the steep Idle Valley side, with no need to pedal, did he fly? Did he spread his wings and fly?

He flew headlong into an oncoming bus ... and died.

His death will go unreported, but it changed my life.

In the middle of England, in the middle of summer, in the middle of the war, what could the British public be expected to feel about the loss of one enemy, when his countrymen are still mowing down 'our boys' in their hundreds?

Back at Camp 52 Nether Headon Prisoner of War Camp, Palmiro La Banca felt the loss as sadly ironic. Many of his thousand or so fellow Italian prisoners at Nether Headon had been reluctant combatants in the folly of Mussolini's empire building adventure in North Africa. Indeed, many had been captured without firing a shot – there had been no shells to shoot. A hundred and thirty thousand of them had been captured by the British, who had no need to even disarm them.

Capture took them out of the war and mostly out of harm's way.

The beginning.

Background to writing the book:

In 1989/90 I carried out an anti-racism social education project with young people from the villages around Headon in Nottinghamshire. A lot of racism was shown by the predominantly white rural teenagers. They were surprised to learn that the 'Camp' they passed every day coming in to school had once been a Prisoner of War camp which hosted enemies from all over Europe - and that many stayed and lived among their own families.

We decided to make a video based on interviews with Prisoners of War from each of the main cohorts held at the Camp 52 Nether Headon, who had settled in the area - Italian, German and Ukrainian.

We received a handsome grant to pay a professional video producer.

Palmiro La Banca showed the young people the site and even found his, by then, very dilapidated hut. We recorded his interview inside that hut.

Günter Arnold Rahn and Ivan 'John' Pasaniuk followed on the video. Bernhard Pönicke sadly died before we interviewed him, but his wife Betty was very interested in the POW story herself and gave us lots of information, photographs and contacts.

We did further research, visited the Imperial War Museum and collected many more stories, anecdotes and documents.

The title page was designed - 'The Untold Story'.

Unfortunately the product was valueless, and even one of the two camera tapes was lost.

When I finished in the Youth Service I turned to writing. After completing two books, I decided to try to edit the video material with the technology now available to the amateur. Looking for more background material I found very little was written, especially about the Italian experience, so I decided to write up Palmiro's story. His sons were able to share many photographs, stories and experiences. The most exciting item to me was the Work Permit inviting him back from Italy sent by Conscientious Objector who had befriended him whilst they were billeted together at Egmanton.

As I developed the story, I thought it best to tell the whole story of the POWs and of the Conscientious Objectors in an accessible popular history book.

I decided to have the material I had gathered, 'discovered' contemporaneously by that Conscientious Objector, Eric Chapman. Despite considerable effort, I could not find anything about the real Eric, so I have created his story from research. His experiences are authentic and genuinely happened to Conscientious Objectors. Over the four years of writing, Michele Gallucci's daughter, Giuseppina 'Josie'/'Pina' Sanderson has pointed me in the direction of numerous useful contacts. She knew little of her father's story.

I dedicate this book to her.

Main Characters

Family:
Eric Chapman, Sheffield steel worker, Conscientious Objector
- Cousin Queenie Thomas.
- Jack Saunders, Royal Tank Regiment, Queenie's boyfriend.

Eric's 'created' family:
- Mam, his Mother.
- Dad, his Father.
- Mummy, his Wife.
- 'Pina', his Daughter.
- 'Uncle Frank', family friend.
- Grandpapa, his Father-in-Law .
- Grandmama, his Mother-in-Law .
- Maisie Matchless, his motorcycle.

Featured Camp witnesses:
Italian
- Palmiro La Banca, Italian Infantryman.
- Luca Ritucci, Italian Infantryman.
- Joe Santacroce, US Air Force, Luca's nephew.
- Michele 'Michael' Gallucci, Italian Infantryman.
- Umberto 'Bert' Ferrarelli, Italian Infantryman.
- Antonio 'Tony' Dalla Riva, Italian Infantryman.
- Filippo 'Phil' Bruccoleri, Italian Bersaglieri.
- Vincenzo Aversa, Italian Artillery.

German
- Bernhard 'Hardy'/'Bernard' Pönicke, German Infantryman
- Rudi Stenger, German POW, Camp Musical Director.
- Günter Arnold Rahn, Lufwaffe Pilot.
- Georg 'George' Rasp, Kriegsmarine.

Ukrainian
- Fedir Walter Wacyk, SS Galician Regiment.
- Ivan 'John' Pasaniuk, Polish Infantry and SS Galician Regiment .
- Ivan Andreculak, SS Galician Regiment.

Polish Free Forces
- Czezlaw 'Chez' Kowalczyk, Polish Air Force.

Camp and military personnel
- Colour Sergeant Willy 'Constant' Kohnstamm, POW Camp Interpreter.
- Sgt Tom Collis, Home Guard.
- June Collis, his daughter.
- Joe Bennett, Royal Navy.
- Lieutenant Ferguson, POW Camp Commandant.
- Henry Faulk, POW Re-education expert.
- QMS Guy Reckin, POW Camp Guard.
- Harold Saunders, Conscientious Objector, Pioneer Corps, POW Camp Guard.

Farmers and civilians
- Alec, Sally and Barbara Fox, Egmanton.
- Charlie, Emma and Betty Gregory, South Leverton.
- Joselyn 'Josie' Husbands, Librarian.
- Leslie Marshal, Farmer, Mattersey Thorpe.
- Gordon Tasker, Farmer, South Wheatley.
- Harrises, Market Gardening firm, West Stockwith.
- Mr Walker, Farmer, Gringley-on-the Hill .
- Mrs Agnes Walker, his wife.
- Harold Hardy, her son, Farmer.
- Les Hardy, his son.
- Georgina 'Gina' Christmas, Land Army, Gringley-on-the-Hill.
- Peg, Land Army, Gringley-on-the-Hill.
- Eric 'Duckie' Ducksbury, Farmer, Tuxford.
- Gwen Faulkner, Butcher's Arms, Laneham.
- Clarrie Mumby, driver, Treswell.
- Mavis Mumby, his niece.
- Betty Jones, Rampton Hospital Nurse.

Passing reference
- Dennis Lovell, Derby Conscientious Objector.
- Richard Hannay, hero of '39 Steps' fictitious.
- Paul Temple and Stevie - Radio detectives fictitious.
- George Orwell, author.
- Clement Attlee, Prime Minister.
- 'El Duce' Mussolini, Italian President.
- Winston 'Winnie' Churchill, British Prime Minister.
- Krebs, Mellanby - Sheffield, Sorby Medical Research Institute .

Main appearances in the text = Chapter of first reference in *italic bold*

1. *Palmiro 'Palmiro' La Banca, Eric Chapman, Mummy.*
2. Palmiro, Mummy.
3. Palmiro, *Grandpapa.*
4. *Dad.*
5. Palmiro.
6. Lord Acton, *Grandad*, Chamberlain, Churchill, Hitler, Fritz.
7. *Sally Fox, Alec, Barbara, Queenie*, Bevan.
8. Palmiro.
9. *Jack Saunders*, Winnie.
10. *Pina.*
11. Alec, Mummy, *Eric 'Duckie' Ducksbury,* Lord Haw Haw, Alec, *Joe Bennett*, *Sgt Tom Collis, Dau June.*
12. Palmiro.
13. Palmiro, Pina, Sally.
14. Mummy, Palmiro, Grandma, Grandad, Dad, *Uncle Frank.*
15. Palmiro, Mussolini, Churchill.
16. Palmiro.
17. Palmiro, *Grandmama* and Grandpapa *Maisie Matchless* Palmiro.
18. Palmiro.
19. Palmiro, Queenie and Jack, *Chapman.*
20. (Scrooby Carlton and other camps discovered).
21. My Dad, *Mam* and Uncle Frank.
22. Queenie and Jack, Fred Rist and Jackie Wood, Father Finneran
23. Palmiro, *Miss Joselyn* 'Josie' *Husbands, Betty Jones.*
24. Tom Collis, June Collis.
25. Sally, Alec.
26. Joe Bennett.
27. *Filippo 'Phil' Bruccolerri.*
28. ....
29. Palmiro, Sally.
30. Palmiro and Alec.
31. *Luca Ritucci, Joe Santacroce, Leslie Marshal.*
32. Dukedom.
33. *Gordon Tasker.*
34. *camp.*
35. Alec, Sally, Barbara, Palmiro.
36. Alec.
37. Sally Barbara *Clarrie Mumby.*
38. Leslie Marshall, Luca, *'Palmiro'*, Queenie's Jack.
39. Sally and Barbara, tour of camps. *Michael Gallucci + Bobby, Chez and Antoni - Poles,* Miss Husbands.
40. Mummy, Grandmama.
41. Mummy, Grandmama and Grandpapa.
42. Barbara, Sally, Alec.

43. Queenie.
44. Mam, Grandpapa, Mummy, *Willy Constant.*
45. Alec, *Charlie Gregory.*
46. Queenie, Mam, Queenie *Thomas*, Jack *Saunders.*
47. Alec, Sally, Barbara; Charlie G, *Emma Gregory, Betty Gregory*, *Lieutenant Ferguson, Karl and Bernhard 'Hardy'. Pönicke.*
48. Charlie, Miss Husbands, Krebs,. *Mellanby*, Mummy and her Papa.
49. *Harold Hardy and Les*, Maisie, *Mr Walker at Homestead*
50. *The first Pina* Mountbatten.
51. Les and Harold Hardy and Mr Walker, *Georgina Christmas, Gina, Peg, Mrs. Walker, Agnes.*
52. Doodlebugs.
53. Gina, Hardys, Barbara Willis, Peg, Bernhard, *Emil Kölmel.*
54. Queenie and Gina.
55. Fox household - Buchenwald.
56. ...
57. Queenie, Jack, Josie, Harold *Saunders,* Gina.
58. *Willy Kohnstamm*.
59. Uncle Frank, Mam.
60. Attlee.
61. Carburton, Joe Bennett, *Faulk*, Norton Cuckney, Sheffield's Norton.
62. Lesley Marshall, Luca, Gina, *Umberto Ferrarelli,* Maisie Matchless, *Harrises 'Antonio' Tony Dalla Riva, 'Stephanie'.*
63. Palmiro, Jack, *Guy Reckin,*
64. *Günter Rahn.*
65. Alec.
66. Palmiro.
67. Sally and Barbara.
68. Willy, *Rettig, Schmittendorf and Kuehne, Kathleen Evans*
69. 'My Johnny'.
70. ...
71. Queenie, Jack, Willy, Rettig, Harold.
72. Charlie Gregory, Betty, Bernhard, *Rudi Stenger , Mr Spittle.*
73. Gina Christmas and family.
74. Mam, Palmiro.
75. Palmiro.
76. Josie, Maisie Matchless, Alec.
77. Palmiro, Alec, Sally.
78. Palmiro, Mam, Eric, Sally and Barbara.
79. Palmiro, Lesley Marshal, Luca, Alec.
80. Sally, Josie Husbands, *Richard Hannay, Paul Temple , Stevie,* Palmiro, Bernhard.
81. Sally.
82. Mummy, Grandmama and Grandpapa, Alec, Marshal, Luca.
83. Mummy.

84. Queenie, Harold Saunders, Willy.
85. Alec, Charlie Gregory, Luca, Gina, Les Hardy
86. Josie, Foxes, Palmiro, Harold, *Miss Joselyn* Husbands, Hannay, Bernhard, Gregory family, Günter Rahn, Josie, Betty's Rudi.
87. Maisie, Gina, Peg.
88. Tony Dalla Riva, Attlee, *Dennis Lovell.*
89. Mummy. Grandmama and Grandpapa, Mam.
90. No names.
91. Günter, Alec, Rommel, Tommies.
92. Barbara, Sally, Alec, Mummy.
93. Mummy, Mam, Günter Rahn, Grandpapa, Grandmama
94. Charlie Gregory, Betty, Mr Chapman, Bernard, Günter Rahn, Rudi, *Georg Rasp.*
95. Alec, Mam, Harrises, Tony Dalla Riva, Stephanie, Gina, the Hardys, baby Susan, Georg Rasp.
96. Günter, Alec Fox.
97. Willy Kohnstamm, Kathleen, Mummy, Fritz Zimmer.
98. Alec Fox, Josie Husbands, Mummy, Palmiro, *Ivans, Fedir Wacyk. Walter, Ivan 'John' Pasaniuk, Ivan - Andreculak, Ivan Besjuk.*
99. Gregorys, Charlie, Emma, Betty, Bernard 'Hardy'.
100. Grandpapa, Faulk, Alec.
101. Palmiro.
102. Günter Rahn.
103. Lesley Marshal, Palmiro, Luca, Ritucci, Joe his American cousin, *Giuseppina, 'Nina'- from Giovannina, Vincenzo Aversa* and Filippo Bruccoleri.
104. Palmiro, Alec, Charlie Fox.
105. Tony Dalla Riva. Luca, Palmiro, Joe Bennett, Freddie (U-Boat) Captain Walker of HMS Wren, Chez and Antoni, Italian 'Phil', Willy, George Orwell, Günter.
106. Mummy, Grandmama, Grandpapa, Giuseppina, Pina
107. ....
108. Georg Rasp, Barbara White.
109. Josie Husbands, Günter, Gwen, Charlie Gregory, Fedir 'Walter' Wacyk, Ivan Andreculak, Farmer Proudley, Mr Jim Lister,
110. Josie Husbands, Walter, Stevie, Paul Temple.
111. ....
112. Betty Gregory, Bernard.
113. Palmiro, Joe Bennett, *Vincenza Fascia.*

Prisoner of War Camps - number = chapter featured:

1. Camp 52 Nether Headon (and throughout the book).
4. Redmires/Fulwood/Lodge Moor Camp, Norton (Sheffield), Barnes Hall /High Green, Parsons Cross.
8. Ely camp.
11. Ecclesfield, Lodge Moor Camp, Sheffield; Langwith, Derbs; Edwinstowe, Notts.
19. Ely, Friday Bridge, Wisbech, Cambs.
21. Carlton-in- Lindrick and (separate) Serlby Hall, Blyth, Notts.
25. Rufford Abbey, Notts.
29. Alexandria 'Alessandro' and Suez 'Swiss', N Africa; Durban, South Africa.
33. Potter Hill in High Green, Bracken Hill at Burncross on the Barnes Hall estate, Sheffield; Eden Camp, Malton, Yorks; Ravenfield Hall, Rotherham, Yorks.
39. Crowle, Lincs; Sconce, Winthorpe, Caunton and Little Carlton, near Newark, Notts; Allington, Lincs; Saxondale, Bingham, Langar, Tollerton Hall, Wollaton Hall, Bulwell Hall, Woodborough (Arnold), Nottingham.
51. Grisedale Hall, Cumberland; Old Mill, Oldham.
54. Ranby Camp, Retford; Bridgend, Wales.
61. Carburton; Norton Cuckney, Notts;
64. Boughton, Ollerton Notts.
65. Haltwhistle, Featherstone Castle, Yorks.
71. Sherifhales, Shropshire.
80. Wigsley (also known as Thorney) at Drinsey Nook, Lincs. US and Canadian camps.
98. Rimini, San Marino, Italy.
99. 'The Marches' - Le Marchant Camp, Devizes, Wiltshire.
113. Indian camps.

REFERENCES

I will be uploading original documents, full-stories and photographs of many elements in the story to www.kevanpooler.com Click follow to get notification of updates.

This is a true story based on testimony to myself Kevan Pooler, transposed as if given contemporaneously to Eric Chapman.

      Eric himself was a Conscientious Objector who befriended Palmiro La Banca. Palmiro told me about Eric. I have a very few biographical details from Palmiro's sons. I built Eric's story from research into the experiences of Conscientious Objectors.

Sources:

Family:

- Eric Chapman, Sheffield steel worker, Conscientious Objector: Palmiro and Egidio 'Gee' La Banca, Dennis Fox.
- CO experiences from Peace Pledge Union, PPU, particularly Sheffield references and Bernard Hicken
  http://www.ppu.org.uk/learn/infodocs/cos/st_co_wwtwo6.html
- Steel work in Sheffield: Peter Phillipson; 'Grinders' - cutlers - Brian Harper.
- Dad, Eric's father, is based on the experiences of my Grandfather, J.F. 'Jim' Pooler, Lancashire Fusiliers, Bantam.

Featured Camp witnesses:
As a true story, this book is based on the actual testimony of the following. However, they themselves may not have accurate recall.

Italian
I dedicate the book to Giusepina 'Josie/Pina' Sanderson, née Gallucci, daughter of Michele Gallucci, who found and made contact with many of the witnesses for me.

- Palmiro La Banca, Italian Infantryman: himself and on video 1989, plus his wife Vincenza 'Nancy', sons Egidio and Christopher and many friends in the Italian community.
- Luca Ritucci, Italian Infantryman: his daughter Giovanna 'Nina' Wakelin, Josie Sanderson and many friends in Italian community
- Joe Santacroce, US Air Force, his cousin: Nina Wakelin
- Michele 'Michael' Gallucci, Italian Infantryman: his daughter Giusepina 'Josie/Pina' Sanderson.
- Umberto 'Bert' Ferrarelli, Italian Infantryman: his son Peppe Ferrarelli, Josie Sanderson and friends in Italian community

- Antonio 'Tony' Dalla Riva, Italian Infantryman: his daughter Susan Denman.
- Filippo 'Phil' Bruccolerri, Italian Bersaglieri, his daughters Pia Anderson and Jenny Whelan.
- Vincenzo Aversa, Italian Artillery: his wife Giulia née Golop.

German
- Bernhard 'Hardy'/'Bernard' Pönicke: his wife Betty Pönicke, née Elizabeth 'Betty' Gregory.
- Rudi Stenger, German POW, Camp Musical Director, Betty Pönicke.
- Günter Arnold Rahn, Luftwaffe Pilot: himself 1989 video testimony, and further interviews; his daughters Janet Shipley and Davina Gull, and grandchildren Becky Brown and Robert Hood.
- Georg 'George' Rasp, Kriegsmarine: his daughter Caroline Springer and granddaughter Imogen Barnett.

Ukrainian
- Fedir Walter Wacyk: himself and his wife Josie 1989, his Daughter Anna Mayfield-Key and DR Potter, Diplomat.
- Ivan 'John' Pasaniuk, Polish Infantry, SS Galician Regiment: himself on 1989 video testimony.
- Ivan Andreculak, SS Galician Regiment: his son Ivan Holden.
- Ivan Besjuk, SS Galician Regiment: his cousin Ivan Holden.

Polish Free Forces
- Czezlaw 'Chez' Kowalczyk, Polish Air Force: his travel diary from his son Robert Kowalczyk.

Camp and military personnel
- Cousin Queenie Thomas: herself, and Margaret 'Peggy' Mortimer, Jack and Harold Saunders' sister.
- Jack Saunders, Royal Tank Regiment, Queenie's boyfriend: himself and Queenie, and Margaret 'Peggy' Mortimer.
- Harold Saunders, Conscientious Objector, Pioneer Corps, Camp guard: his sister Margaret 'Peggy' Mortimer, his daughter Ruth and son Mark Saunders.
- Willy 'Constant' Kohnstamm, Camp Interpreter: his son Mike Kohnstamm.
- Sgt Tom Collis, Home Guard: June Ibbotson his daughter.
- June Collis, his daughter: herself.
- Joe Bennett, Royal Navy: himself.
- Lieutenant Ferguson, Camp Commandant: photo only on Welchman Archive, Bassetlaw Museum.

- Henry Faulk: 'After the Ides of March' (The Nottinghamshire Historian article) Robert Ilett, and general internet.
- QMS Guy Reckin, Camp Guard: his own 1946 film, held by Imperial War Museum - personal viewing only by permission of son Paul Reckin.

Farmers and civilians

- Alec, Sally and Barbara Fox, Egmanton: Palmiro and Egidio La Banca, and Dennis Fox Alec's nephew.
- Charlie, Emma and Betty Gregory, South Leverton: Betty Pönicke, née Elizabeth Gregory.
- Joselyn 'Josie' Husbands, Librarian: herself and daughter Anna Mayfield-Key.
- Leslie Marshal, Mattersey Thorpe: Giovanna 'Nina' Wakelin.
- GordonTasker, South Wheatley: his son Alec.
- Harrises, West Stockwith: Seymour Harris, Susan Denman nee Dalla Riva.
- Mr Walker, Gringley-on-the Hill: stepson Les and Dot Hardy.
- Mrs Agnes Walker, his wife: Les Hardy her grandson.
- Harold Hardy, her son: Les and Dot Hardy.
- Les Hardy, his son: self and Dot Hardy.
- Georgina 'Gina' Christmas, Land Army Gringley-on-the-Hill: herself, niece Carole Swallow, Les and Dot Hardy.
- Peg, Land Army Gringley-on-the-Hill: Georgina 'Gina' Christmas.
- Eric 'Duckie' Ducksbury, Tuxford: Children Ann and Paul Ducksbury.
- Gwen Faulkner, Butcher's Arms Laneham, self and daughter Janet Shipley.
- Clarrie Mumby, Treswell: Betty Pönicke.
- Mavis Mumby, his niece: Betty Pönicke.
- Betty Jones, Rampton Hospital Nurse: daughter Sue Smith.

Sources of background material:
The main sources of background material are Wikipedia and Local discussion and Local History forums - too numerous to mention.

Egmanton Village: Peter Stead, editor of 'The Egmanton Villager', from which reminiscences from Dorothy Cupit and particularly the Mary Needham Diaries.

The Camps - particular help and details:
- Camps - several aerial details and layouts and Gringley Bomber - Milan Petrovic.
- Gringley Blitz, POWs and Land Army - Les Hardy, Gina Christmas and Alan Hickman.
- Doodlebug V1 raid - Les Hardy, Milan Petrovic and Peter J.C.Smith.
- Crowle - Angus Townley, Jean Kohn née Parker.
- Nether Headon - from 1944 only (German with barely a mention of Italians): National Archives.
- Nether Headon Camp and village - Janet Landon, Kathleen Champion WAAF, Robert and David Dodds, camp site owners.
- Edwinstowe - Joe Bennett, Shirley Moore.
- Langwith - June Ibbotson.
- Norton Cuckney - June Ibbotson and Milan Petrovic.
- Serlby - Robert Hood.
- Wigsley - Giulia Aversa. Wigsley at Drinsey Nook - Bob Garlant of Saxilby local history group, National Archive - Headon camp re-education inspection report May 1946.
- Lodge Moor - Willie and Mike Kohnstamm; Redmires POW Camp Community Heritage Project (Facebook); www.chrishobbs.com, Prof Bob Moore of Sheffield University

National Archives has a good section of Re-Education at Nether Headon and its satellites. A single thorough report, confidential at the time, inspired the subterfuge of chapter 80μ. They have only a few notes on Lodge Moor, and almost nothing I could find on any camps or satellites featured in this story, including the huge 3 section camp at Wollaton Hall. There are other records elsewhere, but for the purposes of this story, they were not sought out.

'Prisoner of war camps (1939-48) by Roger J C Thomas. (English Heritage 2003) The most complete list of camps as at 1946 - is still incomplete, especially of earlier Italian camp sites.
'Churchill's Unexpected Guests' by Sophie Jackson, uses this list and is the only 'popular history' I have found. I discounted one published in 2012 because on the blurb it says by the time the War ended, there were over 600 (camps) - it misses the above report by almost 100%.
'Enemies Become Friends' and 'The Germans we Trusted' by Pamela Taylor (Germans only.)

German Prisoners of War in Britain - good article:
http://www.radiomarconi.com/marconi/monumento/pow/pows.html

The Italian POWs' story:
I have been unable to find a popular history of the Italian POW experience in Britain, so I hope I have written it.

The Authority on the system is Professor Bob Moore of Sheffield University:
'The British Empire and its Italian Prisoners of War, 1940–1947' by Bob Moore and Kent Fedorowich, is the leading record on its subject, but it is an academic journal, and not easily or cheaply accessible. I am grateful to Bob Moore for his support on Italian issues.

Corriere del Sabato - Alec Tasker.

Italian captives on Pathe http://www.britishpathe.com/video/italian-prisoners-arrive-in-south-africa

Queen Mary April 1943
http://ww2troopships.com/ships/q/queenmary/cruiserecord1943.htm

Midnight Mass: Peter Giblin.

Conscientious Objectors:
I can find no proper story of the CO/Conchie experience except on the Peace Pledge Union (PPU) website:
http://www.ppu.org.uk/learn/infodocs/cos/st_co_wwtwo2.html
They say 3000 WW2 COs did go to prison.

The PPU holds copies of just two WW2 Tribunal Application forms containing the Tribunal findings and their 'Sentence'.
Chris Lovell shared his father's with me:
- Dennis Lovell, Derby Conscientious Objector: son Chris Lovell.

I can find no overall numbers of WW2 COs, nor where the Tribunals were held.

BBC's People's war contains some experiences:
www.bbc.co.uk/history/ww2peopleswar/

Prison (only) experiences of COs: 'These Strange Criminals: An Anthology of Prison Memoirs by Conscientious Objectors,' Edited by Peter Brock. Valuable contribution to the book title.

Because of the rationale I chose for Eric, I was able to fashion an experience which was authentic, and touching on the whole wider issue.

COVER PICTURE:

Lino print by Heinz Georg Lutz while at Lodge Moor Camp, Sheffield, used by permission of Sheffield Archives and History and Heinz's friend Mr Ludlam who holds the copyright.

Back: Nether Headon Camp photo: Mrs Elizabeth Pönicke.

.

Reader suggestions:

Find your camps. This story is based on experiences of POWs camped all over the Empire, but mainly in East Midlands camps, and shared with me, Kevan Pooler. The whole experience happened in your area of Britain, too. There were 80 purpose built Standard Camps and perhaps 3000 other locations where a large number of men were camped.
40,000 Germans stayed, many having families. 200,000 Italians were recruited to work here after the war, including many POWs returning to their camp localities. How many descendants might you know?

The list below for England alone is extracted from the English Heritage project carried out in 2003. I found many more not on the list of 1029. How many can you find in your area? The full-list by country and county is on www.kevanpooler.com

England

Total numbers of POW camps by county 1944-1948

Bedfordshire	8	Herefordshire	1	Shropshire	16
Berkshire	9	Hertfordshire	9	Somerset	7
Buckinghamshire	6	Huntingdonshire	3	Staffordshire	13
Cambridgeshire	8	Isle of Man	2	Suffolk	7
Channel Isles	2	Kent	15	Surrey	8
Cheshire	9	Lancashire	12	Sussex	6
Cornwall	4	Leicestershire	9	Warwickshire	13
Co.Durham	6	Lincolnshire	16	Westmorland	3
Cumberland	4	London	5	Wiltshire	13
Derbyshire	7	Middlesex	7	Worcestershire	5
Devon	12	Norfolk	10	Yorkshire	33
Dorset	4	Northamptonshire	7		
Essex	12	Northumberland	8		
Gloucestershire	9	Nottinghamshire	9		
Hampshire	21	Oxfordshire	7		

Thank you for all the support during the four years researching and writing this story:

Editing final draft: Bernie Gatt, Dominic Murphy, Ces Baird, James Murphy, Barrie Purnell and Kaye Locke.

Help all along the way - members of Bassetlaw (Worksop) Writers' group and my own Retford Writers' group - Retwords, too numerous to mention, but you all know who you are.

Love: My wife Diane who has had to put up with all these strangers joining our family, my vacancies when I have 'been away with them', and my changes to the landscape of every trip - 'that was one of my camps.'

Also by Kevan Pooler

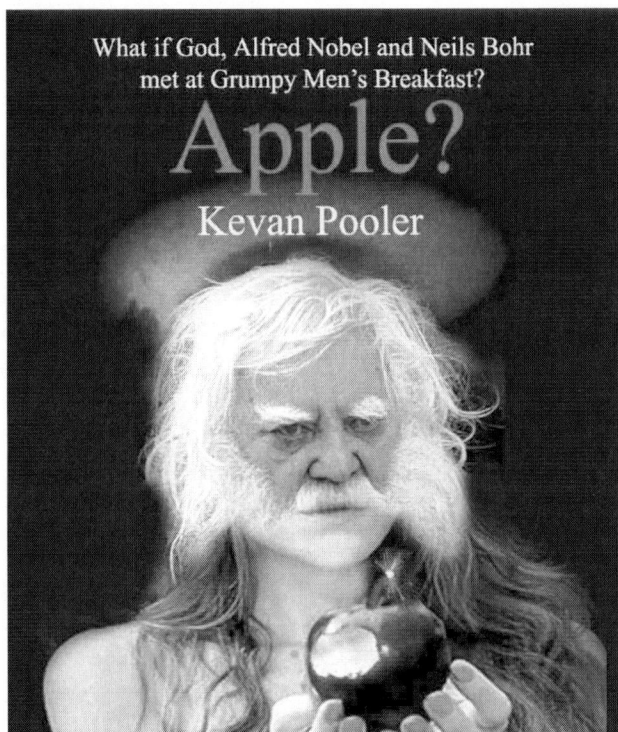

What if God, Alfred Nobel and Neils Bohr
met at Grumpy Men's Breakfast?

Apple?

Kevan Pooler

WMDs - Dynamite, Nuclear Power and Sex.
Their 'inventors' bemoan that their finest inventions
have been turned into Weapons of Mass Destruction, but which is the
worst?
Our hero listens but does not hear.

A year later he is in Africa helping childhood ex-Boy Soldiers
to regain a childhood through the language of Circus Skills.
Will he discover from personal experience which WMD is the worst?

Re-edit for paperback edition pending: Perhaps working title retained:
'A Lethal Weapon Too'

www.kevanpooler.com

Also by Kevan Pooler

The body of a blond is found in the Jacuzzi.
Detective Inspector John Blundell and his new Sergeant Iruna Bahadur take a long time to discover what even happened.

A Chocky and Badder crime mystery set in a Youth Service partnership with a church charity, just as austerity budgets really bite.

The demand for Safeguarding young people was never greater.

Youth Officer Leo Nicholas feels compromised by the challenges he has to make within the criminal record Disclosure and Barring Scheme (DBS) as to what is disclosed.
He asks 'who should really be Barred?'

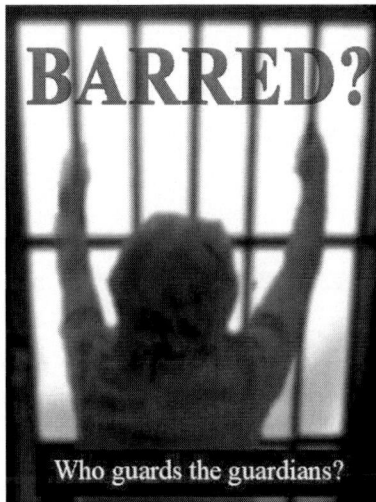

Not one to take on holiday because you have to find out what happened next.' C.M.E.Baird
'Outstanding - a non stop, well written page turner.' P. Naylor-Morrell
'A refreshing change from the usual run of contexts in which many whodunnits are set.' Maggie Lees
'A captivating well researched plot held my attention to the very neat end.' M. Yore

www.kevanpooler.com

Kevan Pooler is a School Governor, ex-Safeguarding trainer, Friar, English Teacher, and Youth Worker. He runs a Nottinghamshire writers' group.

Born in Oxford to Patrick Murphy and Edith née Pooler, he spent his teens training to be a Franciscan Friar. He 'missed the sixties,' but has been trying to catch up since.

Being Editor of the college magazine and Social Secretary helped him to beat Peter Hitchens and Andrew Linzey to President of the Student Union in Oxford. From that experience he discovered that Youth Work was a career.

After unqualified success in Potters Bar, he decided to train in Liverpool. He taught English and Drama on Merseyside and Humberside before returning to Social Education.

Following national recognition in Rural and Mobile Youth Work in Notts, he took on Mansfield District, one of the most deprived urban areas in Britain. His management of a multi-disciplinary team of youth workers in Sexual Health, Homelessness, School Truants, School Excluded and Knife-Crime, helped to secure the highest ever grant for youth work.

He could not stop the slashing of Youth Work budgets.

Kevan had accumulated so many stories, that he decided to turn to writing them up. Needing to hone his skills he joined one writers' group and started another. This has been running for seven years.

He wrote 'Apple?' working title, 'A Lethal Weapon Too', in response to the Weapons of Mass Destruction debate, child soldiers in Africa, and rape as a weapon of war.

This was followed by 'Barred?' a crime thriller set in a youth project, questioning quite who is safeguarding young people and should some of them be barred.

Kevan then returned to a Youth Work anti-racism project started in the late 1980s, where he saw the kind treatment of Prisoners of War as a starting point for our multi-cultural society. Finding little widely accessible information, it took four years to research and results in this full history of the POW camp system, contrasted with the treatment of Conscientious Objectors.

Kevan lives with his wife in Nottinghamshire. They have four grown children.

www.kevanpooler.com